Water Gypsies

Annie Murray

Water Gypsies

MACMILLAN

First published 2004 by Macmillan
an imprint of Pan Macmillan Ltd
Pan Macmillan, 20 New Wharf Road, London N1 9RR
Basingstoke and Oxford
Associated companies throughout the world
www.panmacmillan.com

ISBN 0 333 98947 3

Typeset by SetSystems Ltd, Saffron Walden, Essex
Printed and bound in Great Britain by
Mackays of Chatham plc, Chatham, Kent

PART ONE

1942–3

One

August 1942

'There we are, my dear.' The midwife leaned over to receive the baby from the doctor after the cord was cut. 'And it's another little lady!'

In a moment the screams of the second twin joined those of her sister, who was already lying, wrapped in a scrap of sheet, in an apple box on the side bed of the cabin.

The young mother's groans of pain had ceased and she lay back, drained of strength, without even the energy to raise her head and look at her babies. Her eyes were glazed with exhaustion, the dark hair slicked to her head. She seemed barely conscious as the doctor stitched her up. The second babe had been awkwardly positioned and he had resorted to forceps.

Miss Lyons, the midwife, stepped outside onto the counter at the back of the boat while he finished off, pleased to be out of the blasted man's way. She was running with sweat, her hair damp round her temples and the nape of her neck, but it was blazing hot outside, the breeze so sluggish that it was barely more than a ripple against her clammy skin. She perched on the gunwale, wiped her face with her hanky and let out a long sigh. Thank heavens that was over! She could scarcely remember a labour that she had so dearly wanted finished, such was the distress and fragility of the mother. And birthing women in these cabins was a challenge all of its own, with it being dark and no more room than a shoebox, and the stove lit – in this weather! – to boil water. It was like a furnace in there. Even so, the doctor had done more than his fair share of complaining, she thought.

When she'd realized it was twins and sent to him for assistance, only one of them could attend to Mrs Bartholomew at a time and neither could stand up fully without hitting their head on the ceiling. The doctor, who was new to delivering boaters' babies, had cursed disbelievingly at the lack of space.

At last he emerged from the cabin with his bag, clothes crumpled and puce in the face.

'All yours,' he said curtly. 'Everything's as it should be.'

The air in the cabin smelt rank with sweat and blood.

'Let's get you all cleaned up now, shall we?' Miss Lyons said kindly, pouring water from the kettle. Poor lamb, she thought, watching the silent figure lying limply on the stained bedding. Many of the boatwomen she saw were hardened and robust, born to the life, but this one was finding it all a struggle, though she certainly tried hard. She occasionally saw Mrs Bartholomew standing at the helm of the *Theodore* in her long, dark skirts with a colourful scarf round her hair, a slim, wiry figure, chin jutting out at a determined angle. There were usually one or two of the kiddies up on the cabin roof. Course, she'd had a bad time losing that last little one, and now she looked so beaten down. The cabin floor was covered in filth and the crochet work along the shelves, which the most houseproud boatwomen kept scrubbed white, had turned a jaundiced grey. As she washed the young woman's body, talking soothingly to her, she couldn't help but see the bug-bites on her skin. The bed was obviously alive: she'd have a little word once things were sorted out.

Maryann could barely even manage to open her eyes, even though the babies were crying for attention. Miss Lyons gave each of them a quick dunking, which made them roar even more, then wrapped them securely in the old bits of sheet and blanket Maryann had put ready.

'Come on now, lovey – these little ones need you,' she said gently. 'Let's get you sat up a bit. We'll get a nice cup of tea down you and I'll show you how to feed them both at once, shall I?'

She helped Maryann position the infants to suckle, and the cabin suddenly went quiet, except for one of the babies making tiny squeaks as she fed. Miss Lyons perched beside her as the tea brewed.

'Well, you've done it. And these two look fit as fiddles. How d'you feel?'

Maryann looked up at her, lank hair falling down each side of her thin cheeks. She tried to smile.

'As if I've been under a tram!' But her eyes filled and her mouth wobbled. 'Oh, Lord above – twins! Whatever'm I going to do?' Tears rolled down her face. 'I can hardly manage the other three as it is – what with everything else.'

'It's a shock, I know.' The midwife touched her hand comfortingly. She was about thirty, not much older than Maryann herself, though she seemed far more mature, a motherly person, with a round, pink face and blonde hair. She had delivered Maryann's last son, Harry, and had wept with her when eleven months later Harry, sick with pneumonia, gasped out his last breath on a November day as grey and hard as the steel billets they were carrying in the boats. When she came this time to attend to Maryann in early labour, she put her instrument to

Maryann's ripe belly and kept moving it about, frowning.

Eventually she said, 'I'm sure I can hear two heart-beats.' She looked into Maryann's eyes. 'Did you know you were carrying twins?'

Maryann stared down at them now, each suckling a breast. She was very sore underneath from the stitches, and the babies' feeding made her belly contract so that she winced with pain. The midwife had shown her how to hold them facing her and latch them on with their legs back under her arms, supported by a pillow just behind her on each side. The girls sucked greedily. The larger of the two was dark haired, but the other had ginger colouring like their father. The combination of the pain and her confused emotions of wonder at her new babies and dread of what their arrival would mean made her cry all the more.

'Here –' Miss Lyons helped her sip the sweet tea – 'let's get some energy into you. Husband off with a load today, is he?'

Maryann nodded, managing to free a hand to wipe her eyes. 'Only to the Light. He'll be back soon.'

'They're a good size, anyway, the two of them,' the midwife comforted her. 'Both over five pounds – that makes things easier. You've done ever so well. There's just one thing – you know you've got a little problem with vermin in the bed, don't you?'

'I know.' Maryann blushed miserably. 'Only we've been so pushed on this last trip and I was so heavy and tired and there was all that rain on the way up . . .'

'Of course, of course – I just thought I'd mention it. You can stove the place as soon as you're on your feet again. And you *will* cope, dear, I'm quite sure. I know you boatwomen – you're marvellous.'

6

With further words of comfort and advice she left, saying she'd come back later and urging Maryann to 'have a nap while you can, lovey'.

Stepping out onto the path in the sultry afternoon, she looked back at the tiny cabin and shook her head. *Good luck to her*, she thought, *because, my goodness, she's going to need it.*

Though she was exhausted, Maryann found it impossible to sleep. Childbirth sent her into a high, jangled state from which it took time to come down, and she was conscious of the two snuffling bundles on the bed beside her. Carefully, wincing at the pain from her stitches, she leaned up on her elbow and looked into their tiny, squashed faces. So sweet, they were, so beautiful! And healthy by the look of them, thank heavens.

'Hello, our girls,' she whispered tenderly. Tears filled her eyes again. 'I just hope you're not going to be the death of me.' She felt so worn down, so alone. She'd had no idea how hard this life would be, and harder all the time as they had more children. Other boatwomen – *real* boatwomen – always seemed so tough and capable. Some boats were more rough and ready than others, of course, but they had grown up seeing their mothers cope with all their offspring in these cramped cabins, which were only nine feet long by seven wide. They'd grown up used to the life, whereas Maryann was increasingly coming to feel she couldn't cope any more. Joel, bless him, was such a loving husband, but he often seemed to forget than she was not a narrowboatwoman born and bred. Even after eight years on the cut, she still felt she was having to prove herself, and lately all she had felt was that she was making a miserable job of it.

She lay back, feeling as weak as a baby herself and about to give in to a good weep, when she heard distant voices on the path, and a moment later someone leapt onto the counter of the butty and knocked on the open hatch.

'Coo-ee! Anyone home?'

Maryann's heart beat faster with pleasure. 'Nance?' She pulled aside the red gingham curtains which screened the bed. 'Oh, Nance, am I glad to see you! Get yourself in here, quick!'

A pair of worn, brown boots appeared on the coalbox, and then a long black skirt fastened at the waist by a belt with a brass buckle and a dark blouse scattered with huge, scarlet flowers. A second later, Nance's face followed on, weatherbeaten and brown as a berry, topped by her unruly black curls. In her ears were large, gold hoops. Following her was her daughter Rose, a two-year-old, robust, curly-haired copy of her mother.

'We've only just got in. They said you was here. You've had it then?' Her brown eyes were full of delight and anticipation. 'Thought I'd come along and find you screaming blue murder!'

Maryann pulled back the shawl covering the two infants and Nance's mouth gaped open.

'Two? Oh my word – twins? Look, our Rose, two babbies! Oh, Maryann!' She sat down on the edge of the bed, staring at them in astonishment, then leaned back and let out her loud, deep laugh. 'Oh my God! Ooh, they're beautiful, Maryann, that they are –' She wiped her eyes. 'But you're going to have your work cut out for you, aren't you? – No, don't poke them Rose, gentle now! – What are they? Wenches?'

Maryann nodded. Seeing Nance had made her feel better already. They'd been friends since childhood in

Birmingham; their men, Joel and Darius, were brothers from the Bartholomew family, from generations of boaters. The two women knew each other back to front and they were both from 'off the bank', not born on the cut. In Nance's company, Maryann was completely at home. With the life on the cut of long journeys and chance meetings, they sometimes didn't see each other for weeks on end and she was always overjoyed to see Nance, and never more so than now.

'Twins – fancy. And you never knew?'

'Not till the midwife said. Got a hell of a shock – I still can't take it in. Though, thinking back, carrying them was like having a flaming great octopus squirming about inside, so I should've guessed.'

'What you going to call them?'

'I've hardly thought yet.' Maryann eased herself up, grimacing.

'Bit sore are we?' Nance said sympathetically, but then pulled a mocking face.

'Stop making me laugh!' Maryann groaned, laughing anyway and trying to find a way of sitting comfortably.

'So where's your old man – he taken a load up?'

'Mr Veater's sent him to the 'Lectric Light.'

Maryann was lying in her usual sleeping quarters on the butty boat, *Theodore*, one of a pair which she and Joel worked for the carrier S. E. Barlow. They were moored up at Sutton Stop, the boaters' name for Hawkesbury Junction at the meeting of the Oxford and Coventry Canals, where they usually received their carrying orders from Mr Veater, the traffic control officer. Many a child came into the world at the 'back of Mr Veater's shed', and Samuel Barlow and Mr Veater would kindly send the expectant father on short-haul trips while his wife and 'mate' was indisposed. Joel and Bobby, the lad who worked with them, had taken the motor boat, the *Esther Jane*, on a local trip to Baddesly colliery to bring coal back for the Coventry's Light – the voracious power station at Longford. With them they'd taken Maryann's other three children – Joley, who was seven, Sally, five, and Ezra, three.

'We've just come up from the jam hole,' Nance said, referring to the jam factory at Southall, which was always hungry for coal. 'And we brought a load of cement up for some airstrip they're putting in, worse luck – filthy lot that was. I'll have to get back and clean up. Here – let's have another cuppa first, though.' She reached up to the cabin roof for the painted water carrier – to the annoyment of Spots, one of the family's two cats, who had been snoozing in its small patch of shade – filled the kettle and set it to boil again on the tiny range just inside the door. 'I'll go and fill your cans for you and get your groceries in – and I'll bring a bite to eat round later for you and Joel. The kids can come and eat with us tonight. Save you moving.'

'Thanks,' Maryann whispered, tears welling in her eyes. 'You're golden you are.'

'Nah,' Nance said easily. 'It's not every day you have twins, is it?'

Maryann was ashamed of the state of the stove, all grease and rust spots. She hadn't got round to cleaning or blacking it. She watched Nance move about so capably. Nancy had taken to the life and never looked back, especially as she'd had to risk so much to be with Darius, leaving her violent husband, Mick, to whom she was still officially married. Except during the unhappiest time of her marriage, Nance had always been full of wiry energy, a tomboy as a child, who now managed the all-weathers, ever-demanding work of the cut with vigour and enthusiasm. She even looked the part, with her dark hair and earrings glinting in the light from outside. But just as Maryann was about to pour out her woes, her fear of how she was going to manage, Nance turned, the teapot in her hands.

'I've got news for you an' all – I'm expecting again!'

Maryann swallowed the lump in her throat and tried to smile. She knew how much this meant to Nance. Her marriage to Mick had been childless and she'd ached for babies of her own. Now she already had Darry, Sean and Rose, but at the turn of the year she'd miscarried and Maryann knew how upset she'd been.

'Oh, Nance – that's lovely!' Maryann hoped Nance couldn't hear the tears in her voice. 'I'm ever so pleased for you both!'

They spent half an hour, snatched away from Nance's chores, drinking tea, and Nancy handed her a good hunk of bread with more butter than the scraping of wartime frugality allowed.

'You should have triple ration today!' she said, as Maryann ate ravenously. The twins slept and for the moment Maryann felt quite lifted out of herself and less desperate as she reminisced with Nance. She even managed to doze for a little after Nance left, and the twins, exhausted from the process of coming into the world, slept on.

Joel got back in late that night when Joley, Sally and Ezra were already asleep on the *Esther Jane*.

'Two little 'uns, then?' he said in wonder. His thick beard glowed bronze in the lamplight and he sat, his burly form perched on the edge of the bed, staring at the two little girls. In the light from the oil lamp, the look on his tired, gentle face at the sight of his new daughters filled Maryann with a deep, poignant joy. There was such pride, such tenderness, in his eyes. She told herself how ungrateful she was being to feel so burdened by the arrival of these little ones. She'd made Joel so happy! He was always cock-a-hoop at the births of their children. And she couldn't help remembering the last one, when he first saw their little Harry with his pale hair, now in his grave in a Banbury churchyard. Joel had been heart-broken when they lost him. It was the only time she had seen him cry like a child himself.

'I think that one looks like an Esther,' Maryann said, pointing at the dark-haired infant who was lying dozily beside her. 'And madam here – ' the ginger-headed one was at her breast, a tiny fist flailing in the air – the fidgety one – well, she seems more of an Ada to me.'

Joel's eyes met hers and he reached over to stroke her head, drawing her closer to kiss her lips.

'Thanks, my little nipper. Thanks, my lovely.'

Maryann smiled back at him, her feelings twisting inside. He was so loving, his children meant so much to him after his years of struggling on alone with his father. How could she ever deny him this joy and satisfaction? But couldn't he see it was wearing her down, all of it, week by week, until she wondered if one day she would just drop with exhaustion and sink under the waters for good?

Two

'Hello, my sweet little bird.'

Joel's warm hand moved over her in the darkness. They were in their bed in the *Theodore*, the babies Esther and Ada deep in a snuffling sleep together in a nest of bedding on the floor. The other children were with Bobby on the *Esther Jane* to keep them from being disturbed by the twins' nightly squalling when they woke to be fed.

Maryann lay facing the back wall, the bulwark between cabin and cargo, eyes squeezed closed. Joel's hand brushed her hair back and kissed the nape of her neck. This whiskery tickling used to make her giggle so she couldn't keep up any pretence of being asleep. And the girls were nearly six weeks old now; her stitches had healed. Her husband wanted her. What reason could she find for depriving him any longer? Yet the thought filled her with dread.

Opening her eyes, she turned slightly towards him. There was nothing to see. The lights were out in the cabin, checked curtains drawn across the bedspace.

'My girl . . . My lovely . . .' He was easing up her shift, kissing her breasts, and she stiffened against him. She was alarmed at herself. Hadn't she always loved his caresses? Loved being held and cuddled close? Making love with Joel was such a solid, reassuring thing. She loved lying with him in the cosy light from the lamp, taking time to look into his face, stroking the strong hairs of his beard, seeing the love in his eyes. She would run her hand across the firey hair on his chest, down over his belly, its comforting softness into which she could burrow, teasing, nuzzling, yet tight like a drum when he tensed. She had been so afraid at first, at the thought of lovemaking, after her stepfather. But she had pushed those memories away, buried them deep and learned how to love Joel.

And yes, she did love him, with all her heart, and would have turned to him happily, tired as she was, if it was not for the thought of another child. She lay beside him stiffly, frightened to respond. She couldn't face all that again. Not the sickness, the feeling so done in that sometimes she nearly fell asleep at the helm of the butty, the gruelling agony of birthing them . . . and all that even before the constant worry of their little lives. Of them toppling off the boats, catching in the locks, or falling sick like their poor Harry, who never got better.

'Joel?' she whispered. 'I can't. Not another babby. Not yet.'

He nuzzled her, stroking her belly. It was stretched now, used. A place for people to stop in for a while, she thought, like a cabin. She felt like a battered old boat, trying to keep moving on.

'You won't, will you? Not so quick after the last?'

'I don't know,' she pleaded. She knew nothing about how her body worked, what she could do to keep things under control.

Joel lay back with a long sigh which cut right through her. Her ghosts, her insecurities, crowded in. She hated to hurt him, to refuse him anything. She knew how kind he was, how loving. He didn't complain about any of her shortcomings. But what he called his 'bit of loving' was so important to him. He never tired of her: she was his wife and he needed it from her. What if she couldn't give it to him? What then? He had taken her in, saved her, and her greatest fear was that of being without him.

'Joel?' She reached over and kissed him and Joel took this as a sign that he should continue. They clung together in the darkness and soon she heard his quick gasps of need and pleasure as he moved on top of her, and she felt the bite of him entering her, that pain of the first time after a birth. But the sharpness did not last and she held him close as he rested in her afterwards. He laughed softly, close to her ear.

'Back to normal,' he whispered. 'My dear one. With our lovely family. We'll make Number Ones out of them again – you'll see. We will.'

His arm round her waist, he fell into a deep, satisfied sleep.

The next day they set out to take coal to Birmingham. Bobby Jenks, a twenty-year-old lad from another boating family, had been working with them for a couple of years. Working a motor and butty two-handed with children had soon proved too much for Maryann. 'Bow-hauling' the butty, having to haul it by hand with ropes into locks, was almost too much for her small frame, and she worried constantly about the children's safety. They needed a third hand. They'd had a succession of helpers, but now Bobby had stuck – he was a good worker who'd been steering boats solo by the age of seven or eight. He was a strong, cheerful lad, with a head of wild hair and a sudden, cheeky smile. His family, the Jenks, were a much respected family of Number Ones who had been working boats for generations, but had now also sold out to Samuel Barlow. Bobby had been schooled in the true boatman's qualities of agility and hard work, as well as a quiet courtesy, and Maryann had never had any problems with him joining them. Though she was only a few years older, she had developed a motherly fondness for him.

Joel had worked short trips with the monkey, or motor boat, during those weeks. Maryann stayed tied up at Sutton Stop to get to grips with looking after two extra children and to go and be churched in the parish of Longford. One day, when Nancy and Darius tied up there again, she was able to leave the twins with Nance and go into Coventry to collect new ration books and indulge in a beautiful long soak in the public baths. She knew she'd had more rest than most boatwomen had after their births.

The twins took it out of her good and proper and she often felt weak and tired, but Nance had been a marvellous support. Darius had left her with them for a couple of days, working his boats two-handed with a lad on board, and she helped Maryann stove the cabins and scrub and clean them. She'd washed the curtains and crochet work, hanging them in a flapping line along the *Theodore* to dry in the August sunshine, then polished the brass strips on the chimneys and knobs on the doors.

Maryann sat feeding the babies, watching helplessly, but with relief and gratitude as Nance whisked about, while Joley, Sally and Ezra played with Darry, Sean and Rose on the bank. Darius had tied a rope to the branch of a tree and knotted a stick onto the bottom to serve as a seat. The older ones were having a fine time, swinging and whooping as they did so.

'You can start off nice and fresh now, can't you?' Nance said, blacking the stove.

'It looks lovely,' Maryann said, gloomily wondering to herself how long it would last. *What's the matter with me?* she asked herself. She never seemed to feel she could get on top of things somehow. She'd wanted to keep such high standards on the boats, like some of the boatwomen whose curtains and pinners were immaculate, their brasses winking in the sun against the bright colours of the boats. She dreaded their scorn. They seem to accept her because she had married Joel, who was so respected, one of the old families of Number Ones who owned their own boats, even though the declining trade had forced them to sell out to Essy Barlow before the war.

'You'll soon pick up,' Nance said. 'Eh – ' she turned to look at Maryann, cloth in hand – 'I hope Darius's going to get us a load up to Brum one of these days. I want to go and see our mom.'

Maryann nodded. She couldn't say she felt the same about seeing her own mother.

'Still gives me a shock when I go there – the mess! Great holes and that all over the place. I'm glad we were out of it, really.'

They had been aware of the Blitz, of course. Who couldn't be? And there were a few hairy nights round Birmingham, Coventry and the London docks when the bombing had come frighteningly close. But in many ways life went on much the same on the cut, war or no war, except for identity cards and ration books. The sides of the locks and the bridge-holes were painted white, and they'd had to keep the hatches closed at night and paint over the lamps on the boats for the blackout regulations, but in the countryside and along the cut things went on much as usual, except that now there was an increase in traffic. More loads to fuel the war effort:

to make munitions and vehicles, to build air strips and shadow factories.

They travelled into Birmingham from the north side, along the Bottom Road or Birmingham–Fazeley Canal. Maryann knew this was most people's least favourite trip. They came in from the collieries, their boats loaded up and low in the water. Once they'd got past Minworth, coming into Brum, the cut became more and more filthy, walled in by factories and warehouses and built over so heavily that it seemed steeped in muck and gloom. On top of that the locks were all single, so instead of being able to breast up the motor and butty side by side and put them through, the butty had to be bow-hauled in with a rope, which was exhausting. Thank heavens they had Bobby with them!

It was here you could see a few more signs of the war. She caught glimpses of fat, fish-shaped barrage balloons in the sky. As the city closed in, she was filled with an increasing sense of unease. Her mother still lived here and her two brothers, and it was where she came from, yet Birmingham could always arouse the painful memories buried inside her, which she tried strenuously never to think about. Above all, she dreaded ever seeing *him*. What was he calling himself these days? she wondered. To her he had been Norman Griffin, undertaker, wrecker of her family, thief of her childhood, and the man responsible for her sister's death. He had disappeared afterwards, and none of them knew where he was. But he must be somewhere, could easily still be in Birmingham.

Once, just once after all this time, she thought she saw him. It was a few months ago when they were tied up at Tyseley, one smoky, drizzling winter night. A figure walking along the wharf caught her eye, making her freeze inside. Moving along the row of warehouses ahead of the boats was a dark figure, burly, hat pulled down so that she could see nothing of his face except the glowing tip of a cigarette. There was something in the build, the gait ... Maryann stepped down onto the coalbox and peered out.

'Mom – what're you doing?' Joley asked, puzzled at his mother bobbing in the hatches.

'Nothing – just eat your piece,' she snapped.

Narrowing her eyes, she watched, heart thumping, as the figure moved further along then out of sight. Joley had squeezed in front of her.

'Who was that?' he said, following her gaze.

'No one, Joley. Come on – let's see if we can find a scrape of jam to go with that, eh?'

It was ridiculous, she knew. He was long gone with his foul, cunning ways. With his disfigurement he wouldn't be able to con his way into another family to trap its daughters in fear and shame. Margaret had seen to that. Little Margaret, whose widowed mother had innocently taken on the 'respectable Mr Lambert' as he was calling himself then, after he left Maryann's mother. Margaret, whom he had pushed past the bounds of sanity. Margaret, who was in the asylum now ... The feelings began to rise in her, swelling until her very veins seemed ready to burst with rage, with shame. She was breathing as if she had been running. No, she must push this away! All the memories he brought with him of her past, of her dead sister Sal. That wasn't the man she saw – it was a mistake. Norman Griffin belonged to the past and there he must stay. Ever since that day she had frozen out those thoughts. She was never going to think about the past again.

When they tied up that afternoon at Tyseley Wharf,

19

she left the babies and Ezra with Joel and took Joley and Sally with her to pick up groceries, the ration books pushed into her pocket. As they crossed the wharf, she caught sight of a gangling young man in dark clothes which appeared too large for him passing in through the gates. Tucked under his arm was a thick, black book.

Sally tugged on her arm. 'Who's that?'

Maryann barely glanced at him. 'Dunno. Some holy Joe I s'pose. Come on – let's get going.'

They shopped as fast as the queues and length of young children's legs would allow. Sally solemnly carried the bread. Joley staggered along, insisting he could manage the vegetables. At seven years old, he was already very strong.

'Now then,' Maryann said, 'shall we go and see Mr Osborne?'

Joley and Sally perked up.

'Will he have summat for us?' Joley asked.

'You'll have to wait and see, won't you?' She grinned at them. 'I think Mr Osborne must have filled his cellar with sweeties before the war like a squirrel, don't you?'

Mr Osborne owned a butcher's shop in one of the streets near the wharf. Maryann had switched to buying her meat from him over the past few months as she found him so cheerful and kind that she always looked forward to seeing him. He made a point of remembering their names, invariably had a treat to offer the children and tried to stretch the ration for her as far as possible, unlike some other shopkeepers, who would scrimp on it. He seemed to have taken a shine to her, so that now Joel teased her whenever they reached Tyseley. 'Off to see your fancy man then?' and she'd protest, 'He's old enough to be my father, you daft thing!'

Osborne's shop had an entry along one side and Joley

and Sally always liked to run up and down it. Houses, with their warrens of entries and back yards, were an exciting novelty for them, coming off the cut.

'Come on,' Maryann scolded. 'I want to get home today!'

The shop window was bare, denuded of its peacetime array of joints and chops. It was hard to get hold of anything but essentials these days. As the door opened with a 'ping', they walked into the smell of meat and sawdust and saw that Mr Osborne still had a decorative pig's head on the counter with an apple in its mouth, something that always fascinated the children.

'Ah, hello there!' Mr Osborne cried. He was a short, comforting looking man in his white overall, balding crown lapped by soft white hair. Despite his friendliness he had a hesitant, shy way with him, barely meeting Maryann's eyes, but he was always very attentive towards the children.

'Down at the wharf again then? Seems a long time since you were last here. Now, you youngsters, before your mother and I get down to business, how about a chocolate lime each?'

Joley and Sally nodded with delighted smiles.

'Thought you must be sold out as there's no queue,' Maryann said as he handed out the pale green sweets.

'Oh – never you fear.' Mr Osborne went briskly back behind the counter, while Joley and Sally drew patterns in sawdust with their feet across the black and white tiles.

'There, just a bit extra,' he said, eyeing the scales as he weighed her mince and began parcelling it up. 'Everyone well on board?'

'Yes – thanks.' She told him about the twins and Mr Osborne went quite soppy, marvelling at the thought.

'No wonder you look tired. I thought there was something – dark rings under the eyes. Well, well. Bring them in and let me see them next time, won't you? Nothing like new, young life.'

Maryann asked after Mrs Osborne. The couple lived a few streets away rather than over the shop.

'It's the smell, you see,' Mr Osborne had explained once. 'It's a silly thing, really, but the wife's almost a vegetables-only sort of eater. We're a bit like Jack Sprat and his wife! She can't tolerate the smell, you see, not living here . . . So I rent out the upstairs, off and on.'

'Anyway.' He smiled now. 'I'm glad all's well. What're the names of your boats again?'

'The *Esther Jane* and the *Theodore*,' Joley and Sally piped up.

'Of course, of course,' he laughed. 'Now – ' he held up one finger like a magician about to perform his most demanding act – 'I've got something special for you. A little treat – no charge.'

Disappearing out the back for a moment he returned with a male pheasant, fully feathered.

'Here we go – no questions asked. Have that to be going on with.'

It was the season, of course. Out in the country they kept hearing the sharp squawk of the birds across the fields. If they'd had a dog they could have nipped one in the bag more often, but they only had cats now. Jep the old dog had died years back. And all food was welcome.

'Thanks ever so much,' she said, taking the dead weight of the bird from him across the counter. 'Are you sure you don't want anything for it?'

'No, no. Growing family you've got . . .' He seemed almost bashful. 'Will you be coming up this way again soon?'

'Oh – you never know.' She gave the children a look that indicated it was time to go. 'Pick up your bags,' she told them. 'We can never be sure where we'll be off to next.'

'See you again, then,' he said.

They pinged their way out, Maryann saying, 'Ta for the bird,' once more.

'I think he must like us,' she said to the children as they headed back to the wharf. 'Not sure why, though.'

'I think he likes *us*, not you,' Sally said smugly. 'He gives us sweets, not you.'

'Huh!' Maryann said indignantly. 'He gave me a pheasant, didn't he?'

'He says there was a bloke round looking for you!'

The lad ran out of the toll office the next morning, urgent with a message which he had remembered at the last minute. He pursued the butty, shouting to Maryann.

'Me?' Maryann squinted across at him, with Esther held in one arm and the tiller under the other. 'Oh – ta. That'll be my brother. If he comes again, tell him I've had twin girls. I'll drop him a line when I get a minute!'

The boat slid away faster, her words unfurling behind it. She attempted a weary smile, as Bobby, who had been checking the snubber, climbed back towards her over the sheeted-up planks and took the tiller. Her younger brother Tony was the one person in her family she had any contact with now. She didn't know if the message would get through, but it was nice to think of him coming to look. It gave her a feeling of ties, however slim. Joel's family, the surviving members of the Bartholomews who had not been taken by war or sickness or the dangers of the cut, shared strong bonds. Being with them made her feel safe and protected.

Maryann stood in the hatches for a few moments cradling Esther, while Bobby steered the butty. Joel, as normal nowadays, had their sons aboard the *Esther Jane* with him. Sally was on the roof of the *Theodore* next to the chimney, smudging her fingers in the dust and murmuring to herself. The cut was busy with joeys and other working pairs, and the sounds of traffic clattering over bridges, a train, a screech of metal from a nearby works, filled the air. It was a beautiful, early autumn morning, and even the weary, soot-choked walls, the glamourless industrial buildings cramped shoulder to shoulder, took on a pleasing mellowness in the rich light. A feeling of sudden, swelling contentment rose in her and after the past weeks of feeling so drained and tired she felt more optimistic. The night had not been so bad – she had only been up once with the girls – and with more sleep and in the freshness of morning she looked at her old home with fondness and a touch of regret.

It'll be all right, she thought. *At least today. I can manage today* . . . She didn't want to count her chickens too soon, but it was a moment of lightness after so many exhausting weeks. She saw Joel ahead of her and watched him tenderly, doing so expertly what he had always done. What he was born for. *Nothing like this life*, she thought, suddenly full of optimism. *Maybe I can manage. I can get by, so long as* . . .

The worry was there, always, the deep pang of dread. So long as she didn't fall with another child. Not yet. Preferably not ever. But please God – she repeated the prayer she'd made in the church at Longford – no more babbies for a long time yet.

Three

The trip down to Oxford was always Maryann's favourite. The cut followed a beautiful, winding route along
the toes of hillsides, past Braunston and round the curves
south of Napton, where the sails of the ruined mill on
the hill appeared then disappeared with each bend, only
to appear again unexpectedly a few wiggles later. They
were blessed with glowing autumn days, early morning
mists over the water, berries clustered red in the hedgerows and early frosts.

This route was the first Maryann had ever travelled
with Joel and his father, many years ago now, it seemed
to her, when as a desperately unhappy child she'd run
away from home and asked to stay on the boat with
him. There were always ghosts of her former self along
the way. There were also, along the route at Claydon,
Cropredy, Fenny Compton, the familiar faces of lock-
keepers and lengthsmen and their families, other boat
families and smiles and hellos from behind the counters
of pubs, tiny grocer's shops, and bakeries, greetings of
'Nice to see you down this way again!' and exclama-
tions at the sight of the twins. Sometimes the cut and
its people felt like an extended family, one in which
Maryann had always done her utmost to try and belong
and be accepted.

Joel knew this section of the cut so intimately that a
newly felled tree, a section of the path more or less

overgrown than usual or a silted bend in need of dredging where the propeller struggled and threatened to go aground – all these details he noticed at once. And it was this cut, the Oxford, which Maryann knew gave him the most poignant reminders of what had been lost. Though he seldom spoke of it, she knew it cut Joel to the heart that the old ways were slipping into the past: that he was no longer a Number One like his father had been, with his own boat, a king of the cut, gliding along silently, accompanied not by the relentless grinding of the engine, but pulled by a horse, its hooves and the chink of the harness or flick of a rope the only sounds, except for those of animals and birds and the swish of water. There were certainly compensations for working for an agent like Samuel Barlow, one of which was not having to chase loads. Essy sorted those out, as well as maintaining the boats and paying tolls and insurance. For Maryann these seemed adequate compensation. They still had the *Esther Jane*, after all. But for Joel being *owned*, having S. E. Barlow painted across the panel of the *Esther Jane* amid her roses and castles instead of the name Bartholomew and No. 1 – no, she knew there wasn't a day that passed without him still thinking of this painfully.

It wasn't just ownership. The demise of horse-pulled boats meant that a way of life which had previously supported all sorts of other tradesmen – stable hands, saddlers, blacksmiths – was also disappearing. A number of them had gone off to war. Even some of the lock-keepers were now in the ARP. Though the cut was now busier than it had been for years, friendly faces were gone. And Joel had plenty of time to brood on the fact as he steered the monkey boat up front, still with the proud, upright stance of a Number One, but feeling aggrieved, diminished inside.

When the boats were empty they travelled with the butty tied up close behind the motor, which meant that the butty needed little steering. This was usually not for long, between dropping off one load and collecting another, and Maryann made the most of her hands being free to get ahead with cleaning or cooking and feeding the twins. The *Theodore* was their family butty now since, not having a motor on board, the cabin was a little bigger. So when she wasn't steering she could duck inside and put the kettle on or see to the babies' napkins.

Once there was a load on, however, the butty was towed further behind, the snubber or towing rope extended seventy feet between the two, and it was necessary to steer almost all the time to prevent the butty veering from side to side, out of control. On a long pound with no locks Bobby came back and steered, jumping off the *Esther Jane* under a bridge-hole where the cut narrowed right down, then leaping easily onto the *Theodore* as it came past.

Without Bobby life would have been impossible. Even before Ada and Esther were born, Maryann found the days a long succession of strains and stresses. There never seemed to be a moment when she could relax. As well as keeping the boats moving and steering, there were constant thoughts of *Oh, I must make a cup of tea* or *I must get the dinner on*, or *the stove and floor need cleaning*, or *Sally and Ezra are bored and roaring on the cabin roof*. Not to mention all the washing, mending and shopping she had to to catch up with when they stopped to unload. She had forced herself to develop the other boatwomen's ability to perform several tasks all at once. Everyone did it – there was no choice. You'd tuck the helm, or 'elum' as the boaters called it, under one arm, and with the dipper full of water and potatoes on the roof, stand and peel them as you went along. Or you'd sew or splice ropes – whatever was needed. There was one woman she saw sometimes with a sewing machine in action on the cabin roof while she steered her butty boat.

This particular trip they had a 'good road'. There were so many possible calamities and delays on the cut – clogged propellers, other boats stuck in locks or bridge-holes when the water was low, locks all set against you, not to mention foul weather – that they had developed a patient fatalism which overlay the general need to get a load on and keep moving.

They reached Juxon Street Wharf in Oxford a bit later than hoped, after a delay on the second day with a snarled propeller south of Duke's cut. As the men began unloading, Maryann set off, a twin under each arm and Sally and Joley beside her, to go and 'find Granddad'. The chores could wait a few minutes while she went to the little terraced house in Adelaide Street nearby to tell old Darius Bartholomew that they'd tied up at the wharf. The old man never missed possible moment on his old home, the *Esther Jane*.

The door was opened by his sister, Mrs Simons, a rosy-cheeked, sweet-natured woman, who still had a look of the boatwoman she once was, her stout body dressed in a dark blue skirt, topped by a rusty red woolly. Her feet were pushed into baggy old slippers to ease her bunions.

'Oh, *hello*, moy dear! Oh, my goodness me, look what we have here?' She gazed, astonished at the sight of Maryann's face smiling out between those of the two babies. 'Come in, come in! Hello, Joley, Sally, Ezzy – how're you, moy dears? Darius – look who's here!

You'll be wanting to see! – Come on through – he's having a snooze by the fire,' she added.

Though Mrs Simons had not lived on the cut for many years now, her backroom looked like a home from home, a larger version of a narrowboat cabin, with its gleaming range and colourful peg rug, and plates, their filigreed edges threaded with ribbons, and photographs and brasses displayed all over the walls. Maryann's father-in-law was getting out of his chair by the fire. Darius was in his shirt sleeves and adjusted his braces as he smiled shyly. Maryann was always delighted to see him. He looked just the same, she thought, lined face suntanned even in winter, the white beard and long white hair round his bald crown, the same sinewy, if slightly stooped stance. His deep blue eyes lit up with pleasure at the sight of them all.

'Well now, lass – what've we got here?' Though he knew Maryann had been expecting, this was the first time they had been to Oxford since the girls arrived.

'Look at these two!' Alice Simons exclaimed. 'Here, your arms must be pulled out of their sockets. Put them down on my chair!' Maryann laid the girls down and they kicked and gazed round, stimulated by the faces looking down at them. Esther smiled and blew bubbles. Ada kicked and moved her head, trying to see everything.

'This one is Esther,' Maryann said softly. The old man's wife, Joel's mother, his 'best mate' for years on the cut, had been called Esther Jane. When she died, he had renamed the boat in her honour. 'And this is Ada.'

A wistful smile appeared on the old man's face. He watched the babies, fascinated.

'Two of them,' he said eventually. He shook his head in wonder. 'With the best names.'

29

Tears came into Maryann's eyes. She could tell how moved this reserved old man was at the sight of his granddaughters and she loved him for it. He stood for a long time, eyes fixed on them.

'Bonny,' he said eventually. 'Very bonny, the pair of 'em.' As he passed Maryann, for a second she felt his hand pressed warmly on her shoulder. He went to the front and they heard him putting on his jacket and old trilby. The front door opened and closed. Darius didn't want to be away from the *Esther Jane* a moment longer.

'Well now,' Mrs Simons said, 'we'll have a nice cup of tea. Let those men do the stroving – you stay here and have yourself a rest, moy dear.' She filled the kettle and set it on the range, where it whispered as it heated up. 'Now – I want a nice long hold of these lovely babies.'

They passed a happy hour together. Joley and Sally always enjoyed the novelty of being in a house, which seemed like a palace to them in comparison with the *Theodore*. Mrs Simons found them some bits and pieces to play with and they went out the back to see the chickens. Maryann settled contentedly with the old lady, who had always been kindness itself to her. Whenever they came to Oxford, Maryann felt she was truly coming to see family. Alice had been heartbroken for them when they'd lost Harry.

Alice Simons cuddled Ada and Esther in turn, talking to them, making them smile. When they started squalling she handed them back to be fed.

'Our Nancy's expecting again,' Maryann told her. 'Pleased as punch about it she is.' Nancy and Darius had been working the Grand Union a lot recently and hadn't been down to Oxford.

She had Alice Simons's immediate attention. 'Oh well, isn't that nice! Marvellous. You girls've been such a blessing to Esther's boys. She keeping all right, is she? And how're you managing, Maryann dear?'

'Oh – I'm all right,' Maryann said. There was a silence. The clocked ticked. She so longed to pour out her worries to someone. She'd met boatwomen who'd brought up fifteen children, more even, on the boats. Was that what Joel wanted? Children and more children in a never-ending line? She had some better days now, but come the hard winter, the times of heavy rain, of ice, she knew she'd start to feel herself sliding under it all again.

Hesitantly she said, 'I don't know how I'll manage if we have any more, though.'

'Oh no, dear.' Alice Simons snapped to attention, sitting forward to perch on the edge of her chair. 'Dear me, no. Thin as a railing you are already. No – child-bearing's all very well in its place, but you have to call a halt somewhere. My mother died after she'd had her eleventh. I saw her slip away – worn out she was, with it all. Now you know I was the eldest daughter, so of course I was landed with it all.' She shook her head.

Maryann thought bitterly for a second of her mother. Even if Flo had been prepared to see her, she'd never've been able to talk about anything like this. There'd be no sympathy there. Flo's attitude was always, 'I've had to suffer, so why shouldn't you?' Since she'd met Alice Simons, though, the old woman had always been on her side.

'I wasn't having that – not for me,' Alice went on. 'When I met moy William down here and we was wed I told him straight: "William, I said, "I'm not marrying you to be a brood mare like my mother." Well – as you know, we had the three, and they was enough for me. Quite enough. You want to look after yourself, dear.'

31

Maryann looked down at the colourful peg rug by the range, longing to ask the unspoken question which now hung between them. *But how did you keep from having any more?*

'Joel's a good boy – I've always said so,' Alice Simons was saying. 'I know the men in my family and we've never had a bad 'un. Not really. But they're men – you know what I'm saying, dear.' Maryann could feel a blush rising up her neck to her ears. What was Mrs Simons going to say next?

Just then Sally ran in from the back, her coat flying open, and clearly full of excitement.

'Them hens want some food!' she said. 'Can Joley and me give them some corn?'

Maryann clenched her hands, desperation rising in her. The moment was lost. She couldn't ask now.

'You go out to the privy,' Alice Simons said. 'And you and Joley take a couple of handfuls from the bag out there. Let Ezzy have a go too, there's a good girl. Shut the back door now!'

Sally's boots clattered out again in a great hurry.

Alice Simons leaned forward. 'I wouldn't normally say such a thing –' she touched Maryann's arm – 'because I know people don't go for talking about it. P'raps they *should*,' she added fiercely. 'Only I don't want to see you waning away in front of my eyes.' She lowered her voice. 'You'll have to have a word with Joel and get him to change his habits. You have to get them to pull back before they goes the whole way. That way you don't catch, see?'

The blush had taken over what felt like Maryann's entire body by now, but she looked back at Alice Simons with gratitude.

'Are you sure? Oh – I don't know if Joel . . .'

'Well, tell him it's that or nothing,' Alice said with a sniff. 'That'll make him think.'

Maryann looked down again, trying to imagine. *Is that really how you do it?* she wondered. *Joel gets so carried away. How am I going to ask him to stop?*

But she heard the urgency in Alice Simons's voice as she spoke again. 'Sometimes what it comes down to is it's them or you. And you don't want these children growing up without their mother, do you?'

Four

Old Darius Bartholomew was up to watch them pull away from Juxon Street Wharf early the next morning. Maryann saw him fade into the mist of an Oxford dawn, his face lined by time, just standing still in his coat and hat, eyes fixed on the boat as it moved away, putt-putting gently past the other moored craft. The sight of him wrung Maryann's heart, as she knew it did Joel's.

'He goes down to the wharf every day,' Mrs Simons told Maryann each time they visited. 'Every day without fail. Stands there watching. Poor Darius – he'd give anything to be young again.'

Maryann feared that the same fate – being left behind on the bank – would befall her husband and perhaps at a much earlier age. Joel's chest was weak from a dose of gas in the last war so his health was fragile. She had come to dread winter and the first cough. The crackling wheeze in his chest, which was always there, even in summer, was made far worse by the wet and cold which crept up on them through the autumn. She always hoped for Indian summers and mild winters, dreading his racking coughing fits, the risk of him falling so sick he could no longer work his boats. It was too painful to imagine Joel stranded on the bank with that deep, longing look she saw in his father's eyes. Darius, at least, was old. He had known it would come to him one day and he still

34

had the comfort of knowing that his two sons and their families were working the cut.

They loaded a cargo of stone for Birmingham. The following days were wet, and in parts where the locks were widely spaced Maryann sat in the *Theodore* with the children, while Bobby took the helm. In between her chores she tried to teach Joley his letters.

'Oh, Mom, do I have to?' he'd complain as she tried to get him to stay at the table with a scrap of paper and a pencil.

'Just sit still for a minute and have a go,' Maryann urged. 'You don't want to grow up and not be able to read, do you?'

Joley shrugged, resting his chin wearily on his hand as if to say, 'Oh well, if I *have* to.' Maryann was unusual in being a woman on the cut who was a 'scholar'. Having been brought up on the bank, she had been to school until she was fourteen. She couldn't imagine what it must be like not to understand any of the signs in the shops or to read a newspaper, and she wanted her children to be able to do the same as her. But, to Joley, what counted in his everyday life was being able to catch a rope, jump on and off a boat or have the strength to shaft the fore end off the mud. Why did he need to know letters? With a long-suffering air he wrote his name, JOEL BARTHOL-OMEW, laboriously with the stub of pencil, tongue curled back over his top lip. She taught him to write THEODORE and ESTHER JANE and the names of other boats they passed, which he did under sufferance, wriggling wrestlessly all the time he was made to sit on the bench. Sally was quite different. Her clear blue eyes took in everything and even at three she had been keen to copy everything, struggling to mark erratic lines on the paper. At five, now, she had overtaken her brother.

'Look – I'm *writing*!' she'd proclaim proudly. Joley would scowl at her eagerness, and Maryann often found it tempting not to bother with him and to concentrate on Sally. But Maryann was determined that all her children would at least be able to read and write. What if they didn't spend all their life on the cut?

Those first days of the trip the rain fell and fell. Joel was delighted. The cut was low, the 'bottom too near the top' as some of the boaters put it. At least they weren't pumping out water to put out fires as they had in Birmingham and Coventry during the bombing, but it was never good news when the water level fell and Joel was glad to see some water coming in. They pushed on through the wet. Once they were well into the Midlands, though, the rain stopped and the sky cleared. By the time they reached the bottom of the great flight of Hatton locks up to Warwick, the afternoon was bathed in mellow autumn sunshine, weeds and grass shining with water droplets and the air heavy with moisture.

Maryann was at the helm, with Bobby on the bank ahead, lock-wheeling. Another pair of boats had gone up ahead, which meant that the locks would all be set against them. Maryann sighed. For a few seconds she dashed down into the cabin, brewed tea and fetched Joel's soaked corduroy trousers to lay on the cabin roof in the sun. When she came out, she could see Joel signalling to her that he was going to tie up and wait for another pair to come down. Even when the locks were set for them it was a good two to three hours' work getting to the top of Hatton. The great flight of locks, the 'Stairway to Heaven', towered above them, the black and white beams of the gates and the paddle ratchets rising up the hill towards the sky, looking as if they were stacked on top of one another. The combined rise of the twenty-one locks would lift them almost a hundred and fifty feet to the fringes of Warwick.

They waited at a distance from the bottom lock, drinking tea and eating bread and lard in the sunshine. Joley and Sally got off and scampered about on the bank and Maryann sat holding Ada. Bobby stood ahead by the lock, watching for boats. Something would be along soon.

'Once we get up here, we'll tie up before Warwick,' Joel said. 'That'll do us for the day.'

Quite soon Bobby called to them, 'Pair coming down!'

The two boats from the Grand Union Canal Carrying Company appeared eventually out of the bottom lock, side by side, loaded and sheeted up. As they emerged from the last lock, the butty was released skilfully so that the snubber extended gradually to its full length and the motor boat went on ahead. As they passed, the man at the helm of the motor started waving and shouting about jossers coming up, and turning to look, Joel and Maryann suddenly realized that there was another pair of boats from the Fellows, Moreton and Clayton company steaming up behind them. They hadn't heard the engine over the sound of the Grand Union carrier.

Eyes fixed on the approaching green-and-orange painted boats, Joel slammed his tea mug down furiously on the *Theodore*'s cabin roof. There was no sign of the pair slowing down.

'I don't believe it. Them buggers ent going to stop!' It went against the etiquette of the cut not to wait if another boat was lined up for a lock. 'Right.' Joel's voice was grimly determined. 'Bobby!' he roared. 'We're coming in.' He ran along the bank to the *Esther Jane*, whose motor was still gently turning. Maryann looked round for the children.

'Joley – Sally! Come back on – we're going. Quick!'

They children hopped aboard in seconds. Maryann speedily deposited Ada in the cabin and pushed the butty off as Joel pulled away.

If this other pair were determined to push their way in without waiting for them to come up, they'd be back to square one, with all the locks set against them. And besides, there was a principle at stake – how dare they try and steal the flight of locks!

The jossers (nicknamed after Joshua Clayton, a founder of the company) were almost upon them. Their fore end was almost touching the back of the *Theodore*.

'What the hell d'you think you're playing at, you silly sods?' Maryann yelled, furious, and frightened that the boat was going to ram them.

Seeing Joel had managed to cut in front just in time to take his rightful place in the lock, the man steering the josser motor flung it into reverse, which was the only way to stop a boat apart from driving it into the bank. Joel and Maryann, their skill honed by anger and determination to prove their point, breasted up the boats in quick time and edged side by side into Hatton's bottom lock. Over the engine they could just hear a trail of filthy oaths and abuse being flung their way from behind. As Bobby swung the gates closed, Joel turned to Maryann, lifted his cap and saluted her for an excellent job of work. Maryann grinned back and put one thumb up and Joley stood on the counter with her laughing and cheering.

'We beat those sodding jossers!' he piped.

'*Joley!*' Maryann ticked him off, but she was laughing. It was such a good feeling to beat someone who was trying to put one over on you. She had felt better and more energetic in those moments than she had in weeks.

After that, they were full of energy for the Hatton flight, and always a few locks ahead of the jossers, who had to empty every lock they entered since they were in too much of a lather to get on to wait for anyone else to come down. Every time the crews caught sight of each other there was yelling and sparring, triumphant on the Bartholomews' part, but with genuine resentment on the part of the jossers. Joel grumbled about them thinking they owned the Grand Union. Thought themselves above an S. E. Barlow boat.

The afternoon stayed warm and sunny, and halfway up the locks they received unexpected help. As Bobby was leaning on a gate to open it and let the boats through, he was joined at the other side by a man in shapeless, ill-fitting clothes, who pushed against the beam with solemn concentration. Bobby called out his thanks in his usual good-natured way.

As they waited for the next lock to fill, Maryann watched the man. It was difficult to guess his age. He could have been in his thirties, perhaps older. The sleeves of his jacket were far too short, barely reaching down below his elbows, yet his trousers were loose and too long. He walked with a strange, lumbering gait. He was a large man with heavy features and a slow, childlike look to him.

He'll have come from the asylum, Maryann realized. The Warwick asylum loomed to the left of them, a little further up. On fine days some of the more capable inmates did come out at times and help boaters work the locks.

A couple of locks later she took her turn on the bank, moving from lock to lock with the windlass tucked in her belt. The man kept pace with her, carefully watching her movements to see what he needed to do next. As she crossed over a pair of gates to raise the paddles on the other side, she said, 'Ta – I could do with some help.'

The man nodded and gave a sudden laugh. He had narrow, dark eyes and his hair was receding at the front, two smooth inlets curving back into his hair line as if water had washed the hair from his scalp. 'I can help,' he said in a wooden voice, but she could see the eagerness behind it. 'I can help.'

'You from the asylum?'

He nodded, pointed at the high, forbidding building.

'What's your name?'

He thought for a moment. 'Thomas.' And snickered again.

'Well, ta, Thomas. You're doing a good job for us.'

All the way up the remaining locks, Maryann chose to stay on the bank, as Bobby signalled to her that the twins were asleep. Although the lock-wheeling was tiring, it was good to be off the boat, walking the bank. But she was filled with a sense of unease, which increased as the afternoon went on. Her feeling of buoyant well-being earlier on seeped away and she felt strange and tight inside, brushed by memory. She knew what it was: the asylum. Seeing the buildings, meeting Thomas, brought to the surface another thing she preferred not to think about. Little Margaret Lambert, the child whom Maryann's stepfather, Norman Griffin, had brutally degraded. As her sister Amy was helpless to protect her, Margaret had tried to end her tormentor's life in order to save her own. Margaret had been nine then. Now she'd be fifteen, a young woman. Instead of being sent for trial she was consigned to the asylum in Winson Green. One prison instead of another.

Maryann fastened her windlass onto the ratchet of one of the final set of paddles and pulled it round with all her strength, feeling the muscles work in her arms, stomach and back. She tried to let out the fury and grief which rose in her when she was assaulted by thoughts like these. Margaret in there, locked away all these years of her young life – because of him. Beginning to sob, she crossed the gates and flung herself at the second paddle. Once the gates were open, Thomas peeled off and vanished down the hill again without waiting for thanks. As the pair emerged from the lock, Maryann called to Joel, 'I'll walk on.' She saw he had noticed her tears. But she knew he wouldn't ask. Joel was cowed by emotion.

Maryann walked slowly behind the boats, glad of time to be alone. Just a few minutes away from the children, from the non-stop demands, the cabin being in a mess and the washing not done – the feeling that she just couldn't keep up. Now thoughts of the past welled up, raw and bitter, as she walked, pushing weeds and tussocks of grass away with her feet, trying to force the past back to where it belonged: behind her. Hadn't she come to this life to get away from all of that? To be with Joel and begin again? It was all years ago: there was nothing she could do about any of it now, so why couldn't the memories leave her alone? But this evening her mind wouldn't obey her, wouldn't fold its old emotions away, and dark thoughts followed her all the way to the spot where they tied up for the night.

She had been quiet all evening. The lamp was lit and Joel sat on the side of the bed as Maryann stood undressing, legs straddling the twins, who were bedded down on the floor because she worried about them rolling off the side bed.

She could feel Joel's eyes on her as she unbuttoned

her blouse, loving him watching her, yet dreading what it might mean. She felt desperate. She loved Joel so much, but every time he touched her now she felt worried, angry that he couldn't see how terrified she was of catching with another baby. *Why does it have to be like this?* she thought.

She had her back to him, and his warm hands reached for her, pulling her back onto his lap. He sighed with pleasure, kissing her neck, watching, over her shoulder, as his hands parted her blouse, lifting and stroking her pale breasts.

Maryann's mind flailed from side to side like someone locked in a cupboard.

She wanted to . . . to . . . She scarcely had a name for their lovemaking. To give in to him, to give him pleasure, give him everything he wanted. But all that went with having babies crowded into her memory. Even him touching her filled her with dread and she felt panicky. She'd never felt like this before with Joel. *It's just because I don't want to catch for another one*, she told herself.

As Joel laid her back on the bed, Mrs Simons's advice rang in her head. 'Get him to pull away . . .' Last time she hadn't found the courage to say it. But she had to do something or she'd be expecting again, sick and worn out – no, she couldn't stand it.

Hands under his shirt she stroked his wide, strong back, felt the muscles in it working as he moved in her, his excitement gathering. She struggled for words. Quick, she had to say something or it'd be too late!

'Joel,' she burst out desperately, 'don't go all the way in me – pull out before you finish.'

But her words seemed to have the opposite effect and it was too late. With a low groan her husband completed the act which gave him seconds of pleasure and her weeks of fear. He stayed on top of her, face pressed close to hers.

'What did you say to me?' he asked, contentedly.

Maryann's cheeks burned. She managed to make herself say, 'I asked you to pull away – before you finished.'

There was a silence. Joel lifted his head at last, frowning. 'What? You mean – when I'm going strong?'

'So's I don't have a babby every time,' she whispered.

She saw genuine puzzlement, hurt almost, in his eyes. She was learning about her husband, that while he was the most kind and tender of men there were certain things you couldn't get past him on: boats and babies.

'But we'll get by. We always do, don't we, eh? And think of little Harry. What if summat happens to them, eh? Then where'd we be?'

'But I can't do it again – not yet,' Maryann said, stroking his face, her eyes pleading. 'I can hardly drag myself about some days and I never get everything done.'

'Course you do. You're a good 'un.' Joel kissed her. 'Best wife and best mate a man could ask for. I've no complaints, my little bird.'

Tears in her eyes, she looked up at him.

'Please. Just see if you can!'

Doubtfully he said, 'Well – I'll try it. But that don't sound natural at all to me.'

Five

'Ah – Mrs Bartholomew, how nice to see you. I'll be with you in just a moment!'

The woman in front of Maryann in the queue at Osborne's turned and gave her a nasty look.

Maryann, her shopping bag in one hand, Sally's hand in the other, gave a faint smile, feeling a blush rise in her cheeks. It was embarrassing to be singled out like that, but at the same time she couldn't help being pleased. It was nice to find such a welcome. It almost gave her a sense of family.

'Come on, let the ladies off the cut through first, they've got work to do!'

'Well, so've the rest of us,' someone grumbled from by the door.

Maryann and another boatwoman in the queue gratefully produced their ration books and the butcher served them straight away. As he put together Maryann's rations, he was full of questions. Tied up at Tyseley Wharf again, were they? Loading up this morning? Pity the weather wasn't nicer for them, wasn't it? Wouldn't be staying tonight then?

Handing her the bag of meat, he said, 'And how are those two fine babbies of yours?' As Maryann answered, he winked at Sally and beckoned her closer, slipping something into her palm.

'One each for your brothers as well – and mind you hand them over!' he whispered.

'Oh – say thank you!' Maryann instructed her daughter, and blushing even more deeply. 'Mr Osborne's ever so good to you.'

By the time they stepped out into the cold and rain clutching the meat rations, Sally's cheek was already bulging with the lump of toffee Mr Osborne had given her.

'Well – wasn't that nice?' Maryann said to Sally, stopping to retie her scarf round her head to keep out the wet. 'Though I don't know what those other people must've thought.'

The child wasn't taking in anything she was saying, but was gazing dreamily round her at the street, the shops and houses. She was a sturdy, solemn little girl. Her coat, which Maryann had made herself out of a piece of wool tweed, was too big and trailed almost to the ground.

I never was much good at sewing, Maryann thought gloomily. *At least I remembered to wipe her face before we came out.*

You could only just see her little boots below the coat. Sally's thick blonde hair looked as if it had long been stranger to a comb and her hands were grimy with coal dust, but her face was round and glowing pink in the cold. Maryann suddenly bent over and pressed her lips against the chill, peachy skin of Sally's cheek.

'You're my little bab, aren't you?' she said fondly.

'Why don't we live in a house?' Wide eyes looked up at her, topped by a slight frown.

Maryann took her hand. 'Oh – because we're a boater family. We don't live in houses. But when I was a little girl I lived in a house. Over there – a few miles away. In

45

a place called Ladywood.' Your grandmother lives there even now, she could have said, but kept the words to herself. Her children had never met her mother.

'Can we go there? See your house?'

'One day. D'you remember your uncle Tony? We'll go and see him one day soon.'

Sally and Joley were intrigued by life on the bank. She could see Sally excitedly drinking in the sights around her, even though they were in the drabbest back end of Tyseley. On Maryann the streets of Birmingham had quite the opposite effect: they filled her with a profound sense of anxiety. The later years of her childhood here had been so unhappy, tainted by experiences which robbed her of her innocence. When she went to live on the cut, hard as the life was, it gave her back something of herself. She found love, a sense of safety, enchantment even, out in the open air, with nature all round them once they were away from the cities with their soot and grime. The routine of the cut and the birth of her children had given her back something of her own childhood sense of life again, before it was spoilt and corrupted. But back here in these grey streets shadows of the past seemed to lurk, waiting to pull her down again, breaking through the peace that she'd struggled for. She liked to come back to Birmingham, but there was always a sense of relief, too, when they slid out again from between its black, confining walls. Instinctively, she took Sally's grubby hand as they turned back round the corner into the wharf.

'Mrs Bartholomew!' The voice cut through her thoughts, and the clattering of chains on the hoists, the heavy thud and rattle of cargoes being loaded and unloaded around the wharf. Maryann smiled in recognition as one of the men from the toll office came over to speak to her. He was a friendly fellow, a few years her senior, with arched eyebrows which gave him a perpetually humorous look and a grin from which every other tooth seemed to be missing.

'All right, Charlie?'

'All right,' he panted, adding, 'hello, little 'un,' to Sally and patting the top of her head. 'Just thought I'd tell you – there was this bloke come looking for you a couple of days back.'

'That'd be my brother . . .' Maryann frowned. She'd written to Tony not long ago and had a message via the toll office saying he'd be glad to see her whenever she got round to it. He was married now, Tony was, with a baby daughter. Could there be something wrong? 'Thin fella, dark?'

'Oh no,' Charlie said. 'No – it weren't him. This were an older man, in a big coat, like . . . That's what I came to tell you. Bit of an odd bloke, I thought. Kept his hat pulled right down, wouldn't look at you. When he turned to go, I saw he had this scar all down his neck – like a burn or summat.' Charlie frowned. 'Hey – you all right?'

Maryann felt him catch her arm and guide her backwards, letting her sink down onto a pile of wet sacking as her knees gave way and the wharf seemed to swim round her. She saw lights at the corners of her eyes, a wave of heat rose up in her and, knowing she was about to faint, she pushed her head down between her knees. Sally was pulling at her, saying something, and from somewhere in the hazy air above her she could hear the man asking her questions. After a few moments the sick dizziness passed and things round her became clear again.

'Sorry.' She gathered her wits, brushing down her

coat as she tried muzzily to stand up. Charlie took her hand.

'You awright, bab?' While concerned for her, he couldn't help noticing what a sweet, handsome wench she was. Bit of awright, he thought, feeling her rough little hand in his as he helped her to her feet. She made him feel soft and protective.

Maryann nodded. 'But that bloke you said came looking – he asked for me by name?'

'Must've done.' He was taken aback by the intense way she questioned him. 'D'you know who he is?'

'Oh yes,' she almost spat the words. 'I know who he is all right.' Her limbs still felt weak and shaky with shock. Who else could he be, a man with a burned face, a man who had decided to come looking for her? She looked round, suddenly overtaken by fear, everything out of proportion. The very wharf seemed sinister now. 'Sally?' she cried. 'My little girl – Sal? Where are you?'

'She's here – just behind you.' Charlie spoke gently, as if soothing an infant, for the young woman seemed like a terrified child in those moments, as she grasped her daughter's hand and pulled her close. He resisted an impulse to put his arm round her, as if she were one of his own. 'Look, are you sure you'll be all right?'

'Promise me' – she clutched his arm – 'that if he ever comes here again you won't tell him anything. You've never seen me – we never come here. I don't want him knowing anything – I never want to see him again. Tell the others in the office – for God's sake don't let him near us, *please*, Charlie.'

'Course,' he said, frowning. 'I'll tell them. Who is he, anyroad?'

'No one,' she snapped, her voice full of loathing.

'He's *no one*. And I don't want him anywhere near me or my family.'

She walked away fiercely, holding tight to Sally's hand, then she turned.

'I don't want him knowing anything – not about us, not the names of our boats . . .'

'Oh, he knows them, I'm afraid,' Charlie said. 'When he come in, as far as I remember he said he was looking for the Bartholomews on the *Esther Jane*.'

Disturbed by the look of despair which crossed Mary-ann's face, he said hastily, 'But I won't tell him anything if he comes again.'

She nodded, whispered, 'Thank you,' then turned away. He saw her draw her coat more closely round her as if a deadly chill had infected the November air.

'What's the matter, Mom?'

Sally's eyes were wide with alarm as her mother sank down on the bed beside the twins in the *Theodore*, deathly pale and shaking.

'Nothing.' She struggled to compose herself. 'I just come over a bit funny, that's all. I'll be all right when I've had a cup of tea, bab. You sit and do a bit of your drawing.'

Sally retreated into her favourite activity and Maryann sipped her tea, trying to steady herself. She was raw with shock. She was certain that the man who had come to the wharf was her stepfather, Norman Griffin, and the layers of security she had built round her during the years of her marriage seemed to peel back all at once, leaving her trembling under the gaze of the past. That time she thought she saw him before – it *must* have been

49

him, though she'd tried to make herself believe she'd been mistaken, or at least, if he had been there, that it was a coincidence. He was after her. He had asked for their boats by name . . . But why was he looking for her? What could he possibly want from her now? Whatever his reasons, they would be warped and cruel. After these years of peace and safety his disfigured features were raising themselves to look at her again and the thought chilled her to the core. But to tell Joel meant bringing the loathsome creature into the centre of her family again. Even the sound of his name repelled her. She didn't want to say it, not on the cut, her refuge. He had no place here.

She put her cup down and held her hands out in front of her, angry at their tremor, at the thought that he could still do this to her.

We'll be out of here in the morning, she thought, *and we shan't be back in a while. I shan't say anything to Joel. Not unless we're given another load to come back up to Brum. Then I'll tell him.*

Six

'Christmas at Sutton then,' Joel said.

He had hauled the *Theodore* in alongside the *Esther Jane* and was tying them both up. It was Christmas Eve and they weren't going to make it to Oxford after all. But their disappointment was soon dispelled.

'Look!' Maryann called, jumping with excitement on the counter of the *Theodore*. As Joel and Bobby were securing the boats, her eyes were searching the narrow-boats already in at Sutton Stop, and immediately she spotted the *Isla*, with its butty the *Neptune* breasted up neatly beside it. Nancy and Darius were only two boats away from them, Darrie and Sean scampering towards them on the bank. 'Joel – they're here – look – the *Isla*! Nance! Hull-oo! You there?'

Nancy's dark curls appeared immediately out of the *Neptune*'s cabin and she waved back madly, cleaning cloth still in her hand. She had a bright red jumper on and her cheerful grin lit up the day, despite the cold and leaden sky. Maryann beamed, full of happiness. Joel waved as well. The moment he could reach the bank, Joley was throwing himself off to join his cousins before his mom could say anything about letters and book learning. That was the last thing on Maryann's mind, though – her best pal was tied up nearby!

Nance was across in seconds, politely calling out that she was coming across and averting her eyes in the customary way as she moved over the counters of the two boats which lay between them. She stepped nimbly onto the *Theodore*.

'Look at you!' Maryann laughed, laying a hand on Nance's round stomach. 'Well out at the front, aren't you? You look ever so well, though – don't know how you do it, that I don't.' Nance's abundant energy never ceased to amaze her.

'I went in to see Sister Mary on the way back up,' Nance said. Sister Mary was the nurse who lived by the Grand Union at Stoke Bruerne. She was much loved among the boat families for all the care she gave them. 'She says everything's going perfect. I should be coming to town with him March time.'

They saw Joel's brother Darius coming back along the towpath and both waved. His arm came up in greeting. Joel favoured his mother's looks, with the auburn hair and more rounded face. Darius was the image of how his father, old Darius, must have looked as a young man, with his peaty hair and sharp, chiselled features. He wore a cap and a colourful scarf knotted in the neck of his shirt. With Nance beside him, with her dark looks, bright clothes and gold earrings, they looked an exotic pair. Their children were as striking as they were, Darry and Sean both dark-haired and agile as monkeys, and Rose already sultry-eyed under her own mop of curls.

The two brothers greeted one another on the bank. Maryann and Nance watched them fondly.

'Our two old chaps.' Nance laughed. When they were all together they often teased their men about their age and the 'young wenches' they'd managed to persuade to run off with them. Joel was sixteen years older than

Maryann and the gap between Nance and Darius was even greater – almost twenty-two years.

'His age don't mean anything,' Maryann often said. 'He's just Joel – he's always looked the same to me.' They liked to make a joke of it, though. The two of them chattered nineteen to the dozen, before they managed to tear themselves away to get on with their mountain of chores. Maryann spent the afternoon racing to the shops, washing on the bank beside Nance and some of the other boatwomen, pounding heavy clothes in dippers and galvanized tubs, sharing a mangle and exchanging news, all the while surrounded by their children. Maryann fitted in as much cleaning as she could, getting Sally and Rose polishing the brass strips round the chimneys. She sang to herself that evening as she went about her work, full of a burst of Nance's infectious energy. The children looked quite startled, coming upon her humming 'The Sheikh of Araby' and 'I'm always chasing rainbows'. *I feel better*, she thought at last. *More myself.*

'We're going to have a nice Christmas,' she told Joley and Sally as she tucked them into bed on the *Esther Jane* and kissed them both. 'Sleep tight.'

One of the best things about Christmas was that it was a rest and a change, a chance to celebrate and socialize in what was otherwise a life of almost non-stop work. The family of Ernie Higgins, who worked with Nancy and Darius, were tied up at Sutton too and he and Bobby went to them for the day, leaving all the Bartholomews together. They congregated instinctively in the family's old boat, the *Esther Jane*, somehow squeezing everyone in out of the cold. Maryann cleared the bedding off the back bed and stowed it in the *Theodore* so that the younger children could perch on the bed while they all ate chicken and plenty of spuds and cabbage, with a good jug of ale to wash it down and Tizer for the children. It got so hot inside that they slid the hatch open, until an icy rain began to fall and they had to close it again. And all the while they talked, about recent journeys, of bad bends and hold-ups and engine trouble, wharves and lock keepers and news gathered in passing from acquaintances met on their journeys. They reminisced about how things had once been on the cut and about the time when they had all met. Their favourite story, one they never tired of retelling, was of the morning Nance had finally escaped from her old life and her miserable marriage to Mick Mallone to join them on the cut, dashing after the boat at dawn as they pulled away from the basin at Gas Street.

'Happiest day of my life, that was,' Darius said. He sat back, content to be on his old boat, well fed, a cup of ale in his hand. Maryann watched him fondly, the dark, wavy hair round his face, his powerful, almost eagle-like features. He was, like his father, a man of few words, but his eyes, when he looked at Nance, conveyed everything that needed to be said in the way of affection and regard.

Maryann felt Joel take her hand under the table and their eyes met for a moment. Seeing the way he looked at her, she was startled by a rush of desire for him, an inner throb as if their bodies were connected by something even more powerful than touch, and she was filled with relief. She could still feel for him – it was not lost! In the early days of their marriage, trusting and loving him as she did, she had let him caress and wake her body to the discovery of shared pleasure, of excitement, to

54

lovemaking instead of the forced pain and revulsion which was all she had experienced before. It took time. Often she could not enjoy it; sometimes, when she could feel very little, and could not seem to concentrate, she knew it was his pleasure she was enjoying, not her own. But that was all right. It was not *bad*, not terrible as it had been before and she was grateful for that. She still liked the closeness, the comforting warmth of him. She longed for children then and they had soon arrived. She had no idea how quickly lovemaking would become fraught with fear of its consequences, a bittersweet intimacy of desire and dread. How she would find herself doing anything to avoid it – pretending to be asleep, saying she was too tired ... And now, though her gaze as she looked back at him held love and gratitude, her mind raced ahead ... *Oh Lord, he's going to want it tonight. Will he remember what I asked? Oh, please let him just fall asleep straight away!*

'Maryann?'

Even in her heavily pregnant condition, Nance seemed to land in the hatches of the *Theodore* as if she'd flown there. Her laughing features appeared between the doors.

'Still feeding them gutsy little so-and-sos are you?'

Maryann was pinned to the bed by the twins.

'You can laugh,' Maryann retorted. 'It'll be your turn soon. What makes you think you haven't got two in there, eh?'

'Oh Jaysus, no!' Nance rolled her eyes. 'Listen – Mr Barlow's sending us down London again, but he's asked Joel if you'll do a long haul and come down with us?'

'What – the Grand Union?'

'Yep – he's even giving you the choice, you having

your hands full and that. Anyroad, as I was coming back, I told Joel I'd check with his missis! If we got ourselves sorted out right we could all go down there together.'

Maryann brightened. Today was Boxing Day and after yesterday's celebrations it felt very flat. Now all that faced them was work and more work. The thought of being able to do it alongside Nance cheered her no end. Though they had good relations with most of the other boatwomen, they were always a bit conscious of being 'the Brummies from off the bank' and they shared the same sense of humour. Maryann sometimes found she would crack a joke to another of the boatwomen, only to be met by a solemn, slightly mystifed stare. On the other hand a gaggle of them might be splitting their sides about something which she couldn't see the funny side of. With Nance she could really share a joke. And the children, who enjoyed switching families and travelling on another boat for a change, would be delighted with the idea.

The journey down was reckoned to take a week or so, depending on delays and calamities. They loaded up at the coalfields, spending a freezing morning sheeting up to keep the cargo dry. The side sheets, which when not in use lay folded along the gunwales, had to be pulled up, hard and crackly as they were, and knotted over the top of the planks which ran the length of the boat over the cargo. Then, their hands cracked and chaffed from the cold and from pulling and knotting the rough strings, they had to work the main tarpaulin along the boat, making their way backwards, tying it at the sides. By the end of helping to sheet the *Theodore*, Maryann's hands were so stiff and sore she could barely move them. Joley had disappeared somewhere when she wasn't looking and Ada and Esther were screaming to be fed. She wanted to weep, but just then Nance appeared with cups of cocoa.

'I don't know where Joley's got to – have you seen him?' Maryann was looking round anxiously.

'Oh – 'e's in the *Isla* with Darrie and Sean. Don't worry, kid – he's not run away to sea. Not yet, anyhow!'

As they chugged south, the weather grew colder. Frosts turned the ground to stone and the morning trees to sparkling works of art. For most of the time the boats managed to keep together. In the long pound from Hawkesbury to Rugby they moved smoothly on as a convoy. Once they reached flights of locks they would see each other only intermittently, Joel and Maryann, who were the second pair, having to wait for other pairs to come through and set the lock for them, or reset them in their favour before they could continue. But they would catch up later and tie up together for the night.

The burden of work was no less than usual and the temperatures harsh and cold, but for those days Maryann's heart was lighter. She felt almost carefree. Having Nance around lifted life more into a pleasurable realm, a game almost. They bow-hauled the buttys through the double locks at Rugby, Maryann scolding all the way, telling Nance she shouldn't be pulling at all in her condition, Nance arguing that Ernie was really doing all the work, she was only helping. At other locks they raced to canalside shops for supplies, moving bulkily in their layers of winter woollens and coats, bright scarves tied over their hair, arriving back just as the last butty was being pulled out of the lock, both of them panting and giggling, cautious on the frosty stones, their breath furling white on the air. They climbed into their respective homes with armfuls of bread, eggs and vegetables. In the mornings they waved blearily to each other, stepping out of their cabins as the dawn light reflected off the perfect mirror of water, their movements the first disturbance in the deep stillness of morning.

'It's nice travelling like this,' Maryann said to Joel the first evening. 'With Darius and Nance, I mean. Can we do it again, d'you think?'

He looked up, surprised at the enthusiasm in her voice.

'It'll depend on the loads,' he said, 'but I'm happy with it. It seems to suit you, so that's all the better.'

At Stoke Bruerne the two of them went to see Sister Mary in her surgery by the cut. She wore a white coat and her kindly face, looking out from under a long white nurse's veil, broke into a delighted smile at the sight of Maryann with her twin daughters, wrapped up plump as sausages, in her arms.

'Well I never!' Sister Mary helped Maryann lie them down so that she could examine them. 'Goodness me, you have got your hands full now, haven't you? But what lovely healthy babies!' She made a fuss of Joley, Sally and Ezra as well, before turning to their cousins.

'And you, Nancy – are you still keeping all right?' Sister Mary had delivered Nance's last two babies.

'Yes, ta,' Nancy said cheerfully.

'You do look the picture of health,' Sister Mary chuckled. 'You were obviously made for this life. I don't think there's anything I need to do for you – except remind you not to go pulling those boats about. D'you hear?'

'I hope she'll listen to you better than she does to me!' Maryann said.

'Yes, Sister.' Nancy grinned at her. They were all very fond of Sister Mary. She did such a lot to support the women of the cut and keep them and their children in good health.

Seven

It was a long haul down to London.

'Blooming long journey – started in 1942 and ended in 1943!' Nance quipped. After the New Year arrived they eventually slid between the green sides of Cassiobury Park, then past Regent's Park to the docks, or 'Limehouse' as it was known to the boaters.

Maryann and Joel had seldom worked the Grand Union route. As they travelled the last leg east, Maryann stood on the gunwales in the cold wind, looking round as Bobby steered. The cut was so wide down here that it felt quite intimidating. Along the Regent's Canal, boats were tied up on each side, sometimes two deep, but this still left plenty of room in the middle of the channel. Travelling along this wider cut came huge river barges, which would loom in front of them suddenly, making Maryann's pulse race with panic at the thought of a collision. The further south they had travelled, the more barges they seemed to meet.

And London itself came as a shock. She had seen some of the effects of the bombing in Birmingham, and the skyline of Coventry was drastically changed. At one period it had seemed diminished every time they came back to it. But, as Nance told them, London had 'taken it' for weeks on end and she and Darius had been down a couple of nights after the great fire storm raged almost up to St Paul's cathedral. The further east they went the more devastation they saw, whole neighbourhoods lying smashed apart.

When they got to the last lock, the lock keeper examined their loading orders and told them which wharf to go to. The gates swung open and Maryann looked round, awed at the great vista unfolding in front of them. Their boats seemed dwarfed and humble in this vast steely-coloured pool, flanked by wharves where lighters, barges and narrowboats were loading and unloading, cranes spiking up into the sky.

The boat was emptied that night and they were due to be loaded with a new cargo in the morning. After their tea of stew, the Bartholomew brothers and Bobby went to find the pubs outside the dock gates while Maryann and Nancy settled the children for the night. Then Nance came over to the *Theodore*.

They brewed tea and Maryann sat on the back bed with Esther and Ada, and Nance lay along the side bed with her feet up. Occasionally they heard voices as people passed outside.

'I shouldn't want to live down here,' Maryann said.

'No – me neither.' Nance reached over and poured from the old brown teapot. 'Dunno why, but I've always been glad to head home again. Specially when the bombs were coming down. Weeks of it, they had – how their nerves stood it I'll never know. A couple of nights of that almost finished me off, I can tell you. We went into one of them shelters one night. Never again. It was like a bleeding madhouse in there – and the pong! You'd rather die in your own bed, honest you would. Here—'
She handed Maryann her tea.

'Ta. I could get used to being waited on!'

'Best not – not if you're staying on in this life!'

They sipped the hot tea, laughing and joking. *Why do*

I get so down in myself? Maryann wondered. When Nance was there she cheered up and everything seemed all right.

'This is nice,' Nance said, settling back. Her earrings shone in the lamplight. 'Won't last long, though – I can't get comfy anywhere when I'm this far on.' She soon had to shift her position again, giving a comical grunt and laying a hand on her swollen belly. 'This one's on the go like mad tonight – kicking and thumping about. Must be another lad.'

Maryann smiled. 'I'm pleased for you, Nance. Can't say I'm envious though.'

But Nance looked contented. Comfortable in mind, if not body.

'Ah – nothing like it. New life – kiddies. I know it's all hard work, like, but I wouldn't change it, not for nothing.' She looked across at Maryann's pale face in the shadows of the bed hole. 'I mean, what if I'd stayed with Mick? If I hadn't run down to the cut that morning? If I'd done the right thing and stayed with the man I married? 'Cept it *wasn't* the right thing, staying with him. I know our mom says I could go to their new priest, Father Ryan – get an annulment. But I don't even know where Mick is. They think he went up Liverpool, but no one knows for sure. And the Church takes no end of time over it. We'd all be dead by the time they got round to it. None of that seems to matter out here, anyway. We're a family, Darius and me. That's the important thing.'

A blush rising in her cheeks, Maryann asked, 'But Nance – are you just going to go on and on having babbies?'

Nance sat forward, easing her back. 'I've not really thought. I s'pose so. Darius always wanted a big family and he's not a young man any more. Who knows what might happen. And I like giving him babbies, Maryann. His face when he sees a new life. As many as God gives. Seems what's natural to me.'

Maryann fell silent. Natural. The natural thing. That was what she kept hearing. Was she not natural then, feeling that she couldn't just go on bearing more and more children until it killed her?

'You been over Ladywood recently?' Nance was saying. 'Seen Tony – or your mom?'

Esther was beginning to wake, snuffling, and Maryann took her on her lap.

'I saw Tony a few weeks back. The babby Joanie's a nice little thing. I don't know as they're getting on all that well, though. Dolly gets mithered about the smallest thing – goes on at Tony no end. Don't know how he stands it. And no – I've not seen our mom. To tell you the truth I don't even know if her house is still standing. I'm not going to see her, Nance. I've been bitten that way before and I'm not going back for more. She's made it very clear where she stands. As a matter of fact . . .' She gasped. 'God, Nance – I've just thought . . .' She stopped, a new suspicion forcing into her mind.

'What?'

'The other week when we was tied up at Tyseley, one of the wharf men come to me and said someone was asking for me.' She related to Nance Charlie Dean's report of the visitor to the wharf.

Nance sat up straighter, her face turning deadly serious.

'He was asking for me by name, knew the name of our boats and everything . . .'

'You don't think it's – not *him*?'

'Well, who on earth else could it be, looking like that?

But how would he know where I was? Someone must've told him and now – I've just thought – what if he went back to see our mom?'

'She *wouldn't*?' Nance's eyes were wide with horror at the thought.

'Oh, I wouldn't put it past her,' Maryann said bitterly. 'She blames everything that's happened on me.'

'But after all this time? What would he want?'

'I don't know.' With a shudder, Maryann cuddled Esther more tightly to her. The tiny lighted cabin of the boat now felt like an island of safety surrounded by threatening, icy darkness.

'Well, he won't be looking you up to take you dancing, will he? Have you told Joel?'

Maryann shook her head. 'Joel doesn't know the half of it. I don't want him to know – I don't want him near us, even the thought of him!' She was getting worked up now, panic rising in her. 'He's like poison – he eats away at you until there's nothing left. Oh, Nance – what d'you think he wants?'

They left before midday next day, after craneloads of long, rusty steel billets for Tyseley were swung from the wharf and came crashing down into the boats. Even that late in the day a freezing mist hung over the cut like a ghostly grey blanket. Maryann made sure she kept the kettle constantly on the hob. Bobby was feeling the worse for wear from the night before.

'How much did you let him drink?' she scolded Joel teasingly. 'Look at the state of him – he'll have to go in and sleep it off, looking like that! Never mind, Bobby – only a hundred and sixty-six locks to go!'

Bobby, groaning, was allowed to recover until the

flight at Marsworth, when he was turned out onto the bank to recover by doing some vigorous lock-wheeling.

Maryann was very uneasy when she heard that they'd been detailed to go to Birmingham again. But they couldn't turn a load down because of her fears, could they? Fears of a grim phantom from her past life? How would they explain that to Essy Barlow? She said nothing to Joel.

The journey back was going well until they got to the lovely green stretch at Tring summit. It was a brighter day than the one on which they'd started off, one of sunlit, dazzling cold. The *Isla* and *Neptune* had steamed on ahead of them after their descent down the locks the other side of the summit. When they were breasted up to go down, Joel called across.

'There's summat not right with her!' He pointed to the engine hole and the chimney, which was issuing blacker, angrier looking smoke than usual. There was a sinister knocking sound.

'She sounds bad!' Maryann yelled back.

'We'll try and make it to the bottom and then I'll see to her,' Joel shouted.

As Bobby shoved the last lock open, the *Esther Jane*'s motor was making ever more bronchial sounds and Joel pulled over and tied up. Darius and Nancy's boats were already well out of sight, and by the time Joel had spent two frustrating hours leaning and squatting in the engine hole over the ailing Bolinder engine, the other pair were irretrievably lost to them. The cats, Spots and Jenny, strolled along the gunwales of the *Theodore* as if bemused by the delay. Bobby kept the children entertained on the bank, letting Ezra jump and climb all over him. Maryann was thankful for the umpteenth time for his kindly nature. Ezra was a real handful to keep an eye on and Bobby often helped out. Eventually Joel said, '*Ah!*' Hands black, oil on his face he started up the engine again and after a couple of coughs, it shuddered into life.

Maryann kissed his oil-smeared beard. 'Clever clogs.'

Joel grinned. 'Not letting that blooming moty beat me.'

A mile further along the sound of the motor became clogged and dragging. Joel signalled back to her. He pulled in again and spent a further hour in the bilges, patiently removing thick shreds of rope and what looked like the remains of a wool sweater which were caught in tortuous twists round the propeller. By the time he had done all this they couldn't go much further before the cold and darkness descended and they had to tie up for the night. Maryann was despondent. They were so far behind now that they'd never catch up, and she missed having the *Isla* and *Neptune* tied along the bank just ahead of them. Instead, they were alone in the freezing country silence, under the stars. But as they was falling asleep Maryann heard an engine puttering past outside.

'There go the beer boats,' she murmured to Joel. The Guinness boats worked fly – they had a larger crew, which meant they could keep going day and night chug-ging on along the black cut. 'Glad we're not working them.'

Joel, almost lost to sleep, just managed to grunt in agreement.

The morning was bitterly cold, the grass crackling with frost, and a thin film of ice covered the cut. The bright blue sky of the day before had been replaced by an unyielding grey, which seemed to fit like a lid over the fields. Climbing out through the hatches at dawn, they felt the air sting their noses and their breath left them in clouds of white.

Joel drank from his steaming teacup and looked round.

'If this keeps up, they'll have to get the icebreakers out.'

But the ice was thin enough for the boats to nose through quite easily, cracking it into thin, glasslike sheets. The cold and stillness did not lift all day and the ducks, which usually appeared round the boats looking for food, stayed tucked in the undergrowth and reeds. Only a solitary heron braved the cold and flapped languidly ahead of them, landing at intervals on the bank until the motor grew nearer and drove it onwards again.

Soon they were approaching the junction at Braunston, where they would turn onto the Oxford Canal. As they came through the tunnel at Braunston, enveloped in damp darkness, Maryann thought, *Nancy and Darius'll be about at Warwick or Leamington by now.* Would they see them on the way back? She was disappointed and uneasy. She had wanted the reassurance of Darius and Nance tied up near them when they reached Tyseley Wharf.

She only became gradually aware of the shouting ahead because she was in the cabin. They'd made the turn and Bobby was at the helm. She could hear something, but then Bobby's voice came to her: 'Maryann – you'd best come out!'

He pointed as she came and stood outside. They'd tied the butty on a shorter strap to go through Braunston, so she was not far behind Joel on the *Esther Jane*. The first thing she saw was a small crowd ahead on the bank, who were waving and shouting at them, while a tan and white dog ran back and forth about their legs, barking in agitation. It took only seconds to see that something was seriously wrong. Maryann took in the scene in small glimpses of understanding, as if the corner of a large picture was being gradually revealed to her. A space had been reserved for them along the bank and several of the women were beckoning them urgently to pull in. As they drew close, she made out that the boats the gaggle of people had gathered by were the *Isla* and the *Neptune*. Her mind struggled with this: why were they here instead of much further ahead? Then Joel turned and signalled to them that they were pulling in and Bobby was saying, 'Oh my – what's amiss here?' and at that moment, from the cabin of the *Neptune*, Maryann saw Darius appear and step off the boat. There was a stiffness in the way he moved and his face was like that of a statue carved from the hardest granite.

'Oh, Bobby.' Maryann went cold all over at the sight of him. 'Summat terrible's happened, I can tell. Where's Nance?'

Helping hands seized the straps and secured them as they jumped onto the bank, Maryann taking Sally's hand. Everyone stood back and became quiet as Joel went to his brother. Maryann walked behind, suddenly acutely conscious of following Joel's footsteps, the brown corduroy of his trousers above his boots, of turning to reach out to Sally again as she ran up beside her, of stopping as Joel put his hand on Darius's shoulder. The older brother crumpled, lowering his head, a hand going up to cover his face.

No! Maryann was screaming inside herself. *Not one of the children, not Nance, not any of them, O God, please, no!*

Darius looked up again, face twisted with grief. 'Her's

drownded.' His voice cracked. 'My little mate. My Nancy.'

Maryann heard the sound of a woman weeping behind her. Darius, sobbing openly now, led them into the cabin away from the watching eyes. He went and sat on the edge of the back bed. The first thing Maryann was aware of was the three children, squashed like peas in a pod along the side bench, all crying heartbrokenly. It was the most miserable sight she could imagine. She and Joel squeezed inside the cabin. Nancy lay on the back bed, covered with a blanket, its curving line tracing the shape of her heavy pregnancy. As Darius leaned back to allow them closer, Maryann saw that her friend's face was a bluish white, the features lifeless, somehow impersonal. Nancy, yet not Nancy: the power, the spark of life extinguished in her. Maryann stared, unable fully to take in the sight. The children continued to cry behind her.

'Oh, Nance,' she whispered. Leaning over, she reached under the blanket for her old friend's hand and grasped the cold fingers. 'Come on, Nance,' she said, squeezing them. 'Oh, Nance, what've you done? What's happened to you?' She recoiled, a howl of horror and protest trapped in her chest. 'What's happened?' she demanded of Darius. How could he have let this happen to her friend, to Nancy, who was brimming with energy, with joy, her body leaping with the life of another child? She felt Joel's hand on her shoulder and turned to him, his arms clasping her tight. All of them were weeping. Maryann pulled away and put her arms briefly round Darius, then went and knelt in front of Darrie, Sean and little Rose, trying to draw them all to her at once.

Eight

It was some time before they were calm enough to hear from Darius what had happened. They climbed out and stood in a gaggle, the crowd on the bank tactfully retreating.

The previous evening Darius and Nancy had gone on, getting ahead right into the dusk, aiming to get to Braunston for the night. Darkness seemed to fall even more quickly than usual and they were still on the move, persevering on through the gloom with their blacked-out headlamp. They'd get through the last few locks on the Grand Union, they agreed, tie up at Braunston and get a good start in the morning. It was already punishingly cold, ice forming on the ground, making the towpath and lock sides treacherously slippery. Nancy had been inside the *Neptune*, bedding the children down, and Ernie was at the tiller. At the bridge-hole before the locks, though, Nancy had completed her chores and picked up the windlass.

'I'll go out for a bit. I could do with stretching my legs,' she said to Ernie. 'You stay here.'

Before he could argue she'd stepped off. Darius hadn't known that she'd got off instead of Ernie until he looked back, wondering why Ernie hadn't already passed the motor boat, running ahead to make sure the lock was ready. Instead, he saw Nancy puffing and panting along.

'I was a bit put out with her,' Darius said. 'We was

trying to get on and she couldn't move as fast as she can – could – normal like, her being so big. I thought, what did Nance want to go getting off for? But it were too late by then.

'We got through two and Nance was managing all right, she were strong, you know. And nippy, even when she was expecting ... We was breasted up and Nance'd shut the gates behind us.' He shook his head, still disbelieving of what had happened. 'She'd gone and got the first paddle up. I dunno how she came to fall. She knew she always had to hold on. It was second nature. She was crossing the gate to get the other one and ... I wasn't even looking. I'd gone into the cabin for summat. She come off the gates, fell right down.' His distress mounted as he talked. 'I don't know if she hit her head on the gate or on the *Isla* ... But I looked up – the water was only coming in from one side so it was pushing us about and I thought why ent she got the other paddle open? And she weren't there.' His face crumpled again. 'She just weren't there any more.'

It was a silent, grief-stricken cortège which made its desolate way back to Sutton Stop, outside Coventry. Other boaters who called greetings, ignorant of the tragedy, were met by the frozen, unresponsive faces of people lost in their own thoughts and emotions and the one-sided 'How d'you do's?' faded unanswered on the air. Darius stood straight and still at the tiller of the *Isla* as the boats bore the love of his life back to be buried among the people and villages they knew so well.

For Maryann, every chug of the engine seemed to hammer home the pain inside her. Even here, at the heart of her family, she felt very alone without Nancy. Nance had been her oldest friend, and each had linked the other with the past, with their childhood. Now Nance was gone. It was so difficult to believe and hard not to wait expectantly for Nance to pop up through the *Neptune*'s hatches in her bright clothes and shine the brass bands on her chimney with her usual vigour, or wave and make daft faces at them as they followed behind. All the times she would not see Nance now, all the chats and shared chores and confidences poured into her mind, bombarding her with a future of sad loneliness.

She had managed to find a quiet moment before they left. She asked Darius if she could go aboard the *Neptune* alone to say goodbye and had taken with her a few sprigs of winter jasmine and some pretty red berries which, in their colourful flamboyance, reminded her of Nance. She sat beside her old friend's body. Nance's face was very bruised on the left side, her clothes were still damp and her coldness made Maryann recoil – it seemed so foreign to the warm, vibrant friend she had known. But she took Nance's hand and held it. If she didn't hold her now, soon it would be too late.

'I don't know what I'm going to do without you, old pal.' Her throat ached and the sobs began to rise in her. She pressed Nance's cold hand against her cheek and its strange stiffness made her cry even more. 'Oh, Nance – why did you go and get out of the boat? Couldn't you've sat still, just for once? Why did you have to go and leave us all?'

She drew the blanket back a little, and through her tears looked at Nance's distended body. The poor little baby! Did he die when Nance died or after, living on inside his dead mother, not realizing she was not able to care for him any more and keep him safe? It was a terrible thought. Grief tore at her, for herself and for

71

Darius and his motherless children. However would he manage now?

'I'll do all I can for them, Nance, you know I will. For Darrie and Sean and Rose. But oh, Nance, it's going to be bitter hard for us all without you.'

Nancy lay so peacefully, so uncharacteristically silent. If it were not for the bruising she looked as if she were sleeping, enjoying a sweet dream in her cosy little home. Here she lay on this bed, Maryann thought, which was hardly a bed at all, more a board with a few bits of bedding, but which had served as a happy marriage bed for what was not even a real marriage either in the eyes of respectable people. But Nance had been real all right. And what she and Darius had had made a pale shadow of a lot of other people's marriages. The cut and its people had truly lit the fire of life in Nancy, and the cut had also taken it away.

At last she leaned down and kissed the unbruised side of her old friend's face, her tears falling on Nance's pallid skin.

'You rest now, my love,' she said. 'Sweet dreams.' And, before covering her again, she laid the yellow jasmine and the bright berries on her breast.

Maryann sent a telegram to Cathleen Black, Nance's mom.

They were to finish the journey to Birmingham later. All that week the family clung together. Maryann did everything she could for Nancy's children. Darrie preferred to stay with his father and Rose was very young. Of all of them it was little curly-haired Sean who most wrung her heart, asking and asking where his mom had gone. He and Rose seemed to take some comfort from the presence of their auntie Maryann.

Cathleen Black came from Birmingham for the funeral, with four of Nancy's brothers and her two younger sisters, Lizzie and Mary. Cathleen and Nance had been close, as for many years Nancy had been the only girl among a gaggle of brothers. Cathleen's curly hair had long turned from salt and pepper grey to a silvery white. She had on a squashed black felt hat pushed down over it and a brown tweed coat belted tightly at the waist. She wore spectacles now and her eyes, one of which had been crossed from birth, peered out rather rakishly from behind the thick lenses. Her children were all in their Sunday best, Lizzie and Mary in frocks that were too big for them. All of them were pale and strained with loss.

They knew Nance would have wanted to be buried from the cut rather than back in Birmingham, so the funeral was to be at the church in Longford, where so many narrowboat women had been churched and their babies christened. Maryann put on her one and only best dress which she had kept from her wedding, in soft, blue wool. It felt very peculiar wearing it again.

It was a cold day, but dry. Nancy's coffin was lifted with great care onto the roof of the *Isla* and decorated with flowers. Darius took the tiller, Darrie and Sean beside him. Sean looked bewildered and sad, but Darrie, togged up in his best clothes, dark eyed and solemn, seemed older and more dignified than his seven years. Maryann travelled on the *Neptune* with Cathleen and Nance's sisters, Rose and the twins. Joel brought up the rear on the *Esther Jane* with all the other youngsters squeezed aboard, the lads thinking it great sport to cling along the gunwales which were very low in the water as the boats were still loaded with their Birmingham steel. And behind came Ernie's family, the Higginses, on their boat *Dragonfly* and a number of other families who all wanted to support the Bartholomews.

'At least on the way I can talk to Cathleen and explain properly,' Maryann said to Joel before they untied. 'Poor thing – you can just see what this's done to her, can't you?'

Cathleen seemed dazed and not at all herself. Once they'd started, Maryann handed the tiller to Lizzie, who was twelve and thrilled by the responsibility.

'Just hold it steady in the middle. Shout if you're worried.' She went in to make more tea and see Cathleen, who was sitting in the cabin, looking round her in bewilderment.

'God, Maryann, how d'you manage to live on here? I thought our house was cramped! I can't see Nance keeping one of these spick and span! My poor girl . . .' Her eyes filled again. Maryann handed her a cup of tea with a sizable portion of their sugar ration in it.

'She did, though. Loved it. She was always full of beans, Nance was. Better at keeping up with it all than me.'

Cathleen almost managed a smile. 'Well, she didn't get that from me.'

Nancy's little Rose who was now three, came and pawed shyly at Maryann's arm.

'Hello, bab.' Maryann put her arm round her, cut by the lost look in the child's eyes.

'God love her.' Cathleen looked round for somewhere to put her tea down. 'Come here, darlin' – come and see your nanna.'

Rose looked fearfully at the strange lady peering at her from behind thick spectacles, then back at Maryann.

'It's all right, pet – that's your nanna – your mom's mom. Don't you remember Nanny Cathleen? Go to her for a love.'

Eventually Rose consented to be cuddled. Tears came into Cathleen's eyes. 'She's the image of our Nancy, she is. What'll become of the children, Maryann? Whatever's he going to do?'

'I don't know,' Maryann said wanly. She had been so numb, this week of grieving, that just getting through each day had been hard enough. 'I don't know how Darius is going to get along, Cathleen. I've never seen a man look more lost.'

'I know.' Cathleen paused, then looked across at Maryann. 'Our Nancy really loved him – she did, didn't she? I know it really – it's just that if she'd stayed with her husband, with Mick Mallone, none of this would have happened . . .'

Maryann leaned across to her. 'Cathleen, Nancy had more happiness with Darius these few years than she could have had in a lifetime with Mick.'

Cathleen gave a heavy, sorrow-laden sigh. 'I know.' She kissed the top of Rose's curls, holding the child close. 'I know that really. You only had to look at her.'

Nancy's coffin was carried into church with great ceremony, borne on the shoulders of Darius, Joel, Ernie Higgins and three of her brothers, Charlie, Jim and Percy. The rest of them processed behind with the other mourners. Nance had won a great deal of respect and liking among the boating people, for her skill and cheerfulness and her well-scrubbed family; now they had come to support the Bartholomew brothers and see Nancy off in style. Maryann had been surprised and grateful at their reaction to Nance. This community of people were, in the main, sticklers for convention. Because they were different, not readily understood by outsiders, they fought off the insults that they were dirty 'water gypsies' by strict adherence to social codes. Boaters were married and buried in style, and woe betide a boatwoman who associated too much with another woman's husband unless his wife was within earshot as well! But though Darius and Nance had never married, their situation was understood and accepted. Darius was respected and his 'best mate' was respected too.

Maryann walked with Cathleen, whose nose was pink with cold.

'I've never set foot in a Protestant church before,' she whispered, holding Rose's plump hand and gazing fearfully up at the benign facade of Longford parish church.

'It'll be all right.' Maryann squeezed her arm. 'It's nice. Nance liked it.'

'Did she?' Cathleen sounded surprised, then determined. 'Anyway – Father Ryan's not here to see me, is he?'

In their pews in the musty old church, the boaters and Nance's family sang and prayed Nancy to rest. Out of habit, Cathleen took her string of white rosary beads from her pocket and told them throughout. As they sang 'Abide with Me', Maryann felt the desolate, unjust sorrow of it all overwhelm her and she wept with her arms round Rose and Sally, who cried too at the sight of her. After, while the vicar was reciting the service, other words came back to her, spoken to her during her time in service in Banbury by Roland Musson, one of the sons of the family. Roland had survived the Great War in body, if not entirely in mind, and lived as a recluse at home. That morning he had told her about a young lad in his unit who had completed a successful raid in No Man's Land one night, but was killed first thing the next day. For a moment Maryann was back standing in the sun-filled room at Charnwood House, with Roland Musson saying, '... chap stood up for a few seconds and bang – killed by a sniper. So what was it all about? Man grows up, becomes himself overnight, then –' He snapped his fingers. 'Like a bloody butterfly.'

And what was it all about? Maryann thought bitterly, when they watched Nance's coffin being lowered into the ground. God takes the best young, some people said. This enraged her. Why bother with God if he was like that? Why tangle with God at all of he wasn't the sort who'd be there crying beside her because Nance's life had been cut short?

The sun broke through and shone bravely against the cold as they stood there, Joel beside his grief-stricken brother, who broke down over the grave.

'My Nancy,' he groaned, 'my lovely Nancy ...'

'Oh, the poor man,' murmured Cathleen Black. 'Holy Jesus, why did this have to happen?'

Before the family left again for Birmingham, Cathleen asked Darius whether he wanted her to take any of the children to look after.

'They'll all be too much for you on your own, won't they, God love them?'

Darius, already distraught, could not contemplate the idea of losing any more of his family that day, even as a temporary measure. He thanked her a little brusquely, but said he wanted to keep his family together. Cathleen suddenly put her arms round him and pulled him close with affection.

'We've all lost a jewel in our Nancy,' she said, 'but I want to thank you for giving her these few truly happy years. I've never seen her bonnier or more full of life than when she was with you, Darius.'

Finding it hard to speak, Darius managed to thank her for her daughter and shyly embrace her.

'Come and see us whenever you can,' Cathleen said, trying to be brave. 'I don't want to miss my grandchildren growing up.'

After they had waved the Blacks off to catch their evening train, Maryann helped Darius to settle the children, all together in the big bed for comfort. They were tearful and exhausted and soon fell asleep, while Maryann and Darius sat on the side bench. Sean was still snuffling pitifully even after sleep overtook him. Darius looked across at his sleeping children, an anguish beyond words in his eyes.

'Well,' he sighed. 'We'll just have to keep on, somehow.'

Maryann nodded, tearful again, and touched his arm. She loved Darius like a brother. 'I know,' she said, and for them these simple words were enough to acknowledge the chasm of emptiness left by Nance's passing.

'I want you to have these now.' Darius slid a hand into his jacket pocket and laid on Maryann's hand two gold hoops: Nance's earrings, which had belonged to Esther, Darius and Joel's mother. She knew this was an honour, as if to say, you're the only one left in line now.

She nodded again, understanding. 'I'll always wear them.'

*

It had been a gruelling day and her own children were asleep when she got back to the *Theodore*. Joel poured each of them a generous tot of whisky, which they drank gratefully, along with their tea, and sat on at the table, somehow reluctant to go to bed.

Once lying side by side, they seemed unable to sleep, as if loss of consciousness was a denial of life, and after this day of death and heavy sorrow they needed to seize life and hold on to it. Maryann lay with her head on Joel's chest, his arm round her, hearing the whisper of his lungs.

'You sound chesty tonight.'

'I can feel it coming on a bit.' He wheezed, and gave a cough to clear it. 'Bitter today, wasn't it?'

There was a pause, then Maryann raised her head to look at him. 'How's Darius going to manage? He won't be able to, will he? Not with the three of them and no Nance?'

Joel shook his head. 'I don't know what's going to be best. Can't think. But we couldn't say much about it today could us? I reckon we'll need to help him out.'

'Take the children you mean?'

Joel's nod meant 'maybe', Maryann saw with some dismay. But she knew she had to do anything she could to see Nance's children were taken care of. She peeped over at their twins' sleeping faces.

'I couldn't bear it if it was you.' She looked down at Joel. 'I don't think I could go on. Not without you.'

Smiling, his vivid eyes looking deep into hers, Joel reached up and stroked her cheek. 'My lovely,' he said, 'my little mate. We're here now though, ent we? Now is what we've got.'

'Oh, Joel—' A shudder went through her. 'Nancy was so cold! I don't want to die.'

He stroked her back, making loving, soothing noises, and in a moment they were kissing, pressing close together, fierce with desire for each other, for life. As they loved one another it did not even cross Maryann's mind to stop him, to ask him to pull away at the last minute. The heat of their bodies, the joy and healing comfort of it was all, life and its celebration was what mattered. She pulled him close, her arms clenched to hold him tight, and after their lovemaking they slept, curled tightly together in the freezing night.

Nine

'You poorly again, Mom?'

Maryann just managed to grab the dipper in time and leant over it, retching. Though she was secluded in the privacy of the cabin, she was being watched by a row of curious children, Ezra, Sally and Rose, as her morning tea gushed out into the bottom of the wide container.

Maryann wiped her lips and watering eyes, grimacing at the acid taste in her mouth. She nodded absent-mindedly at Sally's question, not having the strength to reply. She knew this sickness all too well. After drinking down a cup of water she went out, amid the shouts and rattling of chains of the wharf, to empty the dipper. The contents met the surface with a glutinous 'plop' and the milk curled in the dark water for a moment before disappearing. They were at Tyseley again, their cargo being unloaded. Exhausted before the day had even begun, she rested for a moment against the cabin, looking out across the piles of deep orange steel, the scrappy wharf refuse of wire, nails, bits of wood and greasy rags scattered over the cindery ground. She'd been too caught up in her present woes to be afraid of coming back here. All she'd been able to think of on the wet trip up from Limehouse was keeping going, trying to get through the day and not show that she felt sick or weak or faint.

It was two months since Nancy's death and the harsh freeze of that winter had given way to March winds and rain. Starting work again after the funeral, they'd all had to make decisions about how things were going to be managed. Should Darius give up his Barlow boats and come back aboard the *Esther Jane*? But Mr Barlow was desperate to keep all his boats and crews working. The war created an almost bottomless demand for coal, steel and other materials. Let Darius keep the *Isla* and *Neptune*, he said. He could work them with Ernie and he'd find him an extra crewman. The man who filled Nance's place – in no other respect except that he was a lifelong boater – was a middle-aged man called Joe Toms. Joe had also been a Number One and had kept on with his own horse until recently, when his wife had died 'of the bronchitus'. Darius already knew Joe quite well and thought they'd be able to work together. He also said that he could manage aboard with Darrie and Sean, but was grateful when Joel said he and Maryann would look after Rose. Sally was delighted with this arrangement as she was two years older than Rose; it provided both another female playmate and a subject to be bossed about. She immediately started teaching Rose her letters. For Maryann she was another child to be fed and protected from all the dangers of the cut, but she was also a link with Nancy and she did her best for the little girl. But during those months of freezing wind and rain Maryann's spirits had been very low, and when she started to be sick she was filled with despair.

They were mostly working the old routes, the Coventry and Oxford cuts, with occasional trips to London and Birmingham. Maryann had said nothing to Joel about her fears that her stepfather, Norman Griffin, was looking for her. This was only their second trip to Tyseley in the past two months and nothing had happened so far that was out of the ordinary. She was beginning to relax again. After all, why on earth should Norman Griffin want to have anything to do with her after all these years? If anyone was capable of leaving one life and starting off again in another, with a new name and identity, it was him. Why would he want to come back, disturbing old memories?

Leaning over the side, she rinsed the dipper out. A dead bird floated, stiff-legged, close to the bank, rotating slowly on a twisting current. Jenny, the tortoiseshell cat, watched it mesmerized, head twitching back and forth.

'Can't we get off yet?' Ezra demanded behind her.

'No!' Maryann snapped, standing up. 'How many times've I told you, you can't be out there running about when we're unloading. See them chains swinging about? They could have your head off.' She softened a little, looking into his eager, if filthy face. 'They've nearly finished, pet. Just stay on a bit more. A wash wouldn't hurt you, would it?'

Back in the cabin she managed to force a slice of dry bread down her throat and feed the children. It would be a relief when the unloading was completed and the cooped-up children could escape onto the bank, scampering over to find Joel and Joley in the offices.

Maryann sank down on the side bed, still feeling weak and sick. Lord, if only she could lie down and sleep again! Everywhere she looked there was muck and mess – jobs staring her in the face, crocks to be washed, a pan gluey with porridge, crumbs and dirt everywhere, the stove all rust and a pail of dirty napkins outside, beckoning with their smell. Ada and Esther had had a feed and gone back to sleep behind the curtains of the back bed. She shut them in to keep it dark, hoping they'd sleep as long as possible. They'd wake soon, though, and while they were tied up here she ought to be cleaning and washing like mad to get caught up with herself! But her head felt muzzy in the hot cabin and her limbs just wouldn't seem to move, however much her head ordered them to. Her ribs and stomach felt tender from retching. She sat, staring dully at the stains down her skirt, her innards still turning uneasily.

Ada and Esther were seven months old now. Really bonny, everyone said. Esther's hair had grown into dark curls, her eyes big and blue, cheeks rosy and plump. And Ada was still the live wire, smaller featured, red haired and with a nose-wrinkling smile. But only seven months since they were born! How could she have caught again so soon? Her despair sat in her, cold as stone. She felt pushed down too low even for tears. So far she had managed to hide the fact that she was expecting from Joel. She was ashamed of not telling him. She would have liked his happiness, his sympathy, when she felt so ill, but she hid her exhaustion and poorliness as well as she could. Because Joel would never forgive her if he knew what was in her mind. To Joel his children were the fruits of his manhood, his success, his pledge for the future. She couldn't confide in him, not this time. Though she was now certain she was expecting, she didn't allow herself to think of the infant as 'he' or 'she'. She pushed away any imaginings of it as grown up, running among her other children, hand in hand along the flowery towpaths of the Oxford cut. Because having another child was unimaginable. It was impossible. There were already six infants on board. Her whole over-whelmed being cried no! It could not be. In that cold, hard place inside her, she knew she could not do it. Not now. She'd give Joel more children later, but not so soon. She needed more of a gap or she would go under, and then, as Alice Simons had said, where would the rest of the family be?

Moving carefully so as not to lurch her insides about, she eased herself to her feet, rinsed the dipper out again with clean water and piled the family's few crocks in it. All the time, shouts and clangs came from outside. Her ears were cocked for sounds of the twins waking. She must get some things done before they woke! She was so slow, fighting sickness and faintness when she stood up too quickly. All the time, as she poured hot water and soap over the dishes, while she hurriedly rinsed out the napkins and strung them along the empty hold of the *Theodore*, her mind worried frantically at her problems. Bobby usually went and filled the water cans for them when they tied up. But maybe if she went to fill them, lugged those arm-breaking eight-gallon cans back and forth, would that do it? Would that be a way of starting things off? Doing away with . . . it?

Scraping porridge from the sides of the pan, she tried to recall fragments of conversations overheard in her childhood, the things women whispered over the grimy walls of Ladywood backyards. These were the scraps of wisdom and hearsay she called upon when the children fell ill: tea-leaf water for sore eyes, goose fat for bad chests, the middle of a boiled onion in the ear when they had earache. But it was more adult, whispered remedies she tried to remember. Drinking water which had had pennies boiled in it, pennyroyal syrup, gin? Wasn't there something about gin? And, whispered more quietly, more shamefully still, 'putting something up inside'. Once she'd followed her mother into a house where she was helping another woman who'd 'had a miss', and before Flo shooed her out again she'd glimpsed at the foot of the bed the po' half full of blood. The image made her innards contract with fear. Round and round spun her thoughts. What could she do? Oh, if there were just someone she could ask, could confide in! If only Nancy were still here! She couldn't have told Nance, though, not about this. Not life-loving, Catholic Nance – she would've been horrified. But at least she would've been here, the comfort of her, not gone for ever. She ached with loneliness, the tears running down her cheeks and dripping into the washing-up water, but when she tried to stop, wiping her face with her sleeve, the sight of a fraying tear in her old brown cardi made her cry even harder. *If only I had someone to talk to*, she wept. *God, the way I nearly blurted everything out to that preacher last night. That would've given him something to pray about, all right.*

They'd reached Tyseley in the late afternoon and Maryann had hurried out without the children, to get to the shops for their rations before everything closed. Even a brief chat with Mr Osborne hadn't lifted her spirits. As she came back across the wharf with her bread, meat, spuds and tinned milk, she saw the pale young man whom she had caught sight of with his bible on the wharf a few months back. He was speaking to one of the other boatwomen as she stood on the counter of her butty boat, lifting out the tiller to upend it for the night. The man was dressed shabbily in black and wore a trilby hat. His one flash of colour was a red tartan scarf, the ends of which were blowing back over his shoulder in the breeze. Maryann saw the woman nod politely, say something which was evidently dismissive, and disappear into her cabin.

And as Maryann moved across to the *Theodore*, he was suddenly beside her.

'Good evening, madam,' he said, touching the brim of his hat.

'Evening,' Maryann said brusquely. She knew nothing about the man except that he must be one of those 'holy Joes' and they were people she had long found disquieting. She remembered the odd figure of Jimmy Jesus, who used to stand shouting out his message in the Bull Ring. And as children they were frightened of running into the Mormons because people said they would steal away young girls and force them to be brides in Salt Lake City.

'May I presume upon a moment of your time, madam?' he persisted. From his accent, Maryann could tell he was not from Birmingham but from somewhere further north. He held out to her a pale, thin hand and when she felt forced to stop and glance into his eyes, she saw they were large and dark grey and somehow melancholy in a way which made her soften a little towards him. He had well-pronounced brows and lips so full that she found them off-putting, they looked so plump and moist. But she felt obliged to push her packages into the clasp of her left arm and shake hands, conscious of her rough, callused palms.

'I'm Pastor Owen,' he told her. 'James Owen.' Instead of releasing her hand, he turned it over and examined it.

'A hand that knows a hard-working life,' he said, giving her another of his deep, mournful looks. To her consternation, Maryann felt tears pricking her eyes. She pulled her hand away, making out that she was about to drop her shopping.

'What d'you want?' It came out sharper than she had intended.

'Only a moment of your time to share with you the good news of the risen Christ. I'm quite new to the Lord's work in this area.' He spoke so humbly and

87

sincerely that she felt guilty, but had no idea what to say in reply. In her head, her mother's voice admonished, 'Tell him to bugger off!'

Instead, she said, 'Oh, I see.'

From the pocket of his coat he drew a small, plump bible. Without opening it, but holding it out on the flat of his hand as if proffering a plate of sandwiches, he said, ' "Come to me, all ye that labour and are heavy laden, and I will give you rest." The words of our Lord Jesus – and I am very certain that upon Him alone you can lay all your burdens, Mrs . . .?'

'Bartholomew.'

'Mrs Bartholomew.' He went on to tell her how Jesus was the only gate to eternal salvation and to ask whether she had any pressing burdens upon her soul.

Maryann almost quipped that if he had a couple of hours to spare she could tell him a few, but she was prevented by the genuine sense of sympathy coming from the young man, along with his gangly, rather pathetic look. He could only have been in his early twenties and looked as if, had she laid the burdens of her soul upon him as he suggested, his knees might have buckled under the strain.

'I don't think so, not today, thank you,' she said, as if refusing wares from a fish salesman.

'Well, just remember – Jesus is the way,' he said earnestly. 'And I will pray for you, Mrs Bartholomew. I trust you will do the same for me.'

As she nodded, he touched the brim of his hat again and turned away, and she watched his long, skinny form move along the wharf, looking out for other boaters who would stop and listen to his message. Boaters whom he no doubt saw as the unschooled and unsaved souls of the cut whom he must rescue.

Thinking of him now as she struggled through her chores, Maryann knew how close she had come to blurting out her woes to him – a young man, wet behind the ears and a complete stranger! But in her fear and loneliness he was the one person who had asked about her concerns, and who might listen. But then, on hearing, how sharply he would have condemned her! She was contemplating nothing less than the murder of a child in her womb! She was a terrible mother, a terrible woman. But, she thought defiantly, what did that young lad know about being a mother? How could he judge her?

More tears ran down her cheeks.

'Oh, Nance, come back! O God, forgive me for feeling like this!'

She pushed her hands down into the bottom of the dipper and straightened her arms, leaning over the warm water. She was so lost in misery that she didn't move until she heard Joel's voice talking to the children as they all came across the wharf.

Ten

Joel Bartholomew stood at the tiller of the *Esther Jane* later that morning as they made their way, empty for the moment, through Birmingham and out to the coalfields. It was grey and overcast, the warehouses and factories black as shadows as they closed in on each side, and the air darkened by a pall of smoke. Joel breathed in the fume-filled air, then coughed. The Birmingham sky was cluttered with chimneys, the tallest and blackest being those of the fires of industry, belching aggressively into the clouds and creating further clouds themselves. Many more belonged to the endless rows of houses, which seemed to Joel so gloomy and confining. But he only caught glimpses of them: the cut showed him little of Birmingham's life, and it saw little of theirs.

Joel took in less than usual of his surroundings that morning, beyond an automatic watchfulness for the care of his boats, because his mind was restless. Men steering the horse-drawn corporation refuse boats out from the centre of Birmingham to Small Heath tip or to the incinerator at Hay Mills would have seen the *Esther Jane* and her butty heading towards them, washing flapping over the hold of the *Theodore*, and Joel at the tiller, burly, bearded, cap pushed down over his thick hair, his wide-sleeved brown jacket buttoned against the cold. They might have heard his racking cough as he drew nearer, from the damp getting into his lungs. But as they drew alongside and shouted, 'Mornin'!' or 'How d'you do?' as was customary among the politer boaters, they received only the vaguest, most half-hearted response.

When they were approaching Camp Hill locks, Joel signalled back to Bobby. The boats were on a short strap as they were empty, so they were not far apart. Bobby jumped off the butty at one bridge-hole in Sparkbrook and ran forwards to jump aboard the *Esther Jane* at the next.

'You come and steer her through,' Joel ordered, pushing his windlass through his belt. 'I'm going off for a bit.'

'But . . .' Bobby tried to protest. Maryann said the exertions of lock-wheeling made Joel's cough worse and that Bobby should stay off and do it, but Joel was not in the mood to be argued with.

'Can I come, Dad?' Joley called, but too late as another bridge passed and Joel was on the bank.

'You stay on,' he called tersely.

All the way along the flight at Camp Hill he worked with fierce energy, turning the paddles, cursing when his cough doubled him up and made him stop, fighting for breath. He felt taut and explosive inside, his blood hammering in his veins, and he wanted a way to release the tension inside himself. As they worked along the fast-filling locks, he kept his eyes on the immediate task, only casting his glance over the boats in a general, instinctive way, to make sure all was going smoothly. His muscles pulled and strained on the windlass as he turned the paddles.

Every step of the way, though he did not allow his eyes to meet hers, her presence, the white-faced figure of his wife seemed to burn itself into him. His Maryann, his little bird, at the tiller of the *Theodore*, Sally and Rose perched in their coats in front of her on the cabin roof. Once or twice he heard her speak sharply to them. He could hardly avoid catching glimpses of her, in her black skirt and boots, a scarf tied over her hair and her old tweed jacket over her woollens, upright and stony-faced at the helm. Round her had grown up an aura of such misery and loneliness that, however much Joel loved her, he couldn't seem to break through it and now could hardly bear to see it. He knew it was over the loss of Nancy, and he was full of pain and grief too, for Maryann, for his brother, for himself. And Nancy was the one person who knew Maryann from deep in the past, knew her in a way in which no one else did, and Joel knew Maryann's grief cut sharp and raw. But he sensed it was more than that. Over the past few days he felt that something else was troubling her, something he couldn't understand, and he couldn't seem to reach her.

Last night, when they'd lain together in the warm, stuffy air of the *Theodore*, the bitter smell of coal mingling with their breath, he soon realized that though she was silent she was lying awake beside him. The bed was very narrow and no small movement or catch of breath could pass unnoticed if you were awake. Out of the darkness he heard a long, only half-suppressed sigh. For days her face had worn a strained, unhappy look, a frown constantly on her face, sometimes a look of pain. He knew that pale, sick look from when there was a child on the way, but she had said nothing. He knew she was worried about that. Once or twice she had, very shyly, said something about could he pull away – before the last moment. He wasn't sure if she really meant this. It seemed to him such an unnatural, perverse request to ask him to withdraw at the moment when he was giving himself to her and was least able to control himself. He had managed it a couple of times, the second when she cried out, begging him to move away, and with a huge effort he had wrenched himself from her, almost too late. He found it so hard, such a denial of what he needed, that it hadn't always worked. But when he asked if there was a child she shook her head.

'No.' She looked away. 'I've just got a bit of an upset tummy.'

He knew she found the life hard, especially since the children had come along, but in the past she had always reassured him about how much she loved him and how she would not exchange this way of life for any other. But something was eating away at her, he knew, and her quiet suffering made him feel tense and helpless. What should he say? How was he to understand her?

Hearing her sigh in bed, sensing the burdened spirit behind that small outrush of breath, he had reached for her, hoping to achieve with his touch what he could not seem to with words. He felt the comfort of her slight, strong body, his hand sliding over her breast, its soft rounded shape, utter pleasure to him. With his lips he found her neck, moving closer to her, wanting to love her, to give affection and comfort. He stroked her back, her breasts, his hand working downwards over her belly. As he eased his fingers between her legs, her voice burst into the darkness in a wail.

'Oh, Joel, *please* don't!'

She was shaking beside him, sobs breaking out of her like waves taking their time to reach the shore. Weeping brokenly, she turned her back on him.

Having no idea what to do or say, he pulled away, keeping only his hand on her back as she wept in an attempt at comfort, swelling inside with feelings of help-lessness and rejection. When her crying abated, she fell into an exhausted sleep, leaving him restless and frustrated.

He stayed on the bank for a long time that afternoon as they set off along the Bottom Road. He bow-hauled the butty in and out of the locks, through Aston, amid the black, enclosing walls of that part of the cut, the towpaths clogged with oily filth and cinders and its narrow, slime-choked locks. Despite Bobby's repeated offers to exchange places with him, and Joley hopping off to walk warily at his side, he worked on like a dynamo, coughing, working the paddles, tugging on the line to haul the butty, his spirit in turmoil.

Never before in their marriage had he felt this distance from his Maryann. There had been times when the poor, troubled child he knew, before she came back to him as a woman, had closed off from them all and sat sunk in misery. And on many occasions, amid the stress and physical struggles of the boating life, their tempers had crackled and exploded at each other. But that was temporary, was about something he could grasp the meaning of and was over in moments as the annoyance or danger passed. He had never before felt her to be so wholly distant, so completely wretched, and, as if she were his lodestar, he felt thrown off course and afraid.

Is it because she's from off the bank? he wondered. She *was* baffling at times. He often could not work out what was going on in her head. If he'd married a boatwoman born and bred, would it have been easier? Were they more straightforward, the women of the cut, having been known no other life? Was Maryann finally discovering that she couldn't endure it any longer and secretly longing for a house and unmoving days on the bank?

Joel stood at Garrison locks as the water roared

through the paddles. This was the filthiest, most demoralizing part of the whole journey. Overhead, railways criss-crossed over black, clattering bridges; warehouse walls hemmed them in on each side so that the rodent-coloured sky was almost out of sight altogether, but, like a grim reflection, several dead rats were bobbing in the cut amid the scum and oil of the water. A crewman from one of the joey boats waiting to come through the other way bawled along the path, waving his arm.

'Get bloody moving will you?' and Joel realized the water had levelled and he was still standing, staring.

Passing onwards, he tried to imagine any other life than the one he had known. His only time on the bank had been two years in the army, most of it away in France. He had volunteered the year after his mother's death in 1916 in childbirth, when Ada was born. Joel's twin brothers Ezra and Sam had already gone and he left his father and Darius to man the boat, and his sister Sarah to keep house and tend to Ada. Joel was nineteen when he left for France. By the time he returned with his injured lungs, both Ezra and Sam had met their deaths on the Somme without him ever seeing them again, and soon afterwards Sarah had died of the influenza.

Before France, Joel had a part-time sweetheart. Part-time in the sense that boating courtships were capricious affairs, meetings dependent on the movements of cargoes and criss-crossing of boats which might or might not meet. By the time he came wheezing home to what was left of his family, Clara had married one of the 'joshers' and gone to work the Grand Union. Very occasionally, he caught sight of her now, looking across from one of the orange and green Fellows, Moreton & Clayton boats, face hardened by work and weather. A stiff, restrained salute was their only acknowledgement that they had exchanged youthful kisses and – Joel had believed – promises in the Warwickshire meadows all those years ago.

The years after the Great War had been a time of survival for the Bartholomews. By then the family consisted of three men, all numb with grief, and one infant girl, Ada. Ada grew up to be an adept boatwoman. She had been ten years old when a dark-haired girl just a couple of years her senior, skinny as a foal and fiery with mutinous emotions, wandered up to the *Esther Jane* one white, frozen day and announced fiercely to Joel that her name was Maryann Nelson and always would be. Only years later, as a grown woman, had Maryann consented to change her name to Bartholomew, and Joel knew what a store of trust she had invested in him.

He knew it wasn't easy marrying into his way of life, which, before the war began, had been under threat. The boaters kept moving their cargoes, pushing onwards, knowing that if they didn't shift a load they wouldn't get paid, whatever the season, whatever the weather. For Joel, boating was the life he knew in every cell of his body. Any length of time walking in city streets, caught between high buildings and away from the veins of the cut, made him feel fidgety and lost. Family history was a matter of word of mouth, with nothing written down, nor, until his marriage to Maryann, had any photographs ever been taken of his family. Now a framed photograph of that day, him smiling joyfully beside his young bride, hung in the cabin of the *Theodore* amid the ribbon-threaded plates. What he did know, though, was that for at least three generations, back into the haze of those days when Queen Victoria was a young bride herself, Bartholomews had worked the cut and, in particular, the

Oxford cut. Joel's landscape, inner and outer, was marked by winding contours, the black and white beams of locks, the graceful tilt of road bridges which leaned aside to let them past, by those soft, green hills. On that cut, for as long as anyone could remember, they had been Number Ones, working their own family boats, and Joel longed deeply to be a Number One again, for his sons and daughters to work the cut and to feel the dignity and self-respect which had been owned by the previous generations. And he could feel it slipping away from him.

Maryann, too, was so much a part of him now that her deep unhappiness weighed him down. What was troubling her? What could he do to lighten her, to make her smile again?

That night they found a place to stop at Minworth, out beyond the aerodrome. When he went to the *Theodore* after tying up, the three older children were out on the bank. From inside he could hear what sounded like both the twins crying. Timidly, he looked down through the hatches. Maryann was sitting opposite the stove, where bacon was frying in a pan, the fat spitting loudly. In a bowl nearby rested five eggs. She leaned forward to jerk the pan by the handle, her face white and impassive. His heart went out to her. He knew it was hard, that she had so much to do. But that was the life, wasn't it? That was how it was.

He climbed down and squatted on the coalbox and the screams battered his ears. Maryann didn't even look at him.

'Pass us one of them over,' he suggested.

Maryann leaned over and lifted an irate Ada into his arms while she latched Esther onto her breast, still jiggling the pan with one hand.

97

'We've got out through there, anyway,' Joel said. It was always a relief to get past that bit of the cut, even though soon they would reach the coalfields, where everything, landscape and people, was blackened by its dust. He spoke feeling nervous of her, though. He could tell there was something coiled up inside her.

Maryann nodded, still not looking at him. She leaned forward and flipped the rashers over with a knife.

'You all right, little mate?' he asked eventually.

She turned to him then, and in her eyes, for a second he saw a look of utter desperation. But then, by a miracle of will, a smile appeared on her face.

'Yes,' she assured him. 'Course. Tea's nearly ready. Tell Bobby, and the others, will you?'

Eleven

Maryann found herself jerking into consciousness now before dawn, sweating from her dreams. There was a recurring one in which the boats were tied up at Limehouse dock. Maryann was standing on the bank, her boots poised at the edge of the wharf, watching the tide go out, the sea sucking the water back rapidly, boats sinking deeper and deeper down until they seemed much further away than they would be in reality, tiny specks of colour at the foot of the grey wall with its clinging weed and slime. Round them stretched a sea of thick, oozing mud. She felt herself launch forwards over the edge, down, down, knowing that she was going to land smack across the empty hold of a boat and that her belly would pop open like a seed. Except it was the sickening feeling of falling which woke her every time so she never reached the bottom but woke, gasping.

God forgive me, she thought, lying trembling beside Joel's hot, oblivious body. *Just let me be free of it this one time. I'll be able to manage another babby later on, but they're all so close together. I can't. I just can't.*

As the days passed, Maryann knew she had to act. Fear held her back. What was she going to do? If only there was someone she could go to, someone kind like Sister Mary to whom she could pour out all her troubles. But they weren't going down through Stoke Bruerne, and in any case, how could she ever go to Sister Mary

99

and admit what was on her mind? That she had reached such a pitch that she wanted to do away with her baby?

But if I'm going to do it, I've got to get on with it, she kept saying to herself. She could think of nothing else. The thought of it, the dread of childbirth, of another child to cope with possessed her. And supposing it was twins again! In front of Joel and Bobby she tried to act normally, to be cheerful and hide her sickness, though she was constantly pale and strained and she knew Joel had noticed. When she denied that anything was wrong, though, he didn't press her.

Her thoughts wouldn't leave her alone. The cold, closed-off feeling returned, which had come over her when she had run away from home as a young girl and come to Joel and his father on the cut. It had been like that later, for a time, after baby Harry died. If only she could tell Joel how she felt. But that was completely out of the question. If he knew what was in her mind ... Well, she couldn't bear to think how he would react. She felt more desolate and alone than she had for years.

The easiest way, she thought, would be water with pennies boiled in it. And she slipped into a chemist in Birmingham for pennyroyal syrup. Both tasted vile and made her even more sick, but neither had any result at all. She couldn't bring herself to jump, or pretend to fall, not like in the dream. She knew she'd never have the courage. There was only one way left now that she could think of, and a cold shudder of fear passed through her every time she thought about it.

They were on their way south now with coal for Oxford. It was a while since they'd been down there and Joel was pleased, as it meant meeting up with family. By the time they left the coalfields, the grit catching in their nostrils, clothes and hair, the family were all as black and begrimed as ever, especially the children. Maryann felt another deep wave of despair. They looked like a load of chimney sweeps! The old taunt of 'dirty families' haunted her. But how was anyone supposed to keep clean in these conditions, especially feeling the way she did?

Joel and Bobby had sheeted up and put the top planks up over the hold. As well as keeping the rain off, the tarpaulins stopped so much gritty dust from blowing back in their faces.

On the way south they found themselves followed closely by another pair of Barlow boats occupied by the Higgins family, whose son Ernie crewed for Darius. Mrs Higgins was an older woman – it was impossible, Maryann thought, to guess exactly how old – with a wizened, leathery face and a terse but not unpleasant manner. She had a scarf dotted with brightly coloured flowers tied over her hair and her forearms were as knotted and muscly as branches.

'You going down the paper mills then?' she asked as they were untying. When Maryann said they were, Mrs Higgins shook her head.

'Ah well, watch that there river. Can be a booger down there.'

They knew she was right. To reach Wolvercote paper mills they had to go through the lock at Duke's cut and onto the Thames. There was nowhere to turn the boats at the mill, so they had to wind them on the wide Thames and take them down backwards on the rushing current. Maryann never did that part of the trip without her innards turning with fear, and most other boat-women were prepared to admit that they felt the same.

'Least I'll get a good wash done, though,' Maryann said. There was plenty of hot water on offer at Wolvercote Mill and most of them tried to get their wash tubs out.

Mrs Higgins gave her a sudden, gappy smile. 'That you will,' she agreed. 'We're off to the aloominum works, down Banbury.'

With the Higginses on their tail so much of the way south, Maryann felt somehow on display, even though they were as respectful of the privacy of others as anyone could be. But for the first two nights they were all tied up nose to tail along the bank and Joel went out for a drink with Mr Higgins the first night, while Mrs Higgins stayed aboard with the two youngest children, who still worked the boats with them.

Mrs Higgins was one of those women beside whom Maryann felt weak and inadequate. She couldn't forget that Ernie had been the ninth of her thirteen surviving children, who'd all grown up on the cut. It made Maryann dizzy just thinking about it. Where had they all slept? They must have been stuffed under the cratches, she thought. The cratch was replaced on some boats by a very small forecabin in which a couple of young children could be tucked out of the rain for the night. But Maryann felt that women like Mrs Higgins were somehow a different and hardier breed from her altogether. Whatever would Mrs Higgins think if she could see into her mind now?

The days were grey and dull, though the clouds let out nothing more than drizzle. As they wound along between pastures and ploughed fields, Maryann saw that spring was coming in the buds pushing out on the trees, the fuzz of green shoots along the furrows, all the spring promise of new life. But she felt so ill, so unequal to giving life herself, that the sight made her feel even more lonely and desperate than before.

102

On the second afternoon she sat in the cabin as Bobby steered the butty; Joel was way ahead of them with the motor. Maryann was positioned opposite the stove, cooking and feeding the twins in turn. She could balance a baby on her lap and let her feed, keeping her hands free to chop onion, carrot and beef, though it made her back ache. Suddenly the smell of onions filled her with nausea and she had to snatch Ada from her breast and lean over the waste bucket as Ada lay back roaring on the bed.

Spent, she sat with her head down, too tired to move, even after the retching had stopped, the smell of old potato peelings unpleasant in her nostrils. A sob escaped from her.

'I can't go on . . .' she whispered. 'I just can't. Not like this . . .'

They left the Higgins family behind at last and headed south. When they reached Thrupp, Joel found a spot to pull in for the night.

'Don't want to be starting down the Thames in the dark,' he said. 'Best start fresh for that in the morning.' He lifted the water cans off the roof and went off to fill them.

The family ate their stew and potatoes without speaking. Meals were often silent at the end of the day when they had all been up since before dawn and sometimes worked on until after dark. Joel scraped his plate clean and made a satisfied sound.

'Ready for a quick one, Bobby?'

So the men went out to the pub, which nestled among the pretty stone cottages of Thrupp.

Maryann cleared the crocks away, her hands trembling as she stacked the plates. There was no Higgins boat tied up behind them tonight and the place wasn't busy. She knew the time had come.

'Joley, Ezra, Sally, Rose. Come on.' The four of them bedded down on the big bed on the *Esther Jane* still, while Bobby squeezed onto the side bed. Still in their clothes, they snuggled down together, Joley and Ezra at one end, heads in the cupboard into which the bed could be folded up when necessary and the two girls at the other end.

'Night, night.' Maryann kissed them all. She tried to be as affectionate to Rose as to her own children, which wasn't difficult as she was very fond of the little girl. Poor little mite – no mom and now separated from her real brothers as well.

'Night, Mom,' they said. Even Rose called her Mom already.

'Oh, Nance.' Maryann found her lips moving as she closed the hatch and went, shivering, back to the cosy cabin of the *Theodore*. 'I know you'd never understand what I'm about to do, but if you're watching, don't be too hard on me. I won't be able to carry on being a mom to any of them if I have another one now. It'd just finish me off, Nance, heaven forgive me.'

Inside the cabin she continued muttering to herself. The twins slept on on the side bench, and she tried to keep herself calm.

'Now or never. I've got to do it – it's got to be now or they'll be back. Oh, please don't let it hurt too much. Let it just be over!'

She knelt down and reached into the monkey hole under the bed, where Joel kept a few of his tools. The screwdriver felt heavy in her hand. It had a sturdy wooden handle and a long metal shaft leading up to its flattened end, which was about a quarter of an inch wide.

Maryann knelt there, turning it round in her hands, which she noticed were trembling. The metal was tarnished, dotted with rust. She knew she could have sat there for hours putting off the moment, but then it would be too late. It had to be done.

Feeling something was necessary in preparation, some ritual, she poured a cup of hot water over the metal part of the tool and wiped it on her skirt. As she went about these humble preparations, tremors began to move through her body, as if she was running a fever; her teeth started chattering. With difficulty she adjusted the wick of the lamp and the shadows shifted round her.

'It'll be all right,' she whispered, trying to steady herself. 'Calm down ... Steady ... Tomorrow it'll all be over. I've just got to do it ...'

For a moment she stood by the bed, holding the screwdriver, at a loss. She realized suddenly that in order to begin she would have to remove her bloomers. She wore the full, old-fashioned kind still, for warmth. To do that she'd have to take her boots off. Perched on the edge of the bed, she struggled with the laces. Her hands were shaking so much that this seemed to take for ever, but at last she pulled off her boots, placing them silently on the floor, then rucked up her skirt and pulled down her bloomers, feeling vulnerable, embarrassed even, at finding herself standing there with no drawers on and no shoes either. It was a relief to let her skirt fall down again over her thighs.

'Come on, come on,' she urged herself through chattering teeth. It had to be done quickly or she would lose her nerve.

Again, she sat down on the edge of the back bed, the implement with its sharp, square end in her hand. Everything felt unreal, as if she was dreaming. Her legs twitched convulsively and she couldn't control them. She opened them shakily, closed them again. How was she going to manage this? She had to prod hard enough to make sure she started bleeding. The only way, she saw, shuddering, was to lie back, to get in the right position. Shifting her weight, she lay diagonally across the bed so that her head was pressed right into the darkest corner. She could smell coal strongly. It got into every crevice of the boats. The hard wall pushed against the top of her head, the blanket was scratchy against the back of her neck.

Her skirt fell back as she lifted her legs and at once lying in this position filled her with horror. It was unbearable. The air felt somehow indecent about her private parts and she felt helpless and full of shame. She was a child, lying pressed to her mom's front-room floor by Norman Griffin, when he had forced her dress up. She began to sob, but she made herself remember what she was doing. She couldn't stop now: it had to be done to free her of the child. Just this one, she promised. She'd never, ever do anything like this again.

Quick. It had to be quick. The steely end of the screwdriver felt cold as she eased it into herself, guiding the handle. Her breath was coming in loud, juddering gasps. In a couple of seconds she felt it reach in as far as it would go. What now? Push in further, slowly? No, quickly . . . Do it, do it, the blood throbbed in her ears.

She pulled the handle out a little, trying to take aim. Without giving herself any more time to consider she jerked her hands back towards her with all her strength, driving it into her.

The pain was instant. Her eyes stretched wide at the shock of it and she heard herself giving off screams and moans. She thought she knew pain, but this was not the coming, going waves of labour pains but an appalling sharp agony which was getting worse, tearing at her. Waves of heat and nausea swept over her. Unable to control her cries of agony, she tried to sit up, to pull the thing out, but she could hardly keep her hand still enough to get a grip on it she was shaking so much. God in heaven, what had she done? It wasn't supposed to be like this!

Sweat soaked her chest and back. Grinding her teeth, she grabbed at the handle and tried to pull on it, but it wouldn't come. She tried to get to her feet, easing forwards, the thing still in her, but her legs wouldn't stand the weight and she nearly collapsed onto the stove. Sounds came from her mouth, whimpers, groans.

Crouching half upright, she felt a hot surge over her hands, running down to drip from her wrists, over the handle of the screwdriver to the floor. It took her a moment to understand why her hands were red. From somewhere she could hear a baby screaming, and she knew it was the baby inside her crying out in pain, the tiny life to whom she'd done this terrible thing.

'I'm sorry, little one . . . sorry . . .' she managed to say. She slumped back across the bed and in seconds a thick, rubbery darkness had covered her face.

Twelve

Something was pressing on her eyelids. It was not painful, but warm, and seemed to have weight. Next she felt her left ear, that it was pressed down into a pillow. Maryann became aware of herself piece by piece, as if a thaw had set in throughout her body, each part of it warming slowly back to life. She could feel the air passing in and out through her nostrils. There were unfamiliar smells. Her head, the central core uniting her eyelids, ears and nostrils, was throbbing with pain.

She moved her fingers and, somewhere far away, her toes. Pressure mounted inside her which it took a moment to recognize, its urgency increasing so rapidly that her eyes snapped open and seeing a bowl on the chair beside her bed, she grabbed it and leaned up on her elbow, suddenly aware as she moved, that there was a tube attached to her arm. Her innards contracted until a miserable spurt of liquid was wrung from her and she lay back, unable to control her moans. There was a sick banging in her head and in the lower part of her body raw, tearing pain.

She squeezed her eyes shut, waiting for it to subside and struggling frantically to make sense of things. Where, from this white glimpse of her surroundings, was she? A hospital, that much was clear, but where? What had happened to her to cause this agony? Had she fallen in and been hit by the butty? She forced her eyes open, squinting, the bar of sunlight from the long window opposite still falling across her face. She saw the tube running into her arm, and then another bed next to hers. Panic flooded her. How did she get here from the cut? And where were Joel and the children?

Gradually her life poured back to her. She'd been in the cabin, that much she knew. She remembered kneeling there in the lamplight, that she'd been alone. Then blackness. Lord above, what had happened?

A face leaned across from the neighbouring bed, a skinny brown plait draped over the shoulder. Narrow grey eyes stared at her, unashamedly curious.

'You've come round then?' the young woman observed. 'Took your time. You've been out for ages.' She sounded neither friendly nor unfriendly. 'Only had my appendix out, me. What're you in for?'

Maryann wondered if she could make her voice work. 'Wh . . .' she attempted. Her mouth was dry and sour. 'Where am I?'

'Where *are* you? Don't you even know that! The Radcliffe, of course.' Seeing Maryann's blank look undispelled, she added, 'In Oxford. D'you want the nurse?' Self-importantly she called out to one who was not far off, sitting at a table in the middle of the ward. When the woman came she was tall and very thin, with porcelain skin and pale eyes.

'Ah – ' she stood over Maryann – 'you're back with us. How're you feeling?'

'My head.' Maryann pressed her hand against her forehead. 'I've been sick,' she added wretchedly.

'I don't suppose it'll be the last time either.' The nurse had picked up Maryann's other hand and was taking her pulse. After a short silence she nodded and released her hand. 'Good. Yes – it's the after-effects of the anaesthetic. Makes everyone feel ropy.'

She removed the bowl and Maryann watched her willowy figure go along the ward, before coming back with it empty and rinsed.

'She's not so bad, that one,' her neighbour said during the nurse's absence.

'The doctors will be in to see you soon,' the nurse told her. 'Drink plenty of water.'

Evidently it was morning. There was a flurry of bed-making and bed baths, although Maryann was left alone. Then the doctors came. The nurse drew screens around her bed and a middle-aged man, with a clipped voice and a moustache, and two very young men came and stood in a row at the bottom of her bed. Maryann lay looking up at them. The older man had papers tucked under his left arm. The two younger ones looked uncomfortable and their glance kept flickering towards her and away again.

'Well,' the older doctor said, 'I hope you're ashamed of yourself. You've managed to do yourself a great deal of damage.'

Maryann tried to fight the tears which welled up in her eyes. Why was this man accusing her in this cold, cruel voice? What had happened? And where were her family, all the people she cared about and most wanted to see?

He flicked through the notes, while the two students stared at the wall above Maryann's head.

'I'll tell you, I take a very dim view of this sort of thing,' the doctor went on. 'You damaged your uterus beyond repair and we've had to carry out a complete hysterectomy. You've lost a good deal of blood in the meantime and we've had to transfuse you.' He spoke as if these medical necessities had been a huge personal inconvenience.

'Of course, there was no possibility of saving the child.' Abruptly he pushed the notes back under his arm. 'But then I don't imagine that was what was required, was it? Anyway – ' for the first time he looked directly at her – 'there won't be any more babies for you, that you can be sure of.'

To his two underlings, he said, 'Ten-inch screwdriver – still in place when they brought her in. These women are beyond belief.' Shaking his head, he pushed the screen out of his way and moved on without a further word to Maryann.

Tears streamed down her cheeks. The way he had spoken made her feel lower than nothing. She hadn't understood a lot of the words he used but he had made her remember what had happened. Of course. She was expecting . . . she remembered the light in the cabin, her legs bare to the air, the screwdriver . . . and then those dying cries of the child, which seemed to ring in her head. Oh, God above, what had she done? She covered her face with her hands. The screens had been taken away and there was no privacy now. She felt so exposed in the long ward with eyes all around her, when she was used to her tiny cabin. And she hadn't meant any of this to happen! Not like this. No one was supposed to know. How would Joel ever forgive her if he knew she'd murdered their little babby?

She pulled the thin covers over her head and lay weeping bitterly, her body hurting with each wrenching sob, but it was the thoughts which filled her mind that caused her the greatest agony of all.

*

That day was punctuated by sickness and misery and sleep. Maryann didn't take in anything around her or notice time passing. All day her head throbbed. But when she woke the following morning, still very battered and sore but at least free of the thumping headache, she was more alert and able to take in her surroundings and she saw that the tube had gone from her arm. It was then she began to realize that, when the nurse had drawn screens round the bed for the doctor's round the previous morning, the tiny enclosure of privacy had done nothing to contain the doctor's booming voice. It soon became clear that the words 'baby' and 'damaged' and 'ten-inch screwdriver' had bounced the full length of the ward and into the ears of those occupying the lines of beds. Anyone who had missed the sordid details was soon informed, and there was a lot of whispering and looking. Maryann felt eyes staring at her with fascinated disgust.

The tall nurse who had been on duty the day before treated Maryann with a professional detachment which was neither warm nor disdainful, but this was a good deal better than she received from a few of the others. That morning she raised one hand to attract the attention of a young nurse, who bustled over to her, looking irritated.

'Can I go to the toilet?' Maryann whispered. She hadn't been aware of wanting to go the day before, but now it was urgent.

'No, of course you can't!' the nurse snapped. 'You know perfectly well you can't get out of bed. I *suppose* I'll have to bring you a bedpan.' Every line of her bearing implied that she resented having to do anything for *that* sort of person.

When she brought the bedpan and drew the screens

round, Maryann found the courage to ask, 'I was wearing hoops in my ears before. Gold hoops. Please – ' she appealed. 'I don't know what's happened to them.' She'd missed them suddenly when she sat up that morning, their familiar feel.

'Well, *I* don't know about that sort of thing,' the nurse said haughtily, removing the bedpan. 'I expect they've been put away for safekeeping. Why don't you look in your cupboard?'

Painfully, Maryann leaned round and opened the little cupboard by the bed. Inside she saw her clothes bundled up at the bottom and, on the shelf above, the gold hoops Nancy had given her. She reached in for them, her eyes filling with tears, and lay down again, holding them close to her.

All day she had to endure the knowledge that everyone was talking about her. She felt bathed in shame, as if her very skin was raw with it. She was glad she wasn't allowed to move about the ward because she couldn't bear the thought of people looking at her. No one said a friendly word, apart from the woman with the plait in the next bed, whose nosiness outdid any scruples she might have had. Every so often she leaned over and hissed questions in Maryann's direction. These questions pierced her misery like wasp stings.

'Where're you from then? Not from Oxford, are you?' She had a country accent and a village gossip's manner. Maryann tried to ignore her, but she kept on.

'Not a secret, is it? I'm only trying to be friendly, not like the rest of them in here. You come in from one of the villages?'

Maryann shook her head, keeping her eyes closed. She definitely wasn't telling this tittle-tattler that she was off the cut.

'Sounds as if you've had a bad time of it. A screwdriver didn't the doctor say? Dear, oh dear, there's a thing. You must've been in a fine old state.'

Gritting her teeth against the pain, hand pressed over the scar low on her belly Maryann eased herself over in the bed, presenting her back to her nosy-parker interrogator and pulled the covers over her head. In their darkness, trying to shut out the disgruntled complaint that she was 'only trying to be friendly', Maryann lay picturing her home, the boats with their woven ropework and Turk's heads when they were scrubbed white, the shiny brasses. She longed to be in her cosy bed on the *Theodore* with the cats curled up on her feet, to see her children's faces as they played on the bank or in the hold. Her whole being ached with the need to be at home instead of in this harsh, stark place among strangers who condemned her. Where were her family? Had they all abandoned her?

But the thought of home only increased her pain and shame. If strangers condemned her, however was she going to be able to face Joel? *You've killed his child*, she repeated over and over again. *You're a murderer.* And the thought of Joel's face, of having to see him again after what she'd done, made her long for darkness, for the relief of not being able to feel, to be blotted out.

Later on in the afternoon she sensed there was someone near the bed and opened her eyes. In front of her was the rough blue weave of a coat. A body bent over and a face appeared close to hers, which she recognized: blue eyes, features deeply lined by the years and squirrel-grey plaits coiled round her head. At the sight of her, Maryann burst into tears.

'Oh, Auntie!' She tried to hide her face in shame, but found her hand grasped between two tiny cold ones.

'Now, moy dear, don't you go taking on so!' Alice Simons sat down and stroked Maryann's hand. 'Oh dear, oh dear, I don't like seeing you in this state, I don't at all.'

'I've done such a terrible thing,' Maryann sobbed. She tried to speak quietly, conscious of all the other people around them, but she was becoming hysterical. 'I never meant it to be like this, Auntie, I promise I didn't. Only I couldn't manage. I felt so sick and worn out and now I've done the worst thing I could ever do . . .'

'Shh, dear, ssh now,' Alice said, clutching at her hand. 'You don't want all this lot in on your business do you?'

'They are already,' Maryann said despairingly. 'Where's Joel, Auntie – and all our little ones?'

'They're all safe and sound,' the old lady assured her. 'All the girls are at our house with Darius. I said that'd keep him on his toes when I came out to visit you! At his age he could do with a bit of young life around him. We've given Esther and Ada a bit of that form'la milk and they're happy enough, dear. Joley's gone down the mill with Joel and Bobby, but they'll come up Juxon Street tonight, so he'll be in to see you as soon as *they* let him.' She grimaced over at the sister's desk.

'Oh, Auntie . . .' Maryann couldn't stop weeping. She felt wretched and ashamed, yet it was such a relief to see someone she knew, her family. 'Is Joel very angry with me?'

'I've never seen the boy in such a state,' Mrs Simons said, kneading at Maryann's hand in affectionate

agitation. '"My little mate," he kept saying. "My Maryann." Sat down in my house and cried like a child, he
did, over you. "Why daint she say nothing to me?" he
kept saying. Up and down, he was. Couldn't settle. "I
knew there was summat on her mind," he said, "but
she'd never say. And now look what she's gone and
done."

'"Well," I says to him, "the girl'd had enough. That
were a desperate act she done, if ever I saw one. She
weren't put on this earth to be a brood mare, anyone
could see that by the look of her. There's more to life
than wearing yourself out with one child after another,
Joel," I said. "Look at your mother – and mine. You
don't want to lose her, do you, lad?"'

Hearing this, Maryann wept even more. After the
doctor's condemnation of her she had expected the
whole world to turn against her.

'I heard it crying.' She couldn't control her sobbing,
however much she didn't want to attract attention to
herself. 'It was crying when I . . . when I killed it.'

'Oh *no*, dear.' Alice squeezed her hand tightly and
Maryann was more distraught to realize that the old lady
was trying not to cry herself. Her voice was thick with
tears. 'That can't be right. You can't hear a tiny babe
crying in the womb. I s'pect it was the twins you heard.'
She sniffed, then pulled a handkerchief from somewhere
about her and briskly wiped her nose. 'That'll be it.
Don't think like that any more. What's done's done and
you have to go on.'

'He said I shan't have any more babies. I've damaged
myself.'

'You've had everything taken away, dear.' Alice
Simons was whispering now. 'I had a word with the
matron. I'm not frightened of her. You've been foolish

116

hurting yourself so badly, I won't say you haven't. But you mustn't keep dwelling on it. You've plenty of children to care for – a good-sized family, and that poor young Rose. We must all make sure we take good care of them now, mustn't we?'

Thirteen

Joel walked along the shiny floor of the ward, amid the sickly smell of human illness, overlain by onions and gravy. He held his cap clasped tightly in both hands. When he found his wife, he lowered himself onto the chair by her bed, oblivious to the eyes fastened on him all round the ward. For a time he sat leaning forwards, his sorrowful gaze fixed on Maryann's sleeping face, mauve cresents of exhaustion beneath her eyes.

She seemed like a stranger lying there, as if she had gone somewhere far away from him. Where was it she'd gone, his sweet little bird? What had possessed her to do this brutal act, which had nearly finished her as well as their child? Emotions he could not have named swelled up in him until he had to clench his hands into fists, then hold onto his cap to prevent himself from lashing out. He lowered his head and looked helplessly down between his legs at his boots. Their worn leather, shaped by years of wear into the exact contours of his feet, was pale from the repeated rubbing of mud and rain and cinders. They gave out a whiff of the earth compacted in the soles. It calmed him a fraction: the smell of the cut, of what was real and wholesome. And she was part of that, his little wife lying here in front of him.

He took her hand, which lay outside the covers, and looked at it. The lack of privacy didn't enter his thoughts: these strangers in the ward were nothing to him. He was too deep in his own concerns even to see them. He held Maryann's hand between his own, feeling its hard-worked roughness, warming it, then pressed it cautiously to his lips.

Maryann's eyes opened. She looked bewildered until she turned her head slowly and, seeing him, gasped, trying to sit up. Her face creased with pain and she was forced to lie back again, whimpering.

'Steady,' he said, alarmed. 'Don't move. You just stay still, where you are.'

'O-oh,' she moaned, a hand covering her face, tears of remorse flowing at the sight of him. She was in too much distress to speak. Joel couldn't say anything either. His throat was choked and the tears ran down into his beard. He leaned in close, pressing the back of her hand against his cheek. Feeling his tears on her hand, she gradually pulled herself over onto her side to face him, curling herself up tightly, needing his comfort but unable to look into his eyes.

'How could you've done it?' he managed to say. 'I thought you was dead.' He shook his head, shuddering at the memory. 'When I came back and found you . . . You nearly bled to death – you was that close. How *could* you've . . .?' He saw her hide her face again and he had to lean forward to hear her muffled voice. As he did so, he caught the smell of her body, of his woman. A pang of longing went through him. This was all wrong, her lying here among strangers. He wanted to lift her out of this cold white bed and carry her home.

'I wasn't myself,' she said. 'I felt so bad. Couldn't seem to see a way out. It's too much – the twins, all the kiddies, keeping up with the loads and everything . . . I just couldn't seem to go on.' Her shoulders shook with

119

more sobs. 'I daint want to do it – only I couldn't think of another way . . .'

There was a long silence as Joel fought to control his feelings, all the hurt and fear. Their children were his hope of security in a future which, he knew, looked more and more threatened for the boaters. They were a forgotten people, only useful again for a bit now there was a war on. The cut grew more neglected every year. What would happen when peace was declared? All those road hauliers, who barely knew of the existence of the cut, would they be the new Number Ones? How could they keep the life of the boatpeople going, the only life Joel knew, if there was no one to carry it on? If there were no children to put to the tiller and teach boating instincts, the knack of loading and handling, of splicing ropes and working locks? And children died on the cut: sickness and accidents scythed through them. You needed plenty to make sure enough survived to carry on. He tried to tell himself this was only one child lost, that there would be others.

Yet he looked at the frail figure on the bed in front of him, lying with her face hidden for shame and sorrow, and he saw the young woman he loved with all his heart, who had married him, fresh-faced and full of hope, who had made him happier than he had ever been in his life, and now here she was, felled and exhausted, on a hospital bed.

Slowly he moved his hand and laid it on top of her head.

'Don't cry like that, little mate,' he implored her. 'Please don't.'

The sorrow and kindness in his voice made her cry all the more, but she reached out for him and pulled his hand against her breast, holding him tight, her face pressed to his arm.

'I've done such a wicked thing. I never thought I could do anything so bad . . . Our little babby . . .'

He stroked her hair, trying to find words, wanting to climb onto the bed and love and caress her, but of course he couldn't. Above all, he wanted her home. Wanted things back as they were before.

'We'll have others,' he tried to soothe her. 'Lots more little ones.'

She grew very still suddenly and looked up at him. He could see the fear in her eyes. 'Joel – they say I'll never have another babby. They've had to take it all away.'

He stared, not understanding at first, then closed his eyes as her words cut through him. No more children. No more sons to grow up strong and work the boats.

'Oh. Oh my . . .' He stood up, half-staggering, recoiling from her. 'No more? Never?' He was reeling. 'What've you gone and done?' He heard his own voice, very loud. 'What in God's name've you done?'

'Joel – wait . . .' She sounded faint and far away.

He didn't mean to leave her so abruptly, but he had to get out of the ward, to breathe the fresh air, to steady himself. He strode along the polished floor and out through the heavy doors.

Maryann spent a month in the hospital in Oxford and it was one of the loneliest times she'd ever passed. Her body, as well as recovering from the operation, had lost a lot of blood and needed time to recuperate.

When Joel had come to see her on the ward, looking

121

so out of place in his boots and his working clothes all blackened with coal dust, yet so strong and manly with his broad shoulders and thick beard, he had attracted a lot of stares and also a lot of conjecture about his working life.

'D'you work on the canal then?' Nosy next door asked the following day, after the gossip had spread. Not feeling she could lie, and in any case fiercely proud, Maryann nodded.

'Ooh, well – my word!' The woman stared at her as if looking at a weird new creature in a zoo. 'Well, I've never come across any of you lot before . . . I wondered why your arms look so weathered and brown.'

When one of the nurses had given Maraynn her first bed bath, she looked down sneeringly at the grime of coal dust trapped in the creases of her skin.

'Well, I've never washed anyone *quite* this filthy before.'

Maryann looked away, trying to pretend she hadn't heard.

You try it! her mind screamed in retort. *You try living on top of a heap of coal in all weathers with your kiddies to keep fed and washed. I'd like to see how long you'd last, you starchy little bitch!*

But she couldn't stand up for herself. Not now and not in here. She felt too beaten down. And she wasn't going to say anything about where she came from. The nurse also asked if she always wore 'those gold gypsy hoops' in her ears. All Maryann said was, 'Yes, I do.'

She was glad of the wash, though, and the clean nightdress to replace the bloodstained one she had been wearing. The new one was from the hospital store and was pale pink. But even this small amount of effort exhausted her. She seemed to have an endless capacity to sleep. They woke her to give her meagre platefuls of stew and dumplings or potato pie, and as soon as she'd eaten them and the watery junkets that followed, she would sleep again. As well as relieving her huge weariness, these long, dreamless sleeps were a welcome release from the stark, alien ward and from the hostile stares and prying questions of the woman next door. *'Is it true, what you did . . .?'* And, worst of all, the memory of Joel's back moving away from her, as if he never wanted to see her again.

As much as she could, she kept herself to herself. Within a week the nosy body in the next bed was replaced by a reserved, middle-aged woman, who told Maryann that her husband worked for the university but was now in some army education department for the war effort. She was polite, didn't go poking her nose in and read a great many books.

As Maryann's body gradually recovered from the injuries it had suffered, she began to be able to move about the ward. She could go to the bathrooms by herself and along to the day room at the end. From the newspapers left in there, and from the talk among the other patients, she caught up with news about the war, more than she normally heard on the cut. A great many ships were being sunk in the Atlantic, and she picked up snippets about tighter food rations and how crimes were going unreported amid the chaos of blackout and bombing. She found she enjoyed having time to read newspapers and the few storybooks left in the room. They helped her escape. She tried not to let herself think about Joel and how much she had hurt him.

Easter came and went and spring blossomed outside. As her body healed, Maryann grew more and more restless. When the weather was fine, all she could think of was how it felt to be on the cut on days like these, with the trees all coming out and the sun on her face. She was so used to being able to step straight outside from her cabin, into the fresh air, when they were in the country that she found the stuffy, shut-in atmosphere of the ward stifling. When it rained and the drops blew against the long windows, she imagined the feel of them falling on her skin. Sometimes she would stand at the washroom window, arms folded, glad to be away from everyone and look out, wondering where, beyond those trees and buildings, the cut ran, narrow and barely acknowledged. She missed her home terribly. The fields and trees, the colourful sides of the boats and the familiar faces.

Above all, with an ache that seldom left her, she missed her children. Knowing she had taken away her chance of having any more made them all desperately precious. She trembled sometimes with the need to hold them in her arms, grieving for the children she would now never have. She had wanted to slow things down, to give herself a chance. She'd never meant it to turn out like this. At night she lay picturing them in her mind: Joley and Sally with their blond heads and Ezra's dark one, playing on the bank near Fenny Compton or Aynho, the feel of their urgent little bodies, their grubby faces and hands, eyes full of expectant life and laughter. Did they miss her? Were they unhappy? Alice Simons assured her that they were doing very well. Maryann trusted her completely, but everything felt wrong. The family was scattered and broken up. They should all be together on the cut again. Thoughts of Ada and Esther were the most difficult to cope with. In the early days her breasts ached when they let down milk that no one could drink. As the days passed, she knew the milk was drying up. And the girls would have changed by the time she came out! Sometimes she cried in sheer frustration, which was made worse by the fact that she knew she had only herself to blame. Although a few of the other women on the ward were kind, she knew how most of them saw her. She was a wicked woman who'd done away with her baby. When they looked at her it increased her sense of shame, of being dirty in a way which water could not touch. Shame seemed to pulse like through the blood in her veins.

The days passed slowly and miserably. She did not see Joel again in all that time. Mr Barlow had sent Joel and Bobby back up to Hawkesbury Junction to do runs to the power station.

'He's taken it hard,' Alice told her after his visit. 'He said, "I ent going in there again – I can't do it."' Seeing Maryann's distraught expression she said, 'Give him time. He's a good boy, Joel is. He just needs to go on in his own way for a bit.'

But could Joel ever forgive her, Maryann wondered, for what she had done to herself and to his family?

Joley and Ezra had gone with their father, but the girls were still in Oxford. Children were not allowed to visit the wards, but fortunately the hospital was only a couple of roads away from Adelaide Street and Alice Simons came to see her as often as she could. Maryann was overjoyed to see her as she brought news of them. She would try to press Alice for details, but scarcely ever got more than, 'They're quite happy but they miss you.' She returned to them with the simplest little notes written by Maryann for Sally: HELLO SALLY. BE A GOOD GIRL. LOVE FROM MOM XXX Sometimes Sally and

Rose scribbled little pictures to send back and Maryann treasures these small masterpieces. Her favourite was Sally's attempt at Alice's fat black cat. She'd given it a gigantic tail, curved up over its back like a crescent moon.

Every time Alice stood up to go home, Maryann said, 'Tell them I'll be home as soon as I can!'

In the first week of May, Maryann finally stepped out through the hospital gates onto the Woodstock Road. Too excited to stop and take stock of her surroundings, she hurried towards Adelaide Street.

It felt strange to be wearing normal clothes again. Alice had brought her a pretty frock which she had bought secondhand, in bold blue and white checks which fitted nicely at the waist, or would have done had she not lost so much weight. It hung loosely on her for now, but she put her cardigan and coat over the top. She had no stockings, but enjoyed the feel of the air on her legs. Her hair had grown and she coiled it up at the back and pinned it. She only had a small bundle of belongings to carry.

The row of snug terraced houses in Adelaide Street looked very inviting, the patches of brick which still showed through the soot glowing a warm colour in the slanting sun. Almost running in her impatience, though her long unused legs felt wobbly, she finally arrived at Alice Simons's front door.

'Home at last!' Alice greeted her. 'Well, you've come just in time – I've got the kettle on, and potatoes baking in the oven...' Their delicious smell was drifting through the house. But Maryann was hungry for something else.

'Where are they, Auntie? I can't wait to see them!'

She ran through to the back. 'Sally and Rose are in the yard feeding the hens.' Alice called after her. 'But there're the twins – good as gold, they are, bless them. Told you they was crawling, didn't I?'

In the pretty cabin of a back room, Maryann found the two little girls busy with an assortment of objects to keep them amused: a handful of clothes' pegs, a wooden spoon, an enamel bowl and a couple of cotton reels. Esther was sitting chewing determinedly at the end of the wooden spoon and Ada was crawling across the floor aiming for the open door.

'Oh!' Maryann cried, full of joy at the sight of them and flung herself down on her knees, scooping up Ada. But the child gave a squeal of alarm and her face crumpled. She squirmed so much that Maryann had to put her down.

'Esther?' Maryann pleaded. The other twin stared at her with mild curiosity and continued to chew on the spoon.

'They don't know me!' Tears filled Maryann's eyes. She felt cut to the heart. 'They don't know I'm their mom!'

'Don't you worry,' Alice Simons reassured her. She carried in the tea tray and set it on the folding table with quick, birdlike movements. 'You sit with them a while and they'll soon come round. They're just not used to you, dear. Why don't you come and see Sally and Rose?'

They stepped out into the tiny garden. At the end of it the two girls were leaning over the chicken run, scattering seed through the wire.

'That'll do now – come and see who's here!' Alice called.

The children turned, and Maryann saw an expression

in Sally's eyes that she would never forget. There was a tiny pause as she registered who was there, then a breaking in of relief, of absolute happiness, like a light going on.

'Mom?' she faltered. 'MOM!' And her little legs couldn't seem to carry her fast enough, her wheat-coloured hair flying, face stretched with eagerness. Rose, less sure, toddled behind, dark curls bobbing, and Mary-ann squatted and gathered first one then the other into her arms.

'Thank God,' she heard herself saying as her tears wet their firm cheeks. 'Oh my lovelies, my lovely little girls!'

Fourteen

'It's our dad!'

Sally's shriek of excitement rang through the house seconds after they heard the knock at the door.

'Let's let him in then,' Alice Simons said, hurrying along the hall as fast as her stiff hips would allow. 'No good keeping him on the doorstep.'

Maryann tensed. She was feeding Esther in the back room – to her great relief she had been able to get back to breastfeeding – and heard the giggles of excitement as Joel gathered Sally and Rose into his arms. She heard Joel's father come downstairs and his voice; then light footsteps hurried towards her and halted hesitantly at the door.

'Joley!' She was overjoyed at the sight of him. He looked bigger to her, and older, and his fair hair had grown down to his collar, thick and curly. His clothes were filthy, but he looked healthy and strong, standing there in the doorway, and she saw with a pang just how much he was trying to be a little man.

'Come 'ere, bab.' She held out her spare arm and Joley's solemn face broke into a grin in spite of himself. He ran to her and she pulled him close, kissing him. At that moment, Ezra's swarthy face appeared round the door and he launched himself at her.

'Mom!'

'Hey!' she laughed, trying to cuddle them both, kissing Ezra's black curls. 'Mind our Esther!'

'You awright, Mom?' Joley's blue eyes looked deeply into hers.

'Yes –' she squeezed him round the waist – 'and seeing you has made me properly perfect! You been helping your dad?'

Joley nodded proudly, the soft, little-boy moment over as he tugged away from her. 'Been steering the *Theodore* with Bobby. I done all sorts!'

'I been steering an' all!' Ezra piped up. 'And sheeting up and making tea!'

'*Have* you?' Maryann said admiringly.

'Can we go and see the hens?' Joley ran to the back door and Ezra followed. The children loved coming to Adelaide Street.

A moment later Joel was the one standing at the door, his eyes uncertain. Maryann felt herself twist inside. She felt acutely shy of him, as if the time of separation meant them starting all over again, like young lovers. Except that they were not young lovers, there was a history between them, so much to be ashamed of. She looked up timidly, moved by the sight of him back here, steadfast, in his worn old working clothes.

'Ready to come home? he asked gently, and she saw the need for reassurance in his eyes.

Silently she nodded. There was nothing she could say now to make things better. It would have to wait.

However much she longed to be back home with the family, it was hard saying goodbye to Alice Simons and old Darius, who had been so kind to her during that week she stayed after leaving the hospital. Both of them came down to the cut. They made quite a family party that warm afternoon, Joel and Maryann each carrying a twin and everyone else bringing their modest bits of luggage.

130

When they got to the wharf, they saw Bobby, bucket in hand, just finishing off giving the boats a swill down. A line of washing hung along the *Esther Jane*.

'Hello, Mrs Bartholomew.' In his shyness he turned formal with her. Usually he called her Maryann.

'You've got them looking nice,' she told him, a smile breaking across her face. It was so lovely to be back, to see the boats and smell the cut again! And in the cabin she exclaimed, 'Oh, Joel – you've got it so clean! It looks ever so nice!'

She had been bracing herself a little, knowing the men had had to work hard and two-handed and wouldn't have had time to keep house. But everything was tidy and clean, the stove was blacked and the brasses shining.

'Bobby and I had a bit of a set-to,' Joel admitted bashfully. 'Couldn't have my wife coming home to a pigsty, could us?'

There were more surprises. From the empty hold of the *Esther Jane* Joel lifted out two little dolls' prams. Maryann gasped.

'Look Sally, Rose! Look what your dad's got you!'

'Well, look at them,' Alice Simons said. 'Their eyes're nearly popping out of their heads!'

'Put your dolly in, Rose,' Sally ordered, and the two were immediately busy. Joley and Ezra showed Maryann the fishing rods Joel had found for them. He'd been round secondhand shops in Banbury and found the prams, and one of the lock keepers had given him the old rods.

'It's like Christmas,' Maryann laughed. She felt like a queen coming home to her palace.

'And we'll have fish and chips,' Joel said. 'Don't you go stroving tonight.'

They said their goodbyes to Darius and to Alice Simons.

'You've been so good to us,' Maryann said, kissing Alice's soft cheek. She felt a great rush of fondness and gratitude towards her.

Alice kissed her back and took her hands. 'You look after yourself now, dear.' Very quietly she added, 'You'll be all right now, you'll see.' Their eyes met. Maryann knew what she meant. Even amid the shame, there was the relief of no more worry about having baby after baby.

Maryann also went and kissed Darius and thanked him. He blushed, coughed and looked at his boots. 'G'bye now, girl,' he said, pushing his hat down more firmly onto his head.

Joel put his arm round Maryann's shoulders as his father and aunt walked away, Darius with his slow, loping gait, like an old crow in his black clothes, and Alice, limping slightly, but neat and spry in her hat and coat. They didn't look back.

Alone in the cabin of the *Theodore*, Joel drew Maryann into his arms. She leaned against him, breathing in his familiar smells of old wool and engine oil and his own Joel smell. She began to feel the hard twist of dread which had burdened her for weeks, begin to unwind itself.

'I'm sorry, love,' she said into his chest. 'So sorry for what I've done.'

When he spoke, she felt the vibration of it against her cheek.

'If we had any more, I might not have a wife, might I? And she's worth all the little 'uns in the world to me.'

His arms wrapped round, holding her close and she felt him draw in a great breath, his chest expanding. Releasing it, she heard him say, 'Home, my lovely,' on

132

the long exhalation of breath which spoke to her, without further words, of all his longing, his relief.

For the next few weeks after Maryann was back, Mr Barlow kept them on short runs out of Hawkesbury Junction, up and down the Coventry cut to Griff and Baddesley collieries and back to the Electric Light, its maw ever open for coal, its chimneys like huge nostrils snorting out smoke.

The boat families who worked round Sutton Stop greeted Maryann warmly and seemed glad to see her back, asking if she was well recovered. Their kindness lifted her a little, making her feel accepted, as if they were all part of one big family. Joel had reassured her that no one except him knew exactly what had happened that night. He was the one who had found her when he and Bobby came back from the pub, and he had shouted to Bobby to go back and get them to call an ambulance. So far as everyone knew, Maryann had suffered a miscarriage followed by an operation.

They wouldn't be so sympathetic if they knew, Maryann thought. But she tried to bury her feelings of loss and shame and revel in being back with the family, close to her children. The time away recuperating had given her an opportunity to appreciate how much happiness she had with them. The early summer was beautiful. The hedgerows were full of birds, the mayflower and elder blooming at their most exuberant, surrounded by the vibrant green of grass and trees. She steered the *Theodore*, drinking in the feel of sunlight on her skin, the breeze ruffling the leaves, animals in meadows along the cut, and the ducks clamouring for food alongside the boats. Ada and Esther were old enough to be getting into mischief now so she sat them on the roof, harnessed to the chimney, to play and watch the world go by. It was a treat to see the children tucked up cosily in bed or playing out on the bank with hoops and rods, with the prams and on makeshift swings. And, as the warm days passed, her energy returned and she felt better than she had in a good while.

But still somewhere deep inside her was a chilled, sad place that she did not like to visit. One afternoon at Sutton she was out on the bank with some of the other women. They had their wash tubs going, with dollies for pounding the clothes and a couple of mangles on the bank. It was a good chance for catching up on chat as well as getting the washing done. Two of the others were heavily pregnant and a lot of of the talk revolved round family and these new lives. Maryann did her best to smile and join in, but she felt sad and lonely. She missed Nancy so badly. Of course, Nance would have found it hard to understand what she'd done, but she would have listened and tried to comfort her. They'd seen Darius a couple of times while they were working round Sutton Stop. He was so silent, so obviously bereft and miserable without her. The pain of the fact that there would never be Nancy to confide in and share jokes with came back raw and fresh now she was back on the cut.

She kept her sadness to herself. She and Joel did not talk about what had happened. It was done. Over. What was there to say? But although the two of them would be able to love one another freely now and without worry once she was fully healed, something had changed. There was a difference in knowing that no child would ever result from their lovemaking. Not now or ever. And in a hidden place deep in her heart Maryann was weeping for all these things.

Fifteen

The summer passed quite peacefully. It was not until the autumn that Mr Barlow found them a longer trip, up to Birmingham. They drew into Tyseley well on into a smoky September afternoon. The wharf was very busy, and the Bartholomews were told they would have to join the queue for unloading and would probably have to wait until morning.

'I'll get down the shops before they close,' Maryann said.

Sally and Rose insisted on coming too and bringing their dollies' prams. As they didn't have much chance to push them about when the boats were on the move, Maryann relented.

'So long as you carry summat home in them,' she told them.

Moving round the edge of the wharf and keeping well out of the way of the roaring trucks, swinging chains and busy wharfmen, she led the girls, both solemn with the importance of the occasion, out onto the Birmingham streets. The bomb-damaged buildings looked a little less raw now, the rubble softened by grass and weeds.

Maryann pressed on quickly from shop to shop. There was no bread – come back in the morning, they said. She bought onions and carrots, stashing them in the little prams, and a bag of potatoes. When they reached the butcher's, the door opened with its usual 'ting' but the shop was quiet. Then Mr Osborne came through from out the back and Maryann saw his expression change to one of pleasure. He seemed quite delighted to see her.

'Well he*ll*o, stranger!' he said gushingly. 'What a long time since we've had the pleasure...' He peered over at Sally and Rose with a mischievous grin. 'And I'm sure I can find something nice for you two young princesses.'

'I want some mince, please,' Maryann said, taking her ration books out of the basket, 'if I'm not too late.'

'I've just the thing.' He held up his index finger and disappeared out the back again for a moment. 'I've been telling them that stocks are finished but, of course, I've got a little put away for *special* customers.'

Maryann frowned, truly baffled. 'What's so special about me?' Surely he couldn't be making advances to her. Look at the state of her – scruffy and covered in coal dust!

'Oh, I like to keep our boatladies happy.' He eyed the needle on the scale. 'There we are. Just over.' Wrapping the meat with a flourish, he kept his conversational patter going. A nip in the air now, wasn't there? Autumn on its way. At Tyseley Wharf again, were they?

'Yes,' Maryann said absently, wondering whether there was anything alse she should be buying.

'I can throw in a pair of pig's trotters as well. That suit you?'

'Oh – ta very much!' The food was welcome, of course, but for some reason she couldn't identify Maryann felt suddenly uneasy. He's just being kind again, she told herself. Mr Osborne had never given her the heeby-jeebies before, as men did when they seemed to be after something, but today she sensed something forced in his kindness to her.

'There we are.' He handed her the package and dipped his hands into his overall pocket. 'And – for you. Butterscotch!'

Sally and Rose took the sweets with eager hands.

'Say thank you to Mr Osborne,' Maryann told them.

Just as they arrived back at the boats, Charlie Dean from the toll office came over to her in the dusky light, smiling, his cap clinging to the back of his head. Maryann put the potatoes onto the counter of the *Theodore* and waved in greeting.

'All right? Long time no see!' He called a greeting to Joel, who was splicing ropes with the boys on the *Esther Jane*. Charlie stood leaning against the cabin, smoking as they chatted. Maryann was pleased to see him, but she also felt fraught and distracted. One of the twins was crying in the cabin and she hadn't even begun on the tea yet.

'Where've you been then?'

'Essy kept us on short trips,' she told him. He didn't need to know more than that. She kept up a conversation while lifting the groceries down into the cabin, kettle on.

'Shall I fetch your water for you?' Charlie asked, seeing how busy she was. He ground his cigarette butt into the ground with the ball of his foot.

'Would you?' Maryann rewarded him with a brief smile. 'That'd be a godsend.'

He was just turning, the empty water cans in each hand when she heard him say, 'Ey-up – old Weary Willie's back again.'

Standing in the hatches, Maryann narrowed her eyes and saw, coming across the wharf, the slight, tense figure of Pastor Owen.

*

'Good evening, Mrs Bartholomew!'

Pastor Owen approached them raising his hat.

'I'm off – tara,' Charlie muttered, slinking away. 'Don't want to get stuck with him.'

'Evening,' Maryann replied, struck afresh by the foreignness of the young churchman's northern accent. But she was surprised and unexpectedly affected by the fact that he had remembered her name. And he spoke with disarming simplicity, looking hard at her. It made her feel she mattered.

'And how are you today?' he asked.

'All right – not so bad.' She wasn't sure what else to say. She saw Joel look round from where he and the boys were perched on the cabin roof and counter of the *Esther Jane*.

'Family all all right?'

She nodded. 'Yes, thanks.'

'I'm very glad to hear that.' Pastor Owen pushed his hands down into the pockets of his threadbare black coat, and for a moment Maryann thought he was about to bring out his bible again, but instead he kept his hands in there and hunched his shoulders. She saw that he was cold.

'There's tea in the pot,' she said, feeling sorry for him. He looked so thin and underfed. 'Would you like a cup?'

'Oh – ' his lips turned up in a nervous smile – 'that'd be right grand. I've been out and about. I can't say it wouldn't be welcome.'

Maryann poured a cup, sugared it and gave it to the young man, who curved his hands round it gratefully and drank it down at high speed. She found herself wondering in a maternal sort of way when he'd last eaten and why he was so quiet. He hadn't mentioned Jesus once yet. Wasn't he supposed to? Standing in the hatches of the *Theodore* as he drained his cup, she tried to decide whether he was ill.

'Thanks very much.' Wiping his mouth with one hand, he handed the cup back with the other and she saw how long and bony his fingers were. The sight of them made her shiver, but when he looked at her with those large grey eyes, again she saw in them a kind, straightforward sympathy.

'Last time we met you seemed burdened, Mrs Bartholomew. I have a feel for a troubled soul. You know that you can find ease for your mind by laying your cares at the feet of our Saviour? He makes no exceptions in forgiveness.'

'I – yes, I know.' Maryann stumbled over her words. His eyes seemed to look right in her, to the cold, heavy shame which was curled deep inside her.

'There will be a service tonight – of prayer for healing,' Pastor Owen was saying, 'where repentant sinners can lay their cares upon the Lord and listen to the blessed assurance of His Word proclaimed. It's only a few minutes' walk from here. Would you care to join us?'

'I don't—' she began. Out of the corner of her eye she saw Joel step off the *Esther Jane* and walk towards them, as Pastor Owen was telling her the address.

'Come and be with us.' Again, his eyes seemed to penetrate right through her. 'Please.'

'How d'you do?' Joel said. Maryann heard the curtness in his voice. He wasn't keen on outsiders who came to give advice, whether they were welfare people coming poking their noses in and trying to make the children go to school, or holy Joes with their missions to the boat-people. He came from a tradition of self-reliance and preferred to stick to his own people.

139

Pastor Owen returned the greeting and held out his hand, which Joel shook reluctantly.

'I was speaking to your wife about the redeeming love of the Lord.'

'Were you?' Joel said, sounding neither approving or disapproving.

'If you should decide to come it'll be eight o'clock.' The young man backed away, raising his hat. 'God bless you.'

And he walked away along the wharf looking, Maryann thought, as if the cares of the world had been laid not at the feet of his Saviour but on his own thin shoulders.

'I've got a pain in my belly.'

Joley sat beside Maryann on the side bench as she stirred the mince and gravy on the stove; every so often he screwed up his face in pain. 'Don't want any tea tonight.'

'You must be sickening for summat.' Maryann felt his forehead, but it wasn't hot. 'Best get you to bed soon.'

When the food was ready, Joel and Bobby brought the other children in, Joel lifting Ada and Esther over onto the boat. They could toddle about outside now, holding his hands or on reins. Bobby said he'd take his plateful back to the *Esther Jane*, while the family squeezed into the *Theodore*.

'S'coming down thick now,' Joel told her, rinsing his hands in the dipper of warm water Maryann had put out for them all on the counter. She peered out. Fog was curling round the wharf, rising over the dark water so that the outlines of everything were blurred and uncertain.

'Should be ready to unload us first thing, any rate.'
He climbed down and sat on the back bed next to Joley,
while the others squeezed round the table, telling her
bits of news he'd picked up from the boats round about.
A new baby in one of the families, a Mr Baines had had
his leg crushed. Maryann responded with as much
interest as she could, but her thoughts were preoccupied
with Joley, who was now dozing uneasily on the back
bed, and in another, distracting side alley of her mind
with the idea of walking the streets until she reached the
address Pastor Owen had given her. She tried to dismiss
the thought. Of course she wasn't going to go! Joley was
poorly, there was a pea-souper gathering out there and
the man was most likely barmy anyhow. But all the time
the thought kept coming back, refusing to be chased
away. A feeling of need kept rising up in her. It was
connected somehow with the way the young man had
looked at her, had seemed to see into her. The argument
went on in her head as Joel lit the lamp and she spooned
out mince and potatoes onto plates. She *couldn't* go!
What would Joel say? And what did she want to go for
anyway? *For relief . . .* the answer floated up from inside.
From how I feel.

'Best have this one sleeping in with us tonight,' Joel
was saying, eyeing his son beside him on the bed.

She nodded, settling to her tea. 'Joel?'

'Ummm?' He reached over and his hand pressed
warm and heavy on her thigh.

'I want to go. To that place Pastor Owen was talking
about. Just for a bit.'

He looked across at her, baffled. 'Do you? What for?'

'I can't explain, love.' She looked at her plate. 'It's just
– for Nance . . . And everything else that's happened . . .'

'Well –' he shrugged – 'if you want. But it's come

141

down bad out there. D'you want me or Bobby to come with you?'

'No, ta.' She managed a wan smile. 'I'll be all right. It's not far.'

She would be a bit late, she thought. She could just hear a clock from somewhere distant striking eight as she set off along Wharf Road. Almost immediately she stepped out through the hatches she had regretted saying she would go alone. The fog was very thick, making her cough, and was tinged with yellow where it met the light escaping from the cabin.

'Tara-abit.' She parted from Joel and hurriedly closed the hatch, tying her bright scarf with the red flowers on over her hair to keep her ears warm, pulling her coat close round her and hurrying as fast as the murk would allow. The road was dark and deserted, hemmed in by warehouses. *Left, left and left again*, he'd said. *Can't go wrong – it's no distance*. It felt a long way, though, groping her way through the noxious fog, thick with chemicals and smoke. The only sound she could hear was her own footsteps until she reached a pub and was grateful for the sound of voices and laughter and the whiff of ale on the air. She could still hardly explain to herself what it was that drove her on, shivering in the cold, the need that forced her along these dismal streets.

The chapel was in a side road. Between a toolmaker's and the end of the houses, he'd said, and from what she could make out of the buildings on either side he seemed to have described it faithfully. From the front window, high up, a tiny thread of light was escaping round the blackout, and once more she was relieved to hear the sound of voices, only this time they were singing. The

142

meeting had obviously begun and Maryann was glad. She could slip in during the hymn and she wouldn't feel so self-conscious in her old coat and dirty boots if she sat at the back. If she didn't like it, she'd slip out again and no one'd be the wiser.

To her relief the door opened silently, but when she pushed inside she was dismayed to see how small the chapel was. On each side was a row of pews, only eight or so deep, pressed up against the walls on each side with a narrow aisle in the middle. They looked outsize in the place, as if they had been passed on from a bigger church, and she saw that they were only occupied by a small scattering of people. The singing, of a tune with which she was not familiar, was thin and strained.

The back row of the pews on the left was empty so she slipped into it, moving half way along so she could see round the heads in front and loosening her scarf. Standing with the others while the singing carried on, she looked round. At the front was a raised dais with a plain wooden lectern on it. On the back wall, which was pale green, hung dark blue curtains drawn apart. Between them a wooden cross was fixed to the wall and to the right of it was a door.

Maryann saw that one of the two men standing at the front – dressed in just their own sombre suits – was Pastor James Owen. She was surprised at the sudden sense of relief she felt in seeing him in this strange place. She wasn't used to public buildings or meetings now. She was used to the cabins of boats. Pastor Owen was not wearing his hat and she saw that his hair was a sludgy brown and obviously not recently aquainted with the barber's, as it hung in a bedraggled fashion down to his collar. His eyes moved soulfully over the pitiful little congregation as they sang, though his own voice was drowned out by that of the other minister beside him, who seemed to think he had to compensate for the feebleness of everyone else and was booming out the words. 'Blood ... ransom ... die ...' came floating to Maryann. She took in the all-over roundness of the man. He had no need of a barber as his head was completely bald and his cranium, cheeks, nose and stomach all had a cheerful, doughnut-like rotundity. She was just taking in another realization, that all the congregation were women, bar one pale, intense-looking man whom she guessed to be in his thirties, when Pastor Owen caught her eye. To her consternation she saw him leave his place and walk down the aisle towards her.

God Almighty! she thought, her hands going all clammy with nerves. *What's he doing?* Her heart was pounding. *What's he coming over here for? He's not going to show me up in front of all these people is he?* But Pastor Owen simply gave her a faint smile of acknowledgment and stood in at the end of the pew. When the singing stopped he stayed there.

Maryann sat down on the hard seat, which seemed to have been designed to deny any possibility of comfort and forced her to sit bolt upright. She couldn't get away now, could she? He was blocking one end of the pew and the other was hard up against the wall! Again, she had an unnerving sense that he could see into her mind. There were prayers. Maryann put her hands in her lap and closed her eyes, but didn't take in a word of what was being said. Her mind was fluttering between the worry that she was sniffing all the time and had nothing to wipe her nose on and noticing that the room smelt of a rank mixture of camphor, urine and frowsty clothes. All the time she was acutely aware of the long shape of Pastor Owen to her right and wondered why had he sat there. What did he want? It had not, before, occurred to her that he wanted something from her.

Next, the minister stood up and loudly, with dramatic sweeps of his arms, preached about the paralysed man whose friends let him down through the roof to be cured by Jesus. Every time he said the Lord's name, in his Black Country accent, he emphasized it: *JESUS*. On and on he went, about being paralysed by our sins, but the only time Maryann took in anything was when he hammered home the word *JESUS* . . . *JESUS* . . . She felt her mind seize up with boredom. What the hell had she come here for? *JESUS*. She should be back at home with her lad, who was poorly, not sitting here on this flaming hard seat with her backside . . . *JESUS* . . . turning numb!

At last, after endless prayers and another dismal hymn, the service ended. She found herself feeling angry and cheated. Where was the sense of forgiveness, of release she had come to find? She rearranged her scarf over her hair and tied the ends, but as she did so, Pastor Owen slid along the pew towards her and looked into her eyes in that way which always made her feel stripped naked.

'I'm glad you came.'

As Maryann couldn't truthfully claim the same, she said, 'So this is your church, is it?'

'I work with Pastor Joyce, yes. Though, as I'm not in charge of the mission here, I have a little more freedom to go out to the needy instead of waiting for them to come to me.'

Was that what she was then? One of the needy?

There was a pause as she looked down into her lap and Pastor Owen sat forward with his lanky arms resting on his thighs. Maryann just wanted to go, to be at home, but she wasn't going to be able to get past him yet.

145

Other people were leaving, gathering up their hats, walking sticks and torches, nodding and smiling at him as they went.

'There's someone here I'd like you to see,' he said, staring ahead of him at the cross on the wall. 'Someone whose soul is also in need of succour and healing – as I believe yours is.' He looked deep into her eyes again and Maryann felt herself tremble inside at this close attention. 'That's why I especially hoped you'd come.'

'To see? Who?' She felt panicky now. What was she letting herself in for? She felt suddenly as if Pastor Owen, young and unlikely a prophet as he seemed, knew every single thing about her, that she was dirty and wicked, that she was a woman who had taken the life of her unborn child. And who on earth was he going to present to her? Some ill-used woman whom he'd picked up on the streets, bulging out at the front with some bully's spawn? A lady of the night that he wanted her to reform? Was he out of his mind? She had come to him for help but he was the one making demands on her.

'I don't think . . .' she tried to protest.

'There's nothing to be afraid of. It's just a member of our congregation who carries a weight of sorrow in their heart.'

Maryann thought of the ladies who'd been sitting around her. She couldn't imagine what possible help she might give any of them, but they hadn't looked all that fearsome had they? She hoped it wasn't the intense young man he'd got lined up for her with some odd request, but she was pretty sure she'd seen him leave.

Pastor Owen stood up and turned to her. 'Assist me – just for a few moments – please, Mrs Bartholomew. It would make a great different to someone, and I believe it would give you rest in your own soul.'

146

She was drawn in. How could she refuse him? If he had held out his hand to her then, she would have taken it. Instead, he indicated with a movement of his head that they should move along to the front of the chapel. Aflutter with nerves, she followed him.

Sixteen

Pastor Owen led her to the front of the chapel, towards the door which opened off to the right of the cross. Just as they reached it, it opened and Pastor Joyce came out. His big mixing-bowl face took on an expression that was grave about the eyes but smiling at the mouth, the sort of smile he might give to someone bereaved.

'Ah!' he cried. 'Good evening to you! You've come to see our poor friend then?'

'The healing grace of the Lord may well be seen in this place tonight,' Pastor Owen said. The combination of this pronouncement and the other man's coffin-side expression made Maryann want to run down the aisle and escape through the back doors. Bewildered, she followed Pastor Owen into a small, dimly lit room. It was bare: a wooden floor, small table in the middle, over which hung a dimly burning light bulb with no shade. There were a couple of hard chairs. The only other thing she noticed was the jaundiced colour of the light, for the walls were yellow. She took in all of this in a couple of seconds because what snatched her attention from anything else, was the figure kneeling sideways on in the far corner. The sight stole the breath from her. She stood quite still, unable to move.

'Our friend is a spirit deep in remorse,' Pastor Owen was saying. 'He has come regularly to our congregation, pouring out to me his misdeeds, his sorrows, which weigh him down and blacken his soul in the eyes of the Lord. All he needs to free him now is to feel the forgiveness of the people he has transgressed against. Without that forgiveness . . .' But Maryann wasn't listening. For her the only thing in the room was the broad-shouldered figure in the black coat, trilby hat pulled well down, raising itself to its feet with a heavy, lumbering movement and beginning to move towards her.

Everything seemed slow, dreamlike. Closer he came, his shape, the gait so utterly familiar, the figure that had haunted her days and polluted her dreams for so many years. He reached the table and loomed over her, his body like a box, filling the room with his square shoulders. The bulb dangled over his head, and with the unhurried relish of one who enjoys inflicting pain, her stepfather raised his head slowly, turning his face out of the shadow to the light and looked into her eyes.

The features were more disfigured than she had even imagined. She began breathing again, with a gasp of revulsion. That night when little Margaret Lambert, driven by his cruelty, had smashed a lamp over his head, the oil had poured out and burned fiercely on him. The left side of his face was completely altered, a mass of puckered flesh reaching right down his neck, where raised ridges alternated with flat areas which had an unnatural shininess. His left eye was completely hidden in the contorted skin. The right side had been burned, though less severely, and it was into Norman Griffin's lashless right eye that Maryann found herself looking back. She gripped the edge of the table, afraid her legs might give way.

'Maryann – you came then.' His voice hadn't changed. Oh, heavens no, it hadn't! Now it contained a humble, wheedling tone, but it was still the voice that had whispered to her through her bedroom door, had spat such vile words into her ear as he laid his weight on her, forcing, fouling her. In those seconds a flare of rage lit in her that had lain dormant all these years. She was suddenly possessed by it, shaking all over as if she was running a fever. Turning to Pastor Owen she lashed him with it.

'What the hell d'you think you're playing at bringing *him* here? How *dare* you deceive me into coming here to meet . . . *this*?' She could only finish the sentence with a gesture of revolt, slapping her hands down on the table. 'What d'you want from me? You're mad! You've no idea what he's like – what he's done . . .'

Pastor James held his hands out as if he thought he was Jesus calming the storm.

'Mrs Bartholomew – please. I beg you. Don't reject this man. He knows he has done terrible things. He's full of remorse for his past sins. He has told me of them and he needs to express his sorrow. To repent and begin afresh.'

'Maryann – please.' Norman Griffin's voice came out brokenly, hoarse with contrition. 'You've no idea what it's been like all these years living with this.' He pointed at himself, at his scarred face. 'Like a leper – the sign of my guilt. I need to know forgiveness. To be able to live at peace with myself.'

Maryann looked from one to the other, having to grope for words. 'To live at peace?' In order to speak normally at all, instead of raging or screaming which her whole being felt tuned to do, she had to lower her voice to a snarl. 'You don't deserve to live at all. Yes, you're guilty all right.' Again she turned on Pastor Owen. 'I suppose you think you know about him. I s'pose he's told you some soft soap about a few little pinches and

smacks, about his wicked, ungrateful stepchildren? You
think a few smacks would drive a child to do *that*?' She
pointed at Norman's face. 'D'you want to hear what he
did? What he really did? You poor, stupid, little man –
you really think you're doing something grand, saving
his soul, don't you? Well, let me tell you – you've picked
on the one person on this earth who doesn't have one.'

'Please – let me say I'm sorry. I want to make amends
for what I've done.' Norman Griffin started to move
round the table and Maryann backed away from him.

'Don't come near me!' she shrieked, losing control of
herself. 'You make my flesh creep. You're vile and
disgusting. Keep him away from me!'

To her surprise, Norman stopped, standing still, lowering his head. For a moment she was at a loss.

'No deed is beyond our Saviour's forgiveness,' Pastor
Owen pleaded, holding his hands out towards her. He
seemed really distressed, his eyes like huge pebbles under
the light. 'Forgive for your own sake, Maryann. If you
can't forgive, your soul is trapped in darkness. Forgiveness is new life.'

A sound broke through the room, something so foreign and unknown that Maryann at first could not
recognize it. It came to her that it was a sob, that it had
come from Norman Griffin, from beneath the lowered
brim of his hat.

'He lives day by day in hell.' Pastor Owen declared
emotionally. 'And you too will live in hell if you don't
forgive him.' He went to Maryann and attempted to take
her hand.

'Don't you touch me, you bloody nutcase!' She
backed away, tightly folding her arms. She'd had quite
enough of Pastor James with his earnest Mancunian

pleading. 'What's it to you? You don't care about how I feel – you just want to be able to show off about how many souls you've "saved".'

But she was deflated. The room felt very cold and she was suddenly full of doubt, seeing the scarred, broken figure with his head bowed, across the room. For those seconds, she was the one here who was made to seem cruel. But other pictures flashed into her mind, rescuing her: of Sal, her older sister, on the bed that day she'd found her lying in the dark, the blood still dripping from her wrists; of Margaret, dead-eyed in the asylum.

'Can you find it in your heart to forgive him?' Pastor James pressed her. 'To free this troubled soul?'

Maryann looked across at the young man in his poor, sagging clothes and pitied him his naive ardour.

'You've no idea, have you?' She managed to speak more quietly now. 'He can't just change in one night. Not someone like him. It won't just drop off him. If he lives in hell, it's where he belongs. He put himself there – no one else did it.'

To Norman she said, 'I don't know what you want with me now. But whatever it is, you're not getting it. I was the one who was never fooled by you, remember? I know you, and I know you don't have a remorseful bone in your body.'

She moved towards the door. 'I wouldn't tangle with the likes of him,' she told the young man. 'He's beyond redemption.'

As she turned to leave there came a sudden movement and she found the door pushed shut by Norman Griffin's hand. He was upon her suddenly, and so close to her that she could feel his breath on her cheek and she recoiled, but he moved closer, forcing the door shut.

'Don't go – not yet,' he entreated. The voice was soft,

caressing. She couldn't look at him. She kept her eyes down, fixed on his black boots, her own brown ones. 'It's all right, Maryann. Don't worry. I can wait.' And then he let her open the door.

She fled out through the chapel, to the dark street. It was difficult to hurry outside, even though her whole being cried run, run! The night fog swirled round her, seemingly full of threat, of unknown presences.

'Turn right, and right!' She was muttering feverishly to herself. It was hard to see where she was going, to hurry. 'It's not far. Keep going . . .'

Every so often she stopped, but there was silence as soon as her own footsteps were stilled. She knew really that Norman Griffin would not come after her. If he had run out of the chapel behind her, Pastor Owen would surely have followed as well. And knowing Norman Griffin as she did, she knew he was a man who would bide his time. After all, if all he'd wanted was to jump out on her, why go through all this rigmarole of repentance in order to see her? But even so every nerve in her body seem to jangle, her breath sobbing in her lungs as she scurried through the dark streets. Oh God, she knew she had seen him on the wharf all those months ago – and then someone else had said he was asking for her? She knew she had not imagined it – he was after her. What did he want with her?

Most of all, what she could not get out of her head were his final words, speaking in that remorseful, patient tone for the benefit of the young missionary: *Don't worry. I can wait.*

Seventeen

By the time she arrived back at the boats, Maryann was in such a state she could hardly get the hatches of the *Theodore* open. Once she had managed to, she almost fell inside and slammed the doors shut again, panting so hard that she was sobbing.

Joel's face appeared round the bed curtain. He'd been lying down but was not asleep and the light was still burning.

'What's got into you?' It took him a moment to realize she was seriously frightened.

'*He* was there!' She spoke in a hoarse whisper, trying not to wake Joley and the twins. 'Norman Griffin! That preacher's a right stupid bugger.'

Joel gave her a look which said, 'Well, I could have told you that.' With trembling legs, Maryann climbed over the sleeping toddlers in their nest on the floor, where Jenny the tortoiseshell cat was curled beside them, and went to sit by Joel, shivering. She turned to look at Joley on the bed behind them.

'He's been sick a little while back,' Joel told her.

'Poor lamb.' Frowning, her own preoccupations calmed for a moment she stroked his head. Beside it lay his precious tobacco tin of cigarette cards. 'He doesn't feel feverish. Maybe that'll be all for tonight.' She snuggled close to Joel and he put his arm round her.

'What's up with you then?' He squeezed her tight, trying to still her shaking.

She felt jarred with shock and anger. Now she could let it out and tell him what happened, tears came as well.

'Seeing him again was *horrible*,' she wept. 'His face is such a mess and there he was, pretending to be all sorry, as if he's changed and I know he hasn't. He's got that Pastor Owen wrapped round his little finger – I bet he told him to come and find me. Oh, Joel, what does he want? When I was leaving he told me he could wait – as if he's going to keep coming after us.'

'Eh, there.' Joel wrapped his arms round her, rocking her, her head pressed against his chest.

'What can he do to us? He's an old 'un, must be nigh on seventy, ent he? And we're hardly ever up here in Birnigum. Don't you worry about him – we'll be loaded up and gone in the morning and he won't know where to find us then, will he?'

'I know.' She looked up at him, tearful like a child. 'But I thought we were safe after all this time.'

Maryann could see Joel was right about the facts of the situation, at least. They'd be gone. What could Norman Griffin do to hurt them? All Joel said to comfort her was right and reasonable. But Joel did not know about Norman Griffin. Not really. She had never told him, fully, what her stepfather had done to Sal and to her. She felt she couldn't speak of it to anyone, had never wanted Joel to know, and Joel had never asked. He didn't truly understand the horror that Norman Griffin could arouse in her, the thoughts of him like tentacles forcing her back into the shame and fear of her childhood. He might travel with her every mile of the way, even though he was not physically present. Though externally calmer, she was left feeling completely

155

churned up inside and knew she'd have trouble getting any sleep.

There was no room to move round the cabin, so she and Joel took it in turns to undress, standing in the tiny space, which was enough to put two feet down at the edge of the bed.

'I'll move Joley over now,' Joel whispered.

Joley stirred as Joel set him down on the side bench, a coat bundled under his head. Maryann passed over the tin of cigarette cards. Spots, the other cat, had been asleep at the end and got up, rather disgruntled, then settled back at Joley's feet.

'Mom?'

'I'm here, pet.' Maryann peered round the curtain at him. 'You awright Joley?'

'I been sick,' he murmured sleepily.

'I know. Your dad said. How d'you feel now?'

'Bit sick . . .' But he was almost asleep again.

Maryann got out to let Joel settle on the far side of the bed, and kissed Joley's cheek. She put the bucket in the corner by his head and made sure the torch was handy.

'Sleep well, son.' She blew out the light and climbed in beside Joel. 'Maybe he'll be all right by the morning.'

'Hope so.' Joel was almost asleep. It had been a long day. He kept himself awake long enough to wrap his arm round her, and his beard prickled her face with a kiss.

'It'll be all right,' she just heard him say, before he was lost to sleep.

Maryann lay curled under Joel's arm, her body bent to his shape. Usually, tucked in this warm proximity she fell asleep almost instantly, but tonight her mind was jangled, darting from one harsh thought to another. For once she didn't mind if the children woke up, since she didn't seem likely to get to sleep anyway. The scene in the chapel ran vividly in her mind's eye. Pastor Owen's pleading, rock-pool eyes. What a silly fool the man was! How he'd been taken in, thinking he could deal in forgiveness as easily as that. His naive ignorance, the glibness of his thinking, made her feel violently angry. But worst of all was the thought of that voice, Norman Griffin's terrible face, his ruckled skin, the cold gaze of that one eye boring into her. *I can wait.* The words came whispering through her mind, over and over.

All she managed, for a short time, was a restless doze. She jerked awake later at the sound of a high, seagull wail and realized it was Ada. She didn't need the light on to see the child, knowing her cry and where to find her, and she leaned over and brought her up into bed to suckle her. She still fed them herself from time to time, more for comfort than anything as they had long since eaten other food. She sat up, holding Ada's slight form until she was sleeping again, then tucked her back in bed.

She had no idea how much later it was when Joley woke. Once again she was washing back and forth along the shoreline of sleep when his voice, a frantic 'Mom!' came out of the darkness.

'You getting sick, Joley?' With a pang she heard herself say 'getting sick' the way Nancy used to. Nance was always popping up, never far from her thoughts.

'Yes!' Joley wailed.

She was just in time with torch and bucket and Joley heaved until no more would come. Maryann perched on the bench beside him, wiping his forehead.

'Don't like it,' he said miserably.

'No – I know. Here – have a drink of water.'

She climbed to the door and let herself out quickly to empty the bucket. Joley lay limply down again.

'Will I be sick more?'

'Don't know, bab. You might. Look, I'll turn this light off and sit here with you for a bit, awright? Till you're settled.'

Shivering, she reached for her cardigan at the end of the bed and pulled it round her. She already had socks on. The nights were very cold on the cut now once the heat from the range had died out. She sat in the dark, fiddling with the ends of her hair, enjoying the peace and quiet. She could hear Spots purring at Joley's feet, Joel's breathing, the light snuffles of the twins. Every so often she caught the lapping sound of the water against the wharf outside. Her hand gently stroked her son's thick curly hair. *He's such a little boy still, really*, she thought. As the oldest, and a boy, he spent a lot of time with Joel and was given the most responsibility. Joel was deter-mined he was going to be an expert boatman. After all, there was Ezra coming up too, but now they knew there would be no more sons ... She knew Joel tried to hide his grief over this. Touching Joley's cheek, she thought about the hospital, how much she had ached for this cosiness – warm bodies to kiss and stroke, the breathing of loved ones around her at night. She must make the best of all they had now, she thought. She had six children to bring up, after all.

She was gathering herself to get back into bed when something jolted her fully awake again. There was another sound, something that didn't belong, not at this time of night. Yes, there it was, outside. Footsteps along the wharf. A chill went through her and she held her breath, fear swelling. Who was out there? She tried to calm herself, reminding herself to breathe. There was a watchman on the wharf gate at night, so surely no one could get in? It was probably him wandering about, checking that everything was all right.

There it was again. Movement, a slight crunch underfoot. The footsteps came closer, treading quietly, obviously cautious. Had she been asleep she would never have heard them. The side of the wharf was just behind her head, beyond the thin cabin wall. The footsteps moved along a little, then stopped. At last she heard them moving away.

Impulsively she pulled herself up and over the twins onto the coal box. Clenching her teeth, praying to make as little sound as possible, she slid back the hatch far enough to poke her head out.

'Sod it!' she cursed under her breath. Of course it was very dark and still foggy and she couldn't even see the front end of the *Theodore*, let alone anyone moving further away. The only thing she could see clearly was the tiller beside her, upended for the night. But standing very still, yes, surely she could just hear footsteps dying in the distance along the path? Shuddering, she pulled the hatch closed and climbed into bed beside Joel. The darkness outside felt full of threat. It was a long time before she slept.

Joley was sick twice more in the night, and the final time Maryann got up rain was drumming on the cabin roof. It was still raining in the morning, the sky low and burdened. She was feeling quite energetic despite the poor night, though she knew it was a nervous, jumpy sort of energy. Joley was pale and floppy but past the worst and she left him on the back bed to continue recovering.

The unloading began early, as promised. Joel and Bobby were outside with steaming cups of tea soon after seven when it was barely light, untying and stowing away the top cloths. All the supports that held the planks and tarpaulins over the load were thrown onto the bank, the cranes were swung into position and the unloading began.

Maryann fed the rest of the children aboard the *Theodore*.

'Sally – just keep an eye on them for me will you? I'll be back in a couple of ticks.'

Pulling her coat and scarf on, arms folded, head down against the rain, she set off across the wharf, which was fast turning into a quagmire. The place was full of activity: the wharf men shouting and horse-pulled wagons and trucks all arriving to pick up loads, with muted headlights still on to see through the dark and rain. She passed Charlie Dean, who called, 'Morning!' to her chirpily. 'All right are you? Manage to get shot of that holy Joe, did you?'

She turned as they passed each other, rain running down her cheeks. 'Oh, I don't think I'll be seeing him again!' She raised a grin. The sight of Charlie always cheered her. She hurried over to the nightwatchman's hut, wondering if he was still there, but he was in the doorway, talking to two other men. They moved back, seeing her approaching.

'There's a lovely lady here to see you, pal!'

'I thought you might've gone by now,' she panted.

'I should've done, bab, but I got held up canting to these two!' He was a big, cheerful bloke, the backs of his hands hairy like an ape.

'Only – I wanted to ask, like – was anyone else in here last night?'

'What – in my hut?' The three men laughed. 'No, love – I didn't get that lucky!'

Maryann smiled patiently. 'No – up and down the wharf, I mean. Did you go out and walk about?'

He frowned, seeing she was serious. 'Me? No, I can't say I did.'

'I heard someone. They were walking round our boats.'

She could see he was struggling to believe her. 'Well, I s'pose it's possible. But I don't know how anyone could've got in or out past me.'

Maryann knew what she'd heard, that she wasn't imagining it, but obviously they weren't going to get to the bottom of it. 'Oh well,' she said. 'Ta anyway.'

'Tara-abit,' he said easily. 'Don't worry. No one can get in here.'

She hurried back, boots sloshing through puddles. There was water to fetch, kids to see to. She raised her head, letting the rain fall cold on her face as she watched the crane swing high over her head from the hold of the *Esther Jane*.

Yes, she urged the machine, *lift it all out, quick, and let us get out, away from here.*

PART TWO

1944

Eighteen

The days were diamond hard, sparkling with frost. They were travelling south down the Oxford cut, and in the mornings they had to wrench the hatches open, stepping out into a world of white, the trees rimed, twigs gnarled and pale like witches' fingers.

They had to take great care along the icy lock sides. Straps froze stiff as iron and the sheets over the coal were as solid as planks.

The icebreakers were at work, freeing up the channels to allow them to set out, and once they did, often very late, the boats nosed through chunks of floating ice. They stood working the tillers, bundled up in all the clothes they could squeeze into, sleeves pulled down over their hands against the gnawing cold. Maryann kept the kettle on the hob all day, making cup after cup of cocoa or tea to stave off the deep, brittle cold of February.

One day, while she was at the tiller of the *Theodore*, she saw a pair of boats tied up beyond the bridge at Nethercote. It was the section of the cut shared by the Oxford and the Grand Union, and this pair were from the Grand Union Carrying Company. This was nothing unusual and Maryann hardly gave them a glance, until her eye was caught by the figure moving along the bank towards the butty, shouting to an unseen companion in the cabin. The person was very slight in build, and was

165

dressed in slacks and a loose jacket, and wore a strange cap with a peak and earflaps. Maryann sheltered her eyes from the glaring winter sun and stared with blatant curiosity, still turning her head to look after the person had passed behind them. To her amazement, she realized that the lithe, energetic-looking figure was that of a woman – in trousers! And striding about like a man! She'd never seen a woman on the cut looking anything like that before.

Later, when she mentioned it to Joel, he said, 'I saw them. They'll be them volunteers.'

They'd heard mention of them lately in the pubs along the cut. Because of the shortage of crews and the need to keep loads moving for the war effort, there were all sorts coming off the bank to work the cut.

'There's women working in teams by themselves now, so they say,' Joel said. 'Still, they don't mix with the likes of us. They're working the Grand Union, most of them, anyway.' The way he said it made Maryann feel rather superior. Of course, she was 'off the bank' too, but she belonged now, didn't she? She was part of a proper boating family.

It never crossed her mind, then, that she'd ever have anything to do with these strange creatures. These girls in trousers. But later it felt as if that glimpse of them had been a premonition, a warning that she would need to prepare herself for what was to come.

She had asked Joel to try and get loads from Essy Barlow that didn't involve going to Birmingham, and especially Tyseley, to avoid any possibility of meeting Norman Griffin.

Joel tried to reassure her. 'What can *he* do, when you

166

come down to it? He's only trying to frighten you, lass. The man's a bully, born and bred. But he can't hardly go creeping about with a face like that on him, can he? He'd scare the horses all right! Everyone'd see him coming for miles.'

Joel didn't understand how the very thought of Norman Griffin could upset Maryann, could throw her right off balance, but he didn't much like Birmingham and was quite content not to go there. Mr Barlow was a reasonable man, who tried to give them what they asked, so they were working round Sutton again and up and down the Oxford. They'd had a good winter so far, the children were thriving and mostly well, and they'd spent Christmas in Oxford. Their own situation was good. Maryann felt better in herself than she had in a long time. It was Darius's silent sadness and the gap left by Nancy that gnawed at them.

That day was a little warmer. A slight thaw had set in, the trees were beginning to drip and a sheen of moisture lay over the ice on the stones, gleaming in the sun. They'd left Banbury behind, heading south. Joel gave Bobby the tiller of the *Esther Jane* and climbed out to lock-wheel with Joley and Ezra.

The boys waved at Maryann from the bank, and she could hear Joel urging them to hurry. They had to run ahead and prepare the next lock at King's Sutton. She smiled at the sight of Joel's burly figure moving past them. His run, taken in long, unhurried strides, was surprisingly graceful. He had his windlass in his hand and the two boys were pursuing him, relishing their release from the boat's confining space. Soon they were at the lock, Joel and Ezra forcing the windlass round together. Bobby skilfully slowed the *Esther Jane* right down and released the butty, and Maryann steered the

Theodore into the bank and jumped off with a line to pull her in and wait while the *Esther Jane* passed through the lock.

They had filled the lock and Joel was opening the gate to let Bobby in when Maryann was distracted by a loud wail from inside the *Theodore*.

'Sally?' She knocked on the side of the cabin. 'Is that Esther? What's up with her?'

Sally's flustered face appeared. 'She's banged her head and her nose won't stop bleeding!'

'What the hell was she doing?' Maryann tutted, exasperated. Why did things like this always happen when she'd just stepped off the boat? 'Get one of them rags – wet it in the dipper and bathe her face with it.' She was shouting, pulling on the rope to brace it and keep the boat in by the bank. The current moving into the filling lock kept trying to tug it forwards.

The bawling inside the cabin continued. 'It won't stop bleeding,' she heard Sally wail. 'Oh, Esther, just sit still!'

'Just keep the rag on her nose – dab at it till I get back in,' Maryann yelled.

Joel was closing the gate behind the *Esther Jane*.

'Come on, come *on*,' Maryann urged, still leaning back on the rope.

It seemed to take for ever to empty the lock again and for a second she nipped back on board. Sally seemed to be managing.

'I'll come and see to her when we get in the lock,' Maryann said, disappearing out again.

The *Esther Jane* vanished down, down, as water poured out through the bottom paddles. The drop here was considerable as they travelled downhill – about fifteen feet.

She saw it happen as she stood there, eyes fixed on

the lock, willing it to finish emptying quickly, ears pricked to make sure Esther's screams were finally subsiding. Joel was moving away from her, going back to close the paddles on the bottom gates, when she saw him trip. He struggled to right himself, but the foot he put down slipped from under him, taking him over the edge of the lock. He twisted, flailing in the air, then disappeared.

'Oh my God ... *Bobby*!' Maryann screamed.

Joley and Ezra moved to the side of the lock, looking down. Maryann waited for Joel to appear again, climb up the ladder at the side of the lock, but there was nothing, only the little boys, both watching, not moving.

'Sally – get out here, quick!' Maryann yelled at the top of her voice. 'Your dad's had a fall!' She flung the rope into her daughter's hands and tore along the path. Water was trickling in through the top gates. Apart from that it seemed so quiet. She dashed round the arm of the lock gate and looked down into the emptied lock. Bobby had scrambled along to Joel, who was in a precarious position, having slid down the side of the cloths covering the load, and lay crumpled at the side of the boat close to the lock wall.

'Joel? Bobby? Is he all right?' She ran to the ladder and climbed down, then struggled along the gunwale to reach Joel. His eyes were open, but there was a pained, stunned expression on his face. Bobby's normally cheerful expression was very sombre. Squatting close by, he looked helplessly at Joel.

'He fell on his back – hell of a crack – right across the beams, and then he rolled down . . .'

'Joel?' She got as near to him as she could, horrified by the way he was just lying, not moving. 'Love, what's up? What've you done?'

169

'I can't . . .' he raised his head to speak to her, but then lay back with a groan. 'It's no good. I can't move.'

Two days later they pulled into Oxford. Helped by the crew of the boats following behind them, they'd managed to shift Joel onto his bed in the *Theodore*. He cried out in pain as they moved him so that Maryann could hardly bear to hear it, but he refused to let them call any medical help for him there.

'Let me call the doctor,' Maryann begged, beside herself with worry as she saw his face contort with pain every time he tried the smallest movement. 'I can't stand seeing you like this. I don't know what to do.' What if he'd broken his back and could never walk again?

'Just get us to Oxford,' Joel insisted. 'I ent getting left in Banbury or Lord knows where. I'll be all right here for a bit. I'm not that bad. Just leave me be.'

He slept a great deal, groaning with pain whenever he tried to move. Lying beside him at night, Maryann tried to soothe and comfort him. The family had to see to his every need and as Maryann and Bobby took the boats down to Oxford she was willing away every mile of the journey.

At last they arrived, and this time it was Joel's turn to be taken away in an ambulance. Though she tried to control herself in front of the children, Maryann wept as it drove away from the wharf.

'What's he done to himself?' she sobbed. It unnerved her completely to see Joel, who was always so rock-like, in this broken state. 'Supposing he's done summat really bad to himself and he can't work again?'

'He'll be all right.' Bobby tried awkwardly to comfort

170

her, though he was very shaken by what had happened as well. 'He's a tough 'un, he is. You'll see.'

Bobby was a godsend to Maryann in those days. She was surprised because she still thought of him as a young lad, but he had a steady kindness which helped to keep her calm. When she went back into the Radcliffe to see Joel's doctor, he said a whole lot of things she couldn't really understand, but what she did come away knowing was that Joel's back was not broken, but that there had been 'severe damage' to it and that he needed to lie flat and rest it completely.

Timidly, she asked, 'Well, how long for?'

'Quite a long time,' the doctor told her. 'Months, certainly.'

'Months!' she reported, anguished, to Bobby. 'How on earth are we going to manage?'

As ever, Alice Simons came to the rescue. If Joel needed complete rest and care, where else was he to find it other than with his father and aunt? There was no need for him to stay in hospital, so soon he was lying upstairs in the little house in Adelaide Street.

The children were very happy to spend a few days in and out of their auntie's house, but they all knew that if they didn't get moving again soon there'd be no money. Joel lay on his aunt's clean white sheets, fuming with frustration.

'We'll manage for a bit,' Maryann told him. 'Bobby and me. We'll just have to. Joley's a big help now.'

'I know – but I feel a right useless article lying here!' He thumped the mattress beside him with his fist, then winced. 'It's like being a baby again – having to have someone help me, you know – do my business and that every time. Not doing right by my family. I feel a right fool, I do.'

Maryann took his callused hand and kissed it. 'Should Bobby and me look for a load?'

'You'll have to. Get Bobby to go round all the usual and get back up to Sutton and see Essy. Tell him how it is. He can keep you on short trips for a bit.'

Later, over a cup of tea, Alice Simons said to Maryann, 'Look, dear, if you'd like you could leave some of the children behind for a bit while you're short-handed. The twins maybe? We could manage here and they'd be with their father.'

Despondently, Maryann swirled the dregs around in her cup. It was tempting, and was the practical thing to do, but her response was immediate.

'No – ta very much, all the same. It's kind of you, but I don't want them split up if we can help it.' She wasn't coming back to find that Esther and Ada didn't know her again! She wanted to keep her flesh and blood close by, even if they made life harder. It was bad enough leaving Joel behind.

Heavy hearted, she set off north again with Bobby the next day, after a loving farewell to Joel. His words still sounded in her ears.

'Look after them, won't you, little mate?' She knew he meant the family, all the children. But he also meant his beloved boats.

Nineteen

Mr Barlow was not about when they reached Sutton Stop.

'He's up Glascote,' Maryann reported back to Bobby. The main S.E. Barlow offices were at Glascote, near Tamworth. 'I told Mr Veater what's happened and he said he'd have a word with Essy and see if there might be a spare-wheeler going for us.'

She had hoped they might just find the *Isla* and *Neptune* tied up there so that Rose could spend a bit of time with Darius and she could chew the situation over with him too, but there was no sign of them. They were off on a long haul somewhere.

The next morning she and Bobby had begun washing out the boats when she saw Mr Veater's trilby bobbing along the path towards them.

'Morning!' he called, and bent down to stroke Spots, who was standing on the bank with his back arched in a disgruntled fashion, keeping out of the way of the sloshing water.

'I've got a proposal for you,' Mr Veater said, straightening up.

Maryann jumped down onto the bank, straightening the scarf she had tied on to keep her hair back out of the way.

'Proposal?' The only proposal he usually came along with was their clearance papers.

'There's a new crew for you. Two girls. Got a couple of 'em from down London spare-wheeling at the moment. You can have 'em till Joel's on his feet again.'

'*Girls?*' Maryann protested. 'Two of them? But I don't need two – I've got Bobby! Are they them volunteers?'

A smile tugged at Mr Veater's lips at her indignation. 'They've got them trained up, or so they say. What I reckon is, it's best if the two of them stick together, them being birds of a feather, sort of thing. Bobby can go and work for someone else for a bit. That way it won't upset the er ... sleeping arrangements. And it'll keep you three-handed. You've got your hands full as it is.'

Maryann was aghast. She couldn't even begin to put her objections into words. She just gaped at Mr Veater. The volunteers were all very well in their place, but they didn't work with real boatpeople, did they? Not as a rule. And here she was, about to be landed with two complete strangers who hardly knew one end of a boat from another. What in God's name was the use of that?

'But . . .' she began, as Mr Veater started to turn away.

'Apparently they're already on their way from London,' he said. 'Don't fret – it won't be for long. And you'll be able to teach them a thing or two.'

Bobby said his goodbyes and removed his small bundle of possessions to another boat.

'Soon be back.' He winked at Maryann, who was trying, dolefully, to smile. 'Go easy on 'em now!'

Right, she thought, as soon as he'd gone. She was still reeling with shock. *I'd better get to work. I'm not having some posh London misses coming down looking down their noses at my cabins!* While the children played on the bank and made dens in the boats' empty holds, Maryann set to, washing clothes and hanging them in the crisp air and scrubbing every nook and cranny of both boats. She washed the plates and crochetwork and polished the brasses.

Sleeping's going to be a squeeze, she thought, as she polished the stove in the *Theodore*. She planned to move herself and all the children into the *Esther Jane*. It was the smaller of the two cabins, as the *Theodore* had no engine, but it was the family boat, after all, and she'd be in charge of it. Her children couldn't sleep in with strangers: they'd all be in together now. Oh, why had she let herself be pushed into this? She missed Bobby already, with his relaxed, capable ways.

She was on edge all morning, snappish with the children, dreading the arrival of the two women. They were bound to be snooty and look down on her and how was she going to work with them when they barely knew the cut? As the day wore on, her mood darkened to the point where she had to ask herself why she was feeling quite so low and afraid, so angry at what was happening.

'I don't want strangers on our boats,' she fumed, slamming her mattress down on the bed in the *Esther Jane*. 'I don't want them coming here, prying into my life!' She threw the pillow to the end of the bed. She felt raw and exposed. 'I just want things to stay the same. I don't want them here!'

She hurried the children along with her to buy some groceries, then rushed back to begin cooking. By the late afternoon she had the stewpot bubbling away, the kettle on and the boat was well stocked and spick and span. It was only then that she took in the state of herself and the rest of the family.

The twins were smeared with everything they'd had their hands in all afternoon, Ezra looked as if he'd been down a coalpit and all their clothes were dark with grime. Maryann's own frock was filthy and the front of her brown cardigan was coming unravelled. As Nance would have said, *Jesus, Mary and Joseph, will you look at the state of you!* They really did all look like gypsies!

'Come over here and wash your hands and faces!' she shouted to them. 'We've got visitors coming. They'll be here any minute!'

She drew up some cold water from the cut in the dipper and was about to add more hot from the kettle, but it was too late.

'Look Mom – ' Sally pointed – 'they're coming.'

Maryann froze in the hatches, the rag with which she had been about to begin on the children's faces in her hands. Through the smoky dusk she saw two figures moving closer along the towpath, both heavily laden with bags and bedrolls, the taller of the two staggering slightly under the weight. Maryann narrowed her eyes. The taller one had pale, shoulder-length hair. The other one's head was almost hidden behind the bundle in her arms. And they were both wearing trousers.

The family waited, mesmerized by the sight. Maryann had sat Ada and Esther side by side on the cabin roof, their little legs dangling above the counter, knees pink from the cold above their socks. Joley stood balanced on the gunwale close to them and Sally, Ezra and Rose stood on the bank. No one said a word as the two figures drew closer.

Peering at the front of the *Esther Jane*, the taller one said, 'Ah – here we are. At last!'

Maryann felt herself tighten inside hearing that voice. It sounded like high little bells ringing. The way that

176

small utterence was pronounced seemed to open up a vast gulf between her experiences and the kind of life the other woman had come from. It had been different at Charnwood House, when she'd worked in service. Everyone had their place there – family or servants. But now she was expected to live and work with these women!

Then she heard the other one say, in a deeper, booming voice, 'It looks as if we've got a reception committee.'

They came on down to the *Theodore* and now they were visible: one slim with wavy blonde hair, the other round-faced and very plump, dark hair tied tightly back, but with a severe, very straight fringe.

'Well, hello!' the blonde said. 'You must be Mrs Bartholomew.'

Maryann nodded, throwing the rag in through the cabin door. 'That's me.' She couldn't think of a single thing else she might say.

'I say,' the blonde said to her companion. 'Let's put this bally lot down and introduce ourselves properly.'

They were about to dump everything, bedrolls and all on the towpath, but Maryann, appalled at the thought of the mud being transferred into her spotless cabin, protested.

'No – don't do that! It's mucky down there – put them inside. Here – I'll show you.'

She stood outside the *Theodore*, arms folded, as they deposited their things.

'I say, what a *superb* cabin,' she heard the dark one say, and the other woman made some reply. When they came out again, the blonde one climbed down carefully from the counter. Maryann didn't offer to help. The dark one bounced down, landing with surprising agility for her weight.

The blonde held her hand out. Close up, Maryann saw that her hair was rolled back from her forehead and pinned stylishly. She had a wide-eyed, rather birdlike face, not quite pretty, but sympathetic. In the half light Maryann thought, but was not certain, that she was wearing lipstick.

'I'm Sylvia Cresswell. Mrs – normally, anyhow!' Her laugh tinkled into the air. 'I'm awfully glad to meet you, and I'm so sorry to hear about your husband's frightful accident.'

Maryann shook the thin, cold hand and said awkwardly, 'Thanks – how d'you do?'

'And I'm Dorothy Higgs-Deveraux,' the other girl boomed. Her handshake was a lot more forceful. She had a broad, large-boned face and dark eyes. 'Most people call me Dot.'

'I'm Maryann Bartholomew,' she said, as they both seemed to be waiting for her to add something more. She felt so rough beside them: her voice, her manners.

'And these are your children?' Sylvia asked, moving closer to them. 'Goodness me – are they all yours? Who are these little lovelies then?'

'Tell the ladies your names,' Maryann commanded them sharply.

Joley and Sally managed to get theirs out, but the others were too overwhelmed by all the attention from these strangers.

'That's Ezra – he's five,' Maryann finished for them. 'Rose here's four – and the twins, Ada and Esther, are eighteen months now. Anyroad –' she lifted the little ones briskly off the roof – 'you'll be wanting a cup of tea and summat to eat?'

'That'd be *marvellous*,' Dot said. 'I'm parched and I could eat a horse!'

They made as if to move into the *Esther Jane* with the family, but Maryann stood looking down at them from the counter.

'We'll bring you a plateful in your cabin. There's no room in here with all of us.'

'Ah –' Sylvia faltered. 'Yes, of course. So sorry.'

Maryann could see Sylvia had heard the chill in her voice and she felt rather triumphant. She wasn't having them just moving in here and taking over the place!

She got Joley and Sally to carry the plates of stew and cups of tea along to the other cabin. When Sally came back, wide-eyed, she said, 'That lady with the white hair's got some pretty things.'

'Has she?' Maryann said sourly. Whatever fripperies she'd brought with her wouldn't stay pretty long on here, she thought. Not once they got covered in smuts and muck.

'They want to know what time to get up,' Joley said.

Maryann spooned out their stew – a little ration of meat padded out with carrots and turnip. 'Go and tell her, early – by six. We've got a load of coal to fetch.'

From now on she would have to bunk up with Joley and Sally, end to end beside her, and the two younger ones top to tail on the side bench, twins on the floor. Maryann lay in the darkness, hearing the occasional, mournful squawk of a water bird. She ached to be able to reach out and touch Joel beside her. Everything felt so peculiar and sad and she didn't feel safe without him, so solid and true, beside her. She pictured him in his bed in Oxford and sent him a goodnight wish. Then the loathsome thought of the two unknown women lying in the *Theodore* came to her. Even the thought of them filled her with unease. Why had she agreed to let strangers come barging into her life, her family? She and

179

Bobby could've struggled on together. As it was, that Sylvia looked as if she'd break if you dropped her and as for Dot, she was going to be a right bossy one, Maryann could see. What use were they going to be, coming onto the cut from their mollycoddled lives?

She turned on her side and tried to sleep, dreading the next morning.

Twenty

'I say – hello? Anyone up in there? Only we thought you might like a cup of tea.'

The voice came to Maryann in the depths of sleep and she forced her eyes open. Memory flooded in. That voice – of course – those blasted women! The clock by her head said twenty-past six – she was the one who'd overslept! Cursing ripely, she scrambled over the twins to the door, which opened onto a cold, overcast morning.

Sylvia was outside, looking neat and fresh with her hair pinned back, and she held out a steaming cup.

'*So* sorry to wake you.' Sylvia seemed almost to cringe with apology as she spoke. 'I've put a spoonful of sugar in – I do hope that's all right?'

Cheeks burning with embarrassment Maryann leaned over to take the tea, trying to hold the torn neck of her nightdress together: it had a rip in the hem too. Her hair was all over the place, she hadn't lit the stove on the *Esther Jane* yet – and these two clowns had to be up with the lark, sod them!

'Ta. Good of you,' she said, barely able to hide her fury. 'We're nearly ready.'

'Good-oh. Well – I must let you get on. You must have an awful lot to do.' Sylvia moved away, folding her arms, shoulders hunched, as if trying to minimize her presence. Maryann was taken aback at how cowed the woman seemed by her curt response. She got halfway along the *Theodore*, but then, to Maryann's further irritation, turned and came back.

'Er, Maryann, Dot and I brought our rations with us – and Dot's got some extra as well. Of course it makes most sense to combine everything – so how about us doing breakfast for everyone this morning? Dot's already made a start . . .'

'I can manage, you know,' Maryann snapped. She could feel herself frowning and knew she must seem very hostile. But she felt very nervous and under pressure – it was unbearable having these strangers coming and taking over her life! But then Joley pushed passed her and poked his nose out through the door, saying, 'Umm! I can smell bacon – is that for us?'

Forced to swallow her pride Maryann said more politely, 'All right, then – you do it for today. Thanks.'

When the breakfast was ready, Sylvia started carrying plates of it along to them until Maryann ordered the children out to go and collect it.

'We don't need you waiting on us,' she said.

'Oh, it's quite all right!' Sylvia laughed. 'You know how it is. One gets used to it.'

Maryann didn't know how it was, but was puzzled by how cringingly eager Sylvia was to please her.

They all felt well set up after a share of crispy bacon, with wedges of bread and cups of sweet tea. Sylvia and Dot stood outside to finish drinking their tea, and Maryann peered uneasily at them out through the doorway, taking a good look at her new companions in the unsparing morning light, wishing she could examine them even more closely without them seeing. The children kept looking and whispering as well and she had to shush them. She had taken in, this morning, that Sylvia was older than she had supposed the night before. Her thin, oval face looked surprisingly tired and worn, even though she was already made up, with scarlet lipstick to match the wool scarf she was wearing. She had on a pair of workmanlike blue slacks and a loose-sleeved brown jacket. In the neck of this Maryann could just see the neck of a green woolly with the scarf tied round it. She held her tea cupped in both hands to warm them, her long neck bent forwards to sip. She looked to Maryann like a slender, timid deer.

Dot, however, was far more sturdily built – more of an ox, with her plump face, thick arms and chunky thighs encased in brown corduroy trousers. Over these she had on a tweed jacket, and a navy beret perched sidelong on her head. Maryann guessed that Sylvia must be in her late twenties, but with Dot it was very hard to tell. The two women were talking in low voices; every so often Maryann saw them look over towards the open doors of the *Esther Jane* and she tried to pretend she wasn't watching them. What were they talking about? she wondered, full of dread. What *did* women like that talk about?

Then she heard Dot's hockey captain voice cry, 'I say – look at those simply marvellous cats! Do they live aboard, d'you suppose?'

Jenny and Spots were climbing along the cabin of the *Theodore*. The Bartholomew children listened wide-eyed as Dot made cooing, cajoling noises to the cats.

'Oh, aren't you a *darling*!' they heard. Joley and Ezra started giggling and set Ada and Esther off as well.

'Are those ladies living with us now?' Sally asked, bemused.

'Only for a bit,' Maryann said irritably, piling their few crocks in the dipper for washing, with more force than was necessary. She was very anxious about the day

183

ahead. She was skipper of both the boats now, with those two green beginners. She'd only worked with Joel and Bobby and was full of worry that she'd make a mess of it all. What she dreaded most was the thought of all the other boaters watching what was happening to the *Esther Jane* – one of the old, well-known Number One boats. She knew what to do, really, but she was afraid her nervousness would make her do something wrong – and who knew if those two painted birds out there really knew anything about working boats? She was damned if she'd let them make a fool of her and let Joel down. That was how she saw it – she had to do this for him.

'I thought we'd start you off gentle like,' Mr Veater told her when she went to the office. 'Then I'll see about a trip to Oxford.' Seeing Maryann's furrowed brow, the agitated way she was rubbing her hands together, he added, 'They'll soon cotton on – don't you worry.'

Outside, her breath streamed white from her and the smoke from the boats' chimneys hung in long, slowly dispersing banners in the still air. One of the other boatwomen accosted her.

'Who're those two you've got on board with you then, Maryann?' She eyed the Bartholomews' pair, beside which Sylvia and Dot were waiting for her with the eagerness of newly trained dogs.

'Volunteers,' Maryann told her.

'Blimey.' The woman peered at them. 'My eyes aren't so strong now, but if it weren't for that one's hair I'd've said they were chaps.'

Maryann knew the news would spread round the boaters of Sutton Stop at a fast pace. In the seconds it took her to get back to her own pair again, she decided that the only thing was just to get through this period.

After all, she thought, *they'll be on their boat and we'll be on ours. I shan't have to have too much to do with them, shall I? But, Joel, you'd better get right soon and come back. I can't stand the thought of working with these two!*

She knew the women were watching her as she walked towards them and folded her arms to protect herself, as if their eyes were scraping her skin. She wondered how she looked in her frayed cardi, with scuffed old boots. They were waiting for her, all eager like new Girl Guides.

'Morning!' they both chimed, although Sylvia had already seen her once.

'Are we nearly ready for the off?' Dot asked.

'Right.' Once again, Maryann heard her voice come out brusquely. 'Let's get going. We're going up Bedworth for a load for the Light.'

Sylvia and Dot looked at each other in bafflement.

Maryann nodded over towards Longford Power Station, only a quarter of a mile behind them, covered, as usual in a pall of cloud. 'Fuel for that.' She went to climb aboard the *Esther Jane* ready to start the engine. 'It's a day's trip. You steered a butty before?'

'Oh *yes*, of course,' Sylvia said eagerly. 'We've done all our training trips you know. Kit taught us ever such a lot – really threw us in at the deep end.'

Maryann looked up. 'Who's Kit?'

'Oh, *sorry*. Kit Gayford – our trainer. We thought everyone knew Kit by now! She trains most of the female volunteers on the Grand Union. She's absolutely marvellous. Don't worry, Maryann. We shan't let you down. We'll do our very best.'

As the engine of the *Esther Jane* began to turn over, breaking into the morning peace, Maryann thought grumpily that this was yet another instance in the past twenty-fours of someone telling her not to worry.

The first part of the trip passed without a hitch. There were no locks on this stretch and once Maryann was at the tiller she felt better. Of course she could manage! She'd been a boatwoman long enough now, hadn't she? Joley took the tiller, while she ducked inside to do odd jobs and deal with Ada and Esther, and her son's quiet confidence steadied her and made her proud. The day was overcast and they passed through a ghostly land-scape along that part of the cut, a wasteground of former coal tips and abandoned mine shafts. In one spot a group of gypsies had set up camp with their sturdy ponies and coloured caravans, scrawny dogs barking at the boats as they chugged past. The cut was busy with joeys coming and going, and pairs of 'Joshers' and Barlow boats. A family from another S. E. Barlow boat greeted her with waves and the usual 'How do's?' She saw their amazed expressions when they caught sight of the butty with Sylvia at the tiller, now wearing a red and white head-scarf, and Dot perched on the gunwale sporting her navy beret.

'Look at their faces!' Maryann laughed to Joley. 'They weren't expecting that, were they?'

They reached the Bedworth arm and queued for loading. The day had become even more heavily overcast.

During the wait, Maryann fed the children, and she was outside emptying wash water over the side when she saw Sylvia coming towards her and she tensed. Now what did they want? She kept trying to put those two

186

back there out of her mind – pretend they weren't there! Even if she had to suffer working with them, it didn't mean she wanted anything else to do with them. Bucket in hand, she waited.

'We wondered how long we're likely to be here?' Sylvia looked up at her, giving a tight smile. Maryann saw that she had pale blue eyes. She had a naturally vulnerable expression, which softened Maryann's feelings a fraction.

'Shouldn't be long.' Maryann nodded at the pair ahead of them. 'There's only them in front of us.'

'Only, Dot and I have made some cocoa and we wondered if you'd like some?'

'No, ta. We've just had our dinner.'

The smile faded in Sylvia's eyes. She hugged herself as if cold and stood, uncertain, by the boat. For a moment Maryann thought she was going to say something else, but she turned away. The odd thing was, Maryann thought, she looked almost nervous. Surely not about speaking to her? After all, they were the ones with lah-di-dah accents and their clothes weren't running to holes like hers. What had they got to be flaming nervous about?

The afternoon did not go well. They were heavily laden and low in the water, though they hadn't stopped to sheet up the boats: even though the sky was heavy, no rain had fallen yet. Maryann decided to risk it, since they'd deliver at the Coventry Light that afternoon.

By the time they'd reached Sutton Stop again, it had grown colder and a bitter wind was blowing. Ada and Esther had been perched up on the cabin roof, and Maryann moved them inside for warmth.

I hope it's not going to go and rain now, she thought, glowering at the sky. She couldn't remember the last time she'd felt in such a thoroughly out-of-sorts bad temper with everything. All afternoon she'd been acutely aware of the butty behind. She had to glance back every so often to make sure they were following without any hitches. Otherwise she faced ahead, glad of the long snubber between the boats, but still prickling with awareness of the two women at the tiller which for so long had been hers. All the time she felt this inner tension, and that the two of them were watching her from behind.

Sutton Stop was the meeting place of the Coventry and Oxford cuts and the power station was south of the junction on the Oxford. The two waterways met at an angle, which meant taking the boats round two right-angled bends to reach the stop lock dividing the two.

As they approached the bridge before the junction, Maryann slowed to a crawl, allowing the *Theodore* to catch up a bit. She released the snubber and handed it to Joley.

'Get off at the bridge and tell them to pull in and wait while we get round. Then get back and help me. Sally, go forward and get ready to throw him the line!'

Joley leapt off under the bridge-hole and ran back to the *Theodore*. Maryann heard him calling out instructions to the two women.

He knows more than the pair of you put together, she thought. She saw the *Theodore* begin to veer into the bank and Joley running back to join her.

She faced the busy junction nervously, even though she and Joel had been back and forth through it endless times. Sally threw the cotton line attached to the small mast over to her brother and he looped it round the bollard by the iron bridge, playing it round as Maryann brought the boat under. As she kept the engine ticking steadily ahead, the stern swung round nicely, just as required. She smiled grimly for a second. Thank God for that. When they were safely round both bends, she tied up and told Sally to mind the younger ones.

She ran round and over the bridge with Joley, expecting to find the women waiting with the *Theodore* tied up as instructed. Instead of which, by the time she got down to the bank, she found Dot bow-hauling the butty along, almost at the bridge. Dot, who was leaning into the job like a dray horse, had got the butty moving at quite a pace.

'What the hell's she playing at!' Maryann cried. 'She's never going to make the turn like that – how does she think she's going to stop!'

Waving her arms she shouted, 'Stop pulling, you bloody fool! What're you doing? *Slow down!*'

It was already too late. On a monkey boat with an engine, the only way to brake it was to throw the engine into reverse. On a butty with no engine, Sylvia, holding the *Theodore*'s tiller, could only watch helplessly, hauling on it to try and turn the boat in time to make the turn.

'She's going to crash,' Joley said matter-of-factly. 'Good job Dad ent here.'

'If he was we wouldn't be in this bloody mess, would we?' Maryann said furiously.

In those seconds she became aware of several other things. One was that the women had pulled the boat out in the path of a horse-drawn joey, which was bearing down close behind them, the man at its tiller yelling at them, outraged. The other was confirmation of Joley's observation that nothing now was going to stop the

Theodore except a collision. All she could do was watch, hands pressed to her cheeks.

'You cowing, stupid *idiots*,' she breathed.

Instead of managing the left bend, the *Theodore* shot across the turn and rammed, shuddering into the corner of the bank on the other side, leaving Dot with rope scorching through her hands. Sylvia, who had been leaning back, pulling desperately on the tiller, lost her balance on the jolt and fell in over the back into the water, in the company of the *Theodore*'s water carrier, which clunked and sploshed into the cut after her.

Sylvia surfaced, gasping, in the freezing water to see the front of the joey boat coming straight at her. With the speed born of survival instinct she flung herself round to the right of the *Theodore* as the two joeymen shafted and pulled, tweaking the fore end round to the left of the *Theodore* and made the bend.

Dot, standing shaken by the bridge, called to the men in her ringing voice, 'That was a close one. We're most terribly sorry!'

The joeymen eyed her with a contempt more corrosive than even Maryann could have managed and loud expletives trailed in the air behind them. A small but interested audience was gathering on the bank.

Maryann ran to help Sylvia out of the water. Her teeth were chattering convulsively and the black, slimy water poured off her. Her hair had turned an interesting shade of gritty grey. Otherwise she was perfectly all right.

'Come on,' Maryann ordered, holding on tightly to her rage. She led her back over the bridge to help Dot haul the *Theodore* round out of everyone's way. As they joined the *Esther Jane*, Maryann saw all her children

190

perched at various points on the cabin and gunwales, watching the events with fascination.

The three of them went into the cabin of the *Theodore*, Sylvia smelling abominable and dripping all over the floor, and Maryann let rip. She found she was trembling with fury at them making such a spectacle of her and of Joel's boats. She hadn't been deaf to the ribald comments levelled at them from some of the boatmen who'd been watching. After years of trying to prove herself as a boatwoman, a Bartholomew, of trying to belong, these two idiots had humiliated her completely in one afternoon. She let them have it with both barrels.

'When I tell you to wait, you bloody well *wait*!' she bawled at them. 'What in God's name did you think you were playing at, barging out in front of that other boat and bringing her in at that speed? If there'd been anyone else tied up at that corner you could've rammed them and sunk them, d'you know that? And you've gone and lost our water carrier, so unless someone fishes it out we're going to have to get another one. D'you know how long that carrier's been on this boat?' She paused, glowering at them. Dot opened her mouth, then closed it.

'I s'pose you think you know better than people who've been on the cut all their lives, coming along with your airs and graces, 'cause you fancy a little rest from painting your nails? Well, if you're coming to work with me, you can sodding well do it properly or go back to wherever it is you come from!'

'Look,' Dot managed to say. 'It was my fault, not Sylvia's. I admit, I made a mess of it . . .'

'Yes – not half you did!' Maryann yelled. 'I thought you said you knew what you were doing!'

191

They were silent. Maryann was surprised they didn't argue. Sylvia was too busy dripping and shivering, but even Dot, whose face was puce with embarrassment, stood in silence, nursing her rope-burned hands under her armpits.

'Get changed,' Maryann ordered Sylvia contemptuously, finally running out of steam. 'And then we've got the lock to get through. D'you think you can manage that without sinking us?'

Twenty-One

Maryann's foul temper lasted long into the evening. She banged about in the cabin, slamming the pan down as she cooked bubble and squeak, snapping at the children. Her head was thumping and all she wanted was to lie down and forget today had ever happened.

'You gave those ladies a talking to, daint you, Mom?' Sally said as she waited for her food. Maryann knew the child was trying to break the tense silence around her.

'Yes, I flaming well did!' she retorted. 'Coming here with their airs and graces, thinking they know better than anyone.'

'Are they leaving tomorrow?' Rose asked hopefully. Like Maryann, she wasn't very good at coping with change in her life. She liked things to feel unchanging and secure.

'No, bab – no such luck.' Maryann sighed. 'If only Bobby was about I'd have him back like a shot and manage two-handed. I wish to God I'd never let him go, only Mr Veater never gave me much choice.' She turned and started dishing out the food. 'We're going down Oxford tomorrow, so we've got to put up with them.'

Ezra's dark brows were pulled into a frown. 'Ent you allowed no slip-ups when you're grown big?'

'What d'you mean?' Maryann asked, perching wearily on the back bed.

'Our dad says to me when I do summat wrong: when you're starting out you're allowed some slip-ups.'

Maryann sighed into a silence in which the children waited for her answer. She could see they were really puzzled by the intensity of her reaction to the two women. Even with the justification of the afternoon's troubles, she could barely explain it even to herself, how having them there made her feel unsafe and exposed. The tight feeling inside her increased and her temples throbbed.

All afternoon she'd held onto her self-righteous anger. The power station was only a quarter of a mile south, looming huge over the landscape, creating its own pall of cloud from the chimneys and cooling towers which poured out smoke and steam. The afternoon had darkened and, although it was only about four o'clock, already dusk was falling as they slid through the black, refuse-strewn water, in the shadows of the cranes and gantries, to the wharf. Here the coal was lifted from the boat by grabbers onto conveyor belts, to be carried into the insatiable power station. Sylvia and Dot kept out of her way, only exchanging the tersest of remarks about what needed to happen next. By the time they were heading back, gunwales higher in the water, Maryann had calmed down, but her headache was setting in, and a sour, shameful feeling had come over her which she found hard to admit.

Ezra's question made her feel even worse.

'Yes, bab, we all make mistakes,' she said, adding defiantly, 'and there are some people need to learn from them more than others.'

It was a relief to get the children to sleep. Ada and Esther were all but weaned now, just having a drink from her sometimes at night to settle them. Once the children were down, there wasn't much for her to do but go to bed herself, since there was no room to move about in the cabin. They were squeezed in tight as a pea pod. She was about to make herself a drop of hot milk to ease her head, when she felt the boat rock slightly, and there came a soft knocking on the door.

Sylvia was outside, looking solemn and upset.

So you damn well should, Maryann thought, looking up at her. The sky had cleared and it felt very chill outside.

'Look,' Sylvia whispered, 'if your children are settled for the night, Dot and I would really like to have a talk with you. Mend some fences, sort of thing. Will you come and join us for a cup of tea?'

'I was just going to bed.' It came out abruptly again. More so than she meant it to. How was she supposed to talk to these people? She couldn't speak the way they did, could she?

'*Please*,' Sylvia said. To Maryann's astonishment she heard tears in Sylvia's voice. 'We both feel ghastly about what happened today. And we can't go on like this, can we? We've got to learn to work together somehow. We need to try and make friends.'

Maryann knew that what had happened had not been Sylvia's fault. Why wasn't Dot the one here eating humble pie, she wondered. She desperately didn't want to go and sit with them, but she felt sorry for Sylvia and there was something sweet, almost pathetic, in the way she had asked. Grudgingly, she nodded. 'I'll be over in a minute.'

It was an uncomfortable feeling, being invited into what for years had been her own home. She stood out in the cold, starry darkness for a moment, knotted up inside with nerves. Why didn't she just go back to her own

195

cabin and go to bed? She knew suddenly that part of the reason she wanted to hold onto her self-righteous anger was that she was afraid. She realized that it was the word 'friends' that really frightened her. It had been different with Nance, who had known her for years. Of course Nance accepted her. But to try and be close to anyone else felt terrifying. How could she ever show them who she was, what she had come from?

She took a deep breath. They didn't have to know anything about her, she reasoned with herself. Only what she wanted to tell them. All she had to do was try and patch things up so they could manage the work properly. For the sake of the boats. That was all that mattered. She tapped on the *Theodore*'s hatch.

'Here she is . . . Come on in and sit with us for a bit.'

Sylvia welcomed her so kindly that, to her irritation, Maryann found tears in her eyes and tried fiercely to blink them away, though she knew Sylvia had seen them. She sat on the side bench near Dot, who was perched on the edge of the back bed, knitting something with big needles out of thick orange wool. Sylvia came and sat on Maryann's left and poured the tea. She'd obviously managed to wash her hair, as it was pale and silky looking again. She was such a fragile-looking thing, she didn't look strong enough for this life, Maryann thought, sipping the tea. Sylvia could make a good cup of tea, though, she'd give her that. The oil lamp was burning and it was as cosy as ever inside. It felt very strange, though, being here with these strangers with their possessions about: a bar of Pears soap, a pretty mirror edged with shells and a little pink washbag. Sylvia's trousers were hanging over the range, still steaming, and there was a copy of *Woman's Own* on the table, a woman with glossy chestnut hair smiling from the cover. Maryann eyed it curiously. She wanted to reach out and turn the pages, and was surprised by her sudden hunger to see what was inside.

'Look,' Sylvia said carefully, 'we seem to have started off on completely the wrong foot with you. What happened today was our fault entirely . . .'

'No – it was my fault,' Dot said robustly. She looked different with her hair loose over her shoulders, making her look voluptuous and much more feminine. Somehow it looked wrong, as if the hair belonged to someone else. Maryann wondered how old she was. 'I misunderstood your boy when he shouted over to us – I thought you wanted us to follow on. And I must say' – she began to sound rather heated – 'that it wasn't exactly my fault if I could barely understand a blasted word the child was saying. I think it's a bit thin if you won't accept an apology that's genuinely meant. I mean, dammit, I've said sorry. Haven't you ever made a mistake?'

Maryann thought of some of the terrible mistakes she made when she started out on the cut and the shameful feeling nudged harder inside her. How would she have felt if no one had forgiven her? But she felt so lost without Joel, and worried and tense about taking charge of the boats with strangers on board whose background she didn't understand, that it was easiest to take it all out on them! And there was something about Dot especially which made her hackles rise. The way she strode about on her buxom legs and that *voice*. Sylvia was well spoken all right, with her tinkly voice, but she didn't have the posh, overpowering blare that Dot had. She stared back at her, feeling her expression harden, about to make a curt reply.

But Sylvia was saying, 'The thing is, Maryann, we've never worked together before either, and we haven't got used to each other yet – or your family . . .'

Maryann turned to her, frowning. 'I thought Mr Veater said you were a team?'

'Well, if he did, he got it wrong. We only met on the train coming up here. We've done our training trips, but not together. Quite a lot of the girls dropped out and we were leftovers for the moment – spare-wheelers, as Kit would say.'

'We are new girls, it's true,' Dot said, 'but we aren't as bad as . . . well, as we were today. That was me getting the wrong end of the stick and then putting too much oomph into it altogether. But we've both come through quite a few sticky situations on the Grand Union. We'll do our best not to let you down again.'

'The thing is – ' Sylvia cut in again rather intensely before Maryann had a chance to speak – 'we so love the life here, and we think you're *marvellous*, how you manage and everything. I just don't know how you do it with six children. I struggle with only two even when I'm living in a house.'

'*What?*' Maryann was nonplussed. 'You've got children?'

'Oh yes – a girl and a boy. Kay's twelve and Dickie's ten.'

'Twelve!' Maryann blurted. The woman's children were older than her own!

Sylvia gabbled on nervously. 'As a matter of fact I was going to ask you if I might put up some pictures on the walls. Dot, dear, pass my bag over, will you?' She showed Maryann a picture of two smiling faces, a girl and boy side by side. The girl's hair was shoulder length, waving prettily round her cheeks and darker than her mother's, though she had a look of Sylvia.

'Her face is the same shape as yours,' Maryann said, peering in fascination at the picture. 'You can see the likeness. She's pretty.'

'Thank you.' Sylvia smiled. 'Of course, Dickie's the image of his father.' The boy had a squarer face, a rather thin mouth and narrow eyes, but was handsome in his way. Maryann took another look before handing it back.

'And this is my darling Roy.'

The second picture showed a thickset man with cropped, fair hair who looked out of the picture with the sort of half smile which shows no teeth. He was wearing a suit and tie.

'Oh – I see what you mean,' Maryann said. 'Your son *does* look just like his father.'

'Yes.' Sylvia put the pictures back in her bag. 'Though they're not alike in temperament. Oh, I forgot!' She reached over to the cupboard. 'I brought a cake from home. Would you like a piece? It's cherry madeira.'

Maryann wasn't hungry, but she thought she'd better accept a piece out of politeness. And she was beginning to warm to Sylvia, even if she couldn't take to Dot.

'But where are your ... Kay and Dickie then? You left them with your mom?'

'Oh no,' Sylvia said. 'My mother's been dead for a number of years. No, they're at boarding school. I sent them some time ago, to avoid the bombing, of course. They're not far from each other, fortunately – outside Worcester. I've dropped them a line to tell them to send their letters here. Is that the best thing? I so miss hearing from them. I've been told I'll be able to have leave to go home for the Easter holidays.'

199

Maryann was still struggling with the idea of Sylvia being a mother and of sending your children away to the other side of the country.

'How old are you, then?' she blurted out.

Sylvia chuckled at her frankness. 'I'm just thirty-two as a matter of fact.' Maryann was even more astonished. The woman was older than her! 'Dot here's a mere pup – only twenty-one.'

'I think you'll find I'm old for my years.' Dot looked up for a second, somehow challenging them. Maryann wondered why she had to be so aggressive, as if she felt permanently under attack. 'What happened today won't happen again. I can promise you that.'

'And you?' Sylvia asked.

'Me? Oh – I'll turn thirty in the autumn.' Surely she looked older, didn't she? she wondered. Some days she felt as old as Methuselah.

'Were you born and bred on the cut?' Sylvia asked, in rather awed tones.

'No,' Maryann admitted. 'I married into it.'

'Told you, didn't I?' Dot said triumphantly. 'I knew she had a Birmingham accent!'

Maryann stiffened in annoyance. She didn't like Dot's tone, or the fact that they'd been making guesses about her life. She felt prickly about any of her life being exposed beyond her control.

'Yes,' she said, 'I'm from Brum. That's where I met Joel – my husband.' She said it in a way that did not invite more questions and looked down into her lap.

Gently, Sylvia asked about Joel's accident. She said her own husband, Roy, was an RAF officer in Coastal Command.

'Will he get leave at Easter as well?' Maryann asked, trying to get off the subject of herself.

'Oh, perhaps,' Sylvia said lightly. 'I imagine he might. But the poor darling never seems quite sure when he'll be home.'

By the time she went back to the *Esther Jane* that night, Maryann had a picture of Sylvia's life in a nice family home in Wimbledon. She saw a pretty garden edged with roses (this was far more than Sylvia had told her, but she enjoyed embroidering this charmed picture), the two children playing out on the greenest of lawns and her husband coming home, broad-shouldered and handsome in his air-force blue. Of Dot's background she had learned almost nothing, except that she came from Buckinghamshire.

I just don't take to that one, she thought, squeezing into bed beside Joley and Sally. Dot seldom met her gaze, except with a challenging stare. Maryann just couldn't imagine what her real life was like. *I'll just have to try and rub along with her somehow*, she thought. *It'll only be for a trip or two.*

But Sylvia ... course, she was from another life altogether, but there was a nervous sweetness, a sympathy, about her which Maryann had warmed to. And at least Sylvia was a mother: that was something they had in common. It felt new and strange, the company of these women not from the boating life. As if a door had opened, giving her a glimpse into something new.

As she slipped into sleep, she realized her headache had gone.

Twenty-Two

It was true, as Maryann found out on the trip to Oxford, that Sylvia and Dot were not bad boaters, especially for beginners. But they were still early on in their learning and some things took a frustratingly long time.

The first day they travelled back to the coalfields. This time, though, after loading they stopped to cloth up before departing for the long journey south, as the weather looked uncertain. In the past Maryann had usually left most of this to Joel and Bobby, who were quick at it after a lifetime of practice. Now, with Joley's help, it was she who had to cloth up the *Esther Jane*, leaving the others to deal with the *Theodore*.

'Are you sure you know what to do?' she asked them.

'Of course,' Dot said, already climbing along the hold to the cratch at the fore end where they stowed the cloths and tarpaulin. Dot's tone was prickly with resentment at having her competence questioned again.

'I've done it a few times,' Sylvia said. Maryann could tell she was trying to soften the effect of Dot's brusqueness.

'I'll let you get on with it then. Come on, Joley.'

Joley had helped do the job many times. Balanced on the top planks, Maryann shuffled along on her knees, knotting the tough, hairy strings of the side-cloths over the planks, while Joley stood in the hold threading them through in the right places and passing them to her.

'This one needs splicing,' she told him, holding out one that was frayed and in danger of snapping. They had to take constant care of all the ropes on the boat, and these strings had to be pulled very tight and knotted taut; their rough fibre blistered her hands.

She had tied the final string and she and Joley were opening out the top cloth to lay it over when they heard a shriek from behind on the *Theodore*. Maryann swivelled round in time to see Dot hurtling down from the top planks. Her hands reached out, trying to clutch anything to save herself, but she failed and rolled at a very undignified angle over the gunwale and into the cut, her large backside the last thing to disappear under the water. The splash was impressive. A moment later she surfaced like a flustered hippo, spluttering and enraged. Maryann caught Sylvia's gaze as she stood in the hold, a hand clasped horrified over her mouth. As well as consternation, Maryann was sure she saw a flicker of laughter in Sylvia's expression. The Bartholomew children were in fits of giggles, and the man who was clothing up his own boat behind them called out, 'Taking a good look in there, were you?'

Not entirely succeeding in straightening her own twitching lips, Maryann climbed down to help Dot out. Her bun had come loose, her heavy plait uncoiling down her back.

'What happened? D'you have a string snap?'

'Yes, I damn well did.' She took Maryann's hand resentfully and was hauled, gushing water, onto the bank. 'And I don't think it's very nice of you all to laugh!'

'I'm not.' She managed to look sober. 'Sorry, Dot. You awright?'

'Yes, of *course* I'm all right!' She shook herself, almost

like a dog, looking ready to explode with anger. 'Don't be so bloody ridiculous.'

'There's no need to get upset.'

'I'm *not* damn well upset!'

For the second time in twenty-four hours, one of the trainees went dripping into the *Theodore*'s cabin to change an entire set of clothing. Maryann frowned, watching Dot's furiously hunched shoulders disappear through the hatches. There was no need to get that mithered about it, was there? Everyone fell in sometimes. Again, she and Sylvia exchanged glances and Sylvia shrugged, rolling her eyes. For the first time Maryann wondered just how well Sylvia and Dot got on when they were on their own. Just because they were different from her didn't mean they had anything in common themselves.

Maryann had hoped to get past the first set of locks at Rugby that day, but the clothing up took at least twice as long as usual – she helped Sylvia finish on the *Theodore* – and they still had to get past the junction at Hawkesbury again. Dot was silent and morose all day, but with brooding determination completed the manoeuvres round the bends almost perfectly this time. She was still barely speaking to any of them until the evening, though, which added an extra strain, but then she just seemed to snap out her mood.

In a quiet moment that evening Sylvia said to Maryann, 'Kit did mention to me that Dot can be rather touchy, so don't take it personally, will you?'

The next morning, when they reached the double locks at Hillmorton, Maryann gave Dot the mildest of reminders to go back and close a paddle that she'd left open. She got a furious reaction,

'I'm going to!' Dot's fleshy cheeks flushed angrily.

She stomped off with the windlass, calling over her shoulder, 'I do know what I'm doing, you know.'

'Well, if you know what you're doing, why don't you do it then?' Maryann retorted to her back, fed up with her. She'd asked politely enough, hadn't she? Who did she flaming well think she was? She had to admit, though, that Dot was strong. She bow-hauled the butty into the locks at Hillmorton with the force of a man.

Most of the journey went better. There was a hint of spring in the air and the biting cold had softened to mildness. They woke in the mornings to the first, tentative sounds of birdsong. Maryann found that, despite her own burden of being in charge of loaded boats, children and everything, Dot and Sylvia were very efficient at getting shopping in whenever there was a chance to. Sylvia also insisted that she and Dot cook for everyone most of the time.

'How can you possibly do everything – all your washing and looking after the family and cooking? No – you let us do that,' Sylvia said. Maryann had more of a sense that the work was being shared by them all than when she worked with the men.

As the days passed along the winding Oxford cut, Maryann gradually became more used to the women and they to her. She found Sylvia immediately easier – they were closer in age, and Sylvia was always nervously anxious to please. Dot, in spite of her prickliness and determination always to be right, was extremely hard-working. It seemed that her way would have been to push on and on, never stopping for a rest.

'You'll have to go and work the beer boats,' Maryann told her. 'Then you'd never have to stop at all!'

Sylvia was kind and motherly to the children, especially to Rose when once Maryann confided, though without going into too much detail, how the child came to be in her care. She always chose very carefully what she did and did not tell.

'Oh, the poor little lamb!' Sylvia exclaimed. She made a special pet of Rose, always cuddling and spending time with her when she had the chance, and Rose loved the extra attention. Maryann realized that Sylvia needed this. Once she came into the cabin and found Sylvia cuddling Rose, tears running down her face.

'I do miss my own children,' she said wretchedly. 'I love this life here, but some days I just wish it didn't have to be like this.'

To Maryann's great surprise, it was Dot who formed a special bond with the boys. As the children gradually relaxed with 'them ladies', Joley and Ezra shyly showed Dot their fishing rods and she seized on them with great enthusiasm.

'Marvellous. I say, look at those!' She squatted down to talk to them. 'Well – we must give these an airing.'

In spare moments when they were tied up, she encouraged the boys to take up their fishing again, and went to fetch bait for them when they were at Napton, queuing for the locks.

'Nothing like a tinful of squirming beasties to delight a couple of lads,' she said gruffly.

'That's nice of you,' Maryann said, astonished and touched by the trouble she'd taken and the smiles it had brought to the boys' faces. She handed Dot a mug of tea as they stood waiting. The small gesture felt like a friendship offering. The children were clustered round the fishing rods in great excitement, Ezra scolding the twins for nearly tipping the tin of maggots over. 'Joel – their dad – usually gets them doing it. You done much fishing then?'

'Oh, *hours* of it.'

Maryann was still trying to get used to Dot's way of talking. 'Hours' came out as 'ars'.

'We grew up on the Thames, you see. My brother Steven and I practically lived on the river. Steven's a couple of years younger than me. He's in the Navy now – somewhere in the Med. But we were always out and about, he and I. There're just the two of us, you see.'

Maryann saw the softest expression she'd yet seen come over Dot's face as she spoke.

'My two've never been fishing, or anything like that,' Sylvia said, staring out over the water. 'I s'pose I always hoped Roy would take them out and do these sorts of things. But he's always so frightfully busy, of course, poor darling.'

'Well – you'll be able to take them yourself now, won't you?' Dot said.

'Yes.' Sylvia looked pleased. 'I shall, shan't I?'

Sylvia's Roy had been high up in an insurance firm in the City of London in peacetime. Dot, who had been working in London as a secretary in a legal firm, told them her father was a Judge. In other circumstances Maryann would have felt intimidated by this, but now she was getting to know the women a bit better and they were on her territory, making all their beginners' mistakes, she felt better and even risked joking about it when she heard about their backgrounds.

'Aren't I mixing with the nobs these days?'

Sylvia laughed at this. 'Hardly, dear!'

It dawned on Maryann then that, though Sylvia's voice sounded like a tinkling chandelier, she didn't see herself as anything special, and this came as a surprise. And she knew now that they really *had* been nervous of her when they arrived.

'Completely terrified, actually,' Sylvia admitted. 'You've no idea how we all look up to you real boatwomen.'

As the trip progressed, they worked more and more as a team, taking turns lock-wheeling, sharing the cooking and other chores, and Sylvia, especially, helped Maryann with the children.

'I don't mind giving a hand in the least,' she told her. 'It's a treat to be with your kiddies – I miss Kay and Dickie so much. I do hope there'll be some letters waiting when we get back!'

It wasn't so bad, Maryann thought, relaxing more with them as the days passed. It wouldn't be for too long, having them aboard, would it? And when they got to Oxford they could see Joel. Despite what the doctor had said, she couldn't believe it would take him long to recover. He'd always fought back so hard against any kind of pain or illness. As they pushed south to Oxford, she started to feel more optimistic. There were leaf buds on the trees and you could feel the land coming to life all around, the air full of the hopeful scents of spring. Surely Joel would be better soon and they could all get back to normal?

He held out his arms to them as they crowded into the room.

Maryann was holding Esther, the heavier of the twins. Sally had managed to half lead, half carry Ada up from the wharf, cajoling her impatiently.

'Come on, Ada – we're going to see our dad!'

Joel was lying propped up on pillows on the bed upstairs. His normally weatherbeaten face looked pale and, Maryann thought, a little thinner, though he was beaming with delight at seeing them. A strange sensation passed through her at the familiar sight of his body, a kind of inner leap of recognition, as if, having been temporarily stripped of a part of herself, she had found it again.

Apart from a quick hello kiss, she let the children go first, the older ones chattering nineteen to the dozen and Ada and Esther wanting to climb up onto the bed. Joel cuddled each of them in turn on his chest, and the little ones snuggled close, trying hard to be careful and keep still once they'd been told.

'Hello, my little beauties!' Joel kissed and stroked each of them. 'Oh, it's such a treat to see you. And how's our Joley, eh? And Ezra? You keeping your mother in order for me?'

The boys grinned. 'We've got ladies working the butty,' Joley said. 'And Dot likes fishing.'

'Fishing again, eh? You caught anything for me?'

After a time, Alice Simons appeared in the doorway. 'Well, I don't suppose any of you want some ginger cordial and my fresh buns, now do you?'

Left alone with Joel, Maryann knelt by the bed and rested her head on his chest as they held each other. Feeling his arms round her always made her feel safe and loved. She felt herself relax and she reached up for a kiss. Joel's eyes looked searchingly into hers.

'How're you going along, my mate?'

'Oh, I'm all right.' She kissed him again. 'Missing "moy chap", though.' Most of the boatwomen referred to their husbands as 'moy chap'. Maryann grinned. 'My old man.'

'I feel like an old man. I ent half fed up lying here day

after day, I can tell you,' Joel said, wincing as he tried to shift up the bed a bit. 'It's enough to drive you half mad.'

She stroked his face, knowing how frustrated he was and longing to have him back with them, to lie in his arms at night, for things to be normal.

'Isn't it getting better?'

'Well it is, yes. Slowly. I can just about get up now and move about a bit. But I ent fit for the cut. Nowhere near. This ent me – lying about like this. It's boring, hour after hour. Alice's brought this up for me –' he nodded at the wireless set perched on the chest of drawers by the bed – 'so I can listen to all the world's woes. But my head just goes round and round, thinking about where you are and all I should be doing.'

Maryann tried to reassure him and hide her disappointment that he was not more improved. It was so good to be with him again, but she'd hoped he might be closer to coming back with them again than this.

'We're doing all right,' she soothed him. She was proud to be able to tell him how she was managing. 'Bobby's gone off with the Bevans for a bit. Mr Veater got us two of these women trainees off the Grand Union. Sylvia and Dorothy they're called. Well, Dot. You should hear the pair of them talk – it'd make you curl up. Talk about lah-di-dah. They're all right, though. I can't work Dot out, but Sylvia's nice. Seems a bit scared of her own shadow – always apologizing. But she's come on just in this week, and she says she loves living on the cut. She's ever such a good cook too! We'll be awright – I just wish I could take you with us.'

'Not half as much as I do,' Joel said gloomily. His warm hand stroked along her thigh. 'Oh, I do miss you, my little bird.'

Twenty-Three

Over the next few weeks the Bartholomew boats made several trips up and down the Oxford cut to and from the coalfields, and every time Maryann saw Joel he was a little improved, but his recovery seemed long and slow. Then, for a return journey, Maryann was offered a trip to Birmingham. She almost turned it down. If she went to Birmingham she felt, somehow, Norman Griffin would know they were there. But she agreed to it, telling herself not to be so stupid. The load was a consignment of timber for a private wharf in Saltley and they wouldn't be tied up at Tyseley. On a cool morning in March they set off north again.

Things were becoming easier between the women as they worked so closely together day after day, though Maryann still tried to keep her distance, especially with Dot. Sylvia was forever asking Maryann to come and join them in their cabin in the evening and she did go increasingly often, though at first she'd been convinced that they were only being polite and didn't really want her there. Dot and Sylvia seemed to rub along all right, even though they were very different: Sylvia timid and so eager to please and Dot prickly and stubborn. Dot was bullish and determinedly careless of her appearance, while Sylvia never appeared in the morning without carefully applying make-up – her powder, mascara and bright red lipstick, no matter how early it was.

'I feel undressed without it on!' she told them. 'I can't face the world like that.'

One evening, once they'd tied up and finished their evening meal, Sylvia appeared at the door.

'Sorry,' she said uncertainly.

Maryann smiled up at her. 'You'll wear that word out.'

'Oh! Yes – sorry. I mean . . . !'

Both of them laughed and Sylvia climbed down and sat on the coalbox for a few minutes. The older children were all outside except for the twins, who Maryann was washing in turn in front of the range, and Rose, to whom Sylvia held her arms out. Rose gladly climbed onto her lap for a cuddle. Sylvia rested her forehead against Rose's and Maryann heard her give a long sigh.

'What's up?' she asked.

'Oh,' Sylvia raised her head, 'nothing much. Just a bit weary, I suppose.' She smiled at the sight of Ada's little body, standing shiny and wet in the dipper. 'Dot's got the kettle on for a bit more than a lick and a promise too. I've come out to let her have the cabin to herself. Are you coming over later?'

Maryann looked across at her. 'That all right?'

'Of *course*. You're always welcome, you know that. We'll have a bit of a shindig. There's that last nip of whisky to jolly us along. Well, for you and me, anyway!'

Dot seemed to have a deep, almost puritanical aversion to spirits and turned her nose up every time she was offered any.

When Maryann did go to the *Theodore* in the evenings it was after she'd settled the children for the night. The three women were learning to relax together. At first they had been stiff and wary, talking mostly about the events of the day, about the cut. Of course, there was always plenty to chew over there and often a lot to laugh about as well. But now, gradually, they were beginning to learn about each other's lives. Maryann was guarded about what she told them about her early years, only mentioning the bare bones – that her father had died when she was young and she wasn't close to her mother. She never even hinted at the darker, more shameful aspects of her childhood. She didn't have enough trust in them: how could they understand how it had been to grow up in Ladywood, let alone in her family? Sylvia, with her thick blonde hair and English rose face, looked so sheltered and innocent – how could she have any idea of someone like Norman Griffin? And Dot, coming from her boarding school life and going home every holiday to that big house in the country. They were from another world, like the Mussons, who she'd worked for in Banbury. She just told them pleasant little things she could remember – about her brothers and her dad coming home with a bicycle for Tony, and Granny Firkin and her cats. After all, she could pretend she'd had a happy childhood, couldn't she? She couldn't bring herself to talk about Nance either. The pain was still too close.

Sylvia had been a housewife before the war and always maintained that her life was settled and dull.

'Nothing much to say, I'm afraid,' she'd told them. 'You know – house, husband, children. Getting his supper on the table in time and his shirt studs ready in the morning. I have a lady who comes to wash and clean, but I always do all my own cooking. Roy wouldn't have it any other way. He likes me to change before we eat and to make my face up. Our lives are fearfully staid – not like yours, Maryann, coming away to live on the cut!'

213

'But you have now, haven't you?' Maryann said.

'Well, yes – for the moment. I really thought I ought to do something for the war effort with the children away, but it's so tricky with having to work around their holidays. Then I saw a piece in the paper about the training scheme and how they were prepared to be flexible, and I thought, perhaps that's a little chance for me to do my bit. I couldn't really believe I was doing it, even when I turned up at Southall with all my bags!'

'I met one of them,' Dot said. 'One of the first trainees, actually, and she told me about it. Thing was – the work appealed. I've always liked being out of doors – that's what I wanted really. But it was more than that. It was something about the way she talked about the work and the life. She was just full of it and I thought, that's what I need. I was desperate to get out of the job I was in.'

That evening they sat together with cups of cocoa, Maryann's and Sylvia's laced with 'hooch' as Sylvia called it. The chocolatey, whisky-laced steam filled Maryann's nostrils comfortingly. Jenny the tortoiseshell cat was curled on Sylvia's lap and she stroked her, looking at Dot over the rim of her cup. 'I can't imagine you being a secretary at all. Were you really?'

Maryann was taken aback too every time she remembered this. She could much more easily picture Dot doing something with horses, or being a games teacher, running round freezing hockey pitches and bellowing at girls in short skirts.

'Yes.' Dot frowned, fingers still knitting away without her having to look. The orange jumper was long finished and she was making something in soft cornflower blue. 'Detested every moment of it.' Maryann and Sylvia stared at her, taken aback by the anger in her voice.

Maryann thought her cheeks had blushed redder, but it was hard to tell in the dim light.

'It was Daddy, he set it all up through his contacts. Didn't leave me any choice. He said the only thing for a girl was being a teacher or a nurse and he wasn't having me doing either of those "demeaning jobs" as he called them – or a secretary, so I'd best do that. I wanted to get away from home, you see. Once Steven joined the Navy it was ... well, I was the only one left at home and Daddy and I ... let's just say we don't get on. He had marginally more time for Steven, being the boy, though not much. I wanted to go and that was what was on offer.'

'What about your mother?' Maryann asked. It was the first time they had heard Dot open up at all about her family. Apart from her brother Steven, who she was obviously close to, she normally dismissed the others as, 'oh, the normal, sort of thing'.

'Mummy died when I was thirteen.' She turned her cup round and round on the table without looking up.

'Oh, poor you!' Sylvia cried.

Dot talked on rapidly, as if suddenly resolved to let some of it out. 'After that there were housekeepers. Steven and I called them the housemice. Misfits, of course. They always are, people like that. Why else would they take on someone else's family? Same thing with the matrons at school – a succession of the crossed in love, the unmarriageable, the widowed and the barmy – we had them all.' There was a satirical, almost harsh edge to her voice now. 'There was a Miss Gateley, who came to look after Steven and me one summer. She was about fifty and had been working somewhere in Africa. Well, she went down with a frightful dose of malaria and was no use to anyone for days on end! Daddy was furious. He doesn't believe in people being ill. And Mrs Longford – her husband had hanged himself and left her with no money, and she kept taking some sort of medicine all the time and barely ever seemed to be awake. Once I went into her room and she was injecting something into her arm . . . Oh, and there was a Miss Peters. She was tremendously odd – obsessed with birds. She kept the windows open and fed them crusts – she'd have pigeons flying in and out messing on everything . . .'

Maryann listened, astonished. This was not how she had pictured Dot's life in the country at all. And how strange she was, speaking about sad things in that offhand, almost contemptuous way. She really couldn't understand Dot at all.

'Dear oh dear,' Sylvia gave a horrified laugh. 'I do hope they're not all like that where Kay and Dickie are! Didn't you have any other relatives who could have come and helped?'

Dot gave her a scornful look from under her dark brows. 'Help? God no – we're not that sort of family.'

There was a silence, as if suddenly the conversation could go no further and they sipped their cocoa. Then Sylvia said hesitantly,

'Maryann – I wondered . . . I hesitate to mention it and I hope you won't think this rude . . .?

'What?' Maryann frowned.

'It's just that – you are able to read and write, aren't you? I mean I've seen you reading the clearance papers . . .'

'Course I can read and write!' Maryann said indignantly. 'I went to school, you know! I'm not stupid.'

'Of *course* you're not. But it's your children I'm thinking of. Have they never had any schooling?'

Maryann looked down, ashamed. 'No. Only what I

can teach them – and that's not much when there's no time to catch your breath.' She was ashamed, somewhere in her mind, of her children's lack of education, but there was so little time to give it any attention. And here on the cut, where no one's children went to school for more than the odd day at a time or learned more than the very basics, it didn't seem to matter all that much. Being a 'scholar' who could read and add up numbers was unusual. To get by in this life there were other, more important things to learn.

'Sally's the one who likes to try and read. Joley'll only learn summat for as long as he can sit still – and that's not long.' She sighed, looking into Sylvia's face. 'I've done my best but I'm always so pushed and mithered, and with him it's a battle.'

'Well, we could help, couldn't we, Dot?' Sylvia said enthusiastically. 'I mean here you are with all these children – let us help them with their letters. I bet Dot could get Joley and Ezra more interested in reading. They've taken to her. And I'd be very happy to help Sally and perhaps even little Rose, if she'd like to join in.'

'All right – if you want,' Maryann said. She was grateful, but didn't really think the offer would come to anything. Had they forgotten that most days on the cut didn't just go according to plan?

As Maryann got up to go to her cabin that night, Sylvia said, 'Would you like to borrow one of my magazines?' She reached over into the space at the head of the bed, in the cupboard. 'I've got a little stash here – some are a bit out of date, but take your pick.'

Maryann hesitated. She wanted to look at the magazines, but something held her back, some reluctance to be drawn in. She was almost afraid to take too close a look at how things were outside the cut, as if she might discover what she was missing. She didn't want her life disturbed. But seeing Sylvia's eager expression, she picked out a copy of *Woman & Home*, and one of *Home Chat*. A young woman posed on the cover of the second magazine in front of an aircraft propeller, a pair of goggles perched on her head.

'Thanks,' Maryann said.

'Go on – treat yourself to a good read,' Sylvia said. 'It helps chase the blues away.'

Back in her own cabin, beside her sleeping children, Maryann turned the pages of the magazines, surprised by how excited she felt at reading about young women who flew planes, and about fashions and a short story in which she lost herself, oblivious to everything around her. She lay down to sleep with the lives and voices of the story characters still turning in her head.

Whenever they had a spare half hour, which wasn't every day by any means, the trainees took Maryann's older children aboard the *Theodore* and tried to advance their education. Dot took on the boys, schooling them in their letters by trying to make sure that if they were to read and write, it was about something they were interested in, while Sylvia worked with the girls. The lessons were short, but Sally was often still there begging for more when time had run out and there were other things to be done.

What with the extra help cooking and the attention being paid to the children, Maryann could relax a little; her grudging gratitude towards Sylvia and Dot was increasing day by day as they worked closely together. She saw their hard work on the boat and their consideration towards her. Sylvia was less jumpy and seemed to have blossomed over the past few weeks, and Dot, though still prickly, was less liable to fly off the handle at the slightest hint of criticism. Maryann realized they had been rather in awe of her and the physical struggle her life demanded, and needed to prove themselves to be capable and of use. Maryann found herself touched by this.

A few days later they nosed through Birmingham and pulled into the wharf at Saltley to deliver their load.

'Where'll we pick the next load up from?' Dot asked as they snatched a cup of tea while the timber was being unloaded.

'We'll get a load of coal on the way back.'

'I s'pose that means the dreaded Bottom Road?' Sylvia said. Even though they were heading in the Coventry direction they were obliged to return south along the Birmingham–Fazeley Canal, with all its filth and its single locks, and not go back along the Grand Union. The official reason was that this helped to keep the water supplies up on the Grand Union.

'How ridiculous,' Dot muttered. 'We could save hours going back on the Grand Union.'

By the time they had completed the trip along the Bottom Road again, where a group of boys jeered and spat and another hurled stones at them from a bridge, one of which hit Sylvia on the side of the head, they were all confirmed in their view that it was the most dreary and depressing place of any along the cut. But as they moved further away from Birmingham, Maryann felt lighter with relief. It seemed sad, though, that the city of her birth had become such a place of dread.

*

Sylvia was in a state of high excitement. She could hardly wait to get back to Sutton Stop to see if there were any letters waiting for her.

'Kay and Dickie must have written a couple of times by now,' she said. She had posted them letters all along the route, but hadn't heard back.

'Will your husband write as well?' Maryann asked. She'd formed very little impression of Roy Cresswell so far, except that Sylvia had said he was 'marvellous'. He sounded a bit of a stickler for routine, but apart from that she was surprised how little Sylvia mentioned him.

'Oh yes,' she said. 'I expect I shall hear. He's very *good* like that, but he's an adult, isn't he? He has to be able to take care of himself. It's different for Kay and Dickie – those poor darlings are the ones who've been sent away.'

Maryann knew there wouldn't be any letters for her. She had almost lost contact with her brother Tony now, and her little brother Billy barely knew she existed. Joel certainly couldn't write to her. She watched wistfully as Sylvia and Dot went off to the post office to ask after their mail, the four older children trotting along with them, interested in the novel idea of there being letters for anyone. Maryann had to stop Ada and Esther from following as well.

'No – you stay here.' Bad-temperedly, she lifted them into the *Esther Jane*, whereupon they set up a furious, cheated shrieking.

'Stop that racket, the pair of you!' Maryann said fiercely. 'They'll be back in a minute.'

Sylvia came running along the path a few moments later, her baggy jumper billowing round her slender figure.

'Five letters!' she panted, waving them happily. 'Just

220

what I was hoping for. Oh, look – Dickie's drawn a little face on the back of this one!' She raced back to her cabin.

Soon the children came back.

'Where's Dot, then?' Maryann asked.

'I dunno,' Joley said, kicking a stone along the path. He looked very put out as Dot was normally his friend. 'She said to come back – she'd be along in a while.'

'I wanted her to do some writing with me,' Sally complained, looking wistfully along the path.

Half an hour passed before Dot returned. Maryann was just walking along the path with the empty water holders when she met Dot coming the other way, an envelope in her hand. Her fleshy face was pale and set and she seemed lost in thought. There was no reply when Maryann said, 'Got some letters then?'

She'd staggered back with the full water carriers when Sylvia came over, looking worried.

'Maryann – it's Dot. She's come back and she won't say a word. She just came in and lay on the bed. I don't know if she's ill or if she's had a letter or what it is. Maybe she'd say something to you? I don't know what to do.'

Not knowing what she was supposed to do either, but feeling somehow responsible for the young woman, Maryann climbed down into the *Theodore*. In the gloom, she saw Dot lying on the bed, the curved shape of her back covered in a moss green sweater. She was very quiet.

Stepping closer, Maryann leaned over, about to touch her shoulder, but at the sight of Dot's face she withdrew her hand. Dot was lying on her side, curled tightly, eyes closed and her face contorted in a terrible grimace of pain.

Twenty-Four

Maryann sat herself timidly on the bed.

'Dot? It's Maryann. Is . . . are you in pain?'

There was no reply. Maryann could not even hear her breathing. It was as if Dot was paralysed. Maryann's eyes met Sylvia's in a troubled gaze. She felt intimidated by the young woman lying there, and by the power of her silence, out of which something overwhelming seemed to be crying out to them. But she also felt very sorry and maternal, and she found the courage to touch Dot's shoulder.

'Look, love – can you tell us what's the matter?'

But she'd barely got to the end of her sentence when her hand was flung off convulsively by Dot, who then curled herself even tighter, hands over her face. A strangled sound came from her, half whimper, half snarl. Maryann stood up again, stunned and helpless.

Sylvia came over, her face full of pity. 'Dot – Dorothy, sweetheart, don't suffer in silence like this. We just want to help. Can't you tell us what's wrong?'

Abruptly, Dot jerked herself upright. Her face looked altered, tightened. Pushing them out of the way, she sat on the edge of the bed, suddenly gulping, so that for a moment Maryann thought she was going to be sick. Barking the words out savagely, she said, 'My brother's dead. That's all. Daddy wrote to tell me. So now you know.'

Pushing past them, she left the boat and Maryann looked out to see her stride off along the path.

'Oh God, how awful.' Sylvia sat down, unsteadily. 'And there was I rattling on to her about the children and it was an age before I noticed she was so quiet . . .'

'You weren't to know.' Maryann felt sick. Dot's pain seemed to siphon off into her. It all came back in that moment, how she'd felt on losing her sister, Sal, all the rage and helplessness compounding the grief. She stood looking out through the door.

'He's everything to her.' She heard the tears in Sylvia's voice. 'She's such a funny, crusty girl in some ways – her upbringing, I suppose. She doesn't say much about it. But whenever she's talked about Steven, that's the one time you can see how soft she really is.'

Maryann swallowed hard, trying to force down the ache in her throat. It was no good. If she let herself go down into thinking about Dot and Steven, or started opening up the wounds from her own losses, she would drown in sorrow. *Stop it!* she screamed inwardly, clenching her fists, forcing the feelings away. Taking a deep, shaky breath she said, 'We'd better leave her be. I'll go and see to the tea.' When Sylvia started to protest she insisted abruptly. 'It's all right – I'll do it today.'

Arms folded, head down, she marched back to the *Esther Jane*, cursing in her head. Damn and blast these women, these trainees! Why did they have to be here, bringing all their foreign lives, their troubles and grief to her door when she'd had enough already? She'd found peace, hadn't she, hard-fought-for and won. Now everything was getting stirred up with Norman Griffin smashing back into her life, and now this. If only Joel was back and they could forget anyone else existed: go back to the quiet, secluded life they'd shared all these years!

223

Her hands shook as she peeled potatoes and she felt cold and brittle inside, as if she might easily break. The light was dying now and the air smoky grey outside. There was no sign of Dot. Where could she have gone? Where *would* someone like her go? Should they be looking for her? As the darkness fell, her unease grew.

Sylvia ate with them in the *Esther Jane*. Maryann could see she had been crying. For a second she felt angry. She couldn't afford to let herself cry. If she did, there'd be no end to it.

'D'you think we should be looking out for her?' Sylvia whispered to Maryann. 'I thought she'd just go off for a few minutes by herself, but she's been gone hours!'

'I don't know where we'd start,' Maryann said. 'Not now, any rate.'

'Where's Dot?' Joley demanded as Maryann spooned out mashed potato and baked beans. She hesitated, glancing at Sylvia.

'We're not sure where she is – she's gone for a little walk.' She paused in her serving, holding the spoon. 'Dot's had some bad news.' Gently she told them about Steven.

'Is he her little brother?' Sally asked.

Maryann nodded. 'A couple of years younger, I think.'

'Like Harry?' Joley turned his eyes on her with such solemn intelligence that once more Maryann had to fight off her tears. She could see Sylvia watching, puzzled.

'Harry?' she asked gently.

'I had another son.' Maryann finished serving the

224

food and sat down on the step to eat. 'Before Ezzy. We lost him before he was a year.'

'Oh, Maryann, how dreadful,' Sylvia said, shocked. 'I'm so sorry. I had no idea.'

Maryann acknowledged the sympathy with an abrupt nod.

'Anyroad – ' she forced herself to stay in control – 'I s'pect Dot'll be back soon. She's just gone off to take in the news by herself.'

All evening she tried to keep her mind from straying to the worst that could have become of Dot. Sylvia went back to her cabin. Maryann busied herself with children and chores.

It was after ten when Sylvia tapped on the door. Her face looked pale and tense in the moonlight. 'She's back,' she said softly.

'Where's she been?' Maryann began to feel some of the tension unknot inside her.

'Round the fields was all she'd say. Then all I could get out of her was, "Leave me alone." I've left her to get to bed. A good night's sleep should help – if she can manage it.'

Over the following days they could get nothing out of Dot. She just wouldn't talk about anything.

Soon after they heard the news, Maryann asked her, 'Don't you want to go home and be with your dad?'

Dot was pulling fiercely on the rope to untie the *Theodore*.

'Oh, don't be so ridiculous!' she snapped. 'Of course I don't.'

She worked with a crazed energy. They were sent

north along the Ashby cut, a long, lockless stretch to Measham colliery. The stretch was gradually silting up, neglected like all the cut these days, and some of the bridge-holes were a very tight fit with empty boats, not weighed down in the water. They had to take everything off the cabin roof and lay the chimney flat to get through, but otherwise it was easy going. Maryann could see that Dot, the state she was in, would rather have had steep flights of locks to toil through, such was her need to burn up and down, expending her energy. But it was uncomfortable to be with her. Her silence was far from serene: it was full of unspent emotion. Maryann and Sylvia kept exchanging worried glances when they were within sight of each other. Sylvia told Maryann that she'd found Dot one evening hacking furiously at her fringe with the blunt scissors. Her fringe had grown and looked softer on her face, but she insisted, 'It's too *long*. It's got to go.' Now it was severe and uneven and Maryann warned the children not to say anything about it.

Next, they set off down the Oxford. After the first day on the move, Sylvia came to Maryann and said,

'I don't think I can stand much more of this – it's awful!'

More and more tension built up between them all. Dot insisted on lock-wheeling, storming along the towpath and throwing herself at the paddle mechanisms. They could see she was explosive and both Maryann and Sylvia became almost afraid to speak to her. When they did, she answered abruptly, angrily. Sylvia looked pale and strained. She had told Maryann she was finding it hard to sleep with Dot lying close to her and so knotted up in herself. She was at her wits' end to know what to do. They reached Fenny Compton late one afternoon when the sky was heavy with cloud. They had tied up at a reasonable hour and fetched in supplies. Sylvia suggested that they go over to the pub for a drink.

'It might help her to have a break – make her feel a bit better. If I can persuade her to come out.' Dot was usually game for a trip to the pub even if she never drank alcohol.

'You go,' Maryann said. 'I'll stay in. I've got umpteen things to do.'

'Well,' Sylvia said doubtfully. 'I'll see if she will. But it'll be hard going!'

She must have eventually persuaded Dot that a change would do her good because the two women stopped at the *Esther Jane* to say they were leaving.

'It's getting pretty awful out here!' Sylvia said from under her sou'wester. The wind was getting up and the drumming of rain on the roof accompanied Maryann as she worked through her evening chores. Maryann was relieved not to be with Sylvia and Dot. She found it hard to bear the weight of Dot's silent agony and had no idea how to break through it. The strain was telling on all of them and tonight she didn't want to think about anything. She undressed, got into bed and picked up one of Sylvia's magazines. It had become her nightly treat to cuddle up on the tiny bed with her family all round her, hair loose, hugging her old cardi to her, reading and re-reading the articles and stories. The magazines presented her with a world of feminine things she had barely been aware of over the years. Even though fashions and clothing were very limited now by shortages and rationing, to her it seemed exciting reading about patterns and sewing tricks and make-do-and-mend.

She gradually grew sleepy, but struggled to keep awake to finish a story. As she sat with the magazine propped against her knees, a strange sound came from outside in the dark. Maryann raised her head. For a second she thought it was an owl, but that could hardly be in this pouring rain. It was followed by more noises and her heart began to beat fast.

Pulling on her coat and boots, she let herself out, jumping down onto the squelching bank, the sound of the rain all round her, the plop and gurgle of it in the cut. A little way ahead she could make out the bobbing light of a torch, and as she moved closer against the wind, she could make out Sylvia leaning over the figure on the ground. In gusts there came to her the wrenching, almost retching sound of weeping.

Dot was kneeling on the ground, one moment curled forward, the next throwing herself up onto her knees, swaying and moaning, as if trying to work the pain out of her body.

'Dot, sweetie – oh, do get up! Let's go inside...' Sylvia sounded distraught, as she begged Dot not to kneel out here in the rain. But Dot couldn't seem to hear her, or anything. She was lost in her crying, and the sound of it cut through Maryann. She felt herself swell with pity at the little figure, wrestling in the darkness.

When Sylvia saw her she cried, 'Oh, Maryann! She just – I don't know what happened. I can't get her to hear me, she's in such a state and she's getting caked in mud...'

Maryann didn't need to think what to do. She flung herself onto her knees beside Dot, rain running down her face, the wet soaking through her nightdress, melting inside with pity for the girl's distress.

'Come here...' She embraced Dot's lunging, weeping form in her arms and held her, managing to still her a little, tender, motherly words falling from her lips.

'It's all right, Dot, you're all right, have a good cry, that's it – you let some of it out, my love.' She rocked Dot back and forth like a child, feeling her shaking and sobbing.

Broken words and groans of pain were snatched from Dot's lips by the wind. 'My Stevie ... my lovely Stevie...' There was a long moan of pain, before she cried, 'Oh God, he was all I had!' Then her sobs would empty her of breath and she quivered, gulping until she managed a great, gasping breath.

Maryann's own tears came then and Sylvia came up and hugged Dot from behind. 'Poor darling,' she kept saying. 'Oh, poor love.'

Holding each other, crying, the three of them were soon soaked. Maryann lost track of how much time they crouched there. Then Dot's crying quietened to shaking and gulping and she seemed to come to, as if from a trance.

'Sorry.' She struggled to her feet, regaining some of her gruff self-control. 'We must all go in. This is ridiculous of me ... only I...' She lowered her head and began to weep helplessly, but more softly than before.

'Come on.' Sylvia took her hand and, sodden and shivering, the three of them all went to the *Theodore*.

For a moment, in the light of the cabin, they were at a loss what to do. Water ran from them, forming puddles at their feet.

'We'd better take these wet clothes off,' Sylvia said, suddenly brisk, as if the emotions released just now should be swept away now that they were back in the light again. Dot perched numbly on the side bench, as if exhausted. Maryann sat beside her and unbuttoned her coat for her. Dot didn't resist. She suddenly looked very young and beaten, her chopped fringe slicked to her forehead, her cheeks wet and eyes red.

'Let's have a cup of cocoa,' Sylvia said. 'Dot – you going to have some?'

Dot looked up slowly and nodded, her eyes filling. 'I'm sorry – I can't seem to stop now I've started,' she said. 'Oh, Steven . . .'

Maryann put her arms round Dot's shoulders and held her close.

'What're you saying sorry for, you silly so-and-so?'

Twenty-Five

Easter was drawing near. Daffodils rippled bright in the spring breezes in gardens backing onto the cut. Soon it would be time for Sylvia to join her children for their school holidays.

During that time Dot allowed herself to begin to grieve. In fact grief took hold of her and would not let her hold it at bay any more.

'I don't know what's come over me,' she would say, finding tears running down her cheeks at unexpected moments. 'This just isn't like me at all.'

'Dot,' Sylvia would say, 'you've lost your brother, who you loved more than anyone in the world and you don't know what's come over you!' Their sympathy made Dot cry all the more. Maryann and Sylvia, both so much older, had developed a big-sisterly affection and protectiveness towards Dot in her unhappiness. It had changed everything.

On those chill, lamplit evenings they sat in the *Theodore*, and Dot began to talk about herself and her family in a way that she never had before. Things just seemed to come pouring out. One evening, to Maryann's astonishment, she told them that her mother had died in her forties of a diseased liver and alcohol poisoning. When she came out with this in her strange, abruptly matter-of-fact, Dotish way, Maryann saw shock register on Sylvia's face too and their eyes met for a horrified second.

'It took Stevie and me years to work out what was the matter with her. That she was a tippler.' Dot kept her eyes on her knitting. Her hair was loose over her plump shoulders and Maryann suddenly thought how young she looked. She could imagine her as a little girl of seven or eight, with her big eyes, rosy cheeks and sudden vulnerability.

'How terrible!' Sylvia murmured. Dot glanced up and Maryann could see she found sympathy hard to accept, even now. She had been so accustomed to burying her feelings.

'When you're young you accept things the way they are, don't you? Stevie and I just knew that at times – in fact much of the time – our mother had to be left alone, or that she seemed to spend such a lot of time asleep. Passed out was nearer the truth. Then, other days she'd turn on us like a hyena. Poor Stevie – it was far worse for him. He was such a shy little boy. Clingy. Cowed, really. He needed a nice, soft, attentive mother.' Dot gave a harsh laugh. 'I suppose I got by by being his protector, poor little chap.

'Of course, as we got older, we began to put two and two together. There was that smell our mother had about her: Scotch was her poison. Other things would do if there was none going, but that's the smell I remember.' Dot grimaced. 'When she smelt like that, you left her alone. She gave up trying to hide it long before she died. We had housekeepers and *they* didn't smell like that . . . And, of course, we'd hear them talking. One of them, I heard her say to one of the maids, "Mrs Higgs-Deveraux – proper dipsomaniac she is, if you ask me." I went and looked it up.' Dot sighed and stopped knitting, hands in her lap. 'D'you know, I can still see the dictionary. It was a big, heavy thing, the edges of the pages all brown. I sat with it in my lap, in the parlour. I was about eleven. And I just sat there reading the word over and over again. Dipsomaniac. It was almost like discovering you've got a brother or sister you've never been told about, but somehow you always knew was there – things suddenly making sense. Stevie and I had always kept out of her way – if we weren't at school we were out somewhere. And soon after that, I remember, was one of the times we hid for *hours* under the big bed in the spare room when Mummy was in one of her states. We both lay there on the floorboards, on our backs, looking up at the springs, and the sheets tucked under the mattress and it was all dusty and smelt of mothballs, and we could hear our mother and father. He was so cold and cruel to her. Stevie and I started singing little songs, very quietly. "Here we go gathering nuts in May – " Things like that. We didn't want to hear what they were saying. Or what Daddy was doing to her . . .' Dot's voice faltered.

'Is that why she drank – to get away from him?' Sylvia asked gently.

'I don't know. Partly.' Dot was silent for a moment. 'No – I think she was frustrated. She married young when she really had wanted to have a life of her own, and there was just nothing for her in the country, where we lived. And she was married to a man who was as cold as the grave. A narcissist. Couldn't see anything from anyone else's point of view. He never gave her an inch. He always, always had to be centre stage. If we had visitors, everything revolved around him. He's a completely self-obsessed man. D'you know . . . ?'

Maryann tensed inside, almost panicky, as if she wanted to shout, *Stop! Stop – don't tell me any more! Let me believe that you had a happy, charmed childhood, not one like mine, full of cruelty. Please let something, somewhere, be innocent and loving!* Sylvia was silent as well. They could hear her little alarm clock ticking in the background.

'When Stevie was fifteen, he—' Again she ground to a halt, taking deep, distressed breaths.

'Don't.' Sylvia had tears in her eyes. 'Not if it's too much for you, darling.'

But Dot couldn't seem to stop now. The words poured out.

'He took a rope into the stables. Tied it over the beam. And a chair. Only the chair wasn't really high enough – he left the rope too long. Norris – the man who worked in the garden – found him hanging, just off the ground. It'd only been a matter of seconds, I think. But he'd meant it – to take his own life. Stevie would never do something like that without meaning it. Afterwards he couldn't speak properly for days, he'd bruised his throat so badly. It was a Saturday and my father was in his study, preparing papers for some case or other. My mother ran to him to tell him what had happened, and he refused to come down before he'd finished the piece of work he was doing. It was nearly an hour before he came and my mother and I had put Steven to bed and called the doctor. He was in shock, of course: his neck was red and burnt from the rope. And my father came, finally. He stood in the doorway – he's very tall and thin – and stared at Stevie with such *contempt* and anger. He said, "You bloody little fool."'

Dot stared at the table with the empty cocoa cups on it. She was quivering slightly. Then she looked up.

'So – that's my family. A right jolly old crew. Stevie joined the Navy as soon as they'd have him. I know he felt frightful about leaving me, but I was about to go to London anyway. I was delighted for him. It was far

234

worse at home for him than me. Daddy expected so much more of him.'

Maryann was surprised at how much she was beginning to dread the three of them being separated. Of course Sylvia would be back, and in the meantime Dot would stay and they'd have to rearrange things so that Bobby could come back and crew with them. She wasn't worried about shifting the loads, but they'd got into a routine of hard work and support for each other, of sharing laughter and beginning to share some of their lives during their cosy evenings together, although Maryann knew she couldn't share much of her past. Even the thought of talking about it was too big, too frightening. She felt much easier with Dot, now she had shown her softer, more vulnerable side. Of Sylvia, Maryann felt she knew less, but she thought perhaps there was less to know. She was a sweet girl, settled in marriage, and she was a helpful presence and a good worker. When they reached Coventry, Sylvia would get on her train back to London, to her cosy, suburban life, to her house with a bath, her children and her lawn and roses. Maryann liked to think of that – that somewhere people had lives like that in which there was no squalor and unhappiness, no one like Norman Griffin to cast a foul shadow over them.

She began to wish she could slow down their journey to Oxford, that it might not end yet, so that she didn't have to face any more changes. But time seemed to gallop past.

In Oxford she found Joel still slowly and painfully on the mend. He was able to sit downstairs now and move about just a little. Maryann and the children stayed with him for as long as they could manage, sitting in Alice's little parlour. Maryann sat on a stool beside him, holding his hand (which she teased him was getting soft) and telling him about all the ups and downs of their journeys and snippets of news from other boatpeople.

'You sound as if you're getting along perfectly all right without me,' Joel said, as Maryann laughingly told him stories of Dot's and Sylvia's antics.

Hearing his wistful tone, Maryann reached up and kissed him. 'Not perfectly, no – nothing like! But we're getting by, keeping ahead all right. You've made a boat-woman of me, see? And you'll be back soon, won't you?'

'Doctor says two to three months yet,' Alice Simons said, eyeing Joel sternly. 'Don't you go getting any ideas about taking off, spoiling all that resting up you've done.'

Sylvia was lock-wheeling that morning as they headed north away from Banbury. She ran ahead along the towpath, full of frisky energy, and waited on the bridge beyond, her slim, feminine figure silhouetted against the pale sky. She signalled them to slow down: the lock was busy. Maryann slowed the engine.

'We're out of bread – and milk!' she shouted up to Sylvia over the throaty chug of the engine and saw her nod in reply.

Once they were through Cropredy lock, they tied up for a few moments beyond the bridge while Dot hared off with Joley and Sally for supplies. Once she'd seen them climbing back onto the *Theodore*, Maryann and Ezra cast off the *Esther Jane*.

That evening, after tea, Dot said to her, 'Oh – I picked this up as well when we stopped. Course they were going to use it for wrapping, but I pleaded the cause of us poor, deprived souls.' She held out a copy of the *Birmingham Post*. 'I thought you might like a look.'

Maryann thanked her and put the paper aside until she was in bed that night. Sleepily, she reached for it, only half wanting to bother. Sally was pressed up against her in bed, and she feared the crackly paper might wake her. But otherwise there'd be no chance until the next night.

I'll just look at the first couple of pages, she thought, yawning, and glancing over the first page. Gingerly she opened the paper, watching Sally as she did so. A moment later she read something which banished her drowsiness completely. She jerked upright, pulse galloping.

MURDERED WOMAN IDENTIFIED the headline said. The details were bad enough: the young woman, now known to be aged twenty-two, with auburn hair and a pale complexion, had been found beaten and strangled on a piece of waste ground. She had been reported missing by her mother two days previously. But it was the names of the woman and her mother, who had identified her, which almost seemed to shudder on the page in front of Maryann's eyes. The dead woman's name was Amy Lambert. Her mother was a Mrs Janet Lambert.

In her guts she knew immediately. It couldn't be anyone else. In those terrible seconds she knew that this Amy Lambert was the same Amy, the sister of Margaret, who had been locked away all those years in the asylum. Amy, the strong one, the older girl, who had tried to protect her sister, who had looked to Maryann for help and friendship as a frightened twelve-year-old.

Maryann's hand went to her throat, rereading the

report. Amy was dead. And she knew with sudden, terrifying instinct who had brought about her end. Her stepfather, Norman Griffin, had also been Amy and Margaret's stepfather; he had conned his way into Janet Lambert's family and wreaked his brutal havoc on them. After little Margaret attacked him he had been so badly disfigured that he was barely decent to be seen in the light of day. He'd gone to ground then, festering in obscurity like some foul disease. But now he had crawled out of his hiding place, more twisted than ever before. His was the face she had looked into that night in Pastor James's church. What he had done in the meantime, why he was pursuing them now, she had no idea. But she knew it was him. And that he was waiting.

Twenty-Six

'Dot, I need to go to Birmingham.'

Maryann had not said a word to Sylvia and Dot of the turmoil and horror she was feeling. She had been barely able to eat or sleep since seeing the newspaper, but she had held all her feelings inside her during the last leg of the journey. How could she even begin to explain to anyone?

Dot looked nonplussed for a moment. They were back at Sutton Stop and were expecting to spend the day cleaning the boats.

'Family business,' Maryann said. She could see Dot thinking, *How on earth has this come about suddenly, with no letters, and barely any contact with anyone else?* But Maryann couldn't and wouldn't explain.

'Just for the day. I'll go when Sylv goes tomorrow and be back by the night. Sorry, but I've got to. We'll rest up tomorrow and Mr Veater says Bobby should be back in here tomorrow or the next day.'

'Right-oh,' Dot said cheerfully, and Maryann was immediately comforted by the sense that she would cope with everything. 'I'll get cleaned up tomorrow then. Are you leaving me the children?'

'If you can manage. I'll take one of the twins – Ada. She's the fidget.'

'We'll get along famously,' Dot said. 'It'll be a challenge.'

That night, as Sylvia was about to leave, they had a little party. They were tied up at 'home' at Sutton Stop again. It helped take Maryann's mind off things a fraction. Sylvia baked a cake and they fetched the children's sweet rations and made a nice little high tea, Ada and Esther drooling as they sucked on their highly coloured jelly babies. When Maryann explained to the family that Sylvia had to go away for a while, they were full of questions. Maryann managed a smile, as she listened to them trying to understand that Sylvia's children lived in a big school with a lot of other children. But little Rose, who was tucked in beside Sylvia as usual, started crying.

'Oh, darling!' Sylvia put her arm round her and kissed the top of her head. Maryann was surprised at the pain she saw in her eyes as she did so. 'I'm not going away for long – just a few weeks and then I'll be back with you. I'll bring you a present back, sweetheart, all right? And the rest of you!' With an effort to look cheerful she smiled round the table.

Later they spent their last night together chatting in the *Theodore*. Sylvia had bought a bottle of whisky.

'Sorry, Dot – I like my little tipple – I know you don't go for it.'

'For rather obvious reasons,' Dot said, screwing her face up in disgust at the smell. She unlaced her boots and tugged them off, wiggling her toes in their woolly socks and sighing with relief.

'Well, I like a drink,' Sylvia said defiantly, giving some to Maryann and pouring herself a generous tot. Maryann watched surprised. She saw an edge of tension, of aggression in Sylvia that was not evident in her normally placid personality. 'Sometimes it's the only way to get through, isn't it?'

'*No*,' Dot insisted. 'It's the one thing to avoid getting stuck on, I'd say.'

'Here – you're going back to a nice comfy house and a bath!' Maryann laughed. 'What've *you* got to get through?'

Sipping her drink, Sylvia stared at her over the rim of her cup, as if considering something. She put the cup down. 'Oh – nothing,' she said brightly. 'Don't be silly, it was just a figure of speech.'

But as the evening wore on and they sat reminiscing about their trips together so far, Sylvia went quiet suddenly and they saw she was fighting back tears. Maryann and Dot immediately tried to comfort her.

'I know I'm being a soppy old thing,' Sylvia wept into her hanky. Through all the rush and chaos and often grimy squalor of life on the boat, Sylvia always seemed to have a cotton hanky on her somewhere at the ready. Nasally, she said, 'I just can't tell you how much I've *loved* being here – this time on the cut has been the best time of my life! I'm longing to see Kay and Dickie, of course, but it's so hard to leave you all. I wish I could just bring them back here.'

Dot and Maryann exchanged puzzled glances, but they jollied Sylvia along.

'Oh, you'll be glad enough when you're lying in a nice hot bath, thinking about us having a lick and a promise out of the dipper!'

The next morning Maryann set off, with Ada balanced on one hip, to catch the bus to Coventry station with Sylvia and her bundle of clothes. Before they set off, Sylvia hugged Dot and all the children emotionally.

241

On the bus, Maryann saw her looking out at the wreckage of Coventry, a bleak expression on her face.

'Don't you want to go home?' Maryann couldn't help asking, perplexed by the gloom that seemed to have overcome Sylvia.

'Umm?' Sylvia looked round and gave a smile that didn't quite reach her eyes. 'Home? Yes – of course I do.'

They parted at the station and once more Maryann saw tears welling in Sylvia's eyes. She embraced Maryann and Ada tightly and kissed them both. 'See you soon, darlings.' Maryann watched her walk away, her blonde hair bouncing on her shoulders as she went off to find her platform. What a stranger she seemed suddenly, from quite another world. After all, what did she really know about Sylvia?

Her own train drew into New Street before midday.

'Here we go,' she said to Ada as they climbed down from the carriage. 'Back in Brum.' It was the first time in a long while that she'd been into the middle of Birmingham, and walking along New Street from the station she was shocked by the smashed gaps in long-familiar facades of buildings. It took time for her to orientate herself and find the right bus stop.

Janet Lambert had lived in Handsworth during her marriage to Norman Griffin, who by then was calling himself Albert Lambert. She had long since moved to Erdington, for a fresh start.

I suppose she was trying to get away from the memory of him, Maryann thought grimly, sitting on the Erdington bus with Ada in her lap. The little girl was looking round, fascinated by all the new sights and people's faces. But Maryann felt hemmed in by the city, by its greyness, the lines of low, grime-covered houses and by the shreds of memory which it stirred up for her. Was there no end to this? she thought despairingly. To the pain and damage caused by this man, whose presence seemed to echo like an evil chorus in her life?

The closer she came to seeing Janet, the more the emotions she had been trying to suppress came seething to the surface: the rage and sorrow and horror of reading Amy's name in the *Post*. *Murdered*. Getting off the bus, she felt crazed, as if she might rage and scream in the street, and by the time she reached Janet's black front door she was shaking with the effort of holding herself together. It was a help having Ada chattering in her arms. It steadied her. And she had to remain strong, she commanded herself. For Janet. It was she who had lost her daughters – both of them.

It always took Janet Lambert some time to reach her door. She had a tubercular hip and walked awkwardly with a stick. At last the door opened. Maryann barely recognized the woman who appeared. She had faded hair which showed only traces of the fiery rust colour it had been the last time they met, and her face, which had once been that of a serene beauty, was now battered by life, marked with the scars of grief. She looked out with a dazed expression.

'Janet,' Maryann said gently, 'it's Maryann.'

Janet sagged. Prepared to see a stranger outside, her grief surfaced immediately at the sight of a friend. 'Oh.' It was almost a whimper. 'I didn't know you for a minute ... I'm in that much of a ...' For a moment she seemed quite at a loss, then collected herself. 'Come in, dear.'

Maryann followed Janet's painful progress into the parlour at the front. As in her last house, it was a tastefully decorated room in greens and browns and she had trimmed her own curtains. Maryann set Ada down and she immediately headed for the fireplace, where there were brightly polished brass fire tools in the grate. The two women could not contain their emotion any longer.

'I saw it in the paper,' Maryann said. She went to Janet and the woman crumpled into her arms. 'Oh my God, poor Amy – our poor little Amy!'

They clung to one another, pouring out their anguish, both of them trembling and weeping.

'Why? . . . why?' Janet kept crying. 'Oh, my little girl . . . my baby girl . . . my lovely Amy.' Maryann could feel the force of her sobbing, and she too cried, at last, feeling the pain deep inside herself as if it was being wrung out of her. For a long time neither of them could calm down, but at last, a small portion of emotion spent, they drew back from each other.

'Let me make you a cup of tea.' Janet said dully.

'No – don't bother with that,' Maryann tried to protest.

'It's no bother, love. It'll help.'

And Maryann, too, was relieved to go through the ritual of kettle filling and helping to fetch cups and saucers. Janet had always been ladylike in her ways, and even now, out of habit, she laid the cups out nicely on a tray.

'The funeral's next Wednesday,' she said while they waited for the water. 'They say they should have finished with her by then.'

While they drank their tea in the neat parlour and Ada pottered about exploring, Maryann sat listening as Janet poured out the events of the past days. She kept hold of the handle of one of her walking sticks in her left hand, as if it steadied her.

Amy had gone to work as usual. She had a job in a

dress shop in town and went in on the bus. But that Thursday night she hadn't come home.

'I didn't know what to do.' Janet's agitated fingers bent and straightened round the handle of the walking stick. With her other hand she worried at the material of her skirt. 'I suppose I should have gone to the police straight away, but I thought she'd been held up, or she'd gone out with Geoff, her young man, and forgotten to mention it to me. I wasn't terribly worried to begin with. And then it got late and, well, I waited and waited ... I was frightened to go out. It was very dark and it's a long walk to the telephone box.' She sobbed again, then spoke through her tears. 'I thought it'd be all right. I never dreamt ... I should have gone! I was up all night and by the morning – then I was afraid something had happened. Amy was always such a good girl – didn't stop out of a night, nothing like that. But I was frightened to go and tell anyone because then I'd have to find out there'd been an accident. If I just stayed here, I could go on thinking she was all right. But of course I did go, eventually. I never thought of .. ... not that she was dead.' Her face creased and she began to weep again.

Maryann cried with her, unable to stop. Poor, lovely Amy! She kept seeing her in her mind's eye as she had the first time she set eyes on the girls that day in Handsworth Park, those two silent children full of pain and fear, always beautifully turned out by Janet in their matching frocks and hair ribbons. And though she had only seen Amy occasionally since then, she knew she had grown into a kind-hearted and beautiful young woman.

'They found her up near the hospital two days later. Course I'd reported her missing. I had to go and see her, to identify her as my girl, my baby.' She was silent for a moment, shaking her head. 'He'd made such a mess of her.' Arms folded, she began to rock back and forth in the chair in distress. Unable to bear it, Maryann went to her and put her arms round Janet's shoulders, rocking her gently. She waited until Janet was a little calmer, then went and refilled the teapot and topped up their cups.

Kneeling beside Janet she looked up into her eyes. 'It was him, wasn't it?'

'No!' Janet reacted immediately. '*No.* What're you *talking* about?'

She looked down into her lap, shaking her head. There was a long silence. Once more, she began to rock, unable to contain her agitation.

'I've been trying not to – to think it. To think about *him*.' Her gentle face twisted with loathing. 'It could have been anyone who did it. But then it goes round and round in my head. Why would anyone do that to my lovely Amy? They'd have to be insane. An animal.'

'Have you seen him since he left?'

Janet shook her head. 'He just vanished. Never came back. That was what we wanted, of course. Amy and I moved – we needed a fresh start, but not too far from Margaret. I did hear the odd thing about him. One of my old neighbours reckoned she'd seen him, said he was a mess to look at. He closed that business down in Handsworth. I suppose he must have gone and set up somewhere else – done something to make a living for himself. But I haven't set eyes on him.'

'I've seen him.' Maryann said. She told Janet how he had come looking for her, about the episode with Pastor James, how he'd tricked that foolish man into believing him, about what happened in the back room of the church.

'God in heaven!' Janet laid a hand over her heart. 'I remember that first day I ever saw him, all upstanding and smart. And I was so desperate I just took to him, just like that. Let him into my life, my family. My God!' It came out as a howl. 'Look what I've done. What I've made happen!'

'Stop it!!' Maryann's voice came out loud and sharp. Rage flamed in her at hearing Janet say the thing she still had to fight against perpetually in herself. *It's my fault. All my fault. What happened to Sal, to our mom, to Amy and Margaret – all of it. I'm dirty and shameful and always have been. That's why he did it. I asked for it. It's all my fault.* Why could she see so clearly that this was not true for someone else when she still, deep down, felt she was not like other people, that she must hide from them? When she still blamed herself?

Leaning down, she looked urgently into Janet's face. 'Don't do that! He's the one that did all of this – *all* of it! Nothing's your fault – *only* his. As soon as you start thinking it's your fault he's got you!'

'But what should we do? Whatever can we do?'

'Tell the police about him.' Even as she said it, Maryann felt a sense of despair. How could the police ever find him, let alone prove it was him who murdered Amy, however sure she was that he and only he could be responsible? He was so sly, so slippery. None of them knew where he was or even by what name he went these days. She could see that Janet was thinking the same.

'But his face,' Maryann said. She stood up, her expression hard and determined. 'No one else has a face like that. We've got to tell them.'

*

247

The grey-haired police officer looked at her wearily over the counter as she walked into the dingy light of the police station, carrying Ada in her arms.

'Can I help you?'

Maryann put Ada down and the child instinctively stayed close to her.

'It's about...' Maryann felt shaky, and somehow foolish. It was as if none of this was quite real. 'That murder. The one in the papers – the girl with the red hair, Amy Lambert. I know who killed her.'

She had his attention now. He stood straighter and his eyes widened, but his expression and the way he rubbed his hand over his chin made her see he was wary of her. Did people come in claiming things like that every day, she wondered?

Trying to steady herself, she gripped the counter. There was a gouged wound in the wood under her right index finger.

'It was a man called Norman Griffin – least, that's what he used to call himself.'

She poured out her story, gabbling, desperate for him to believe her. He nodded a lot as she spoke and after a time he pulled his notebook from his pocket and wrote something down, frowning as he did so. When she stopped at last, waiting for something – what? – for him to jump into action, he said, 'Well thank you, Mrs er . . .?'

'Bartholomew.'

'We'll follow this up.'

'Well, I should hope so!' She burst out, her voice loud and shrill now with frustration. 'He murdered her, I know he did! And what're you going to do about it?'

She immediately regretted losing herself as she could see the policeman was thinking she was some silly woman, no doubt funny in the head. Backing away from him, towards the door, she cried, 'You'll see. You go and find him! I know it was him!'

Outside she leaned against the wall, taking deep, distraught breaths, holding tightly to Ada's hand. It was a few moments before she managed to begin walking along the street, trying to tell herself she'd done the best she could. Who else was there to turn to but the police? Surely he had to believe what she'd told him! At least they'd be looking for Norman Griffin, wouldn't they? He would get what he more than deserved at last.

Standing at the tram stop, her mind raced on. What if they couldn't find him? What if – the thought sent a spasm of fear through her – what if he went after Janet next? As the tram swayed into view, the thought chilled through her. Was he coming back after all of them now? Was that it?

Twenty-Seven

A shadow fell on Dot as she knelt in the spring sunshine the next morning, splicing a rope in the empty hold of the *Theodore*. She looked up and saw a young man with dark eyes, a swarthy face and thick dark hair falling over his forehead. He had with him a rusty bicycle, poised with its front wheel at the edge of the cut.

'How do? So you're one of the new 'uns are you?'

Dot stared back. Something about the way the young man was looking at her, the frank appraisal and twinkle of amusement in his eyes made her feel immediately prickly and self-conscious. She clambered to her feet, feeling plump and ungainly.

'I suppose I am, if you insist on putting it like that.'

He laughed, not seeming to take offence, laid the bike down with a clatter, climbed in over the gunwales and held out his hand.

'I'm Bobby. I'll be crewing with you for a bit.'

Dot shook his hand, stiffly. 'How d'you do? I'm Dorothy – Dot. And I've heard a lot about you.'

'Ah – it's the bits you ent heard that are the best!' he laughed.

Dot glowered at him. Why did young men with good looks and easy charm like Bobby make her feel so grumpy? As if her skin was being rubbed over with sandpaper. It was made even worse by the fact that he was a boater born and bred. She knew what they tended to make of trainees like herself. Here she was, just beginning to feel she fitted in, and she was going to have to prove herself all over again. And to make it worse, she knew he'd see her as posh and clownishly plump.

She was saved from further chat by hearing shouts along the bank. 'It's Bobby – he's back!'

The Bartholomew children were charging wildly towards them, raggle-taggle brigade that they were, in their motley collection of clothes. Rose had on an old frock of Sally's that was almost down to her ankles and she had to hold it up to run along. All of them were grubby from top to toe. It was a losing battle for Maryann, trying to keep them clean. Bobby laughed at the sight. Maryann was at the back, being pulled along by the twins, one tugging on each hand, and smiling at the sight of Bobby. Dot suddenly saw for a second a sweet young woman beneath the careworn wife, mother and boat skipper whose face was always lined with tiredness and worry.

Bobby leapt back onto the bank and the older children ran at him, all talking at once.

'Bobby's got a *bike*!'

'Whose is it? Is it yours?'

'Where d'you get it?'

'Can we have a ride?'

'Hello, Bobby – got here at last! All right, are you?' Maryann called out over the children's din. She felt like flinging her arms round him, she was so pleased to see him, but she knew he would just be embarrassed. Her inner heaviness lightened a fraction. Bobby was like part of the family. Having him here for a while gave a feel of things returning to normal. She was puzzled, though, to see Dot looking aloof and rather bad-tempered. *Back to how she used to be*, Maryann thought. *What's got into her?*

'A feller gave me that, down London,' Bobby said, nodding at the bike. 'Thought it'd speed us up a bit.'

Maryann nodded. She and Joel had never used a bike, though the trainees had expressed their surprise at not finding one on the boat when they arrived.

'I s'pose so,' she said doubtfully.

Once they'd swapped their news, Maryann said, 'I'll get the kettle on for a brew and we'd better get cracking.' Bobby had said he could stay with them for as long as was needed, and certainly until Sylvia was due back at the end of the school holidays. They started on re-arranging the boats. It was to be boys in one, girls in the other. Maryann would be in the *Esther Jane* with Dot, Sal, Rose and the twins, and Bobby would have Joley and Ezra bunked up with him in the *Theodore*.

Dot silently carried her belongings onto the *Esther Jane*. The children were all very excited, both with Bobby being back and by the changes, and ran back and forth shouting shrilly to each other, begging Bobby for rides on the bike.

'It's going to be more crowded in here than you're used to,' Maryann apologized to Dot as she carried her belongings in.

'That's all right,' Dot said and smiled. Maryann was reassured. She wanted to ask if there was something wrong but didn't quite dare. Dot had only just begun getting over Steven's death, hadn't she? That was surely what was wrong. Overwhelmed by her own worries, she sometimes forgot.

Dot was quiet all afternoon, but for most of it Maryann was too lost in her own thoughts to notice very much. As well as sorting out and cleaning both boats and keeping an eye on the twins, her thoughts swam round and round all that had happened when she visited Janet, the horror of Amy's death and the visit to the police station. Her nerves were so jangled she jumped at the slightest sound. Bobby stuck his head through the hatches of the *Esther Jane* while she was polishing the stove, lost in thought, and she shrieked, laying a hand over her pounding heart.

'Flippin' eck Bobby! You nearly made me jump out of my skin!'

'I've finished taking my things in. All settled. Good little cabin you got there.'

'You only just noticed?' Maryann forced a grin onto her face.

'Now I've worked a few others I can see how nice you've got it. You should be proud.'

'Yes,' Maryann sighed. 'But – you know Joel. Only thing'd make him proud is if it's his own, with "Joel Bartholomew, Number One" on the cabin.'

Bobby moved a bit further in. 'That Dot's a bit of a rum 'un, ent she?'

'She's all right.' Maryann looked up from her polishing again for a minute. 'Good sort. Don't know what's up with her today. She'll come round.'

'Well, I flaming hope so,' he said. 'I ent said nothing amiss that I can think of and all I get from her's looks – and not very nice ones.'

Maryann laughed at his indignant expression. 'Well, there's a challenge for you, eh, Bobby? Time you found yourself a nice girl anyway.'

'Ooh – not like that 'un! He rolled his eyes, as if to imply that Dot was like someone from outer space.

'You got your eye on anyone yet?' Maryann often felt like Bobby's mother.

He grinned mischievously. 'Might have. Might not. We'll have to see, won't we?'

Mr Veater put them on short trips shifting coal again to begin with, to Baddesley colliery, then Griff. The spring days increased in warmth and the cooling towers of the power station puffed out their clouds of vapour towards a fresh, blue sky.

Bobby took charge of the *Theodore* and Dot chose to do whatever lock-wheeling was called for, often with some of the kids scrambling along beside her. Sometimes now they used the bike.

Maryann found her mind scattered and forgetful. She would find herself standing, forgetting what the task was she was supposed to be carrying out, and she couldn't seem to keep her thoughts together. As she stood at the helm the past kept welling up, however much she tried not to think of it. She could not stop thinking about Amy, especially as the day of her funeral passed. Janet understood that Maryann wouldn't be able to be there, but it was a hard, bitter day for her and, as she worked, her mind was with Janet. Every time she thought about it she was overwhelmed by rage. Round and round it all went in her head. She didn't want to be here, she needed to be in Birmingham, tracking Norman Griffin down, bringing justice upon him. How could they find him? Of course – she could ask Pastor Owen. Why hadn't she remembered to tell the policeman about him? Norman might have let slip to him something about where he lived and worked. *Someone* must know. After all, it wasn't as if you could miss him with looks like that. You couldn't forget him.

She became aware gradually, though, that all was not

well with her crew. A sparring match had begun between Dot and Bobby. They seemed to have started off on the wrong foot with each other and it wasn't getting any better. When Bobby heard Dot's full name of Dorothy Higgs-Deveraux, he'd chortled with great amusement and sent Dot off into a huff by nicknaming her 'her ladyship'. Dot was not showing much sense of humour about this and was now, to Maryann's exasperation, back to being as abrasive as when she'd first arrived. With Bobby behind her on the *Theodore* Maryann didn't notice what was going on a lot of the time, but once when she turned to look as he was bringing the boat through a lock, she saw him making an exaggerated bow towards Dot, who was on the bank, and doffing his cap. Dot completely ignored him on this occasion, sailing past without turning her head. Bobby always seemed to be trying to get a rise out of her and often succeeded. He couldn't seem to find any other way of dealing with Dot or she with him.

At the end of their first trip, when they were back at Sutton Stop, he invited her out to the pub with him. 'Would your ladyship fancy a drink at the Greyhound?' he asked teasingly.

Dot was thumbing through a newspaper and didn't even look up. 'No thank you,' she said coldly.

'There's not much joy for Dot going to the pub – she don't drink,' Maryann excused her.

'Oh.' Bobby frowned, as if finding all this very peculiar. 'Suit yourself. What about you then?'

'No, ta – I'll stay in tonight. You go and find your pals.'

When he'd gone, she said, 'It was nice of him to ask, Dot. He didn't have to. He's all right you, know, Bobby is. He's just a lad. He's got a good heart.'

'I'm sure he has,' Dot said breezily, folding up the newspaper.

'He's just not sure how to talk to you, that's all. He's never met anyone like you before.'

'Come on, Joley, Sal – and the rest of you!' Dot said, as if Maryann hadn't spoken. 'How about a bit of writing practice before bed?'

'You want your heads knocking together, the pair of you,' Maryann grumbled. 'I hope you're not going to carry on like this for a month!'

Twenty-Eight

This is going to be one of those trips, Maryann thought as she climbed out of the cabin again into the driving rain. Dot was at the helm, collar up, huddled under a sou'wester, trousers soaked dark with water. Her boots were over-flowing as she stepped squelchily from foot to foot.

They were on the route down to Oxford and every-thing had gone badly from the beginning. The rain had barely let up for days, slowing, even stopping to allow brief, overcast intervals before starting again and falling hard and steadily. Loading up had gone badly, the coal getting wet as soon as it rattled down into the hold, and trying to sheet up in the wet and in a hurry was always an ordeal, with the slippery boards, the ropes chafing rough and wet against their hands and having to be spliced when they snapped. Maryann kept barking at the children to stay indoors and not get all their clothes wet because, before they'd even started out, the adults' clothes were soaked through. The bedding was damp as they hadn't been able to air it outside for days, the cabin floors were thick with mud and filth and, worst of all, the bedbugs were back and everyone was scratching bites. The snubber snapped on the long, lockless route down to Rugby and then they'd just missed getting through Banbury before the gates were locked up and had to tie up earlier than they wanted. Everyone was wet, cold and bad-tempered.

257

'You go in and warm up – there's tea in the pot,' Maryann said, climbing out to relieve Dot.

'Ooh, marvellous.' Dot climbed down stiffly into the cabin, trying not to bend her legs because of the discomfort of cold, wet trousers.

Things on board had improved only a bit over the past fortnight.

'Don't keep on at her,' Maryann had said to Bobby several times during their trips, when the only way he could seem to talk to Dot was to rile her. 'You're upsetting her. She's only like you and me, Bobby. She's got feelings, you know.'

'I'm not keeping on!' he protested sulkily. 'I'm just having a laugh and a joke!'

Maryann was surprised by the strength of Dot's reaction to Bobby. It was only teasing, Maryann could see that herself, and it was the way his own kind of shyness came out. But Dot seemed hurt and enraged and to take it all terribly personally.

'He treats me as if I'm a complete idiot!' she fumed.

Maryann was bewildered by the pair of them and weary of it all, but they managed gradually to work together with a little more civility. Bobby stopped trying to get a rise out of her and Dot mostly ignored him. The result wasn't the most harmonious crew ever, but at least they'd stopped their constant jibing. Last night, though, sitting in the *Esther Jane*, they'd had a spat about the business of the Bottom Road. Dot said contemptuously that it was quite ridiculous having to trek all round the north of Birmingham to get back when they could turn round and go via Warwick. Bobby, whom Maryann knew perfectly well loathed the Bottom Road as much as any other boater, got on his high horse and said it wasn't ridiculous, if she really wanted to know, it was to save water. Dot said she knew perfectly well it was to save water, thank you very much, but it was still ridiculous and they ought to be able to wind the boats and go back. The two of them got really heated and glowered at each other across the table.

'Oh, for goodness *sake*, you two, pack it in!' Maryann snapped at them at last. 'I feel as if I've got two extra kiddies on board with the pair of you. Bobby, if you don't stop going on you can just get out. Go on! Go back there on your own.' She pointed back towards the *Theodore*.

Bobby got up, wearing a surly expression. 'All right, I'll go. I know when I'm not wanted.'

'But it *is* ridiculous,' Dot murmured to his departing back. 'Whatever you say!'

Never mind, Maryann told herself, feeling the rain plopping endlessly onto the scarf she'd tied over her hair and soaking through it. Water ran down her face. All around was the rank smell of slimy mud. She'd see Joel again in a few days and it wouldn't be many more trips before he was back and she didn't have to worry about all these other people. She did feel a pang at the thought, though. She'd miss them now. They'd had a postcard from Sylvia, sent to Sutton Stop on what Dot worked out must have been her first or second day home!

'I *miss* you both ever such a lot. Children well and happy, but can't wait to get back! Keep 'em ahead! All my love, Sylvia.'

Maryann found it very strange that she had thought to write to them so soon when she must have so much to occupy her, seeing her children and her husband again.

Dot had to leave her half-drunk tea to see them

through the locks at Upper Heyford. But not long after they'd got under way again the engine started to take on a sluggish, complaining tone.

Oh, here we go, Maryann thought. *Something's in there.* Instead of anger and impatience she just felt resigned. *I might've known something like this would happen today.* She slowed the engine, turning to signal to Bobby that she was pulling in.

Dot appeared. 'I say, what's up? Problems down below?'

'We've caught a bundle down here,' Maryann said. 'Joley, stay in – you'll get soaked, else.'

Her son scowled up at her from the cabin. 'But I want to come out and help. S'boring in here.' In the background one of the twins wailed and started crying.

'Well, help by keeping yourself dry!' was all Joley got back from his mother.

'Right –' Dot shoved her wet sleeves up her arms once Maryann had brought the boat in – 'let's have a look in there, then.'

Maryann gave a brief nod and stood back out of the way to let Dot at the bilges. Dot had quite a way with the mechanics of the boat and was willing to get stuck in. Maryann was grateful to her. She didn't seem to have the energy for anything herself.

Now the engine was off, all they could hear was the sound of the rain falling into the water. Dot knelt in the wet, leaning forward and reaching down into the sludge-green water, bottom in the air, tugging at the snarled-up mess round the propeller.

'What the hell've we got down here?' she grunted.

Bobby appeared, splashing through the puddles along the path, water dripping off his cap.

'Let's have a look-see then.'

He climbed up on the gunwales, expecting Dot to move, but she completely ignored him.

'What we got in there?' Bobby was all eager, ready to spring into action. Again he received no reply.

'Whole load of stuff,' Maryann said.

Dot got hold of something and and began to pull, but after a moment the piece of what turned out to be rag tore, leaving only a small fragment in her hand. Dot cursed under her breath and went back to her reaching and grunting, hands in the cold, filthy water.

Bobby couldn't contain himself. 'Come on – move over and let us have a look. I'll soon have her freed up.'

Dot pulled herself upright and stood up, muddy water running down her arms. She was breathing heavily and Maryann saw, to her consternation, that she was brimming with emotion.

'All right.' The words exploded out of her like bullets. 'You do it. You're the expert.'

She pushed past Bobby, jumping down onto the bank, and strode off furiously along the towpath, head bowed against the rain. Bobby swivelled round to watch Dot's receding figure.

'I only said . . . What the hell's the matter with her?'

'Oh, Bobby – you could've given her a chance,' Maryann said, exasperated with all this carry-on. 'She's quite good if you let her get on with it. Can't you just keep your mouth shut for five minutes? Look, you get on with it now. I'll go after her.'

Slipping and jumping around the puddles, Maryann followed Dot. Another pair of boats was passing and she saw the man at the tiller turn to look curiously at her.

'Dot – wait!'

She put her hand on Dot's shoulder and Dot stopped and turned grudgingly round. To her surprise, Maryann saw she was in tears.

'Bobby didn't mean anything. He was just trying to help.'

'I *know*.' Dot didn't meet Maryann's eyes, but looked down at her muddy boots. For a moment she seemed like a child.

'Well, what's up then?' She couldn't help her impatience. Here they were, soaked and getting behind on the trip and now there was all this upset.

Dot shrugged angrily. 'He just . . . He always has to do that, doesn't he? Push you around, show he knows best because he's a man and they always have to be in charge. I *hate* it. And I hate *him*.' She let out a deep, shuddering breath, as if suddenly running out of steam. 'No, I don't,' she said more quietly. 'I didn't mean that.' There was a silence as the rain fell. 'I just – he makes me feel . . . peculiar. That's all.' She shook her head, as if ashamed. 'I can't explain. I feel so stupid.'

Maryann could barely begin to understand and she was shivering with cold. 'Come on. Let's get back. We can't go on like this.'

Dot looked up, shamefaced. 'Sorry, Maryann.'

'It's all right. Come on.'

As they walked back, Bobby stood up and they saw him yanking at something, then he stood upright, a grin on his face, waving a tattered length of some filthy object that had been wrapped round the propeller.

'That was quick,' Maryann said. Her teeth were chattering. 'Let's get the kettle on before we go.'

Bobby looked down at Dot, her round face pink from tears and the weather, hair soaked and flattened to her head. 'I just thought you wouldn't want to be in there, in all that muck and mess, that's all.'

He spoke with such straightforward friendliness that no one could have taken offence.

'It's all right,' Dot said stiffly. 'I was being silly.'

'Not *you*?' Bobby said. Hearing the teasing note in his voice, Maryann tensed. Surely he wasn't going to start the whole flaming fight off again?

But Dot gave a cautious smile. 'Yes, me, I'm afraid.'

Dreaming that night, Maryann was back in the old house in Ladywood, the one they had moved to when Norman Griffin came into their lives. The house was the same as then, except that it had no roof. Flo, her mother, was downstairs and she kept sending Maryann upstairs to fetch things. When she went into her old room, it was open to the grey sky and the rain fell onto the bed, gathering in its sunken dip like a small pond, onto the chest of drawers and her few possessions, her hairbrush and comb. Water washed over the floor and poured down the stairs as she climbed up them. She twisted and turned in her bed, trying to escape, to leave the dream, the place. It was nothing she could see, not anything frightening in itself. But the smell of the house came to her, overpowering in the dream, and the way her mother sat, always with her back to her down in the front room, snapping orders, the way the light fell on the stairs and she knew he was there, somewhere, waiting for her, and she couldn't see him ... All these things filled her with horror and a panic that forced up suffocatingly at the back of her throat. She felt a weight on her chest and woke, moaning, fighting for breath.

'Maryann? What's the matter? Aren't you feeling well?'

She'd sat up, moaning, clasping her arms round herself and rocking, still half inside the dream, although she was half awake and could hear Dot's voice from the other end of the bed. She ached for Joel to be there, to hold her.

'Hey – whatever is it? Goodness, you're shaking.' Dot moved closer, putting her hands on Maryann's shoulders. Her tone was soft and full of sympathy. Maryann could only whimper a reply.

'Bad dream, eh?' Dot's arms came round her now. 'I know. It's lousy, isn't it?'

Dot didn't ask any more questions, as if she knew already that they could not be answered. She just held Maryann until she was calmer, the atmosphere of the dream fading a little. She would have liked to put a light on, to get up and do everyday things to push away the feelings, the oppressive mood of the night, but she didn't want to wake the girls.

After a time she whispered, 'I'll be all right now.'

'Righty ho,' Dot said doubtfully, releasing her. 'But don't be afraid to wake me.'

Maryann lay on her back, looking up into the dark, the sound of the rain insistent on the roof.

It was only when they reached Oxford that she was able to let out some of her feelings. She laid her head on Joel's shoulder and wept until she could weep no more, and he held her close, comforting her as he had always done.

'It's him, I know it is,' Maryann sobbed.

Joel's eyes had shown his horror and reluctance to believe it when she told him about Amy. He was so

264

kind, Maryann thought, looking at his big, gentle form in Alice Simons's little room. She knew it had been hard at first for him to take it in, to believe what effect Norman Griffin had had on herself and Sal as children, and she had only ever told him a little. He knew of Norman Griffin's cruelty. He'd seen the effects of it on Amy and Margaret. But she had never talked, even to him, about what else their stepfather had done to them all, robbing them of their bodies, their sexual innocence. She knew that Joel found even the part he did know hard to believe. He had once told her he found it harder to take in than what he'd seen in the trenches.

'I was there though, then, see,' she remembered him saying. 'You have to believe your own eyes, don't you? And that was war. But what he did – to children – well, that was something else altogether.'

As he held her now, she knew he would be having the same struggle to believe in the further wickedness of what had happened.

'What makes you so sure?' he asked, eventually.

Maryann pulled back and looked into his eyes. He had to believe her. She knew it was the truth. 'Because he's on the warpath. He is – I remember the way he looked at me in the church that night. I don't know what he wants, but he won't stop until he's got it.'

Twenty-Nine

'Maryann?'

Dot leapt up onto the *Esther Jane*, making Maryann almost jump out of her skin. She was sitting on the bench facing the stove, dazed, as if unable to move. She had been about to do something. What was it? She couldn't seem to hold a thought in her head for long and Rose and the twins would keep on, 'Mom ... Mom ...' and she'd get as far as saying absently, 'What?' and then not hear the rest of what they said to her.

'You all right?' Dot asked. She came down and squeezed herself onto the coalbox, looking at Maryann with embarrassed concern. Dot wasn't comfortable with emotions and Maryann felt herself stiffen and go red with embarrassment.

'I will be,' she said tersely. 'Just getting cleared up.'

Dot, seeing she wasn't going to get anywhere, stood up and went again.

But Maryann had seen it in Dot's eyes, the thought, *I know you're not all right, but I don't know what to say* ... Her nights were full of dreams now, fragments of childhood which she forced away from her memory when she was awake, but which made her cry out or wake up sobbing and shaking. It had not been as bad as this for years, not since she first ran away and started working at the big house, Charnwood, near Banbury. A number of times Dot had had to comfort her, and in the darkness

266

she had held Maryann, speaking to her with a sweet gentleness that Maryann was learning to accept instead of pushing her away, but which she found hard to reconcile with Dot's awkward gruffness in the daytime. And in daylight she could not seem to keep her mind on anything, could not remember from moment to moment what she was supposed to be doing. It didn't help that she knew why it was happening to her. Through all the shocks and loss of the past months she had managed to hold onto herself, to keep the past at bay, even when Norman Griffin came back into her life. If any memories had forced themselves at her she had pushed her mind elsewhere, made herself go numb as she had when he was with her, forcing himself on her. But the horror of Amy's death seemed to have stripped her, left her bare and there was no Joel, her support and mainstay, to rescue her and keep her safe. She was frightened, overwhelmed by her feelings. It seemed to take an effort almost beyond her strength for her to stand up and get on with all her chores that morning. The kettle was boiling furiously on the stove. How long had it been like that? she wondered, yanking it off the heat. She must get on – they had to get moving . . .

It had been Bobby's idea that they make the trip down to London. Mr Veater had no trouble finding loads needed for Limehouse. The war effort's hunger for coal was bottomless. Bobby would find a boat to crew his way back on and they could pick up Sylvia for the return trip now that the Easter holidays were over.

Spring had truly arrived over the past fortnight and suddenly the worst of the cold had passed. Standing at the helm, Maryann felt her limbs relax a little in the warmer breeze, after the months of cold. The boats were heavily weighed down with a full load of coal and tidily sheeted up by Dot and Bobby. She tried to keep her concentration together. Once they got onto the Grand Union, you could turn a bend and find yourself nose to nose with the huge river barges, which loomed above tiny narrowboats. To her surprise, Dot had suddenly said she'd take the older girls and stay awhile on the *Theodore*, to give them a lesson with the boys, while they were on a stretch with none too many locks. But Maryann read the worst into this. Normally Dot would have done anything to avoid being too near Bobby. *She wants to get away from me*, she thought. *Can't blame her, I suppose.* But she suddenly felt sad and lonely with just Ada and Esther on the roof. Rejected, almost. As they drew closer to Sutton Stop, she turned to signal that she was slowing down. Bobby was standing in his usual easy fashion, cap perched on the back of his head, tiller behind him, and to Maryann's surprise Dot was standing out there beside him and they were talking, apparently quite amiably. It took her a moment to get their attention.

I should be glad, she thought. It's about time they stopped being so silly and got on with each other. But that day the sight of them together made her feel even more bleak and alone.

The journey south went smoothly. Maryann was astonished at how smoothly, considering she felt as if the days were passing in a dream. She was exhausted. It seemed so long since she had had a really good night's sleep. She felt as if the flashes of memory – sometimes not even memory, discomfort rather – were sapping all her energy. They came south towards Stoke Bruerne and once more she was steering the boat alone. When Dot had said earlier that she'd go aboard the *Theodore* again, Maryann teased her.

'You're getting mighty friendly with Bobby all of a sudden!'

'Oh, don't be so *silly*,' Dot said huffily. 'Joley and Ezra want to fish off the side and I said I'd help.'

'I don't think you'll catch much like that, will you?' Maryann said.

'You never know – and it'll keep them happy for a bit. You don't mind, do you?'

'No.' She wanted to ask, why can't you stay on here with me and do it, but she felt childish and bit back the words. Of course Bobby was the main attraction for Joley and Ezra – he'd always been Joley's hero.

So she steered the *Esther Jane* with no one else on board except Ada and Esther. They were napping in the cabin as the boats came towards Blisworth Tunnel at Stoke Bruerne. The black mouth of the tunnel grew bigger as they drew closer, swallowing the front of the boat. Its cold shadow fell over her and abruptly Maryann found herself in the darkness. She had put her scarf and coat on in preparation, collar up, as the place was permanently dank and dripping, cold water splashing down on you.

She forced herself to concentrate on the steering. It was hard at first, disorientating to be plunged into darkness; it was easy to lose any sense of direction and steer the boat into the opposite bank and end up veering back and forth, crashing into the walls. There was only the boat's dim lamp ahead, with no light from an oncoming boat. She peered ahead, sometimes standing on tiptoe to try and see better, glancing back every so often to make sure the *Theodore*'s light was following behind. In here, if the snubber snapped, there'd be no chance of hearing a cry over the echo of the engine, which roared off the curved brick roof of the tunnel, filling her ears so it was impossible to hear anything but the loudest of sounds over it.

Every so often ventilation shafts in the roof let in a ghostly cylinder of light from above, from the world outside, convincing you for a few seconds that real daylight still existed. Otherwise, for over a mile and a half, all was darkness and engine throb, and the dim yellow beam of light casting forward only a few yards onto the ripples to show the way. A freezing splash of water dropped down the back of her neck.

After a time she saw the far end of the tunnel, a tiny dot of light at first, growing very slowly bigger. *Thank heaven for the motor*, she thought, shuddering at how they would have had to get through here the old way, when the horses would be walked over the top and the men lay out on planks half over the black water, feet pressed to the wall to leg the boat through step by step.

It came over her with no warning, about halfway through. She could not have said exactly what set it off: some half thought or memory, or simply the darkness, the way the white light so far away never seemed to get any bigger, however much they moved towards it. The blackness became suffocating, as if it had weight and was pressing itself on top of her. Her lungs felt crushed, incapable of pumping air in and out. Heat rose in her, her own body seeming to suffocate her and she was sweating and overtaken by panic. She tore her coat off, flung it down into the cabin and bent over the tiller gasping for breath. Her lungs were sobbing as if she had run to the summit of a cold mountain. Her neck and forehead were wet with sweat.

Maryann was jerked back to her surroundings when

270

the *Esther Jane* hit the opposite wall with an awful crack and scrape and she was almost flung over backwards. She just managed to clutch onto the cabin roof, and immediately fought to straighten out the boat and get her running on the right side of the channel.

It was a few moments before she gained proper control again, the tiller was throbbing in her hand and she was trembling with shock. She leaned on the cabin and, knowing no one would hear, let out a great howl of pain which echoed round her amid the throb of the engine.

When the boat finally moved out into the sunshine it was like emerging from a nightmare. She breathed in hard, still shaky but longing for the light, for the sense of release it brought. Stoke Bruerne was busy, and Maryann knew they should press on through, but the moment she saw the familiar buildings along the canal she was filled with longing. It made her think of Nance and the time they'd brought their children in together to see Sister Mary Ward. She wanted desperately, suddenly, to see Sister Mary. Just the thought of the woman's comforting face would make her feel better. She turned and signalled that they were going to stop.

Holding Ada's and Esther's hands, Maryann walked to Sister Mary's little front-room surgery. Another boat-woman, heavily pregnant, came out and then it was their turn.

The sight of Sister Mary in her white overall and long white veil, even the smell of iodine steadied her. Sister Mary was busy over on one side of the room. Maryann heard the clink of glass as she arranged a jar on the shelf. After a moment Sister Mary looked round and gave her warm smile.

'Ah – now I know you, don't I?'

Maryann found herself smiling back. 'I haven't been to see you in a while, Sister. Last time, I came with my friend Nance – Nancy Bartholomew.'

'Of course, the Bartholomews.' Sister Mary came across and gestured for Maryann to sit down. 'You take a rest when you can, dear.' She looked solemn. 'I remember. Poor, poor Nancy. That was a real tragedy. I was so very sorry to hear about it. That must have been a couple of winters ago now?'

Maryann nodded, looking down into her lap as her eyes filled. She spoke more roughly than she meant to.

'Can you look these two over for me?'

'Ah now – ' Sister Mary bent over, putting her hands together almost as if praying and smiled at Ada and Esther – 'I remember these two as babies, don't I? Let's have a look at the pair of you then, shall we?'

As she examined the girls, their heads, necks, ears and throats, she asked after the rest of the family. Maryann told her about Joel's accident, about the trainees.

'Oh – we have quite a few of them up and down here.' Sister Mary laughed. 'You've got a couple of them working on the Oxford as well now, have you? Most of them are marvellous, of course – there's just the odd one or two can get a bit uppity.' She glanced at Maryann as she worked, and after observing that Ada might need her tonsils out one day she pronounced the twins to be fit and bonny.

'And what about their mother? Are you keeping well?'

Maryann nodded, feeling herself crumple, hearing the kindness in her tone. Her throat hurt with the effort of not breaking down. 'Mostly. You know how it is.'

Sister Mary knew all too well. After years of working with the boatwomen she was awed by their stamina and

272

capacity for endurance. Her eyes twinkled down at Maryann.

'No problems, then?'

Problems? Maryann longed just to lay her head on the woman's shoulder and sob out all her need and confusion. She shook her head, but the tears welled up again unbidden. She was getting up out of her chair to leave, afraid of embarrassing herself, but Sister Mary gently took her arm and encouraged her to stay sitting.

'What is it, dear?'

Shaking her head, Maryann felt sobs rising up again. She was so mortified, she wished she could become invisible. How could she even begin to tell Sister Mary what she felt, however kind the woman was?

'I can't say ... it's nothing.' She wiped her eyes on her sleeve and stood up. She couldn't begin crying: if she did she might never stop. 'I'm just being silly. I just feel a bit anyhow today, that's all.'

Sister Mary watched her with concern, but she could see that Maryann was determined not to say more.

'Well, you make sure you look after yourself properly, dear. Don't put yourself last all the time, will you?' She opened the door to let Maryann out. 'Goodbye, dear – I'm always here, you know.'

Thirty

Limehouse Dock was very busy. Once again they moved across the great expanse of water, dwarfed by many of the vessels around them. They joined the queue for unloading and got busy on all the chores and the shopping. By the time they had finished those it was dinnertime, but their two heavily laden boats were still waiting.

'When's this Sylvia coming, then?' Bobby asked through a mouthful of bread and cheese. He was seated casually on the back of the *Esther Jane*, feet on the bank.

'Oh, she's not coming here,' Maryann said. 'She's s'posed to be getting a train up to join us in a day or two. She doesn't know we're down here.'

'Seems silly, doesn't it?' Dot said, perched up beside Ezra on the cabin roof, tea mug in hand. 'Why don't we telephone her? Have you the number?'

'No. Got the address, though.'

'Well –' Dot tipped her dregs into the water and jumped down with a thud onto the platform – 'we'll just have to scout out a telephone directory.'

'Don't you know where she lives?' Bobby asked. 'Dunno why you don't just go and see her.'

'I say –' Dot turned to Maryann, excited – 'how about it? We could surprise her! What if we took the kiddies along? It'd be a little outing for them as well.'

Maryann looked at Bobby, who gave his easy smile. 'I'll see to the unloading. Don't you fret.'

As they began on their journey, having speedily gathered up the children, Dot looked back at the pair of boats and said, 'I never cease to be amazed by Bobby's relaxed attitude to life.'

'Oh, he's a good'un,' Maryann said. 'Nice family, the Jenkses.'

They made their way through the shabby Limehouse streets and got onto a crowded bus, standing all the way, packed in. Maryann saw Dot wrinkle her nose as she registered the strong smell of unwashed bodies pressed close to them. Peering out between people's heads, Maryann caught glimpses of the damage the Blitz had inflicted on the East End. She was glad Dot knew London so well as she guided them onto the Underground. Rose looked really frightened at being led down into a dark, squalid hole in the ground. Dot took her hand and reminded her that they would soon be seeing Auntie Sylvia, and the little girl's face relaxed, her eyes lighting up. Soon all the children were peering out, watching excitedly for each stop. There were a few moments of peace, and Maryann felt she might easily fall asleep here in the warm, stuffy carriage, rocking back and forth, her coat on to cover her grubby frock. She gave a wide yawn, feeling muzzy in the head. She felt Dot looking at her.

'I'm not very good at talking about things and so forth,' Dot said abruptly. 'Thing is, Maryann, you've obviously got something on your mind. Don't want to pry. But – I can't help but notice – bad nights and so forth.' Dot was blushing, looking down at her plump thighs, clad in black corduroy. 'If I can be of any help, you would say . . .?'

Maryann was touched, but at the same time the old panic rose in her. *Don't ask me! Don't let anyone find out!* How could she possibly explain to Dot – how could she name the strange feelings she had? It was true Dot had family problems, but nothing like this. Sometimes she longed to pour it all out to someone. But she couldn't even tell Joel! She sensed he didn't really want to hear it. So far as he was concerned, past was past and they had their own family now. Did anyone, ever, really want to hear the truth? She didn't believe they did. Naked truth was too horrible. She swallowed hard.

'It's all right, Dot. I just have the odd nightmare sometimes. Don't know why.'

It seemed a long walk from the tube station to Sylvia's, but the afternoon was warm and pleasant.

'Is this her house?' the girls kept asking, but then there were so many houses on the way that they gave up and became weary and just stared round them.

'Aren't we *ever* going to get there?' Sally complained wearily, her old boots scuffing along the pavement.

Looking at her children, Maryann was suddenly full of misgivings. Now they were away from the cut and in this neat neighbourhood with its little front gardens with trimmed hedges, they did all look a scruffy bunch with their old clothes and grimy skin!

'D'you think she'll mind?' she said as they looked over the gate. 'I mean us turning up, showing her up?'

Dot snorted. 'Oh, I can't imagine so! Sylvia's not like that, is she?'

Isn't she? Maryann thought. How could they really know what she'd be like away from the cut and in her nice home? The neighbourhood was such a world away from the jerry-built Ladywood houses she'd grown up in that she felt nervous and out of place.

Sylvia's house was painted white, but Maryann was at once disappointed and relieved to see that the roses and shrubs in the front garden looked straggly and there was plenty of groundsel and dandelions. It spoiled her pretty picture of Sylvia's perfect house! But, of course, Sylvia had not been at home to see to any of it, and the fact that everything was not perfectly neat made her feel reassured. The house had a pea-green front door, with a window set into it edged with coloured-glass fruits. A cinder path ran alongside the grass.

'I wonder if her husband's here,' Maryann found herself whispering. 'What's his name again?'

'Roy.' Even Dot was whispering. '*Darling* Roy.'

'Oh yes – how could I forget!' This set them both off into giggles and for a few moments they were both helpless with nervous laughter in the road.

'What's so funny?' Sally frowned at them. 'Aren't we going to knock on the door?'

Ezra ran ahead and started banging his fist on the lower part of the door and Maryann went and dragged him back, saying, '*Sssh!* Don't!'

'One way to find out.' Dot's hand was poised over the knocker. 'Ready?'

Its brass clatter sounded very loud in the silent street. The houses looked down on them from all round, with their anti-blast tape on the windows. Where was everyone? Maryann wondered. The only life about was the lady next door, who stepped out through her front door carrying a cloth bag and peered at them over the wall.

All of them jumped, startled, when the door opened and they found themselves faced with a well-built man with fair hair shorn into a very short serviceman's haircut and a wide, strong face. The man from the photograph.

'Yes?' His voice was clipped and conveyed no expression, either of disapproval or welcome. Maryann could not meet his eyes and kept her gaze on the sharp creases in his trousers, his well-polished black shoes. She saw that the floor was a pale wood parquet. Dot could do the talking. She wasn't going to open her mouth with her Brummie accent and have him sneer at her. She felt instinctively that he might be the sneering type.

'Dorothy Higgs-Deveraux,' Dot announced briskly, though she too appeared uncomfortable as Roy Cresswell looked appraisingly at her generous figure, dressed in her worn black trousers and the brown baggy sweater. The one touch of colour she wore today was a red and green scarf tied as an Alice band to keep her hair back. She pointed at her 'IW' badge. 'I'm a colleague of your wife's – Inland Waterways – National Service. This is Mrs Maryann Bartholomew, whose boat we're crewing. Sylvia's due to join us again tomorrow, of course.'

'I see.' He stood looking at them, holding the door open with one arm, which protruded hairily from his white, short-sleeved shirt.

Well, he's not very pleased to see us, Maryann thought. Though his face betrayed no emotion, she sensed that he was angry.

'Is Sylvia in?' Dot persevered. 'We'd like a word with her.'

'Just a moment.' He swung the door almost closed and they heard him calling, 'Sylvia. Sylv! Someone to see you.'

Dot turned and grimaced at Maryann. 'Not exactly a gushing welcome,' she whispered.

Rose was pulling on Maryann's hand, her face anxious. 'When's Sylvia coming out?'

A moment later the door opened again. Sylvia was wearing a very pretty floral dress with a floating skirt, a white cardigan over the top and leather navy pumps. As ever, she was well made up, with her favourite scarlet lipstick. She looked delicate and feminine. Maryann was quite taken aback. They'd only ever seen Sylvia in her boat clothes and the children looked especially abashed, as if they could barely recognize her. Maryann felt Rose's hand clutching at her skirt for reassurance.

'Oh, my goodness!' Sylvia hissed. She sounded horrified and immediately it all felt a terrible mistake that they'd come here. She glanced behind her and pulled the front door closed and squatted down so that her skirt fell in soft swathes over her knees. 'Oh, Rose, it's all right – come here, darling!'

Rose, whose face had crumpled ready for tears, let go of Maryann and went shyly to Sylvia, who immediately cuddled her, despite Rose's grubby frock. Sylvia greeted all the other children and then stood up, still holding Rose's hand. She looked back anxiously towards the door again and gestured them to move further away along the path.

'Is everything all right?' Maryann asked. There was a tight fearfulness in Sylvia's face that she had never seen before.

'I'm *so* sorry.' Sylvia spoke quickly, in short bursts. 'I'd love to invite you in – only I can't. The children could have played in the garden if . . . but not with Roy here, you see. He's very . . . particular about everything, you see. You do understand, don't you?'

'Where're your children?' Maryann asked. She was filled with unease at the sight of Sylvia. She looked lovely, fresh and well groomed, and she was the same, sweet-natured Sylvia, yet somehow quite different.

'Oh, Kay and Dickie have gone back to school. I put them on the train yesterday. It was a couple of days early, but I thought it was for the best. I wasn't expecting Roy home, you see – not now – and he likes to have me to himself. He had a couple of extra days' leave, you see.' She gave a valiant smile.

'So you don't want to come back with us today?' Dot tried to joke. 'You don't look dressed for the part, I must say.'

'No – it'll be a couple of days. I'll find you – don't you worry. If it all goes wrong, I'll get to Sutton and pick you up there. Oh look – ' she glanced behind her – 'it's so sweet of you to come and I'm longing to see you all properly, but I'd better not stay now.' She began to back down the path. 'Roy goes back tomorrow. I just need to stay and see him off.'

'It's all right – you make the most of it.' Maryann felt herself twist up inside, though she didn't really know why. Sylvia seemed so anxious and unlike her normal self. 'We'll get back and help Bobby with the unloading. You enjoy the rest of your time. Have a bath for us both, won't you?'

'Oh,' Sylvia said yearningly, 'I *wish* I could ask you in, I really do! It's a bit difficult to explain.'

'You're all right – I was only joking,' Maryann called lightly, shepherding the children in front of her. 'TTFN!'

'Cheerio, Sylvia!' Dot called.

Sylvia waved and, as she pushed the front door open, they caught a glimpse of Roy Cresswell standing in the hall, arms hanging at his sides. Then the door closed.

As they went out of the gate, the woman from next door was coming towards them along the pavement. Her bag was still empty and Maryann sensed she had been waiting for them. She was in her thirties, hair scraped into a bun, and wearing a faded flowery frock.

'Could I have a word?' She spoke in a quiet, guarded voice, looking back at Sylvia's house.

'Of course,' Dot said.

'You'll probably think I'm ever such a nosy-parker,' the woman said, fiddling with the frayed handles of the bag. 'My name's Lois, by the way. Lois Parmenter. Are you friends of the lady in that house?'

'Yes,' Dot said. 'What's the trouble?'

'Well, I don't know, that's the thing. Dear, oh dear, you are going to think I'm an interfering busybody.' Her eyes darted anxiously back and forth between Dot's and Maryann's faces. 'You see, I've been wondering because I haven't been living here all that long and there hasn't been anyone in next door for some weeks.'

Dot explained briefly that Sylvia had been away working with them.

'Oh, I see – well yes. But then they came home and the kiddies were playing outside and that was all per-fectly all right. And Mrs – Cresswell, isn't it? Yes, we exchanged a few words. But then her husband's been about once or twice, and he's there now. It's just that, well, he seems a bit of a queer fish. Oh dear, I do feel funny about asking, but I just wondered if everything's all right.'

Maryann immediately sensed that the woman was not just being nosy, that something had caused her to feel real concern.

'We don't know, really,' she said. 'We don't know him either. But Sylvia's coming back to work with us tomorrow.'

'Oh – oh good. Well, that's probably all right then.'

The woman started to back away. 'Sorry to bother you.' She retreated inside her gate. 'Sorry,' she said again. 'Goodbye.'

They retreated down the road, pacifying the disappointed children, who had all hoped to see Sylvia's nice house and be able to run in her garden.

'Look, I tell you what,' Maryann said, fishing in her pocket. There was a corner shop at the end of the road. 'I've got this week's coupons – we'll go and get you some rocks, eh?'

The children cheered up immediately at the thought of sweets.

'Take them in, will you, Dot?' Maryann handed her the ration coupons. 'Get them sorted out. I don't like this. I'm going to go back.'

'What the hell're you talking about?' Dot said. 'Go back? What, knock on the door and ask Roy Cresswell why he's such a "queer fish"? You can't do that!'

'I *know*,' Maryann snapped. 'What d'you take me for?'

'Well, what can you possibly do?'

'I don't know.' Maryann couldn't explain the tight feeling of dread in her chest that Roy Cresswell had given her. 'I've just got to ... to see. Hang on for me a few minutes, will you?'

Full of nerves and afraid she was being stupid, she hurried back along the crescent towards Sylvia's house. To her relief, Lois Parmenter had gone indoors. An elderly man scuttled along the pavement with a hairy terrier, which seemed to be pulling him along at the full stretch of its lead. The man touched the brim of his hat with two fingers and was propelled off round the corner.

Maryann felt very foolish. The house was quiet, just as when they had left. Supposing Sylvia saw her out of the window? What on earth would she say to her? She opened the front gate very quietly and closed it behind her, gritting her teeth. Her heart was banging wildly. What the hell did she think she was doing? She should just turn back now and go: stop being so downright ridiculous. But she felt driven on, partly through curiosity, but also by a sense of recognition. That fear she had seen in Sylvia's face, the instinct that she was hiding something, that there was a dimension to her life that she could never admit to anyone. These were things Maryann knew herself as if they travelled in her blood. She recognized them when she saw them in someone else. And she doubted if Sylvia would ever tell them. She would just suffer on in respectable silence.

There was no sound at the front of the house and all the windows were closed. The front windows were swathed in net curtains. The houses were built in twos, semi-detached. Maryann eyed the little path running round to the back garden. She pushed past a hydrangea bush and stepped into the shadow of the house, its wall to one side, a fence on the other.

This is daft, she thought, heart pounding. *I'll just have a peep at the garden and then I'll go. What am I going to see doing this?*

She heard something then, though. Faintly, from somewhere at the back, she could hear a man's voice. Sliding along the side of the building, Maryann saw there was a window open further along and she moved until she was standing close to it. It must be the kitchen's side window, she realized: she could hear water running, then the clatter of cutlery being put into a drawer. There was a long silence, though Maryann could hear movements from inside, and her curiosity got the better of her. She leaned round and peered through the window, quickly moving back again so that no one should see her. But in that moment she saw that Sylvia was on the other side of the room at the sink, with her back to her, and she just caught a glimpse of Roy Cresswell sitting at the table, bent over something.

Maryann leaned round again. Roy Cresswell had one hand on the table and was holding a cigarette, above which the smoke hovered in an upward swirl. With the other he was holding a box, or biscuit tin, and shaking it, examining the contents. Maryann squinted. She couldn't make out what was in the tin, but there was a shape on the table beside him, and she realized he must be building a model ship out of matches, or small slivers of wood. She could see three masts sticking up from the main hull.

Sylvia was wringing a cloth out at the sink. She hung it over the tap, dried her hands and placed the towel over the back of the chair with slow, deliberate neatness. As Sylvia turned, undoing her apron, Maryann shrank back until she was still just able to peer round the window-frame. Sylvia tugged at the apron strings and there was sharp anger in her movements. For a moment she stood with it crumpled in her hand, then flung it decisively down onto the table.

'D'you know, Roy—'

He looked up, evidently startled by her tone.

'I really don't care what you think. You're going tomorrow, anyway, so what possible difference can it make to you? I'm going back and that's that. And it doesn't matter a fig to me any more what you think about it. Think what you like.'

And she strode out of Maryann's line of vision and left the kitchen.

Roy Cresswell sat for a moment staring ahead of him with the same blank expression. Maryann saw his jaw tighten. With a sudden movement, which made her jump, he brought his fist down on top of the matchstick model, smashing through it. He picked up the tin and hurled it with great force across the kitchen. Matches flew out and spilled all over the floor.

Thirty-One

They were up early the next morning. Dot handed Maryann a cup of tea in through the hatches, and she and Bobby stayed outside on the towpath, hands cupped round the hot mugs, shivering in the early morning chill although the sun was already beginning to break through. Around them they could hear the clanking of cranes beginning to work, the splash of water as men pumped out the holds of their boats and the distant, mournful sound of a ship's siren. Soon the tannoy would start crackling and blaring over the wharves, calling crews to be assigned their loads.

They'd talked it over and over the night before – Roy Cresswell and the burst of temper Maryann had seen through the window.

'I just don't like the look of him at all,' Maryann said on the way home, while the children were quietened by mouthfuls of sweets. 'The way he threw that box across the room – and the way his face was. There's something about him makes my flesh creep.'

'He certainly struck me as *odd*,' Dot said, 'but in the end you didn't really see anything much, and you can't just go barging in on other people's marriages, can you? Sylvia'll be back with us in a day or two, anyway.'

'Darling Roy,' Maryann mused. 'She's ever so loyal to him.'

'Or the lady doth protest too much.'

'What d'you mean?'

'I'd guess she's been covering up for him a bit. She's certainly succeeded up until now, I'll give her that. But she is nervy, isn't she? Maybe that husband of hers accounts for it.'

They busied themselves with the morning chores, Maryann sorting out the children and shooing them outside, then starting on breakfast, and Dot and Bobby readying the boats for loading. Maryann had just begun on the food when she heard a cry of excitement from Rose, who was jumping excitedly on the counter.

'Look – Sylvia's coming!'

'No –' Maryann called up to her. 'Not today, bab. She'll be along soon, though. Couple of days.'

But Rose was off along the path and then Dot poked her head into the *Esther Jane*, looking bemused.

'Sylvia's already here, it seems.'

Maryann climbed out, shading her eyes in the morning glare. Sylvia's neat figure was moving towards them along the path, carrying her bundle of belongings. As soon as she was close enough she threw it down on the path. She looked pale and exhausted. After a second Maryann realized this was almost the first time she had seen Sylvia without her make-up. It made her feel uneasy.

'Hello, stranger!' Dot exclaimed. 'What're you doing here?'

'You're early!' Maryann said. 'How the heck did you get here by this time?'

Sylvia gave a tight smile. 'Oh, Roy decided he ought to get back to his squadron a day early. So I thought, rather than miss you, I'd high-tail it over here as soon as I could. I woke very early, so I walked some of the way until the buses started running. Anyway, here I am. Sorry about yesterday, by the way.'

'Not at all,' Dot said. 'Did your husband get off all right?'

'Oh yes,' Sylvia said brightly, leaning down slowly to pick up her things. As she bent over she gave a little grunt, as if it was a huge effort. Maryann saw Dot glance at her.

'Here, let me take that.' Dot swooped down for the bundle. 'I expect you're worn out already – you must have been up well before the lark! Oh, this is Bobby by the way.'

'I'll get you some tea,' Bobby said.

'Thanks awfully.' Sylvia straightened up, and they all pretended not to see the tears in her eyes, which she quickly brushed away. 'I could certainly do with it. And, Bobby, I'm sorry if this inconveniences you dreadfully. Are you going to be able to get another trip?'

'Oh, I s'pect so,' he said easily. 'Don't you worry.'

'Thanks awfully.' Sylvia's eyes filled again. 'You're so kind, Bobby.'

She held out her arms to Rose, who was waiting expectantly.

'Are you coming with us now, Sylvia?' Rose asked.

'Oh, yes,' Sylvia said. Suddenly she held the little girl close and the tears she had been holding back spilled down her face. She put Rose down. 'It's all right, darling,' Sylvia reassured her, wiping her eyes again, but still unable to stem her tears. 'It's so lovely to see you, but I do miss my Kay and Dickie as well. Oh, I'm sorry – I didn't mean to do this!'

'You're all right,' Maryann comforted her. 'Why don't you just go and settle in? I'll get us some breakfast.'

'Why's Sylvia crying?' Sally asked as Dot helped Sylvia take her things to the *Theodore*. With Bobby gone, Dot would be able to move back in there herself.

'Oh – I think it's just saying goodbye to her children and her house,' Maryann said. But she felt uneasy. Seeing Sylvia's house yesterday and her husband, she had suddenly begun to view her in a new light. She had so much wanted to believe in a perfect marriage and family, a perfect life, but it wasn't like that. Somehow she felt cheated and worried for Sylvia. But she couldn't just ask, could she? Not about things that were private like that. She knew she didn't like it when people asked her questions.

Bobby was taking the last of his things from the cabin of the *Theodore* when she carried food over to them. Maryann felt a rush of fondness for him.

'Here, get that down you before you go.' She handed him a couple of sausages with hunks of bread. 'Thanks, Bobby – you've been marvellous. And we'll be back to normal soon – Joel back and that.'

Bobby nodded shyly. 'S'all right. I shouldn't have no problem finding a trip. We'll all be back right as rain in a few weeks. Sorry to go, though.' He glanced at the cabin of the *Theodore* and just as he did so Dot climbed out.

'Breakfast,' Maryann said. 'Pass the other one to Sylvia, will you?'

'I'll be off then, soon.' Bobby said.

'So you will.' Dot stood, somehow at a loss. She looked down at her boots then back at Bobby. 'It won't be the same – not without you to squabble with!'

A grin spread over Bobby's handsome face. 'You're all right,' he said, then added with a chuckle, 'Dorothy Higgs-Deveraux!'

Dot blushed. 'All right – I can't help it!'

There was a crackle and a hiss and a voice called out harshly over the tannoy, 'Mrs Bartholomew, Bartholomew, of S. E. Barlow carriers – to the office, please!'

Putting her half-finished breakfast down, Maryann hurried over to be assigned the next load.

The office was already humming with activity and the red-faced man at the desk handed her her clearance papers, hardly even looking up at her.

'Steel billets – up to Tyseley.'

Maryann froze. She couldn't seem to force her hand out to take the papers. She could hear the blood banging in her ears.

'Come on – here y'are.'

'But—'

'What's the matter?' He spoke impatiently. 'You're unloaded and ready, aren't you?'

'Yes.' How could she begin to explain why the thought of going to Birmingham filled her with such fear? There was a huge quantity of steel to be shipped to the Midlands and it was one of the main cargoes and a good load. Why on earth would she object? The silence went on and her cheeks burned. She felt more and more stupid, as if everyone in the office was watching her. Forcing her hand out, she took the papers and walked shakily out into the fresh morning. She pulled her old cardigan round her and stood for a moment, looking out across the low tide of the dock. She took in a deep breath, smelling the rank mud.

I won't be afraid, she told herself. *I won't let him make me be afraid.* And she turned and marched back to the boats, where the others were waiting.

'Right, let's get going,' she said. 'We're carrying steel to Tyseley.'

'Can you come?'

Dot was standing out in the darkness. They'd tied up

290

quite late after the first long day of work, of getting used to crewing together again. 'It's Sylvia. In a state. I need you. You know me. Can't think what to say.'

Maryann glanced round her cabin. The children were only just settling for the night.

'I've got to go and see Sylvia for a minute. Go to sleep,' she commanded, fairly certain they would. It had been a hard day and it was late. She felt fluttery with nerves, wondering what was wrong. It was only at times like this that the age gap between Dot and the other two of them became so obvious. Dot hadn't the experience of men and marriage.

It had started to drizzle and Maryann could feel the droplets brushing her face as they stumbled back to the butty in the dark. From inside the *Theodore* came the low sound of Sylvia sobbing. Maryann felt Dot's hand on her arm.

'Thing is,' she whispered, 'she's been all right all day. At least I thought she was. We were just getting ready for bed and I knocked her with my elbow by mistake, when I was taking off my woolly. And she just *crumpled*. I don't know . . . I'm so bad at all this.'

So am I, Maryann thought. She already felt over-wrought because of her own worries, but she was full of unease about what she had seen at Sylvia's house. Not that she'd seen much, but there was just something about the atmosphere, about Roy Cresswell that had disturbed her.

'Let's go in to her,' she whispered to Dot.

Sylvia was sitting on the side bench opposite the stove, on which the dipper stood which she had been using to have a wash. Rose was flat out, asleep on the bigger bed. Sylvia had her blouse unbuttoned down the front and was holding the sides of it together across her chest,

291

arms wrapped round herself, head down and shivering. Maryann cautiously sat beside her.

'Sylv?' she spoke softly, but instinct told her not to touch the woman.

There was a silence before Sylvia said, 'I just can't stop crying.' She sniffed and loosed one arm to search for her hanky. It was the first time Maryann could remember her not having one to hand. She wiped her eyes, but more tears ran down her cheeks, shining in the lamplight. She stared ahead of her. Her shivering seemed to increase in intensity.

Dot picked up the kettle and indicated that she was going outside to fill it from the water can. 'I think we need some tea,' she said.

Into the silence, Maryann whispered, 'What happened?'

Sylvia turned to her, looking into Maryann's eyes as if seaching for something and her own filled with tears again.

'Oh, Maryann, I've tried so hard, for so long.'

'I know,' Maryann said soothingly, sensing it was the right thing to say. 'I know you have.'

Abruptly, Sylvia pulled open her blouse and let it slide down over her shoulders so she was naked but for her brassiere.

'*This* is what happened.'

Even in the poor light Maryann could see the welts, sharp and angry across Sylvia's back and shoulders. Just then Dot climbed back in and stared, wide-eyed, at the sight of Sylvia's back.

'Dear God!' she breathed.

'Oh, Sylvia.' Maryann couldn't hide how appalled she felt either. 'That looks terrible. Why didn't you say before? Those must have hurt so much all day while you were working. Dot, get the kettle on and we'll bathe them for her! Put your blouse on and keep warm a minute, Sylv.' She tried to sound calm, but she felt shaky, horrified at the violence inflicted on Sylvia's back. The marks were big and deep and angry.

'He did most of it with his belt.' Sylvia was sobbing, shaking. She looked up, with frightened eyes. 'The thing is, I think I've just left my marriage.'

The words sunk into the quiet of the room.

'He did that to me last night after we'd got ready for bed. I'd told him I was coming back here, to the boats. He doesn't like me working or doing anything outside the house at all. It's got worse since the children have been away. I suppose he thought they kept me inside, in his control. I never went to bed afterwards, last night. I sat up until he'd fallen asleep and then I got all my things ready bundled up and I left before it was light. Walked for miles. Didn't care. I've . . . I think I've left him,' she said again.

'But – your children?' Dot jiggled the kettle as if hoping this would encourage it to boil faster.

'Well, fortunately they've just gone back for another term.' She drifted off, still hugging herself, rocking slightly back and forth.

'Has he done this to you a lot?' Maryann asked gently.

'No – oh no. Hardly ever. Just once or twice, but never as bad as this. This isn't the worst thing. Not really. At least when he did this he was full of – something that I could see. Something like feeling, any-way.' She glanced at Maryann for a second. 'I'm afraid there's something terribly wrong with my husband. It's taken me years to see exactly. I always thought it was me, you see. That I was doing something wrong.'

293

Dot poured some warm water into a basin.

'Let us see to those sores, Sylvia, eh?'

'There's a clean hanky of mine under my pillow,' Sylvia said. 'And I've got a bottle of witch hazel – over there.' She pointed. 'There's iodine somewhere.'

Between them, with gentle hands, Maryann and Dot bathed all the welts and cuts and dabbed iodine and witch hazel on the cuts and bruises. Sylvia hissed with pain when they dabbed on the iodine, but she didn't complain. When they'd finished, they helped her ease her nightdress very gingerly over her head and shoulders. Dot made and poured the tea.

'Perhaps you could do with some of this?' Dot held out the whisky bottle.

'Yes,' Maryann and Sylvia said together and Sylvia laughed suddenly.

'Look at us!' she spluttered, voice rising hysterically. 'Dot's even handing it out like medicine!'

'Each one to their poison,' Dot said dryly, pouring a tot into each teacup.

'What did you mean, you thought you were the one in the wrong?' Maryann asked.

For a second Sylvia sagged, leaning her blonde head on Maryann's shoulder. Moved by this, Maryann put her arm gently round Sylvia's waist. After a moment Sylvia braced herself, sitting straight again.

'Roy and I were introduced through a friend of my mother and father. We're both about the same age. He was nice looking – handsome really – and polite. A bit stiff – I noticed it even then, but I thought it was shyness. He liked me, I thought. Oh, I was such a silly thing. I was young and I just thought it was astonishing that any man would like me. Hadn't really had any experience, you see – sheltered life, girls' school. He asked me to

294

marry him quite early on and we got engaged, nice ring, the lot. I mean, it took me quite a time into the marriage to see, *really* see that there was something not right. Roy had been to one of those public schools which can make men a bit sort of stiff and humourless. He was never nasty, exactly, not then. It wasn't anything really that you could put your finger on. He was trying to be pleasant and a few months after the wedding I conceived Kay.' She paused for a moment. 'It took me years to work out that it wasn't me. You couldn't exactly fault Roy. He got a good job in town, he worked hard and we had our children. He was quite considerate, but I always found him very cold, in his feelings. As if he was going through the motions but wasn't really there. That's what I mean about thinking it was me. I thought maybe I couldn't make him feel the right things, make him laugh more or be sort of spontaneous. He's very wooden. I barely knew any other men – not well, and I've no brothers, just Ruth, my sister – so I thought maybe they were all a bit like this and if you were a proper wife you could get round it. I tried so hard. He's always liked me to look the part – you know, nicely dressed and made up. D'you know, I've got to the point where I can't stand my face without make-up now! Silly, isn't it? Anyway, he was all right with the children – not demonstrative, but *proper*. A good provider. But he can't stand change. Not without warning, anyway. I moved the furniture round in the sitting room once while he was at the office and when he came home he was absolutely *furious.*'

She took a drink of tea, then stared bleakly into her mug. 'I've been so lonely. I didn't know how much until I came on here with you two. Actually, just a few months before I came I had to go to my doctor about something. He's a nice man, not one of the sort who talks down to you. Roy had been home on leave then as well and I was feeling very low. Really in the doldrums. He'd been worse than usual – perhaps he found the adjustment to coming home again difficult – but he was cold and silent and wouldn't talk to me or the children. It's like living with a machine, really it is!' She stopped for a moment, fighting back tears.

'He just kept on making these wretched models he's forever building. He's obsessed with them. He gets obsessed with all sorts of odd things ... Anyway, I was so miserable and I didn't have anyone to turn to, and I ended up blurting it all out to the doctor. He was rather wonderful, I must say. He listened and asked me some questions. Then he said, "You really shouldn't be blaming yourself, Mrs Cresswell. I do believe it's not your fault." He told me he thought Roy might have some sort of mental condition. He said there were doctors who'd done new research and that some people were born like Roy, and they can't understand emotions like other people. You see, I felt sometimes, if I looked at Roy and smiled, perhaps, that he was sort of reading my face and waiting to find out what to do before he could smile back. As if he didn't know how without watching me. Anyway – I did feel better thinking he really had something the matter. But then he's still my husband and all these years of living with him have made me feel dead inside. And when the war ends I'd still have to live with it, whether it's my fault or not, and I can't.' She wept again for a moment before going on.

'Yesterday he was very edgy. As bad as I've ever seen him. He was having to go back and he can't stand the fact that I'm on here. He more or less ordered me to give it up and stay at home. He was hateful about it. And I just told him I wasn't going to take any notice of him . . . I rather lost my temper. That *stupid* matchstick ship he keeps fiddling about with and never any proper company or conversation. Not ever, really. That was when he came after me.'

She sat silently, shaking her head, before saying, 'What have I done? I can't take in what I've done.'

'But,' Dot said, 'does your husband know you've left? Really left? I mean you could go back – if you wanted.'

'Oh no. No.' Sylvia sat up straight. 'I'm not going back to that. Never. Whatever I have to do – even if I have to live in a potting shed with Kay and Dickie, I'm not living like that any longer. Being here with you two has shown me how much better things can be. I can't go back.'

Maryann watched Sylvia's face, the determined tilt of her chin as she spoke, feeling for her. *But,* she thought, *you can't just stay here! Joel will be back, and Bobby, and we shan't need you.* But she touched Sylvia's hand, and at this sympathy Sylvia's face crumpled again. 'Whatever have I done?' she said. 'What am I going to do?'

Thirty-Two

'Hello there – you're a sight for sore eyes!'

Maryann walked into the toll office at Tyseley, to be greeted by a familiar gap-toothed smile.

'Awright, Charlie?' She felt a grin spread across her own weary features, which immediately froze again as Charlie said, 'Funny you should roll up today. Had a bloke in with a message for you yesterday. Come in special like. Here – what's up with you? Don't you want to hear it?'

'No!' she was already on her way out of the office. They had to leave straight away. How did he know? The very day she was coming back to Birmingham – only hours before and he was here, looking for her! Her chest tightened until she could scarcely breathe and every hair seeming to stand up on her body. *How did he know?* Once more she had the feeling that he knew every move she made, as if he was forever watching.

'Maryann . . .' Charlie ran after her, grasping her arm to stop her. He looked into her eyes and she saw his face change at the fear and desperation he saw there. 'Look – he said he was your brother.' He held her for a moment by her upper arms, then his hands dropped to his sides. He saw her panicky breathing subside a little.

'You all right?' he asked gently.

'My brother? What did he look like?'

'Young. Dark.' Charlie shrugged. 'Thin, like.'

It sounded like Tony. Certainly not like Norman Griffin.

'He said your mom's been took bad – thought she wouldn't last the night. Said if your boats was to come in in the next day or two, you're wanted at home.'

'*Home?*' Maryann laughed bitterly. 'That's a good 'un. Anyroad – ta, Charlie. Sorry for snapping at you.'

He watched for a moment as she set off back along the wharf, arms folded across her wiry form as if holding herself in. She was a smasher, that one, he thought. Worked like a little Trojan.

Maryann slowed her pace and stopped, looking along the wharf towards where their boats were tied up. She stood still, the life of the wharf going on around her, and felt cold and suddenly exhausted. All the way up from Limehouse she'd forced away her dread of coming back here. There was enough else to think about. As well as the everyday busyness of the boats and the family, Sylvia was in pain and Dot was still quietly grieving. She felt for them both and it was easier to think about their problems than face her own. They sat together at night and talked about Roy Cresswell and what on earth Sylvia was going to do, and allowed her to cry and let out some of the anguish over her marriage.

'I never felt loved,' she sobbed one evening. 'Not properly. Not once in twelve years.'

Though they were so fixed on comforting Sylvia, Maryann sometimes noticed Dot looking at her, wondering, and she was sure Dot and Sylvia talked about her, about the nightmares, trying to work her out. But how could she talk to them, bring all the past out into the open? It was dirty and shameful. No one else would ever understand except Janet Lambert. And Amy . . . oh God,

Amy! How could she tell them any of the nightmare that went on in her head day after day?

And now Tony had come. *For what?* she thought angrily. As their mom's messenger? *And what the hell does she want? Me there at her deathbed telling her what a wonderful mother she's been and how she'll go straight to heaven?*

She felt her face twist with hurt and bitterness. If there was anyone she needed to be with while she was here it was Janet Lambert. Janet had been kinder to her than her own mom had ever been. And they were in it together – the hell that was ever having anything to do with Norman Griffin.

But she thought about Tony coming all the way over to Tyseley to find her. He needed her. And she owed him, her little brother, little Tony whom she'd left behind when she ran away from home to join Joel on the cut. She couldn't just ignore him. She'd tell Sylvia and Dot that they would have to delay leaving.

'We're going to visit your grandmother's house.'

She couldn't call her mother any of those pet names – Nana, Nanny, like she'd called her dad's mother, Nanny Firkin. Just the cold truth. Your grandmother. My mother.

'Have we seen her before?' Joley asked, puzzled, as they set out the next day. She took all the children except Rose, who begged to stay with Sylvia. There was enough for Dot and Sylvia to do on the wharf without minding all her kids again, and she wanted them to see Tony. It was a Sunday, but as they waited for the bus into Birmingham, Maryann thought for a moment that the atmosphere of the morning was missing something. It was too quiet. Of course, it was missing the sound she remembered from childhood – church bells. The war meant that they were still not allowed to ring out and the street felt eerily deserted.

It was only a short distance from the middle of town to Ladywood. As they walked through the familiar streets, Maryann experienced the mixture of feelings that returning to the neighbourhood always aroused in her: of recognition, of a deep sense of belonging, but also of anxiety and vulnerability. She was back in the home of her young years and it made her feel like a child again. She didn't want to do the things which might have recalled a happier childhood – to take her own children to the house in Garrett Street and say, 'Look – that's the house I grew up in. That's where me and Auntie Sal played.' Their Auntie Sal was long dead and the house a place of grim memory. Her mother had moved out of it after Norman Griffin left her; forced deeper into poverty, she had gone to a house in a yard on Sheepcote Lane.

Court Two, it said over the narrow entrance to the yard.

'Does she live up here?' Sally said, puzzled.

'Yes, she does – oi, stop that, you'll end up black as the ace of spades!' Maryann snapped at the boys as they rubbed their hands along the slimy walls of the entry.

The children had never been anywhere quite like it before. These houses made even Alice Simons's little terrace in Oxford look spacious and the brickwork was crumbling and caked in soot and dirt.

Maryann saw Tony immediately. He was standing at the door of the house, blowing a blue stream of cigarette smoke from his lips. The other side of the yard, beyond the washing line, from which hung a single pair of limp, yellowed long johns, was a tap, fixed to the high wall and constantly dripping. A rotten smell drifted along the yard from the rubbish heap down the end.

Maryann led her children across the dirty blue bricks, her brother watching them approach, though he didn't move. He looked so much older, she thought. What was he now – twenty-three? A father with a small child, aged and pinched in the face. She felt a pang of pity for him, trapped here in this static life.

'You got my message then,' he stated.

'This is your uncle Tony – remember?' Maryann said as the children stood looking. Ada and Esther loosed her hands and wandered off across the yard.

'Don't go messing with anything,' she called after them, without much hope of being obeyed. 'What's happened?' she asked Tony. 'How is she?'

'She went. Last night.'

Maryann nodded. She felt a lurch of emotion inside her, but that was all. And she knew that it consisted as much of relief as of sorrow that she would not see her mother alive again. 'What took her then?'

Tony shrugged. 'She were bad with her chest.'

The older children waited, taking everything in.

'Are we going to see our grandmother?' Sally asked solemnly.

'No, bab. She's passed on. Last night.'

There was a silence.

'How's your Dolly – and the babby?'

'All right.' Tony crushed the remains of the cigarette under his heel. 'Joanie's getting big. Dolly's got another on the way.'

'Oh – that's nice.' How quickly time passed, she thought, their lives moving on.

'I'd better see her then,' she said, as Tony didn't

volunteer anything else, and he stood back to let her in. 'Joley, you all stay out here and keep an eye on the twins for now. You can come in a bit later.'

Inside, she asked, 'Who was looking after her – anyone?'

'Couple of neighbours. Mrs Biggs.' He nodded towards number four. 'Lives over there. It went quick in the end. Someone came over to fetch me Friday night. The undertaker's coming later.'

Undertaker, Maryann thought grimly, clattering up the bare staircase. That had been the start of it all: her father's death. The undertaker – Norman Griffin. She'd never been deceived by him, even then, she thought. Perhaps that was what had saved her sanity – not like Sal, who'd tried to believe in him, let herself be beguiled by the sweet talking, the outings to the cinema and his offer of a job working for him. Maryann had loathed him from the very first time he had set foot in their house.

Stepping into her mother's room, even now, when there had been so little feeling between them, tears of pity came to her eyes at the state to which Flo had been reduced. The bare room with its crumbling walls, without so much as a peg rug to relieve the splintered grime of the floorboards, was bigger than Maryann's whole living space in the *Esther Jane*'s cabin, but without one iota of its intimate cosiness. This room was bleak, its only furniture the single iron bedstead, a rickety chair by the bed and an old chest of drawers.

Maryann sank down on the chair. She barely recognized her mother. In her prime Flo had been a voluptuous, stately woman with thick hair of a natural blonde which had kept its fine colour until she was well on in years. It was a sickly grey now. She was thinner, yet her face seemed to have lengthened, making her look different, and the flesh of her cheeks had become slightly bloated and puffy. Had it not been for her familiar profile, her large nose, Maryann would have had difficulty in recognizing her.

She sat struggling to think how old her mother would have been. When was she born? 1890, she thought she remembered. Fifty-four then. She stared at the yellowish face there beside her. Flo looked twenty years older.

She hadn't expected her tears. Her heart had been hardened against her mother for so long. When she had left this house it was with Flo's screams of condemnation in her ears, words spat out with loathing – that she had been the ruin of them all, that everything that had happened in the family had been her fault because she was a liar who'd turned their stepfather against them. It was her fault that her mother was reduced to live in utter poverty. Maryann had barely wept over it then, but the tears came now. They came when she remembered other things she had long shut out of her thoughts: how Flo had been when they were all small, during the Great War and after. She'd been harassed and often beside herself with worry, it was true. And when Maryann's father, Harry, came home a shell of the man he'd been, her worry and anxiety increased. But Maryann's father had been a good, kind man and Flo, then, a strong woman. She was never a tender mother, more tough and matter of fact. But Maryann could remember being held in her lap, the rich sound of laughter that could rise up from her. She recalled being sent out with halfpennies for sweets. And, above all, she remembered that once the days had felt normal and untroubled. Back then, such a long time ago, she had felt safe. With her hands over her face, she felt tears run out through her fingers. Sobs were wrung out of her from somewhere deep inside and she knew she was crying not just for her mom, but for her lovely dad as well, for both her parents with all the hardships they'd had to face. And for herself too, for all they'd once been before the war, before that motor car knocked her father down one afternoon and he never came home again.

She didn't know how long she had been sitting there, but after a time she heard feet on the stairs and Tony appeared with a cup of tea, stirring in the sugar as he came into the room.

'Here y'are, sis.'

'Ta, Tony.' She wiped her eyes, dazed. 'Are the kids all right?'

He went and stood looking out through the dirty window, hands in his pockets. 'They're in the yard.' She thought how deep his voice was now, how his skinny body already sagged, as if worn down.

'What's next?' she asked, feeling somehow that he was older now and knew what to do.

'She'll be buried, Tuesday.'

'I don't think I can stay.'

'No.' There was a pause.

'Sorry, Tony.'

He turned. 'S'all right.'

She sipped the tea. It tasted funny now, with stera. She was used to fresh milk.

'It's a shame,' she said.

His eyes followed her gaze round the room.

'She wasn't always like this. Did you come and see her much?'

'She daint like Dolly. I come of a Sunday sometimes – just to see she was all right, like. Billy never come. He hasn't been near for years.'

After a moment she asked, 'D'you remember our dad?'

Tony turned to the window again, his head dark against the light. 'A bit. Not much. I remember the day he passed away.'

'You were hardly more than a babby. And then Nanny Firkin passed on. And *he* was there by then.'

Tony didn't say anything. Maryann knew he understood what Norman Griffin had done to his sisters, that he believed her, had seen and heard things he knew should not have been done. But he didn't want to talk about it. Not again.

'Did she . . .' She trailed off, hardly able to put into words what she wanted to ask. 'Did she ever say anything about him – you know, regrets – that she knew . . . about him? What he did?'

Tony hesitated, then shook his head.

Pain roused itself in her again. 'Nothing – ever?'

'Look, Sis – ' he came over to see if her tea was finished – 'just leave it. It were years ago. She's passed on now.'

Maryann looked up into her brother's dark eyes. 'I know, Tony – but he hasn't.'

'We'd best get cracking then,' she said when they were downstairs. 'The landlord'll want the house after Tuesday.'

She was looking round the tiny downstairs room when the sound of yells and shouts of pain came from the yard. Tony ran out.

'Oi!' she heard him shouting. 'Pack that in! Get off of him!'

'You didn't hear what he called me!' Maryann went

306

to the door to find Joley, fists clenched and puce with fury, being pulled off another, bigger lad by Tony, who had to clamp both arms round him to restrain him. Ezra, though, was busy landing a punch on another boy who'd appeared in the yard.

'Ezzy – stop it!' Maryann ran to him and hoiked him away. 'What's going on?'

'Fuckin' water rats!' the older boy shouted. He had a thin, unhealthy look and was wearing long shorts that looked too tight and no shoes on his blackened feet. Maryann saw his nose was bleeding and he was wiping it on the sleeve of his shirt. He backed away, shouting, 'Water rats, water rats! Gyppos!'

'You shut up!' Sally yelled, defending her brothers. 'You're dirtier than us – what're you calling us names for, eh?'

Joley suddenly managed to twist free of Tony and launched himself on the other boy, who although bigger had not expected a water rat to have the strength acquired by working narrowboats from a young age. Joley ran at him and punched him hard in the belly and he sank with a groan.

'What's all this fucking racket about?' An elderly man with a furious, drinker's face appeared out of another house along the yard. 'Who're you lot? Clear off and stop making all this fucking carry-on!' He waved his arms and there were suddenly two large women there as well, carrying on about gyppos and rough, nasty brats and how the likes of them oughtn't to be allowed near the place, mixing with ordinary people. Maryann managed to get all the children into the house, her temper raging.

'My family's worth ten of you cowing slum roaches! Go on – you can all bugger off back indoors now, you nosy bastards!' She slammed the front door so hard it shuddered.

'I remember why I wanted to get away from this bloody place now!' She was still shouting inside the house. Seeing the children all grinning with apparent approval at this outburst, she lowered her voice. 'Fighting's no way to carry on,' she scolded. 'Don't do it again. Come on, Tony – let's get this house cleared and get out. There can't be much to get through. And you kids'll have to find something to do in here – I don't want you going out in the yard again, d'you hear?'

She found a dog-eared pack of cards in the one little cupboard in the downstairs room and told the children to make do with them.

'It won't take all that long,' she said. 'There's hardly anything in the house.'

'I don't like it here,' Sally said miserably.

'It looks as if most of this is only fit for burning,' Maryann said to Tony, her face creasing with disgust. 'That old chair looks riddled with vermin. How long's she been living like this?'

Tony shrugged. 'I dunno. I s'pose she just let it all go.'

When they had finished, Maryann carried Flo's small collection of clothes down to the pawn shop. She walked back along the road looking around her, curious to see the old houses and entries and hucksters shops, yet still uneasy. She could never be free in this neighbourhood. It was too full of ghosts.

She sorted out the scullery, going through her mother's few pots and pans. Anything useful she and Tony divided between them.

'There's some papers and stuff in here,' Tony said, opening a drawer at the bottom of the small cupboard.

'Don't look like anyfing much. Will you have a look, sis? You were always better at reading, like.'

Maryann sat at the table with the thin sheaf of papers, most of them yellowed with age. The birth certificates of the four Nelson children were there. She stared sorrowfully at Sal's for a moment, then put them aside. *Don't think about it*, she told herself. *Don't start wallowing.* To her surprise, the next sheet of paper was a receipt for payment from her father's funeral all those years ago. Whyever hadn't Flo thrown it out? Perhaps she had felt it was one of the few things she had left of Harry. She stared grimly at the fragile sheet of paper with *N. Griffin & Son, Undertakers* in faded black ink at the top. *Had* Norman Griffin ever really had a son? she wondered, frowning. If so, she'd certainly never met him. She tore up the paper into tiny pieces. As she was looking through the rest of her mother's old, pathetic paperwork, a card fell out from between the sheets into her lap. It was whiter, newer than the rest. In blue ink it read, *Albert Griffin, Toolmakers & Machinists.*

'Tony – come and have a look at this.'

Tony glanced at the card over her shoulder. 'What about it?' he said, moving away.

Maryann frowned at it, the horrible realization only fully dawning on her now.

'It's him, isn't it?'

'Who?'

'Oh, don't be bloody dense, Tony!' She stood up, scattering the rest of the papers. 'You know who! Is this who he is now? Has he been here? Has she been seeing him?'

'No!' Tony raised his voice so that the children all turned to look. 'I mean – I dunno! I dunno anyfing about him or who he is and I don't want to!'

309

Maryann felt as if she'd been punched.

'God in heaven,' she gasped, 'it *is*. I know it's him. After all this – all that happened and she'd *see* him . . .' She looked up wildly at Tony. 'She didn't take him back, did she?'

'No! Of course not. Why the hell would she do that?'

'I don't know . . .' Maryann's hand went to her head, as if rubbing it might make things clearer. Why should she be surprised that Flo would have her stepfather back in her house? After all, she had never wanted him to leave. She had blamed Maryann for driving him away, her source of financial security. She'd never believed anything Maryann said, anyway.

She dragged her eyes back to the card again. The address of the works was in Highgate. Face set grimly, she slipped the card into her pocket.

Thirty-Three

When they got back to Tyseley that evening, Maryann found Dot and Sylvia sitting out on the *Theodore*. Both boats had been unloaded and were riding high in the water. Sylvia stood up on the counter and waved when she saw them coming along the wharf.

'We've got a potful of tea here!' she beckoned. 'Come and sit down for a bit. You must have had a lousy day.' When they'd all clambered aboard, Sylvia put her arm round Maryann's shoulder. 'Poor old you. I remember when my mother died – I felt as if the stuffing had been knocked out of me for weeks.'

'We weren't close,' Maryann said. She spoke so tersely that she was immediately ashamed. 'I mean – I've hardly seen her in years.' She knew Sylvia's sympathy was well intended but she felt like a fraud. What grief and loss did she really feel for Flo? Nothing, but for that glimpse of the young woman she had once been, too long ago for Maryann to remember clearly. 'Me and Tony've cleared the house. There's only the funeral now.'

'Well, I think you're being very brave,' Sylvia said, handing Maryann her tea.

Maryann smiled absently. She didn't feel grief or sorrow at this moment. In her mind all evening, as she sat with Dot and Sylvia and they told her how the unloading had gone and that they'd managed to stove both boats in her absence to get rid of the bugs, was the

311

thought of the card pushed into the pocket of her cardigan with its blue lettering.

Longing to be alone, she told them she wanted an early night.

'We were thinking of popping out for a bit – see if we can find a pub that's not too soul-destroying,' Dot said.

'But we won't if you'd rather we didn't,' Sylvia said hastily.

'No – that's all right. You go,' Maryann said.

Even when she was by herself on the *Esther Jane* later on, the children bedded down for the night, she still didn't give any thought to the fact that she and the children were alone. Her head was too full of other things. She took out the card and propped it against the alarm clock near her head. She lay on her stomach in bed, staring at it in the candlelight. The words seemed to ripple and flicker as the flame moved gently. *Albert Griffin, Albert Griffin* . . .

'Should've been a bit cleverer than that, shouldn't you?' she whispered. 'Calling yourself Griffin again.'

Thinking of him, of all he'd done, she felt herself clench up inside with anger and her own sense of defilement. And Flo had, at some time, seen him again, perhaps had him visit her house . . . However much she told herself she had no feeling left for her mother, that she didn't care what she'd done, now she knew pain and outrage flooded through her until she could scarcely breathe. Once more she made herself force the thoughts aside. If she let them take her over, they would destroy her. She had protected herself from him so far as well as she could – she wasn't going to let it happen now.

Turning onto her side, she looked at Sally's sleeping face beside her, the pale hair in disarray on the pillow, and smiled at the thought of her yelling at those boys in

Flo's yard. She was glad to know her daughter had more mettle in her than she would seem to have from her angelic looks. Very lightly, Maryann stroked her head.

Tomorrow, Albert Griffin, *I'm going to the police*, she thought. *And then they'll have you.* Settling herself, she blew out the candle and the smell of its waxy smoke was the last thing in the darkness before she slept.

She was in a tunnel. It wasn't Blisworth Tunnel or Braunston. She knew that. It wasn't the same: it was much, much longer and there was no reassuring keyhole of light at the end, the tiny beacon to which the front of the boats could be directed. There was a path to one side. As it was completely dark, she could feel rather than see how narrow it was. It was barely more than a ledge and certainly not wide enough to lead a horse. She was making her way along it, moving sideways, her right arm scrabbling forward along the slimy bricks for finger-holds, her left arm stretched out on the other side to help her remain close to the wall and not topple off into the water. She seemed to move so, so slowly, her progress impossible to measure in the dark, and there was no light drawing closer, bringing hope of release. Although the sound of a boat came from somewhere in the distance, she didn't know whose boat it was or which way it was moving. The echoes in the tunnel mixed directions into confusion. All she could hear were the muffled sounds of the motor and the drip of water, close and loud from the roof of the tunnel. She cried out for the boat to come and help her, to get her out, but it was too far away, its engine throbbing and she couldn't make herself heard over its noise. She couldn't make out its headlamp in either direction. As she struggled along agonizingly slowly, she began to hear the other sound: the breathing. She knew it was his breathing and it was becoming louder than anything else in the tunnel, the echo swelling, bloating the sound until it seemed to be all round her. He was there – behind her? In front of her? Seemingly everywhere, not speaking, only breathing, the sound moving closer all the time. Somewhere in the wall she knew there was a door, a niche cut into the tunnel that only he knew the position of. That was where he wanted to take her, to lock her away! Behind the door of the hidden cupboard he kept an upright wooden chair. A chair, the same one he'd had in the cupboard of his undertaker's business. The chair he tied Sal to ... She tried to hurry, nails scrabbling at the wall. Yet she didn't know where he was coming from, her left or her right, and his breathing was moving closer, its secure, unhurried rhythm gaining on her until she was sure she felt his breath on her neck ...

The dream seemed to last for an eternity, as she clung, suspended in darkness, and at last started to fall backwards, throwing herself into the black water, anything to get away from him. She woke with an anguished cry, her body soaked in sweat. For a moment, in her confused state, the rain on the cabin roof seemed oppressive and terrifying. She knew she couldn't just lie there: the darkness wouldn't release her from the world of the dream. She groped for the box of matches and lit the candle, sitting up, tightly hugging her knees, weeping and shivering, rocking herself to try and find comfort. She looked round at the familar lines of the cabin, the range, the coalbox and dipper, Ada and Esther sprawled together on the floor, her clothes, bolts of colour at the foot of her bed. It was a long time before she stopped shaking and could begin to see things more normally,

314

though the dream still lurked close to the surface. When would this ever end? she thought, like a howl inside herself.

It was getting on for five in the morning. It would be light soon. She hadn't heard Dot and Sylvia come back from the pub, she realized. And it was only then she remembered that she had allowed herself to be left alone with the boats at Tyseley! Thank goodness she hadn't thought of it while they were away! She'd been so tired the night before.

As they were staying, not loading up, today, there was no need to rise early. She bedded down again for more sleep, blowing out the candle, dreading another onset of the dream. Its images crowded in the moment she closed her eyes and for a time she fought with them. At last she slept.

'Here we are, my love!'

The hatches opened and Sylvia's face appeared, smiling against the sunlight. Spots the black and white cat tore in past her legs and jumped up onto Maryann's feet.

'Goodness – what's got into him?' Sylvia climbed in, carrying a cup of tea. 'He nearly knocked me down the steps. Here – drink it while it's hot.'

Maryann sat up blearily and looked round at the clock. 'Half-past eight! Ta, Sylv. Where are the twins?'

'We came and fetched them out a good hour ago. And Ezra. Dot and I thought it'd be good if you got all the sleep under your belt that you could. She's taken them off to get more bread. Have a good night?'

Maryann nodded a lie. She didn't want to mention her nightmare. To her discomfort she felt tears come into her eyes at this kindness and managed to mumble,

'Thanks,' feeling frustrated that she couldn't find more words to express her gratitude to them both. When Nance had died she'd thought she'd never have a good friend again, but now she'd been through so many things with these two women that she felt closer to them than she'd ever imagined possible and that was also part of her tearfulness.

'Cheer up.' Sylvia looked tired and strained herself, but she smiled sympathetically into Maryann's face. 'Look – you must go to the funeral tomorrow. It's not right to miss your own mother's funeral, whatever you feel about her. Dot and I were wondering whether we should try and work a day trip today and come back. Only we've left it a bit late now ... Of course, we could come to the funeral with you – help with the children.'

'Don't go,' Maryann heard herself say. She suddenly couldn't bear the thought of being left alone here. 'You have left it a bit late to get going – and I *would* like you to come.' She felt her cheeks go red. 'If you don't mind. It's not much of a treat for you.'

'Oh, don't be silly. Of course we will.'

'I've got a few things to get done today ...'

'Right – well, let's all take it easy for once. And I tell you what – I'm going to treat us all to fish and chips tonight, as well!'

'Mom! Mom – come and look!' Ezra appeared on the steps, his dark eyes wide.

'What's up?' His voice told her immediately that something was really wrong.

'Quick—' He beckoned, and was gone again.

She wasn't yet dressed, but pulled on her winter coat over her nightdress. It felt too hot in the warm May morning, but she followed Sylvia up out of the *Esther Jane*, and on the towpath they looked along and saw

Ezra with Rose and the twins at the front of the boat, standing silently, their eyes fixed on something.

'What's going on?' Sylvia said.

Joining the children, their eyes followed the others' to the little mast. Hanging from a short length of rope was Jenny the tortoiseshell cat. The rope was twisted tightly round her neck and her body dangled from it, stiff and bedraggled from the night's rain. The neck was at an odd angle. There was no movement, no life left in her.

'Oh, Jennykins!' Sylvia's hand went to her mouth. 'Oh, that's horrible! How did that...? Someone must've ... mustn't they? Who on earth would have done that?'

Maryann turned away, beginning to tremble. She could feel herself going to pieces. She'd seen enough to know immediately: could not bear to take in the sight any longer. Even while she'd been dreaming of his hot breath on her skin he'd been out here. He liked to inflict pain. He took relish in exactly this kind of cruelty. She had seen it all before, her own childhood kitten Tiger dead at his hand. She remembered leaving her cold, dead body under a pile of leaves on the bank by the cut. And once again he had known their boats were here. This more than anything chilled her blood. *How did he know?* And what was the message of this? It was all too clear: *I'm here. I'm waiting.*

Sylvia was trying to comfort the children, and as she hurried back to the cabin to dress, Dot had just come back with the twins.

'What's all the kerfuffle about?' she asked cheerfully.

But Maryann was already heading past her, back to her cabin.

'I've got things to do,' she announced. 'I'm going out. Now.'

Thirty-Four

'Maryann – ' Sylvia's voice was terse with tension and anxiety – 'you really must stop shutting us all out. You know who did that to Jennykins, don't you?'

They were all gathered in the *Theodore* that evening and the air smelt tantalizingly of the fish and chips and tangy vinegar that Dot had fetched on Bobby's bicycle, which he had kindly left for them to use. The children were wolfing down the food.

'Sorry,' Maryann said, 'for taking off and leaving you with it all today. The kids and that. I'm ever so grateful.'

'But where've you *been*?' Sylvia burst out. 'We've been beside ourselves wondering what's going on. You do know who did it, don't you?'

Maryann saw all the children's eyes swivel towards her. 'Oh, some nasty man I expect. I don't s'pose he'll ever do it again.' She gave Dot and Sylvia a look which said, *later*. She could only pick at the fish and chips with difficulty, even though they were a treat. She felt sick and full of inner turmoil.

'You can come and have a drink with us later,' Sylvia said.

'No!' Maryann almost shouted. 'I mean – no, sorry. I don't want to leave the kids on their own. Not tonight.'

It had been agonizing enough leaving them in the day. She had spent hours moving round the city.

'I've got to go out again,' she'd told Sylvia in the

318

morning. 'I wish I could take everyone with me, but I can't. Just keep them close – don't let them out of your sight, *please.*'

'I won't,' Sylvia said. 'I promise.' She was obviously deeply unnerved by what had happened. 'Maryann – where're you going?'

'Tell you later.'

First she went to the police.

'This is the man you're looking for,' she announced, handing over the card. She grasped folds of her skirt, pleating them with her fingers to hold herself steady, to stop her screaming and making an exhibition of herself.

'I see.' It was the same policeman she'd seen the last time. He thought she was bonkers, she was certain.

'I grew up with him.' She was almost begging, trying not to weep. *Believe me, for God's sake, someone please believe me.* 'I *know* it was him. He's cruel and violent and . . .' She couldn't go on, couldn't speak, could only squeeze on the folds of her cotton skirt until she thought the bones in her hands would crack.

'We'll look into it,' the policeman said calmly. Why was he so calm? she thought, infuriated.

'He's got a scarred face. A terrible, hideous face . . .' Oh, this sounded ridiculous, like something she'd made up. For a split second she doubted herself. Had Norman Griffin simply been the stuff of her nightmares? Then she thought of her sister, of what he had reduced her to. 'He's dangerous,' she gulped. 'You mustn't let him get away. He killed Amy Lambert – I know he did.'

Afterwards she went to see Janet, Amy's mother, to tell her the news, to try and bring her some comfort, even though she felt so agitated herself. Janet seemed to have turned into an old woman just in the past weeks. With Amy's funeral now over she was calmer, but the pain of loss was written in every line of her face. When Maryann told her she was sure she had found Norman Griffin's new premises, Janet stared back at her fearfully.

'I just wish – ' her already watery blue eyes filled with tears – 'I wish he'd just disappear ... that it was all over ... I just want my Amy back.' She sobbed brokenly and Maryann tried to give comfort, knowing that really there was none.

Late in the afternoon she walked through Highgate. The address on the card was Cheapside, almost at the bottom of the hill. Maryann walked down the long slope of Cheapside, factories on either side all the way down, the clang and clatter, the drone of machines, the shouts above the noise, coming at her from everywhere. Her eyes darted from side to side. She felt as if everyone must be staring at her, at her clothes, her dirty boots, as if her every thread shouted 'boatwoman', and here she was, born in Ladywood, but feeling like a foreigner in her own town! What really frightened her was that she might meet him, that he would appear from somewhere, out of a factory or one of the side alleys, with his box-like body, those wide, square shoulders, hat pulled down to hide his face. That she would have to look into his eyes again.

She saw the sign from a short distance away: *Albert Griffin, Toolmakers & Machinists.* For a moment she doubted herself. Could he really have anything to do with this place? It was certainly a new line of business for him. He'd been an undertaker for years – would he go into toolmaking instead?

The factory had quite a narrow frontage, but the buildings reached back some way from the street. For a moment she stopped, almost paralysed with nerves, as if the factory had an invisible electric fence round it that she did not dare to pass.

For goodness sake, she urged herself, *I'm only walking past down the road. It'll look even odder if I stop.* Her hands were so sweaty she had to wipe them on her skirt.

There was nothing to see. The doors were shut and no one came in or out. She hurried past and turned, relieved, back onto Bradford Street, where the trams went rattling past and things felt safer again.

But I know *it's him*, she told herself, hurrying away. Her heart was still pounding. Why else would Mom have had that card in her house?

She thought again of Jenny the cat, hanging by the neck from that scrap of rope. A chill went through her which grew into panic. All she wanted was to get home.

She wouldn't go back to the *Theodore* with Dot and Sylvia once the children were in bed. The three of them stood outside, coats on against the chilly evening.

'Maryann, we're your friends. At least, we want to be, don't we, Dot?'

Maryann stood with her arms folded, closed in on herself as the others tried to get her to talk.

'You've seen us both through a lot. You've been a real brick – and so kind.' Sylvia stepped closer, as if to embrace her, but Maryann stepped back. She didn't want to be touched.

'It'd make you feel better,' Dot said gruffly. 'To talk, I mean. Goodness knows, I'm bad enough at opening up. But after Steven died – well, you did a lot for me.'

But that's different! Maryann wailed in her head. *You loved your brother and he died. That's natural. It's clean*

– not like this, not like him *and all he's done! How can I tell you? Things like this don't happen to people like you – you're different. Or I'm different: that's what it is.*

She stared out at the water beyond, at the broken light reflected in the ripples. There was a smell of frying onions coming from another boat. Inside her the worst thought of all swelled, unspoken. *If I told you, you'd never believe me. You'd think I was a liar and you'd find me disgusting.*

'What is it, Maryann?' Sylvia said softly. 'Can't you trust us? I saw your face this morning and you were really frightened, I could tell.'

'You're even frightened in your sleep.' Dot spoke with such sympathy suddenly that Maryann felt an unbearable tightening in her throat. A pool of unshed tears seemed to press behind her eyes.

'You know who killed little Jenny, don't you?' Sylvia persisted.

Maryann turned to them. She had to tell them something. It was such an odd, horrible thing to have happened.

'I think it was a man called Norman Griffin. He was my stepfather.'

There was a silence. She saw Sylvia and Dot glance at each other.

'But *why*?' Dot said. 'He must be quite mad.'

'He's not very nice, no,' she said flatly. All energy went out of her suddenly. The tears subsided. She couldn't say more, couldn't begin on it. After the funeral they'd get away from here again and she could feel safe, keep away from Birmingham, leave it up to the police to catch him. She could put it all away again.

'I just don't want him anywhere near my family, that's all. It makes me a bit jumpy sometimes. That's

322

why I asked you to keep an eye on them, Sylv. Anyroad
– it's been a long day. I'm going to bed now.'

She could feel them watching her as she opened the
hatches of the *Esther Jane*

''Night, 'night,' she said.

She knew they were perfectly aware that she wasn't
telling them all of the truth. *They're not stupid,* she
thought, climbing over the twins to her bed. *But I can't
– I just can't. What would they think of me?*

Lying in bed, she felt wide awake. It was a relief
because she dreaded the dreams. She lay in the dark for
ages, listening for any sound outside.

Thirty-Five

They woke early the next morning and a light mist hung over the water, the sky colourless and hazy. It seemed to Maryann that she hadn't slept at all, but she did not feel tired. She was in too wound up a state for that. Even before her morning cup of tea – once more made by Sylvia – she was full of agitated energy.

The night before they had decided that, instead of leaving the boats and resorting to buses and trams, they would take the *Esther Jane* across town to where they could walk to the cemetery. Maryann had sent a message to Tony to say that they were not going to join the modest funeral procession across from Ladywood. Dot got the engine going, while Maryann and Sylvia finished getting everyone dressed.

'Neither Dot nor I have anything really suitable to wear for a funeral!' Sylvia said, slipping a frock over Ada's head. Her wiry little arms thrust up through the sleeves.

'Can't say I have either,' Maryann said. 'Never mind. We'll just have to make the best of it. There'll be hardly anyone there except Tony and Billy.'

She found, almost to her shame, that she was quite looking forward to the day. It was a change, after all – another day off before all the hard work began again, and a chance to see her brothers. Tony had said Billy was coming home on leave for the funeral. Perhaps she might get to know him a bit better, to feel he really was her brother.

They had breakfast moving along. After they'd crossed town they moved onto the Worcester Canal, chugging along past Davenport's Brewery, its bitter, hop smell filling the air. The sun began to break through and melt away the mist, and the air started to feel warm and muggy, so they laid some of the bedding out to air. They passed carriers whom they didn't normally see, clothed-up pairs of boats from the Severn Canal Carrying Company, which transported goods out to the West Country, out through the long tunnel at Tardebigge and down to the Severn.

'I haven't been down here in a good while,' Maryann said to Dot, as she stood out with her eating breakfast. Familiar landmarks moved past them, Sturges's Chemical Works, the tunnel at Edgbaston, the copper works at Selly Oak. It was a stretch full of poignancy for Maryann. It was one of the greenest parts of the cut in Birmingham and today the trees were covered in fresh spring leaves. She remembered coming along here on another lovely day with Nancy and Darius when they were first falling in love and how she, seeing what was between them, had fretted and tried to prevent it: Nancy was married then to Mick Mallone. How ridiculous her worries seemed now, when Nancy had only had such a brief time of happiness with Darius. This sadness added itself to all the rest. For a moment, as they brushed through the green light of overhanging branches, she was filled with a hard, hungry ache for Joel. For him to be at her side, to feel him holding her. She felt surprised, ashamed even, at how little she had missed him in the last few weeks, how she had grown used to his absence. But it couldn't be long now before he would be strong

325

enough to come back. And then, she realized with another pang, she would have to say goodbye to Sylvia and Dot, and she knew how much she didn't want to lose them either.

They tied up at Selly Oak and walked to the gates of Lodge Hill Cemetery in time to meet the carriage bringing Flo's body.

'Well, we look a motley crew, don't we?' Dot said as they set off. It was the first time Maryann had ever seen Dot in a skirt, straight, tightly fitting and navy blue, and she had complained like anything when she tried to squeeze into it.

'I've put on pounds doing this job! Good heavens, I can hardly do it up at the waist!'

'Never mind – you look as healthy as a hunter,' Sylvia told her.

'Well, it's not fair,' Dot protested, going red in the face as she breathed in, trying to do up the zip. 'You and Maryann stay as thin as twigs and I rush about far more than either of you!' She had to resort to leaving the top button undone. They had all put their coats on, even though it was quite warm, in order to look a bit smarter.

The funeral cortège was as basic as it could be because there was no money in the family. In the event, the only mourner apart from the family was a neighbour of Flo's, a middle-aged, corpulent lady called Mrs Biggs, who waddled towards them in front of Maryann's brothers, in her hat and coat. She had dark, thick brows and prominent cheeks, above which her deepset eyes appeared only just able to see out. She nodded with sharp disapproval at Maryann.

'I were a friend of your mother's,' she said, adding tartly, 'somebody had to be,' before turning away.

Walking beside Tony was a tall young man with fair

hair, dressed smartly in Air Force blue. He was the taller of the two and, although Maryann knew it had to be Billy, it still took her a moment to recognize him.

Her hand went to her mouth, 'Oh, my word, look at him!'

As he came closer, she saw that he was handsome and big-boned like their mother had been. *He looks like our mom and Sal*, she thought, *and he must be all of twenty now.* His eyes were vivid blue and he had a cropped RAF haircut.

'Here's Uncle Tony,' she said to the children. 'And this is Uncle Billy.'

Billy looked round at them all and nodded, though he didn't smile. 'Maryann. All right?' was all he said, and that quite abruptly. The cold expression in his eyes made Maryann sink inside and she turned away, hurt. *Well, I suppose I never was much of a sister to him*, she thought. *Or not so's he remembers, anyroad.*

Even though Dot and Sylvia were there, she felt terribly alone as they walked behind the carriage taking her mother's body into the cemetery. Mrs Biggs's hostility and the coldness of Billy's greeting sunk deep into her. *Oh, Sal, you ought to be here with me now*, she thought, *not lying six foot under already, with our mom coming to join you. We should be doing this together.*

They reached the plot that had been reserved beside Sal's and their father's graves. Maryann saw Sylvia and Dot discreetly reading the words on the headstones. Sylvia's eyes lingered on SALLY ANNE GRIFFIN, 1913–28, and Maryann saw her wondering how Sal had died when she was only fifteen. How could she begin to explain?

She barely noticed the undertakers bringing her mother's coffin to the graveside. Standing by Sal's grave again she felt desperate to see her, to be able to pour out all her troubles. Sal was the one person who would have understood.

He's back, Sal, she told her in her head. *And I'm so scared. He's worse than before. He's killed Amy, murdered her, and he's always there. He always seems to know where we are. I can't sleep, I can't think properly . . . I wish there was someone could help me.* Had she been alone she might have broken down and wept then, but Sylvia was nudging her. The burial was about to begin.

'D'you think we'd better pick these two up?' Sylvia nodded down at the twins.

Maryann lifted Esther up and Sylvia took Ada. No good having them running off in the middle of it. The other four children stood solemnly in a line in front of them.

'I am the resurrection and the life,' the vicar was saying. Maryann felt some comfort from the old, formal words and from her daughter's warm, plump body in her arms.

As the body of her mother was lowered into the grave, she glanced across at her brothers, who stood on the other side. Tony had his head lowered, cap in his hand. She saw him wipe his eyes as the earth rattled onto the coffin and felt sorry for him. Poor Tony – he was always the soft lad. He was also the only one who'd been really close to Mom. Billy, however, stood very upright, in a military stance, hands behind his back. His cool blue eyes gazed beyond them all at the trees behind. Little Billy, the round toddler she used to bath and sit on her knee, while he chuckled and bounced. She wanted him to know that, to reach out to him.

When it was over, they walked slowly away from the

family graves through the peaceful cemetery. The children, released at last, began to run and jump ahead of them, loving the open space and the trees to dodge round to let off steam.

Dot and Sylvia walked together, each leading a twin by the hand, discreetly allowing the family to be together. Mrs Biggs collared Tony and Maryann went to walk beside Billy. He seemed even taller than she'd realized, with a long, muscular stride.

'How you keeping?' she asked nervously.

'All right. Going back tomorrow.' She knew he was in Coastal Command. She asked questions, but he wouldn't be drawn about it and they lapsed into silence. Maryann looked down, watching her old boots with their scuffed toecaps moving over the dry ground. She heard Joley and Ezra shouting to each other in the distance, knew she ought to tell them to quieten down, but she didn't want to move away.

'Billy – ' she looked up at him, but he didn't turn his head – 'I know I haven't been much of a sister to you – not being here and that. Only it seems a shame not to try and see more of each other like, now Mom's gone . . . You know, family – keeping in touch.'

Billy shrugged, and in that movement of his shoulders was complete indifference. But what cut her to the heart was the look in his eyes when he turned to face her. She saw that her blond, handsome brother was like a hard-faced stranger beside her, staring down at her with contempt.

'You're not really from round here any more, though, are you?'

And she saw her clothes, her ragamuffin children, her life, through his eyes and how he despised her – for not being there as he grew up, for what she had become.

'No,' she conceded miserably. 'I s'pose I'm not.'

He turned away and went to join Tony and Mrs Biggs. Maryann waited for Dot and Sylvia, forcing a smile to her lips to hide how much Billy's words had cut her. She wrenched her hurt round into a tough, defiant anger. Yes, she'd moved on from here and this was who she was. She was Maryann Bartholomew, a skilled boatwoman, and her family were boater's children and proud! *So sod you, Billy Nelson – you may be my brother, but you're a cold bastard and stuck up with it!*

'You all right?' Sylvia put her arm round Maryann's shoulders.

'Yes. Ta.' Maryann shrugged her off. She couldn't manage sympathy or closeness. Not at the moment.

'The vicar handled it all all right, didn't he?' Dot said.

'I thought he was rather nice,' Sylvia agreed, and Maryann could tell they were just talking for something to say and she was grateful to them.

'Do you want to go back with your brothers – spend the evening with them?' Sylvia asked.

'No.' Maryann just managed to keep the bitterness from her voice. 'All I want is to get back home. Get going again.' *Away from here*, she thought.

They reached the cemetery gates. Billy and Mrs Biggs had already gone. Tony waited, though.

'Bye, sis,' he said. 'Come and look us up, won't you?'

'Course I will,' Maryann said. She knew she would, every so often. But she also realized that probably, she'd never see Billy again, and with a pang, she knew that it no longer mattered.

The twins ran to catch up, skipping along the path. Joley and Ezra were chasing each other in and out of the gate, while Rose was picking up bits and pieces off the ground. Seeing Sylvia coming, she ran to her and took her hand.

'Right – all shipshape everyone?' Dot said.

'Where's Sally?' Sylvia said, headcounting the children.

'Good job someone's looking after them,' Maryann said. 'Shows what a daze I'm in! Where's she got to?'

They called back along the path, but it seemed wrong to be shouting in a cemetery.

'Knowing her, she'll've gone off in a dream some-where,' Maryann said. She frowned. 'I thought she was in front of us.'

'Well, she was at one stage,' Sylvia said. 'But they were all dodging about so much. She's probably got herself lost in there.'

They spent the next half-hour searching the big cem-etery, calling and looking, walking right down to the far side.

'It's not like her to hide and be naughty, is it?' Dot said.

Maryann was bewildered. Sally could be dreamy at times, it was true, but she'd never done anything like this before. And she wouldn't run off into the unknown streets of Birmingham without the rest of them. None of the other children knew where she'd gone and Maryann could see from their faces that they weren't having her on. She became more and more uneasy.

'It feels as if she's fallen down a hole or something,' she said. 'What the hell's happened to her?'

On the far side of the cemetery, in a newer part where there were few graves, they saw a middle-aged man kneeling, mending the fence.

'I say!' Dot called to him. He turned, startled.

'We're looking for a little girl – she seems to have lost

her way in here. Have you seen her? She's – how old is she, Maryann? Seven?'

Maryann nodded miserably. A coldness was beginning to creep over her. Sally had been missing for too long now to be playing up or have just wandered off. Realization was just beginning to dawn in her.

The man frowned. 'I've only seen one girl this afternoon. About half an hour ago. Blonde. Pretty little thing.'

'Long blonde hair?' Sylvia asked, excitedly. 'What – wandering about here?'

'Well, no. She was with someone – walking along the path over there – a bloke.'

'How odd,' Dot said. 'What did he look like?'

The man shrugged. 'Not young. Quite a big feller. Sort of wide-chested. Trilby pulled well down – couldn't say what his face looked like.'

The sound which came from Maryann made them all look round: a sharp exhalation as if she had been punched. She couldn't hide the fact that was trembling all over, everything round her was reeling. For a moment she thought was she going to pass out.

'Maryann?' Sylvia and Dot hurried over to her at once, asking questions, but she managed to stay upright and ran to the gardener.

'Where did they go? Which way?'

She tore off in the direction in which he pointed because it was all she could do, knowing that it was too late, too long ago, that when she reached the gate the road would be empty, but she could only run with desperate prayers streaming from her lips that he hadn't got her, hadn't really got away with her little girl . . .

There was no one on the road. A lone car passed in the quiet afternoon.

Dot, Sylvia and the others caught up with her and it was Dot who ran to Maryann and seized her by the shoulders.

'Who is he? Who's got her? For God's sake, Maryann, you've got to tell us what's going on.'

Thirty-Six

She couldn't be still.

'I've got to go – got to find them.' She pulled away from Dot and started running blindly along the road, unable to do anything else but move in the direction her child had gone. But of course she didn't know the direction. They were gone, they could be anywhere by now. When Dot reached her again and caught her arm, dragging her to a standstill. She felt herself cave in. Everything seemed to whirl round her, overwhelming her as if she was drowning. Her nightmares had merged into the reality of day and there was screaming and crying somewhere in the distance and she could not catch her breath . . .

'Maryann – MARYANN!' Sylvia was there now, shouting in her face. Why was she yelling like that? 'Maryann – I don't want to slap you, but I'm going to have to if you don't calm down!'

She felt herself being shaken hard by the shoulders and at last the world steadied a little.

'That's better.' Sylvia gripped her arms. 'Now tell us – who is Sally with?'

'With . . . with my stepfather – he used to be. I know it's him – I know he's taken her and we've got to get her. You don't know what he might do . . .' Her hands went convulsively to her cheeks and she was sobbing, shaking so hard that she could barely stand.

Supporting her on each side, they asked her over and over if she was sure, if it could be a mistake. *No, no* – all she could do was shake her head.

'Look,' Dot said, 'we must go and tell the police.'

'No!' Maryann cried. 'I know where we need to go. He's got a factory in Cheapside. We'll go there – I bet he's taken her there!'

Sylvia's eyes were full of doubt at how they were going to manage this when she barely knew the geography of Birmingham's great sprawl, didn't understand anything of what was going on.

'Look,' she decided, 'I'll go home with the children. You and Dot go.'

On the tram, the two of them sat side by side in silence, Maryann filled by a numb sense of inevitability that now they could only do small things, one at a time to get Sally back, when her nerves were screaming that she had to find her now, *now*, and have her back safely in her arms. She tried to close her mind to everything but the next step. The tram crawled along the Bristol Road. There was too much to say for them to begin talking now so they reserved speech only for practical things.

They went to the police station in town, where Maryann talked to them with a sense of hopelessness. Yes, her daughter had been taken away and it was by the same man, she impressed upon them, who had murdered the red-headed woman Amy Lambert. She told them the name of 'Albert Griffin's' factory. And they had to look for Sally *now* because otherwise he would harm her. He was evil, capable of the most terrible things. And Maryann wept helplessly in front of the policeman as she described her pale-haired little Sally.

When they left, Maryann stormed at Dot, 'It's no

good. They keep saying they're doing their best, but they're no ruddy good to us. They never *do* anything.' So many of the police had gone away to war that only a skeleton service was operating. 'We'll have to do it ourselves.'

'Maryann,' Dot panted, trotting to keep up as Maryann tore along the street, 'what were you saying to him? About that woman, a red-haired woman, you said. You said *murdered* . . .? What in heaven's name were you talking about?'

'He murdered her, I know he did.' Maryann didn't stop for a second, firing out disjointed scraps of thoughts. 'Amy – and Sal. And Margaret might just as well be dead. It's all him, all of it. And they won't believe me – and we'll have to do it. No one else has ever – no one believes me except Janet because she knows. She's seen . . . she's the only one who knows.'

Maryann couldn't see the expression of appalled sorrow in Dot's eyes, couldn't see her own distraught, pitiful state. Dot knew that this had not come out of the blue. She had lain beside Maryann, known the terrors that haunted her sleep. What on earth did this poor, sweet-natured woman have in her past to cause all this? What had she suffered? Dot was filled with sorrow and tenderness, but she was out of her depth, inhibited by her own youth and lack of experience. Maryann's life was another world to her. All she could do was follow, look for Sally, and try to gather what was happening.

Maryann led her to Highgate, half running along Bradford Street and across to Cheapside, until they stood outside *Albert Griffin, Toolmakers & Machinists*, both of them panting hard. Maryann went straight to the open door. Inside, the long, dark factory extended back from the road. Dot saw a row of women seated at lathes, and a long table surrounded by a mess of packing cases. There was a subdued roaring from the far end of the workshop, over which they could hear the sound of music from a wireless on a smaller table to their left. A man was singing somewhere. The women nearest the door turned and stared at them but didn't stop work. After a moment the singing stopped and a man appeared, wearing a dirty overall.

'You looking for someone?'

'Yes, Mr Griffin.'

Dot was surprised at how collected Maryann seemed suddenly.

'He don't come in much, afternoons. He's not here. In fact he said he was going to a family funeral, now I think of it.'

'Yes,' Maryann said, 'that's it – he's my uncle, see. We've just come from there. We don't see much of Uncle Albert, but I left my daughter with him and he said he'd meet us here. You sure you haven't seen him – with a little fair-haired girl?'

The man shook his head. 'No. Like I said, I've not seen him all day.'

Maryann managed to look bemused. 'I must've misunderstood him. P'raps he's taken her back to his house. What was the address again?' She turned to Dot, who managed to shrug as if she'd momentarily forgotten it.

'Oh dear. I'm sorry to trouble you – would you be able to tell me his home address so's we can catch up with him? Only, we was hoping to have tea with Uncle Albert – get to know him a bit better like.'

'Just a minute,' the man said noncommittally. 'I'll have to ask Doris.' He went to the back of the workshop and vanished through a door. When he came back, he gave them an address: 33 Cameron Road, Acocks Green.

This time they caught a tram along the Warwick Road. When they alighted in Acocks Green, Dot saw to her surprise that they were not far from Tyseley Wharf. She wished, not for the first time that afternoon, that she wasn't dressed in this damnable skirt and court shoes, but in her usual slacks and boots so she could move freely. Maryann, in her full black skirt, was able to stride along unimpeded. She was running, still possessed by an insane energy. All Dot could do was follow, feeling her feet blister as they rushed along the row of terraced houses.

'Here!' Maryann cried.

Dot felt her heart lurch. Whatever was she going to do?

Maryann didn't miss a step. She marched straight up and hammered the knocker with such force Dot thought the door must split. Maryann couldn't stand still for a second. She was moving back and forth, one hand resting on her waist, elbow out. She chewed fiercely at her other thumb. But suddenly she snatched her hand away from her lips and started screaming.

'Come out! Come on – get out here! I know you've got her, you evil bastard! Get out here!'

Her cried sounded frail in the open air and the house felt silent and unoccupied. The windows reflected back the sky's late afternoon light, but inside it was dark and there was no sign of movement.

Maryann hammered again desperately. Again, no response.

'He's in there – I know he is!' Her hands went to her

face and she wept, distraught. Feeling helpless, Dot went to try and comfort her. But Maryann fought her off to begin her pacing again.

'I'm not going till we've been in there! We've got to get in – I'm going to get in if I have to break the door down. He's got to be here – where else can he be?'

Dot knew that Maryann felt it was their last chance of finding Sally today. She went to the door herself and pushed on it, banging once more on the knocker. It felt like a firm, strong door. Then she heard the sound of smashing glass and turned to see Maryann bashing at the front window with a lump of wood she'd found. Having smashed the window, she was clearing away the splinters of glass to climb in.

'Oi – what the bleedin' 'ell d'you think you're doing?' A gaunt woman in an apron had appeared from the next-door house. 'I'll have the coppers on you . . .'

Before Dot could turn and give a reasonable explanation for their conduct, Maryann had stormed over to the low wall and let out the loudest and most colourful string of invective Dot had ever heard. It brought the blood to her cheeks. She'd never heard Maryann so fluent and there were certain words she didn't even recognize. It looked for a moment as if Maryann was going to punch the woman, who eventually retreated back indoors, mouthing oaths. A moment later she was peering out of her front window. Dot didn't dare say a word. She wondered whether the woman would go for the police but, after all, what did it matter? Maryann turned on her, her face pale and taut.

'You coming in with me?' she demanded.

'Yes, of course.'

They hauled themselves in over the sill, Dot wrestling with her tight skirt. She cursed, scraping the back of her

339

leg on the way down. They climbed into the front parlour, and as their eyes adjusted to the light they saw that the room was set out in a stiff, formal fashion, the walls, floor and furniture all varying shades of brown. But there was nothing else to see and they moved quickly through the lower part of the house – back room, kitchen, all very neat and tidy. There was no sound.

Without speaking, they ran up the dark stairs with their runner of brown carpet. Although there was no point in trying to be quiet, Dot found herself wanting to tiptoe. She didn't like the musty smell of the place, its drabness, and most of all her growing dread of who might be here, what they might find.

There were three bedrooms off the landing. The smallest back room was completely empty, without even a covering on the floorboards. Having poked their heads inside they moved on to the middle one. A single bedstead was pushed up against the wall, with no bedclothes on it, only an old mattress, the ticking cover unpleasantly stained.

They exchanged glances and moved to the main bedroom at the front. Again the colouring of the room was brown, and it looked dark and uninviting in the strained light filtering through the nets. In silence they stood looking at the single bed with its coppery brown eiderdown, the bedside chair, chest of drawers and wardrobe, the long mirror on its door reflecting light from the window. The wallpaper was a deep coffee colour, marked with a thin, swirling pattern in black. There was no other decoration except for long moss-green curtains and, on the wall by the bed, a photograph in a frame.

Dot moved over to look and Maryann followed. A woman in her middle years looked out from the picture. Her hair was caught up and piled on her head, topped by a white bonnet with a flower at the side. She had a wide, handsome face with dark, emphatic brows. At the bottom edge of the picture could just be seen the frill of a white, high-necked blouse. She stared steadily out at them, rather solemn, neither smiling nor severe. Dot peered closely, leaning across the bed. The eyes, close up, seemed penetrating, hard, and she stepped back, somehow disconcerted.

'His mother,' Maryann said. The picture had wrung a distant memory from her. He had had it in the room he shared with her mother in Ladywood, but propped somewhere in the room, not on the wall. She only dimly remembered, having hardly been in there after her father died.

With loathing, she added. 'Oh, he'd've done anything for Mother, all right. She was the only person who ever mattered.'

She went to the wardrobe and opened it. Two suits of clothes hung there, smelling of camphor. Maryann was about to shut it again when Dot saw her reach down and pick something up from the floor of it. She turned, her face set grim.

It was a square of cloth, pale blue with a pattern of tiny diamonds in a darker blue. It was clearly torn from a small blouse because one side was part of the fastening edge with two buttonholes.

Dot couldn't make sense of this. A piece of rag?

'This'll be something,' she heard Maryann say, almost to herself. She looked at Dot. 'He always has a reason for everything. He's like a machine.'

She pushed the clothes out of the way and bent over once more. The only other thing, lying coiled in the corner of the cupboard, was a length of rope. Dot felt her stomach turn with dread as Maryann brought it out.

Before she could say anything, Maryann ran back out of the room, taking both the rag and rope with her. 'Cellar – there'll be a cellar.'

Dot followed the sound of her rushing boots down the stairs. Maryann was searching frantically, in the understairs cupboard, along the hall, anywhere where there might be a door to an underground room, and Dot helped, increasingly bewildered but filled with a sense of horrified misgiving. But they could find nothing and no one. The house was empty.

Eventually, once the possibilities all seemed exhausted, Maryann sank to her knees in the hall, gripping the skein of rope in her hands. She slumped forward, letting out a helpless, anguished howl.

'Where are you, you evil bastard? For God's sake, where's my baby? Give her back to me – just let me have her back!'

Thirty-Seven

Sylvia and Dot did everything for Maryann that night. She was in no state to manage. Dot had to lead her back to catch the tram from Acocks Green. All the energy, the fight, seemed to go out of her and she stumbled along helplessly on Dot's arm like someone barely alive.

Between them, Dot and Sylvia took the *Esther Jane* back to Tyseley Wharf. All evening Maryann was in shock, unable to eat, to move or do anything, and the other two women saw to the boats, the food, the children, as she sat, numb, unable to concentrate on anything that was happening. Dot and Sylvia had to try and explain to the children what had happened, to give comfort. Time swam past and when Sylvia came to Maryann, offering a generous tot of whisky in a cup, she found she was sitting on the edge of her bed in the cabin, the family already bedded down.

'Look, darling, get this inside you,' Sylvia instructed. 'You can't go on like this. Dot's going to sleep in here tonight. You come over and bunk up with me.'

Maryann put the cup to her lips, and sipped the pungent liquor. It trickled hot down inside her and within seconds she could feel its effects. Her head went swimmy and she felt as if she was swaying from side to side. Things became even more muddled and unreal. She allowed herself to be led, head reeling.

'I'll never sleep,' she said to Sylvia when they were

343

aboard the *Theodore*. She began to weep again. 'What can I do? I can't stand it.' She tore at her hair, trying to find an outlet for her pain. 'I want my Sally back, my baby – I can't stand to think of what he'll do to her!'

'We'll find her, we *will*! You've just got to hold on till tomorrow.' Sylvia pulled her into her arms. She was crying too and the two of them wept together, Sylvia rocking Maryann as if she were the baby. Maryann closed her eyes, wanting to surrender to this comfort, but instead, her guard weakened by the alcohol, she found that she was suddenly unable to stop herself sliding, sinking into dark, deeply remembered places inside herself, haunts of pain and revulsion so acute that suddenly she was gagging. She had to pull herself up shakily, hand over her mouth and struggle out of the cabin to retch into the cut again and again until she felt wrung out and exhausted. She couldn't move, couldn't think. Head spinning, she rested wretchedly against the cabin, wanting to bang her head against the roof so hard that she lost consciousness, escaped from the pain filling her every pore.

'Come on – I've brewed the tea.' Sylvia's pale head appeared beside her in the darkness. She spoke as if to a child. 'Come back in, lovey.'

The tea steadied the reeling in Maryann's head a little. Eyes swollen from weeping, she looked round at Sylvia.

'How can I sit here drinking tea? I should be walking the streets. I ought to know where to go and find her.'

'We'll do everything we can when morning comes,' Sylvia said. 'What can we do tonight? We've told the police.'

'I can't . . . I can't . . .' Maryann started to lose herself again.

Sylvia grasped her hand. 'Tell me,' she said gently. 'You've never said – about your stepfather.'

Maryann stared blearily across the cabin, seeming so distant that Sylvia thought for a moment she hadn't heard. But then she said, 'He killed my sister. D'you know that? And he's killed Amy. And now he's got our Sally . . . and I've got to find her – I can't sit here like this.'

She stood up and struggled to get out, stumbling up the steps.

'No, Maryann –' Sylvia caught her by the waist and held on, speaking softly, but firmly – 'you can't, not like this. Where're you going to go? Look, the police'll be looking for her – they *will*.' She steered her back to her seat and Maryann sank down.

'Come on – let's get you to bed.' Sylvia carefully shifted Rose from the main bed onto the side and helped Maryann to lie down. Neither of them undressed for the night. In her muzzy state Maryann was just aware of Sylvia easing herself onto the bed beside her. She didn't top and tail as was more normal on the narrow bed, but came in beside her.

'Come here, you poor love,' Sylvia whispered.

Maryann felt the comfort of arms round her, pulling her close, trying to console her.

'What's the address where your husband's staying in Oxford?' Dot asked the next morning.

Without question, Maryann trotted out the Adelaide Street address and a moment later Dot was off across the wharf in the morning sun.

The night had been terrible, almost sleepless, but the

345

brief periods when she lost consciousness were full of fractured, terrifying dreams. Daylight arrived like a reproach. How could she have slept? She was in a fever to be off again, searching, pursuing.

She shrugged off Sylvia's offer of breakfast. Still in her black skirt, an old blue cardigan pulled round her, she hurried over to the toll office. Before she reached it, amid the morning hubbub a voice reached her.

'Maryann – here, Maryann!'

It was Charlie Dean, grinning all over his face.

'Well, you're miles away this morning, aren't you? Must be in love or summat!'

Her expression as she turned to him wiped the smile off his face.

'Oh, have I gone and put my foot in it?' Contritely he took his cap off. 'What's the trouble?'

'It's my daughter.' As she spoke it felt as if words could not begin to convey the horror of the situation. 'She's been taken – by a man. A bad man . . .' She couldn't go on and ended by shaking her head.

'Oh.' Charlie looked nonplussed.

Urgently she moved closer to him. 'Charlie – there was a man before. You said you'd seen him on the wharf, looking for me – ages back. D'you remember? With a scarred face?'

Charlie nodded. 'You wouldn't forget his mug in a hurry I can tell you. Terrible. I've seen him about a couple of times. Not often.'

'When?' Maryann was so urgent to know that for a moment Charlie thought she was going to grab him by the throat. She looked a little deranged. 'Where? Where've you seen him?'

'Well, you know – about the place. In the road, like. I haven't seen him on the wharf again. Just walking about.

Oh – except once. The last time I saw the bloke he was up the shops – in the butcher's, I think. But other than that . . .'

'The butcher's? What – Osborne's?'

'That'd be it, yes. Can't think of anywhere else. Don't s'pose that's much help.'

Once Maryann had hurried on she realized it probably wasn't much help. He went to the butcher's once – well, so what? Mr Osborne would have been his polite, jolly self and have pretended he hadn't noticed the dreadful state of Norman Griffin's face and that would have been all there was to it. She asked a couple of other people round the toll office, but although they thought they'd seen him once they didn't have any more to say. But she couldn't keep still. Someone had to be able to help. That preacher was the one to go to. He might know something.

She found Pastor Owen saying goodbye to a small knot of people dispersing after a prayer meeting and launched herself at him.

'Well, I hope you're pleased with yourself!' she burst out, sending the remnant of the congregation scattering. She was too overwrought to care who heard her.

'Mrs Bartholomew!' He looked very startled. And just as malnourished and dishevelled as ever in his black clothes. She had wondered if he would remember her. Oh, he remembered all right.

'He's got my daughter now. Snatched her away while we were burying my mother in the cemetery and God alone knows what he's doing to her!' To her immense frustration she found herself weeping again. She wanted to hurt him, to make someone else feel the agony she was in, but something in her still responded to his innate sympathy and her anger melted into distress.

'What's this?' Pastor Owen's large eyes widened in consternation. He hovered before her, hands dithering in the air. 'What are you telling me? Can you say it more calmly?'

But she couldn't, could only sob, distraught. Pastor Owen stood before her looking agonized, as if he simply did not know what to do.

'I haven't seen our Mr Griffin in months,' he told her. 'Not since soon after you came that time. I'm very sorry. I've always meant to see you – down at the wharf, but the Lord has had other pastures for me lately.'

Gulping and trying to control herself, Maryann didn't reply.

'You must believe me.' The young man wrung his hands as he talked. 'When he first came to me, he did show genuine signs of contrition. He had a burdened soul. Yes, a burdened soul. He laid his troubles over his mother before me, and—'

'Burdened soul!' Maryann found she was screaming, hysterical. 'He's got a burdened soul all right! He's a murderer, he's filthy . . . oh, I can't even tell you.'

Sobbing, she ran from the church. Pastor Owen was no help to her. She had to go, to run and find Sally before it was too late. Why did she think anyone could ever be any help?

All day they searched. Another boater family looked after the children and Maryann, Dot and Sylvia moved between the police, the factory in Highgate and Norman Griffin's house in Acocks Green. He did not, as they had been assured he would, turn up at the factory that day. The house was empty and did not look as if he had returned to it. The window was still smashed and nothing had been moved inside. Round and round they went, as if on an awful circuit which yielded nothing.

The three of them stood outside the house, burning to keep moving, keep looking, but unsure what to do next.

'His mom!' Maryann said suddenly. 'She had a house in Handsworth.'

'Is she still alive?' Dot asked.

'Don't know – but let's go and find out.'

Across the city they went again.

'You must eat something, Maryann,' Sylvia said anxiously as they moved along on the tram. 'You've barely had a thing. You'll drop with exhaustion if you don't. Here – have this.'

Maryann ate the biscuit Dot offered, scarcely seeming to notice. She had to keep going, had to keep on, not keep still for a moment.

At the house in Handsworth they were told that old Mrs Griffin had died a few years back, having been well into her nineties by then.

'It's no good,' Dot said, when they had been back to the works in Highgate yet again. 'We're not going to find him like this. I vote we head back to Tyseley and get ourselves a meal before we drop.'

On the way back, Maryann left the others and called in at Mr Osborne's shop.

'Hello, m'dear!' he greeted her, beaming. 'Well, I haven't seen you for a month of Sundays. How're you keeping?'

'All right,' Maryann said. 'Look, I haven't stopped by for meat – I wanted to ask you if you've seen a man who's been into your shop lately.' She explained, described. Mr Osborne stood leaning forwards on the counter, considering, beside a plate of pigs' trotters.

'I think I do remember the man you mean,' he said, 'because, as you say, his face was so badly disfigured. You couldn't help but notice him. But he hasn't been in for a while now. No – not that I remember. What's your reason for asking, m'dear?'

'Oh, I just need to see him,' was all she was going to say, but Mr Osborne's kind, twinkly face made it all come spilling out, about Sally and how she knew it was this man who'd got her and *please* to keep an eye out.

'Well –' Mr Osborne stood up straight, looking shocked – 'what a terrible thing for you. Are you sure? I expect you've told the police, haven't you?'

'Oh yes,' she said desperately. 'They're s'posed to be looking too. But you know how it is these days.'

'Don't I just. Goodness me – I'll certainly keep my eyes peeled.'

She walked back to the wharf, exhausted, in despair. All day she had forced herself to think of anything except the reality of her child in the hands of Norman Griffin and what he might be doing to her because if she let herself imagine, she knew she'd go mad. All they could do was to keep searching, keep looking and hope and pray that it was not too late.

Dot and Sylvia were trying to cook tea when she reached the boats, but there was a knot of people round the *Theodore*, talking, asking questions, all deeply shocked by what had happened. Everyone wanted to help. Maryann saw that Charlie was among them, leaning against the cabin. She quailed, feeling she couldn't face any of it, the questions and especially the sympathy. Needing to avoid them all, she went to the *Esther Jane* and picked up the water cans.

'I'll fill up,' she called to Sylvia, who began to protest,

but she waved this away. ''I've got to keep on. It's the only way.'

She stood watching the silver thread of water filling the cans and imagined taking her kitchen knife and dragging it through the flesh of her arm or leg. She almost ached for it. Wouldn't that kind of agony be easier to bear than this? Once the cans were full she lugged them back towards the boats, glad of the harsh strain on her arms and back. The others kept a respectful distance, seeming to sense her need, for the moment, to be alone.

But as she made her way across the wharf she caught sight of a figure moving over towards the boats with a slow but sure stride. For a moment she just stared. It couldn't be! He wasn't supposed to be here! In a second she was almost running with the water carriers hauling on her arm sockets and reached him before he got to the boats, dropping the cans to the floor.

'Oh – you're here, you're here!' Tears streaming down her face, she was taken into Joel's arms, clasped to the familiar smell and shape of him, sobbing her anguish into his chest as he held and stroked her.

Thirty-Eight

Everyone was looking at them. Clinging to Joel, Mary-ann poured out all that had happened in incoherent snatches.

'He's got our Sally – I know it's him and I've been looking and looking and . . . we've got to find her . . . I can't stand it . . .' After holding onto her feelings all day they poured out now, running out of control. It didn't matter who was watching – she didn't even see them. For a few moments she could only dimly hear Joel's rumbling voice trying to comfort her, to make sense of what had happened. He took her face between his leathery hands and made her stop and look up at him.

'It's all amiss,' he said. 'Everything's amiss about this. But I'm here now. We won't stop till we get our Sally back.'

Dot and Sylvia had climbed onto the bank and were standing discreetly nearby, obviously full of sympathy but feeling awkward at the distraught state that both Maryann and Joel were in. Joel released Maryann and turned to them. They had never met him before and came and shook hands formally. Everyone was shy with one another. It was not a good time for Joel to be dealing with new people.

'Pleased to meet you,' Dot said, holding her hand out. 'Except for the circumstances. You received the telegram, then?'

Joel nodded, seeming a little overwhelmed by Dot's powerful presence.

'Came straight away. First train I could.' He looked down at Maryann with pained eyes. Then the others were crowding round, those who knew Joel greeting him, asking if he was better.

'Not quite myself, but nearly,' he said. 'Near enough so's I couldn't sit still there for a moment hearing this news.'

'What're we going to do?' Charlie asked. He seemed full of agitation. 'You can't just have some bloke run off with your daughter . . .'

Others called out their agreement. 'Come on, Joel – we'll come and help you find him.'

'We're ready – let's go now!'

As Maryann and Dot filled Joel in about all that had happened, Sylvia brought them cups of tea. Maryann couldn't seem to stop crying, the tears running down her cheeks as she talked.

'I've been back and forth all day – every place I can think of, his house, his factory and I can't find him. The police're s'posed to be looking but I don't know what they're doing. I don't know where they can! I don't know what else to do—'

'Let's go again.' Charlie seemed on fire with the need to do something. His tender feelings for Maryann were inflamed by seeing her in such distress. Some of the others called out in agreement.

'Let's go and track the bastard down – we'll find him! Come on – where do we start?'

'I'll come!' Maryann cried. 'I've got to – I can't sit still here till we've found her!'

Sylvia came over to Maryann and gently took her arm, speaking both to her and Joel.

'You must have some food first. Maryann, you've been on the go all day with nothing – and your husband must be hungry as well.' She ignored Maryann's protests that they didn't need food, that they should go right away. 'Come on, love, there's some stew ready.'

'We'll have ourselves a bite to eat –' Joel steered Maryann by the arm – 'and then we'll go and get him.'

It was already getting dark by the time they set off. Three of the men said they would go to Norman Griffin's house and see if there was any sign of him. Charlie wanted to come to the Highgate factory with Joel. Maryann refused absolutely to be left behind. Sylvia said she and Dot would stay and put the children to bed. Sylvia stood on the back of the *Theodore*, a neat figure holding Rose's hand, watching as they left. The men had instinctively armed themselves with some of the few things they possessed: screwdrivers, hammers and windlasses.

Maryann walked through Highgate with a sense of hopelessness. She'd been back and back to these places. What could they possibly hope to find? But what else could they do except go round and round, watching, waiting for Norman Griffin to appear, to slip up and give himself away? If he was not at his house or his business, where could he be, and how would they ever be able to find him? A sick, unbearable feeling rose in her at the thought of Sally with him. But she pushed it violently away. If she opened the door to it she would end up tearing her clothes like a madwoman. She must think of nothing but *finding* Sally. At least Joel had come now, and with Charlie's reassuring presence too she felt much less alone.

The evening had clouded over after a warm day and a light drizzle began to fall, which brushed her face like cloud. Charlie tactfully walked a few paces ahead of them. Maryann looked at Joel beside her, noticing with anxiety how stiffly he was walking. She put her hand on his arm.

'Is it still hurting?'

'Not much – not enough to fuss about.' A few seconds later his voice burst out in the darkness. 'Why's he done this? *Why*? What does he want with us, to do this?'

Maryann heard all the grief and anger in his question and in anguish she squeezed his arm tightly.

'That's what he's like . . . what he's always been like.' But Joel had never really wanted to hear it.

Charlie stopped and waited for them. 'How far along is it?' he whispered in the quiet street.

'Down on the right,' Maryann said. She walked ahead. A car was parked ahead of them on the road, but there was no sign of anyone about. A few moments later they were standing in front of the works – *Albert Griffin, Toolmakers & Machinists*.

In Acocks Green, the three boatmen who'd walked from Tyseley Wharf found their way to the house in Cameron Road. Maryann had told them they should be able to climb in through the front window, but they found that a board had been nailed over it. He'd been back then, or someone had. Between them, with their few tools, they quietly prised the board off and climbed inside.

They had no fear of switching the lights on. If they were caught, what did that matter? They were only doing what the police should have done – they had right on their side. Walking round the house, they could see nothing amiss. They looked round downstairs and then went up to the bedrooms. Had they been there before, with Maryann, they might have noticed that certain things were different: the wardrobe door was swinging open and there was nothing inside. Some items had disappeared from the chest of drawers and the walls were now completely bare, where before a portrait had hung above the bed. But these details were lost on the men.

Downstairs they looked, as Maryann had done, for signs of other hiding places in the house. They went out to the back and opened the door of the privy. The flush toilet looked innocently back at them in the gloom. They shook their heads. Nothing doing there.

As they were passing back through the kitchen, one of them noticed something that made him stop. The floor was covered with grey lino, and he stood puzzling, noticing that it had been strangely laid. Instead of being arranged to cover the largest amount of floor with the least number of cuts, there seemed to be a panel of linoleum covering the middle section of the small square room. At one end it met the wall, at the other it was held down by a small cupboard with a meat safe on top.

'Let's have a look here,' he murmured, and shifted the cupboard across onto the other strip. The linoleum easily rolled back, and underneath they saw the square shape of a trapdoor. For a moment they all looked at each other.

It took them seconds only to lift the trapdoor. On a beam just below they found a switch for the cellar's light, and climbed down the brick stairs, each waiting at the bottom until all three of them were down. The cellar was not large, nor did it feel damp; it was very clean and obviously recently swept, though there was a stink in there which they did not recognize as the source of their unease. All they could see were a couple of shelves to their left on which rested bottles and jars and, in the far corner, what looked like a heap of old linoleum.

One of the men went over and, almost idly, lifted up the corner of it. He dropped it again instantly and recoiled, cursing.

'Lord God Almighty . . . oh my word . . .'

The other two went to see for themselves. They looked at each other pale-faced. One clamped a hand over his mouth.

'For God's sake, let's get out of here,' the other said.

They ran, stumbling up the stairs and out into the dark street.

'This his place then?' Joel looked up at the frontage of the Cheapside works.

'There's no night shift, anyroad,' Charlie commented.

'So – you reckon we need to go in?'

Maryann could hear the doubt in Joel's voice. His innocence both touched and enraged her. Joel's life had not contained the darkness of Norman Griffin and in some way he still could scarcely believe that such cruel wickedness as Griffin was capable of could truly exist. It was in the cellar beneath his premises in Ladywood that Sal, her sister, had suffered at Norman Griffin's hands.

'We've *got* to go and look,' she hissed at him, enraged by the doubt in his voice.

Charlie tried to peer down the grating at the front of the factory.

'Can't see a thing – but there's sure to be a cellar. It's just how we get down there . . .'

Maryann was burning with impatience. 'Can't we get the grating up? Climb down there?'

'It's not as easy as all that,' Charlie said. 'Let's have a look round first – see if there's any other way.'

Narrow alleys led down each side of the works. The three of them moved cautiously along the one to the right, Maryann between Joel and Charlie, who was in the lead. He tripped and almost fell over a piece of wire.

'Bugger it! – 'Scuse us,' he said, catching his balance against the wall. 'It's so bleeding dark down here.' They could just make out that there were windows in the side of the building, which must have let in precious little light in the daytime, as they were so close to the wall of the premises next door. Gradually, struggling over the uneven ground, which seemed to be strewn with rubble, they reached the end of the works. There was a thin yard at the back, fenced off from the one belonging to another factory in the street behind. The three of them stood, straining their eyes in the darkness.

'Why didn't we bring a torch?' Maryann said desperately. 'This is hopeless! How're we s'posed to get anywhere like this?'

'Hark – what's that?' Charlie held up a hand and Maryann's heart began to hammer, almost unbearably.

From the street they heard the sound of an engine starting up.

'That's a moty car,' Joel said.

They breathed more easily again.

'Come on – let's move on round,' Joel said.

He led the way round the back of the building, sliding his hand along in the darkness. Maryann was now immediately behind, and when they had almost reached the far end, Joel suddenly gave a gasp and almost toppled forward. He had been unable to see that the ground suddenly fell away and had almost tumbled down a deep cleft in front of him.

Charlie struck a match, and in the couple of seconds' flash of illumination they saw that there were steps down from the corner of the works.

'Why the hell didn't we bring a proper lamp?' Charlie grumbled.

Another match, held lower, showed them that at the bottom was a rusty iron door. When they climbed down they found it was held shut with a chain and a hefty padlock. Charlie shook his head.

'We'll have a hell of a job getting in here.'

Joel tried his strength against the door. It gave slightly, tugging on the chain, which seemed to rattle far too loudly in the quiet.

'If we can't smash the padlock, I reckon we'd be able to break that down,' Joel said. 'If I was up to full strength, I could.'

With their hammer and the windlasses they smashed at the padlock, an erratic process in the pitch dark. Striking another match showed them that they had only succeeded in denting it, and the chain wouldn't break or give. Maryann stood watching, her whole body tensed to breaking point, wanting to smash at the door herself.

'It's no good!' she cried after a few moments. 'We'll never do it like this!'

Joel stood up straight, considering. 'Look, pal – let's go at the hinges. I don't reckon they're up to much.'

They leaned and shoved and kicked. Joel aimed a blow low on the door with his leg and reeled back in the narrow space with a grunt.

'Confound this back of mine!'

'Here – let me.'

With a few kicks from Charlie's powerful leg, the lower hinge came away.

'I can get in through there!' Maryann cried.

'Just hang on.' Charlie kicked at the door again and Joel joined in. Soon the top hinge gave as well and the door fell in with a crash and fell, hanging at an angle from the chain.

They walked into even more profound darkness, straining their eyes to see anything of the space around them.

'This is hopeless,' Charlie said. In the flare of light from another match, they saw they were in a narrow room. Maryann had a brief impression of a large, dark shape to her right.

'Here – there's a light!'

She turned on the switch by the door. The dim bulb in the middle of the ceiling gave off light that strained to reach the walls. The big object by the wall turned out to be a rusting old lathe. Ahead of them was a partition wall with a door in it. Otherwise the space was clear: brick walls, earth floor. Nothing else.

'Oh, where is she!' Maryann wailed. 'What's he done with her? Could she be in there?'

She went to the door in the partition and hammered her fist on it, beginning to sob. 'Sally – Sally, it's your mom. Are you in there?'

Nothing. They stood listening.

'Let's get in there and see,' Charlie said grimly. 'Why's he got so many locked doors in this place? What's there to nick?'

'Sally!' Maryann banged again. 'It's all right, bab – it's your mom and dad.' She turned to Joel. 'Oh, this is no good. She'd call out if she was there wouldn't she?'

Joel nodded miserably. 'Unless . . .' They neither of them wanted to put into words unless what.

'Right,' Charlie said, positioning himself to kick the door.

'What's that?' Joel held him back. From low down somewhere came a tapping sound, getting louder, insistent, frantic.

Maryann went to the door, throwing herself against it. 'Get it open, for God's sake!'

'Mind out!' Joel caught hold of her, shifting her away and he and Charlie set to at once, kicking at the door with all their strength. Unlike the outer door it was made only of wood and one of Charlie's kicks splintered it. In a few moments they'd kicked it down.

Maryann ran in ahead of the men, looking round frantically in the poor light coming through the door. It was a continuation of the long cellar, only twelve feet or so across, partitioned off and empty and completely bare except, except for . . . A cry escaped from her. There in the corner was all she needed to see: lying on sacking, Sally's blonde head, the torn cloth tied round her mouth, the ropes round her ankles and wrists, head straining up, her pleading eyes burning into them.

Thirty-Nine

Joel carried Sally back all the way, cradling her in his arms. Only the deep sound of his breathing betrayed to Maryann the depth of his distress and anger. He sat on the tram back to Tyseley with Sally's head pressed to him like a tiny infant's and every so often Maryann heard him make a low, comforting sound, which seemed to rumble up from deep within him.

For a moment Maryann let her head rest on his shoulder in the tram's gloomy light. It seemed to have been the longest day of her life! All she could feel now was overwhelming relief at having Sally back, alive and safe in their arms. What had happened to her, what state she was in, only time would tell. They would have to go to the police again, to deal with everything, but that could wait until the morning. They had her back – her baby would be home and safe. Tears ran down her face again. She leaned round and laid her hand on Sally's head.

'Mom's here,' she murmured. 'It's all right. It's all going to be all right.' Joel freed one of his hands and pulled her close, stroking her cheek.

After thanking Charlie, they walked home across the wharf. It felt later than it was – barely ten o'clock – and Sylvia and Dot were still up and waiting. Both jumped off the *Theodore* and came running towards them. At the sight of Sally in Joel's arms, Sylvia burst into tears.

'Oh, thank God! I can't believe it! Oh, the little love – is she all right?'

'Where was she?' Dot asked.

Briefly they explained.

'Look, we've got the rest of the children in with us,' Sylvia said, wiping her eyes. 'We thought it was for the best – not knowing what time you'd be back. They were unsettled.'

Maryann knew that in normal circumstances Joel might have bridled at the idea of someone like Sylvia taking charge of his children. Bad enough having them on the boats at all. But tonight everyone felt close, united in relief, even though Joel and the two women barely knew each other.

'Good of you,' he said gruffly, beginning to move to the *Esther Jane*. 'We'd best get this 'un tucked up.'

'Our kettle's just boiled,' Dot said. 'I'll bring you over a drink in a minute.'

Maryann looked at them. 'I don't know how to thank you. You've both been so kind.'

'Don't be silly,' Dot said briskly. 'Absolutely the least we could do in the circumstances.'

Sylvia reached out and squeezed Maryann's arm. 'Is she all right?'

'I don't know. God, Sylv – you should've seen where we found her.' Her voice began to crack. 'But we've got her back – that's the main thing.'

They'd tucked Sally up in their bed and she lay on her back, staring up at the ceiling.

Joel and Maryann looked at each other, eyes very troubled. Ever since they had rescued her she had lain limp and silent.

'Sally?' Maryann perched on the bed beside her and took her hand. It was ice cold. 'Would you like a nice cup of hot milk? Or some cocoa? Warm you up?'

There was no response, except a flicker of her eyes.

'I'll put a bit on to warm anyway,' Joel whispered behind her. Both of them knew they had to have something they could do: they both felt so helpless.

Maryann waited, stroking Sally's hand, her hair, making soft, reassuring noises. She was appalled, wrung out by the sight of her child. Sally looked like a shell of the pretty, lively little girl she had been.

'Here.' Joel handed her a cup of warm, sweet milk.

'Can you sit up and drink a bit of this, pet?' Maryann supported Sally into a sitting position and she managed to take a couple of mouthfuls of the milk before turning her head away.

'All right – you sleep now, my lovely. I'll sit with you. You're safe here. No one's going to hurt you ever again.'

She sat on the edge of the bed, tears running endlessly down her cheeks as the fear and tension gradually drained out of her. Her little girl was here, she was safe! But she was so sad and frightened by the state Sally was in. She held her hand and tried to hum to her, until at last Sally began to drift off to sleep. Maryann sat on for some time, unable to let go.

When Sally had slipped off at last, Maryann and Joel squeezed onto the side bench, their eyes turning every few seconds to the tormented little figure on the bed.

Joel put his arm round Maryann's shoulders and leaned down to kiss her hair. She heard the soft whisper of his lungs close to her and the rhythm of his heart.

'Back home,' Joel said softly, stroking her back. 'With my little bird at last.'

She nodded into his chest, feeling warm and cared for. She kept her head down, knowing that if she looked up he would kiss her, knew he was longing to kiss her, but she couldn't face that. Not now. She only wanted to feel the comfort of him near her.

'I don't know what we're going to do. She looks so bad,' she said desperately.

There was a silence, filled only with the tinny tick of their alarm clock, then she heard Joel's voice, filled with a bitterness she had never heard in him before. 'We've got to get that bugger. That we have.'

It was a few minutes later that they heard the tapping at the door. When Joel opened up, they saw the three boatmen waiting with pale, solemn faces. Beside them was a policeman.

'It's all right.' Joel spoke quietly, standing in the hatches. 'We got her – found her at the works – Griffin's. She's in here with us, fast asleep.'

The solemnity on their faces turned to bewilderment. They looked at each other, seemingly unable to take in what Joel was telling them.

'Are you sure?' one of them said, eventually. They seemed totally confused. Joel climbed out onto the bank into the damp air and Maryann followed.

'Course we're sure!' Joel told them. 'Not going to mistake our own daughter, are we?'

'What's up?' Maryann asked them, a sense of dread coming over her once more.

The policeman, a chubby-faced man, seemed to think he'd better take over.

'While these men were searching certain premises in Acocks Green – according to your instructions, I

365

understand – they found a body in the cellar. A child's body.'

Maryann couldn't move. She clamped her jaws together.

'Thing is,' one of the boatmen said, 'we thought it must be your wench. Only she were . . .' He stopped, face creasing in distress.

'The way the body was,' the policeman said flatly, 'anyone'd have been hard pushed to say who she is.'

'My God,' Joel said.

Now do you believe me? Maryann thought. 'I've been telling them for weeks he's a murderer!' she blurted out. 'So now you know for certain, don't you?'

'Thank Christ it's not your little 'un, Joel,' one of the men said. They all looked extremely shocked.

'But it would've been if we'd left it any longer,' Joel said grimly. 'What're you going to do about it?' he demanded of the policeman.

'We'll find him and arrest him, of course,' he said with dignity. 'As soon as we possibly can. We'll put all the men we can onto it.'

''Bout bloody time too!' Maryann lost control of herself. Her voice was edged with hysteria. 'None of you've ever taken any notice of what I said, have you?'

When they went back into the cabin after thanking the boatmen for their help, she could no longer contain herself but shook uncontrollably, as if she was having one of her nightmares while she was still awake. Even Joel holding her close didn't dispel the terror and despair which filled her.

'We've got to get away from here,' she said between chattering teeth. 'Away from Birmingham – away from *him*. While he's still on the loose, none of us are safe.'

Joel gave a long sigh into her hair, stroking her back.

'I don't s'pose we can just go like that. We need to talk to the police – make sure they get him before he does anything else.'

The whole Bartholomew family moved into the *Theodore* for those days. They towed the butty to a quieter part of the wharf, and Sylvia and Dot took the *Esther Jane* back to Coventry to work short trips out of Sutton Stop and bring in some money. The children enjoyed the enforced break and being able to play on the bank, though Maryann knew the boys were aware of the unease and trouble around them, and she insisted that they never move out of sight of the boat.

All she could think about was Sally. She knew that she might be able to tell them things which would help catch Norman Griffin, but she could not stand the thought of forcing anything more on the little girl. For the first couple of days Sally seemed to be in a trance, sitting or lying staring ahead of her, not speaking, barely eating, her pale face wearing a vacant expression, as if she couldn't bear to inhabit her body. Maryann sat with her whenever she could, holding her hand, stroking her hair, making gentle noises to try and reassure her that she was safe now, that everything would be all right.

Joel was finding it hard to bear. His eyes, when they rested on his daughter, were full of pain and anger at what had been done to her. He was tender with her but also full of frustration that she could not, or would not, tell them what would lead them to Norman Griffin. The weather was fine and to relieve his feelings he took refuge in working on the *Theodore*, scrubbing her out, splicing ropes, doing repairs. Maryann could see that his back was still hurting. She went to him outside on the

367

first afternoon with a mug of tea. Joel was squatting in the hold, looking at the tarpaulin sheets, and she climbed along to him.

'Cuppa for you.'

Joel looked up, letting go of the coarse ropes to take the mug.

'Ta.' He drank some of the sweet tea, then stared out to his left across the cut. At last he said, 'Can't stand seeing her like that.' She saw tears in his eyes, which he wiped away quickly with a rub of his sleeve.

'I know.' She swallowed, unable to comfort him. All the time, inside herself, she was terrified of identifying too much with her daughter. She had to prevent herself revisiting places of pain and horror which she had shut away in herself so long now, or she would fall to pieces. She had to stay calm, to hold herself together for all of them.

The other children couldn't understand why Sally was like she was and kept asking why she didn't come out and play. 'She's poorly,' Maryann told them. 'Just leave her be for a day or two, eh? I s'pect she'll be better soon.'

She felt torn, as if on a rack, between all her family's emotions. And, stretched across the middle of it, she forced herself to remain numb in order to be strong.

The police came several times. They had visited Janet Lambert and now believed that the two murders had been committed by the same man. They had no idea of the identity of the other young girl found in Norman Griffin's cellar. The only clue was her long blonde hair. On Maryann's advice they visited Mrs Biggs, her mother's neighbour, who had been to the funeral. She admitted that Norman Griffin had been to visit Flo a number of times before she died. But they had no idea where he had disappeared to now. Neighbours had been asked to watch his house. So far, he had not returned.

'Where can he be?' Joel kept saying, with more and more pent-up frustration as the days passed. His ignorance of the city, of anything but the cut, only added to his sense of angry helplessness. It was against all his habits to sit still like this, on these calm days in early summer which were ideal for trips, while strangers were working his boat and he couldn't get a load on and get ahead. How much longer would they have to wait?

After a few days Sally seemed a little improved. She had slept a lot and began to eat a bit more. On a sunny morning Rose came to her and asked timidly if she wanted to come and play out and Sally nodded. Maryann felt a leap of hope inside her. Tears came to her eyes as she saw Nance's little girl take Sal's hand and lead her into the bright light, along the towpath to where the others were waiting. Maryann got on with her chores, and about an hour later Sally came back, slipping down the steps into the cabin.

Maryann followed her in and found her sitting on the side bench, her face pale and drawn.

'What's up, bab? Don't you feel very well?'

Sally shook her head. 'I wanted to be inside for a bit.'

Seeing the fear in her eyes, Maryann gently put her arms round her. She knew those feelings; the sense of fear, of panic suddenly taking her over.

'That's a good idea,' she said, kissing the top of Sally's head. 'It's nice and cosy in here, isn't it?'

She felt Sally nod. They sat in silence for a few minutes while Maryann rocked her frightened little girl back and forth.

'Sally,' she said very gently, 'you know when we found you? Had you been in that place for long?'

The child shook her head. Into Maryann's chest, she said, 'He'd just put me there – just before. I was somewhere else before. He left me there, then you came – straight after. He took me there in his moty car . . . I had to lie down in the back . . .'

As she spoke Maryann felt the hairs stand on end all over her body. She pulled back and looked into Sally's face.

'You mean – when we found you he'd only just left you there?' She heard again in her mind the sound of the car engine starting up in the street as they stood at the back of the factory. Seeing Sally nod, she whispered, 'Oh, my God!' A shudder passed through her. He had been there behind the factory as they arrived at the front! As they felt their way down one side of the works he must have been creeping along the other. How was it he always seemed to be invisible, to move like a shadow that no one could find or catch?

Holding Sally close again, she whispered, 'It's all right, my lovely. We'll never let him near you again.'

Days passed and still the police were making no progress. Sylvia and Dot brought the *Esther Jane* back, as arranged. Joel was feverish with the need to get going again, however overwhelmingly he wanted to see Norman Griffin caught.

Maryann had hoped to see Sylvia and Dot off in style when they left the cut – at least to have a little goodbye celebration. As it was, there was too much grimness and worry to occupy everyone and the two women didn't want to intrude any further on the family's problems.

'We're going back down to the Grand Union to be allocated new boats,' Dot said. The children were all very sad to see them go. Rose cried heartbrokenly when she heard that Sylvia was leaving.

'Never mind, darling.' Sylvia hugged her tightly. 'I'll see you whenever I can. And one day I'll have a home where you can come and see me.' Maryann was touched by Sylvia's bravery. Her future was very uncertain. Who knew how she was going to make a life when she had to leave the cut?

Both of them hugged Maryann and even Dot was tearful when the time came to depart.

'This is certainly a time I'll never forget,' she said.

'You've been so good to me,' Maryann told them. 'I shall miss you both – all our chats and that.'

Sylvia put her arms round both of them and they stood together in a tearful huddle, until Dot broke away. 'We'll miss our train if we carry on like this,' she said.

'We'll see you whenever we can!' both of them promised.

The family waved them off as they disappeared across the wharf, bundles of belongings in their arms; they turned at the last moment, each managing to free an arm to wave. Maryann thought of the night they'd first arrived, how strange, how alien they'd seemed. She could see especially how Dot had changed. Even the way she wore her hair was softer, her fringe had grown again and was no longer a hard line across her forehead. She knew them both so well now, knew that whatever their upbringing, their class, and however seldom they might be able to meet, they were friends for life. She blew them a kiss to answer their last wave, then looked up at Joel beside her. It was just the two of them now. Bobby was working the Grand Union and they wouldn't get him back for a while. She was so happy to have Joel back, yet she felt very distant from him, as if shut in on herself, frozen inside. She felt a sudden pang of dread at being alone with him again.

The next day they untied their pair of boats from Tyseley and slipped quietly away from the wharf, heading south in the cool, quiet morning with a load for Banbury.

Later that day, in a Birmingham street, a blackout curtain moved at an upper window. Had anyone been looking they might have caught sight of a face peering cautiously out. It was a face which did not dare venture out into the light of day. The face of someone whose features were so distinctive, so disfigured, that for the moment hiding in an upper room was the only way left to live. The face turned a little from side to side, looking up and down the street, as if waiting for someone. Then the curtain fell back and it disappeared into the darkness.

Forty

The *Esther Jane*'s engine coughed, then jumped into throbbing life in the dawn, scattering alarmed moorhens towards sanctuary in the reeds. The Bartholomews had tied up the boats for the night on a remote stretch of the Oxford cut, and woke to find themselves still alone, no other boats nearby. The water was a deep, muddy green, lightly veiled by shreds of mist.

From the back of the *Theodore* Maryann watched Joel, ahead of her on the *Esther Jane*, catch the rope flung to him by Ezra, who then scampered expertly back aboard before Joel poled the boat off the mud close to the bank. Maryann fixed the helm in place while Rose untied the *Theodore* from its mooring pins. They were in a good position to move off, she noticed with the small part of her mind that was paying attention. The routine of morning departure was so familiar as to be automatic. She steered out behind the *Esther Jane*, smelling the churned-up mud. Ahead of her, Joel stood at the tiller, cap on his head, looking resolutely in front of him.

When we were first married, he kept turning round, waving at me, she thought. *As if he couldn't stop looking, couldn't believe I was really here. And I was the same. Not now, though.* She gave a sigh out of her deep sadness, watching Joel's implacable back, which was turned firmly towards her. *God help us*, she thought. *What's happened to us? How did everything get like this?* Here

373

they were again, Joel with the boys on one boat, her and the girls on the other. That was how it was now – separated by night as well. And, in the daytime, barely speaking. Nothing had been right since Joel came back. The initial shock of events had brought them close for a while, but ever since they had seemed to grow further and further apart.

Distracted by a sound from the cabin, she peered through the hatches to see if the kettle was boiling yet. Sally was trying to wipe over Ada's and Esther's faces and Ada was squawking and fighting her. The twins were a handful, but Sally was managing.

It was her fault, Maryann knew, but she couldn't help it. She wanted Joel close to her, to feel the comfort of him, yet she couldn't bear it when he came near her. At first they'd had Sally with them in their bed, keeping her safe, trying to comfort her. After two nights they had moved her onto the side bench so they could reclaim their marriage bed, and Joel was so hungry for her, so insistent. He was her husband, of course he was – what was wrong with that?

She lay frozen in the roseate light, hearing his sighs of pleasure as his hands moved over her, caressing, pulling her close against him so she could feel how urgently he wanted her.

'Oh, that's better.' She felt his breath against her ear. 'Oh, my bird, I've missed you. I know I'm home now.'

She tried to respond, to lie close to him, her hands stroking his wide back, his hair, trying to desire him, to want what had to happen. Eyes closed, she tried to force her body to cooperate with the sensations of Joel's lovemaking. His breathing became fast, excited. Maryann felt a frightening tightness growing deep within her. She

She broke out in a sweat, not just from the heat of his body close to hers but from utter panic, and she found herself struggling for breath. Forcing her eyes open, she looked into Joel's face. Why did she feel so cold and detached from him? Why couldn't she just love him back? *This is Joel, your husband! Joel, who loves you.* His eyes were shut, his lashes rusty-coloured arcs, closed against her, mouth feeling for her with the blind instinct of a baby, wanting her, kissing, nuzzling . . . The tightness in her swelled and a whimper escaped from her which Joel heard as an indication of pleasure and he rolled over onto her, weighing her down with what felt an inescapable weight. And all at once, in the shadowy light, the lips reaching for hers were not his, the face breathing hotly on her in the gloom not Joel's, but scarred and pitted, horribly distorted and the eyes boring into her with what seemed sadistic lust were Norman Griffin's when he forced her down in the front room in their Ladywood house, heavy as a fallen statue on top of her, trapping her under him so she could not move. Revulsion and panic exploded in her and she tore at Joel's back with her nails, kicking, struggling, letting out desperate, muffled cries under him.

'Get off me – get off, let me out!'

She sank her teeth into his shoulder and bit hard, panting and crying and Joel reeled back from her, clutching at the deep welts she had made with her teeth.

'Darn it! What the—? What the hell d'you do that for?'

Through the blood pounding in her ears, she could barely hear the frustrated anger in his voice. She had curled into a tight ball on her side to protect herself and for some moments couldn't be sure if she was inhabiting her younger self or her daughter. Sally's suffering possessed her, wrapped itself round her tightly with her own memories. She was a child again, trapped in a dark place, terrified of what would be done to her. The horror began to choke out of her. She moaned and sobbed.

'Maryann? Love?' Joel sounded frightened. Cautiously he touched her shoulder, but she fought him off. She was still horror struck and could not see him as he was. He was someone else, someone dangerous. She was so far down in her pain and fear that she barely knew he was there. Joel knelt, watching her, bewildered. Nothing had happened like this before. Not even in the early days, when she was afraid to give herself to him. He had known she was fragile, had suffered something, but he had been confident then that with enough patience, his gentleness and the pleasure of love would thaw her and bring her through. He knew no other way – this was what was natural to him. And it had done, he thought. He had touched her with care and respect and loved her into pleasure. He had never before seen her as she was now.

After a time her crying stopped and she lay quiet. They were both silent behind the little curtains veiling the bed. Maryann looked out from between her lashes, as if emerging from the darkness to see little chinks of soft light, and sensed Joel still close to her, heard his breathing. Her cheeks were wet with tears and she felt exhausted, wrung out. She could not look at him.

'You don't want me,' she heard him say flatly.

She couldn't bring any words to her lips to reassure him.

Eventually Joel pulled up the bedclothes with a heavy sigh, turned away from her and was soon asleep.

It had not got any better. It was a month now. In those early days when Sally was back with them, Maryann had been very gentle with her. At first the little girl wouldn't speak at all and seemed in a trance. Day by day, though, she became more herself as the impact of the shock receded, and she began to get up and play with the others. Maryann had warned them not to ask her questions, and in any case they soon forgot their curiosity about where Sally had disappeared to and she, though quiet and seeming older suddenly, fitted in with them as before. Alone, though, sometimes Maryann tried to get her to talk.

'Did he touch you?' she asked her, one day in the cabin.

Sally stared back at her, wide-eyed. It took Maryann back to the day she had asked the same question of Amy and Margaret Lambert and seen the fear and shame flicker in their eyes.

'That man – Mr Griffin. Did he do things you didn't like? Touch you where he shouldn't?' She wanted to speak calmly but somehow the words came out sounding harsh. 'It's all right,' she added more gently. 'If he did, he shouldn't've done. It's not you that's wrong – it's him.'

She saw her daughter's blue eyes fill with tears. 'I shouldn't've gone with him. He said he'd get us all some nice things – sweeties and that . . .'

'Course he did!' Maryann said fiercely, sitting down beside Sally and putting her arm round her. 'That's because he's a bad man and a liar. Weren't you frightened – of his face and the way he was?'

'A bit. But he spoke to me ever so nice. And he had a little dolly with him in a pretty dress, said he'd give it me in a minute, when we got to where we was going. He never did, though.'

'And where did you go?' Maryann asked, heart beating faster.

'He took me in his moty car, said I could have a ride if I was good and quiet. We went to a shop and bought some mints and he said I could have them when we got home. He never gave them me. Then he took me to a house. Later, when it was dark. I kept saying I wanted to go home.'

'Where was it?' Maryann couldn't help asking, even though she knew that Sally could really have no idea.

'He wouldn't have me sitting in the car. Said it was a game and I had to lie down on the floor and he put a rug over me so I never saw nothing. When we got to the house –' her voice stalled, became halting – 'he said I wasn't to make a noise, wasn't to cry. I don't know where it was. It was all brown inside. And he took me upstairs and there was a bed and a woman's face and he made me . . . he made me . . . she kept looking at me all the time . . .'

'A woman?' Maryann frowned.

'On the wall. I went into the picture with the lady. She was pretty. She had a hat on with a feather in.'

The picture. It came to her. The picture of Norman Griffin's mother with her proud, stern face.

Maryann gently pulled her into her arms. 'Oh, my baby. My poor baby.'

Thoughts of what he had done to Sally wouldn't leave her. Maryann felt scraped raw. She knew now that the fringes of these feelings had begun to surface again when she was in the hospital in Oxford, and she had pushed them away. But now memories kept coming to her at odd times, unbidden except by a chance fall of the light, certain smells: sweat, a whiff of smoke from someone's cigarette, an odd sound or feeling of cold on her skin. Her own wounds tore open, memories she had long hoped to bury seeping out again and, with them, the terrible knowledge of what he had done to her daughter when she had been unable to protect her. Once again he seemed to be everywhere, creeping, oozing into every situation. Life became like a bad dream, in which he was the dark shadow at the end of each corridor, the face at every window.

Yet she couldn't speak of it, or explain it to Joel. Standing at the helm of the *Theodore* that morning, she felt utterly hopeless. Even to Sally she could not bring herself to say that this man had been her stepfather and had committed the very same foul acts with her. It was too shameful, too hard to bring the words out or explain. She found herself longing for Dot and Sylvia. Though she had never brought herself to talk to them about it, now she felt as if that might just be possible. They would try to comfort her, would not demand anything from her. It would be so much easier than trying to speak to Joel, who wanted her love and her body so badly, yet each time he tried to get close to her she suddenly became like a frightened child again, crying out and sobbing with panic. And, she thought, rage flaming in her, he never asked, never tried to understand why she felt as she did. He had just cut himself off from her, hurt and rejected, unable to find any words of comfort for her. She felt utterly abandoned and lonely, even though Joel was here with her only yards away along the cut.

Forty-One

As spring slid into a warm summer, the Bartholomews' boats worked the Oxford cut. As they travelled north this time, on the stretch where the Oxford shared a section of cut with the Grand Union, Maryann kept an eye out to see if she would spot Sylvia and Dot. Last time they came along here, they had spotted each other close to Nethercote and there had been much excited waving and calling out, exchanging scraps of news while on the move. Sylvia, steering the monkey boat, actually jumped with excitement on catching sight of them.

'Maryann, we miss you! Is everyone all right? Coo-eee – Rose! Hello, darling – see you soon!' And she blew kisses as they passed and her voice faded.

And then Maryann spotted that their third crew member, all smiles beside Dot on the butty, was Bobby! The children waved and shouted.

'We need you!' Maryann teased. 'What're you doing on there with them?'

'Keeping these two in order!' Bobby shouted.

'That's what he thinks!' Dot called.

Bobby's grin and Dot's tanned, radiant face came to her and her spirits lifted. If only they could all be together, she thought as they moved apart, calling, 'See you soon – somewhere!'

It was a month since they'd been to Birmingham. They made their way through the city on a muggy afternoon, the air heavy with smoke and fumes. The noise of the place seemed overwhelming to Maryann: the roar of buses and shriek of brakes on the bridges running over the cut, the clatter of trains and racket from the factories along the banks. She felt wound up to the hilt, her nerves assaulted by the noise, and she wanted to ask Joel to turn round, for them not to have to be here. But of course they couldn't turn round when they had a full load of coal to deliver, the laden boats riding low in the water. Even if she called to Joel, who was ahead of her, he couldn't hear her. After all, she thought sadly, when did they ever really speak to each other these days in any case?

While they were unloading at Tyseley, Maryann went to find Charlie Dean. Looking up and down the wharf, she soon spotted his jaunty figure by the cab of a truck, squinting as he looked up at the driver, cap tilted to the back of his head. She waited, arms folded, until he turned and saw her. She forgot for a moment all her grim troubles, when his face broke into a grin at the sight of her in her blue frock and boots, dark hair curling round her face. She was one who didn't half make him wish he was young and free and that she wasn't already wedded to another man!

'Hello there!' He strode over. ''Bout time you got yourselves back here – haven't seen you in weeks!'

Maryann managed a smile at the sight of Charlie's cheerful, coal-smeared face. The sensation of the corners of her mouth lifting felt unfamiliar. God knew, there'd been precious little to smile about recently. But Charlie's features grew solemn again.

'No news for you, I'm afraid. Nothing, even now. The fuzz aren't getting nowhere and no one's set eyes on that Griffin bloke. Not a peep. Sorry, Maryann.'

He saw her face tighten and, as on other occasions, had to fight a desire to put his arms round her to try and give comfort.

'What're they playing at?' she demanded furiously. 'They must've done summat by now! How many more people's he going to do in before they get to him?'

'They just can't seem to find where he's gone to earth. His car turned up, miles out somewhere. But no one's seen hide nor hair of him. D'you think he might've gone away from Brum?'

Maryann shrugged. 'Someone must've seen him.' Her mind seemed to drift. 'Ta anyway, Charlie,' she said and began to walk off, her thoughts miles away. Charlie watched wistfully. Maryann always touched a soft spot in him. And her suffering wrung his heart.

Being in Birmingham tore the wounds back open. Unable to think of anything else, Maryann did the rounds again. One of them must know something: Pastor Owen, Janet Lambert. There wasn't time to go and see Mrs Biggs, her mom's old neighbour. And she didn't see any reason why Norman Griffin would want to go back there now. Nor did she bother visiting the works. If he'd turned up at his factory, they'd have had the police onto him straight away.

She found Janet Lambert even more pale and worn.

'I can't rest until I know they've got him and put him away,' she said, leading Maryann into the back kitchen. In the gloomy light of the little room, her skin seemed to have a yellow tinge and her eyes were sunken. Her hair was a dull mousy-grey now, thinner and scraped carelessly back into a bun. Maryann was alarmed by her appearance. She looked really ill. As she made tea her hands shook, clattering the spoon convulsively against the side of the cups as she put the sugar in.

'Janet.' Maryann moved closer to her and looked into her eyes. Gently she said, 'Janet, love, I know you're going through hell, but you must look after yourself. Don't let him do this to you.'

Janet turned to her and Maryann saw the utter despair in her eyes.

'What more *can* he do to me, Maryann? He's already taken away everything I ever had. He might as well just come and kill me now. It doesn't matter any more.'

They sat in the parlour, the cups on a small occasional table on a cloth embroidered with butterflies. Janet had always kept a genteel home. They talked for a while and Maryann steeled herself to ask about Margaret, Janet's other daughter.

'I want to go and see our Margaret.' Janet looked across with begging eyes. 'I don't go often. Can't stand it. And I can hardly manage the tram and all that now. But it's a visiting day tomorrow. Will you come over there with me so's I don't have to go on my own?'

Maryann felt a plunge of dread inside her. Oh God, not this on top of everything else! The asylum! The very word filled her with horror, let alone the thought of the huge, grim building with its dark gates. She had only seen Margaret there once before and the images she carried in her head of the child were terrible. How could she stand to go and face Margaret now? But how could she refuse Janet, the state she was in? Her mind raced. If she was to go with her tomorrow, they'd have to put off leaving Birmingham after they were loaded up. She'd already left Joel to do everything this evening and he'd be cross at the delay. Joel became angry so easily these days. She knew the pain in his back and his sense of helplessness in the face of her suffering made him frustrated, but it didn't make anything easier.

'Course I will, Janet,' she heard herself saying. She felt melted with pity inside and reached over to take Janet's hand. How could she not meet this desperate request? 'Course I'll come with you.'

Janet accepted the comfort, fingers exploring Maryann's palm, and the feel of the calloused skin distracted her for a moment.

'You lead a rough life, don't you, dear? Hard-working, I mean. It must be tough on you.'

'It doesn't let up much,' Maryann agreed. 'Best never to think about how tired you are.'

'You've a good husband, though.' Janet's eyes searched her face. 'Counts for everything, that does. Look what happened to me. Don't you forget it.'

Maryann looked down to hide her emotion. 'Yes – he is.'

There was a silence while Janet still held her hand.

'You'll come with me?'

'I said I would.'

'Bolt the door tonight, won't you?' she said to Joel. He nodded. Joel had been surprisingly patient about her request to go and see Margaret the next day. For a while that evening she thought things might be getting better, that they could be easier together. But at bedtime he had almost ordered her and the girls out of the *Esther Jane*'s cabin. It felt as if he was afraid to be near her.

She settled the girls in the *Theodore*. Before locking up, she pushed the hatch open and stood on the step, breathing in the night air and gazing round the wharf. With an ache she looked back at the *Esther Jane* and pictured Joel inside with the boys. If only he could just hold her, give her comfort instead of always wanting more when he touched her . . .

The shadows round the wharf seemed to mock her and her flesh came up in goose pimples. Fear grew in her. Was someone standing in those deep pools of darkness? He was out there somewhere. The sense of being constantly watched overtook her and she hurried back into the cabin, feverishly pulling the hatch closed and fastening the bolt.

It was never going to get better, she thought, lying down on her bed. Not while he was still out there. The great darkness outside seemed to be pressing in on the boat and she curled up, frightened, her arm round Sally, trying with her body to protect her from all harm.

Forty-Two

They stood at the asylum gates on a grey, rainy afternoon. Maryann had helped Janet on and off the tram, and the physical exertions of the journey, of struggling with walking sticks on her bad leg, had only added to Janet's emotional distress.

Maryann walked beside her on her painfully slow progress up the drive. Their coats were silvered with rain. As they reached the entrance, Janet faltered. For a moment she stared at the wet ground, then turned to look at Maryann. She didn't speak, but her anguished expression said, *I can't bear it*. Maryann took her arm.

'You're still her mom. She's your daughter. It's not your fault she's here, Janet.'

Janet shook her head, a desolate expression on her face. 'I think that I've come to terms with it until I come back here. She'll never be my Margaret again. Not after all this time.' She squeezed her eyes tightly closed. Maryann saw tiny, convulsive movements in her jaw muscles as she fought to remain in control of herself. 'It *is* my fault. For bringing him into the family . . .'

'No!' Maryann gripped Janet's arm fiercely. 'It's his fault. *All* his fault! Don't ever say it's your fault.'

Janet took a deep breath and looked up again. 'Oh Lord.' She sighed desperately. And after fighting for composure, she said, 'It's all right. Let's get in out of the wet.'

Immediately inside the entrance they were in another world. The sound of the big doors closing behind them made Maryann shudder. Outside they had left the wet air, full of factory smells and smoke, wind-shaken trees and buses and trams passing on the distant road. Now there were other smells, alien and institutional: whiffs of floor polish and disinfectant, stale cooking and another sweet, sickening smell which Maryann couldn't identify. Here they were in a world of high ceilings, of grey, distempered walls, of footsteps echoing in long, gloomy corridors, of locked doors, odd sounds. It felt sealed off and utterly separate from life outside.

The orderly who met them was a bald, middle-aged man who walked with a limp. As he led them to the visitor's room, Maryann saw the silhouette of a male figure moving away along the corridor in the distance, sliding close to the wall, with an odd, slouching walk. It was impossible to guess his age, but the brief glimpse made her feel profoundly unsettled. She shivered, cold even though she had her coat on still. She had a horror of places like this and if it hadn't been for Janet she would have obeyed the impulse to turn and run, to escape from the oppressive atmosphere.

There were three other people waiting in the visitors' room, who sat in silence looking subdued and anxious. A plump lady in a brown pork-pie hat stared at them as they came in, but the others looked away.

'She'll be brought to you at half-past two,' the orderly said, before backing out as if they might all turn on him and shutting the door. Perhaps it was just habit, working here, Maryann thought. There were only a few minutes to go, according to a clock on the wall, but the minute hand seemed to take an eternity to creep round from the five to the six. Everyone waited, not speaking. Maryann and Janet both sat in their coats: although it was June, the room held no warmth. The windows were long but high, letting in cobweb-coloured light. Other than the wooden chairs round the walls the only furniture was a table, pushed up against the wall in one corner, with an empty vase standing on it.

Just after half-past two they heard footsteps in the corridor and three women were brought in: the first a suety, middle-aged woman, her frizzy black hair caught up in a bun, followed by a scrawny girl whose age was hard to guess. There was a pause, and then they heard a man's voice in the corridor saying impatiently, 'No, it's not – it's two women. You going in or not?'

Margaret appeared then, but she clung to the door handle, peering fearfully across at them until she was sure who it was before she came towards them. She was a slight figure, her bright auburn hair tied back into a greasy-looking bunch, grey eyes squinting as she peered across the room, looking, Maryann thought, like a frightened hound. She was wearing a brown pinafore dress several sizes too big which hung on her, the waistband too low and the skirt falling well below her knees. Under it was a fawn blouse. Her face was still freckled, and very pale, not pretty – the eyes were too narrow, her expression dull and vacant. For a moment she stood in front of them staring at her feet on the wooden floor.

'Won't you sit down, Margaret?' Janet suggested. She hadn't got up to greet her. When Margaret was perched, ill at ease, on a chair, Janet went on, 'I haven't been in a while, love. Sorry. I haven't been all that well.'

Margaret accepted this without comment. Her hands, in her lap, were never still, and Maryann's eyes kept being drawn back to their restless movements. Her fingers were thin and red raw, as if she had them constantly in and out of water. Her nails were bitten down to the quicks and there were sores where she chewed and picked compulsively at them, as she was doing now.

And neither was Janet at ease. Her walking sticks were resting at an angle against her legs, and she held the handle of one, her fingers twitching nervously. Janet's discomfort, her remorse, was something you could almost smell in the room, over the whiff of floor polish. Maryann saw, with pity, that she was afraid of her daughter and barely knew what to say to her. From her own instincts as a mother she knew Janet ought to be able to say, I want you with me, child. Let me take you away, take you home. But they both knew Margaret was not going home. She had come here when she was exceptionally young, ten years ago, because of the seriousness of what she had done. Looking at her, Maryann could see she was not fit for life in the normal world out there. She was docile enough, but her mind had been badly scarred as a child, and now she had been here too long. No one was going to plead for her release. The rest of her life would be behind the asylum walls.

'You all right, love?' Janet asked, a tremor in her voice. Margaret was not looking at them, but staring distractedly round the room as if only half aware they were there. 'You remember Maryann, don't you?'

Margaret's gaze returned to them and she looked at Maryann blankly then gave a faint nod. Maryann wasn't sure if she really remembered. It was impossible to tell. She found herself hoping that Margaret *didn't* remember her.

'Hello, Margaret,' she attempted gently. 'You keeping all right?'

Margaret nodded tersely, then looked accusingly at her mother.

'They're giving us that stuff to eat again – gruel like. It's horrible. I don't like it,' she said petulantly. Her voice was thick, clumsy, as if her tongue was unpractised in speech, and her gaze didn't fix for long on the person she was talking to, but shifted about.

'Well,' Janet said, 'I suppose with the shortages and everything—'

'It's nasty.' Margaret cut in across her. 'We had porridge before. I like porridge. I don't like gruel.' She spoke loudly like a sulky child, almost shouting, so that the woman in the pork-pie hat glanced round at them. Margaret couldn't seem to fit her talking properly round the rhythm of anyone else speaking. Conversation with her felt like a jigsaw puzzle in which none of the pieces slotted together properly.

'When's our Amy coming? She hasn't been in ages. Tell her to come.'

Maryann saw Janet's jaw tighten. 'Oh, she'll be along in a few days I expect. She's been very busy. Started a new job, and she—'

'But she hasn't been! She always comes and she hasn't been!'

Maryann sat horrified, watching the two of them. All this time and Margaret didn't know Amy was dead? Whenever was Janet planning to tell her? Janet carefully avoided her gaze. Margaret was chewing her left thumb like a starved person.

'She's my sister!' she cried.

Maryann was disturbed by the look in her eyes at that moment: something fixed and cold, animal, not quite human, or that was how it seemed to her. Margaret pulled her hair forward over her shoulder and tugged at the ends of it, moving her body agitatedly.

'He came. He came to see me.' She was rocking back and forwards now.

Janet cast Maryann a worried, sceptical look.

'Who came?' she asked with exaggerated patience.

'*Him*. My *stepfather*.' This last was said in a mocking, sing-song tone.

'What d'you mean?' Janet's voice rose with panic. 'You haven't got a stepfather! What on earth're you talking about?'

'I have! *Him*. Your husband – you haven't forgot him, have you? He came in here visiting – with that face. Trying to hide – under his hat.' She giggled suddenly, a harsh snicker. 'I did that to him all by myself!'

Janet was on the edge of her chair, grabbing at Margaret's hands.

'What d'you mean?' Janet implored her. 'What're you saying – he came here? Margaret, is this true or are you making up a story?'

'He told them he was my stepfather – well, he was once, wasn't he?' Margaret sneered.

'*When*? When was he here?'

'I dunno.' Margaret looked sullenly down at the floor. 'Since Amy came. Long time ago. Dunno now.'

'Well, what did he want? What did he say?'

Margaret shrugged. Maryann felt a sudden urge to shake the words out of her.

'Talked about his mother. Said he was sorry. I wasn't listening.'

The two of them sat in stunned silence at the preposterousness of this. Rain blew against the window behind them. It was coming down more heavily now, the sky even darker.

'Margaret, did this really happen?' Maryann asked,

though she already sensed that Margaret was telling the truth. She wouldn't have the ability to invent such a story.

'He came. I told you. You could ask that lady.' She jerked her head towards the woman in the pork-pie hat. 'She was here then, an' all. Kept staring at him.'

'But what did he *want*?' Maryann could hear a note of hysteria in Janet's voice and felt something similar rising in herself.

'Dunno. He asked me about the family – where everyone is. I dunno where they are. Asked me about Auntie Maureen and if she was still in Alvechurch. She was the only one I could remember. We went out there, daint we? She had them kittens.'

'What else?' Janet demanded.

Margaret shrugged. 'Dunno.' Her mind seemed to slide away and she looked about the room again, chewing savagely at the end of her finger.

For the rest of the visit, however hard they tried to press her, she would say no more. Conversation flagged. After all, what life did Margaret have to tell them about? Only that she was still apparently doing sewing. Mending clothes.

At last they had to say goodbye. As Janet kissed her, Margaret stood passively and asked if she could bring some sweets next time. She didn't seem to understand about rationing, even now.

The two of them were ushered out and the doors slammed behind them, leaving them to face the rain.

'It's easing off a bit, I think,' Maryann said, trying to sound cheerful. In fact it was still raining just as hard, but it was a relief to get out of the dim, enclosed world of the hospital. She longed to get back to the cut, to get untied and away from Birmingham.

Janet closed her eyes for a second and let out a long,

shuddering sigh. 'I find it hard to believe she's mine any more.' She opened her eyes and looked at Maryann. 'My little Margaret.'

Maryann couldn't stand any more emotion. She took Janet's arm.

'Come on. Let's get home.'

But Janet was staring ahead of her at the steady fall of rain. In a despairing voice, he said, 'What does he want? What more *can* he want from us?'

Maryann was in the fringes between waking and sleep that night when the knocking forced her awake again, knuckles wrapping insistently on the door. Her body tensed in a rigor which left her for several seconds incapable of movement.

'Maryann?' she heard. 'Don't worry, it's only me – Charlie.'

Whatever did he want? She liked Charlie, but felt apprehensive, remembering what she had seen in his eyes sometimes when he looked at her. His attraction to her was not something she found comfortable. And why would he be coming to see her at this time of night?

She opened up the back, pulling her coat tightly round her. The rain had stopped and the night was clear. Charlie must have retreated when he heard her unbolting the door, as he was now standing on the bank. With him was a woman. In the poor light Maryann made out a sweet face and curly hair falling round her cheeks. Was that his wife? she wondered, bewildered.

'Sorry—' Charlie began. Though he was speaking in a low voice, it communicated urgency. 'Only, Liza and me – this is Liza, by the way –' Maryann gave the young woman a faint smile – 'we was out near Osborne's – by

Mulligan's ironmonger's. That's Liza's dad's shop, see – and we was up the entry –' Maryann saw Liza look at the ground and sensed rather than being able to see her blushes. No, not his wife then. Her estimation of Charlie sank a little.

'Anyroad – this motor car came and stopped in the road and these blokes got out. We just heard voices and that. We wouldn't've taken any notice, would we, Lize? Only then there was this noise, like – how would you describe it?'

'It was a kiddie crying out,' Liza said.

'Not just crying – howling,' Charlie said sombrely. 'As if it was in pain. Like a little rabbit. And I said, ey-up, summat amiss here. Didn't I, Lize?'

Liza nodded shyly.

'I looked out the end of the entry, Maryann, and I didn't hear anything else. But I got the shock of my life, 'cause that's when I saw him, just going up the entry to Osborne's!'

'Him?' Maryann's throat tightened. 'Mr Griffin?' Charlie had seen him before, of course, but could he be so sure in the dark street?

'Oh, it was him all right. Hat pulled down like he wears it to hide that fizz-hog of his. There was three of them – another big bloke went in behind him and the other one drove off again after.'

'Osborne's?' Maryann was completely bewildered. Charlie must be mistaken. Whatever could Norman Griffin want with kind Mr Osborne? 'Maybe it was the place on the other side he was going to?'

'Nope. It's Osborne's all right. Heard the door go. And Liza's room's across the road from them and she says she reckons there's someone else living above the shop in the attic.'

'They suddenly put blackouts up a few weeks back,' Liza said. 'There was nothing before. It was all empty. And I've seen someone moving about once or twice in the day. I've never seen anyone come in or out, though.'

The hatch of the *Esther Jane* slid open and Joel came out, pulling on his jacket. Maryann explained what had happened.

'You think they're still up there, then?' Joel said.

Charlie nodded. 'We came straight here.'

'Come on, then.' Joel was all set to go and roust them out himself. 'Let's go and see.'

'But the coppers,' Charlie protested, 'they're s'posed to be looking for him. Shouldn't we get them?'

This was an idea foreign to Joel's self-sufficient ways. He hesitated.

'Well, all right then. But if they don't get on with it we might just as well do it ourselves.'

Forty-Three

Joel and Charlie waited for the police to arrive, standing along the street from Mr Osborne's shop. Maryann had stayed with the boats, the children. She wasn't leaving them alone, for Sally to wake and find her gone.

'Take their flaming time, don't they?' Charlie ground the stub of a cigarette against the cobbles with his heel, then immediately reached into his pocket for his packet of Woodbines and offered it to Joel.

'No ta.' Joel knocked his fist against his chest. 'Can't.'

'Sorry, pal – forgot.' Charlie lit one up for himself. He was too young to have fought in the Great War. 'Gas, was it?'

Joel nodded. His back was giving him a lot of pain too – it hurt far more than he would admit to Maryann. Beside Charlie he felt old, done in.

Charlie peered along the dark street. 'Better watch in case they sneak out again without us seeing,' he said through his cigarette. He took it from his mouth and spat on the ground. 'Filthy bastards.'

Joel said nothing. He was not much of a one for words in any case, and he could not have expressed what he felt towards Norman Griffin. Since his return to the boats from Oxford, his daughter had been taken away, his wife had withdrawn from him, and he knew that the mute misery he could see in Maryann was somehow rooted in what she too had experienced at the hands of

396

her stepfather. Joel had never known exactly what went on while Norman Griffin was with Maryann's family. She'd never said and he couldn't bear to ask, had no idea what to do to make it better. He longed to take her to him in bed, to love and caress her sorrow away, but he knew he couldn't. Since he had been back she had been closed off to him. If he touched her she fought him off or turned away, rigid, weeping. Better in some ways that they sleep on different boats. Then at least the warm shape of her beside him was not a temptation. But it was a sad, lonely state of affairs which he found hard to bear. His fists clenched with fury at the thought of Norman Griffin. He wanted to storm into the house and do him violence, never mind waiting for these duffers, the police.

'Why the hell don't they hurry up?' he burst out eventually. 'Bloody useless idiots.'

A few moments later they saw the shaded lights of a car approaching from the far end of the street. Charlie flagged it down a little way along from Osborne's shop. Three policemen climbed out carrying truncheons and stood looking around them.

'In here,' Charlie said.

The most senior policeman must have been nearly sixty and had a neat little moustache.

'You sure it's him?'

'It's him,' Charlie said. 'You couldn't mistake that face. I only caught a glimpse, but he's the one.'

'All right, lads.' The three of them stood apart by a lamp post and conferred for a moment. Joel saw the two younger ones listen, leaning in for instructions.

'I reckon he's only a sergeant, that one,' Charlie murmured. 'You'd think they'd manage to send a bigger fish along for this, wouldn't you?'

'Right,' the sergeant said as they came over again.

'Only thing we can do is take them by surprise. You think they're up at the top of the house do you?'

'The attic,' Charlie said.

'And how many're in there?'

'Three, I'd say.'

'Right,' he said again. 'Come on then.'

The three men stepped into the pitch black of the entry. Joel and Charlie glanced at one another, then followed. One of the policemen switched a torch on, creating a picture show of jumping shadows. They all crept silently round to the back door.

'Ready, lads?'

The door broke open on the second try and banged back hard. The policemen raced through it and upstairs, making the most terrific racket on the bare boards. Charlie raced after them and Joel followed, up through the dark house, frustrated by his slowness. There was a particular, cloying smell, and he realized after a few seconds that it was of meat. Of course – this was a butcher's shop. Fancy living with that horrible stink all the time!

He heard the other men reach the top of the attic stairs and the door crash open. He paused at the last bend in the stairs, expecting instant sounds of mayhem, of shouts, even fighting. But there was a moment of stunned confusion and during it he followed them into the room, panting from the stairs.

He was in a dingy attic room, with a sloping roof at one side. Three men were round the little table in the middle; a bottle lay on its side dribbling its contents over the table and onto the floor, evidently knocked over as the round-faced fellow facing Joel had leapt to his feet. On one side of him was grey-haired Mr Osborne; on the other Norman Griffin sat hunched, looking impassively in front of him. Under the high, dormer window was an old iron bedstead with a filthy mattress on which crouched a little girl, her distraught face smeared with dirt and tears.

'What d'you think you're—?' Mr Osborne got to his feet then. He sounded frightened.

'Stay where you are,' the sergeant said. 'No monkeying about. You're all under arrest.'

At his nod the other two policemen jumped into action. The round-faced man struggled, panicking.

'No – you can't do this to me! This is ridiculous – a mistake! I shouldn't be here –'

'No – quite right, you shouldn't, sir,' the policeman said, forcing the man's hands behind his back as he tried to struggle. In a moment the handcuffs were fastened on. The other officer had handcuffed Mr Osborne, who stood in shocked, sullen silence.

Norman Griffin hadn't attempted to move from the table so they left him until last. There was something about his brooding stillness and the grotesque distortion of his face that made them hesitate, reluctant to move closer or lay hands on him, almost as if he were an unearthly creature, not fully human. Joel saw him look round and fasten his one good eye on him, and held Griffin's gaze, revolted at what he saw. That puckered, shiny skin – what a horrible sight he was! For a second Joel even pitied him.

Norman Griffin pushed the chair back and stood up slowly. Out of the corner of his eye, Joel saw the sergeant take a step forward.

'So – Mr Bartholomew,' Norman Griffin said. His tone was mocking. 'Little Maryann's husband.'

Anger flared in Joel. 'How do *you* know who I am?'

'Oh, I get about, don't forget. Quite a regular visitor

to the wharves. I keep an eye on things – I like to look out for my old family members.' He made a sound which could have been a laugh or a clearing of the chest. 'Make sure they're not coming to any harm. I've never been sure at all about you, for Maryann. Far too young, she was, when she first took up with you.'

Joel drew his fist back, but in that split second Norman Griffin launched his weight at him, catching him off balance and thrusting him back against the open door. Joel cried out with pain and fury as the hard door crashed into his back. Norman Griffin took off down the stairs.

'Well, get after him, you gormless clods!' the sergeant yelled, furious at himself for hesitating. 'How could you let that happen?' The other two let go of the scowling Mr Osborne and the third man and took off in pursuit.

'They'll soon catch him up – he's twice their age,' the sergeant said.

'Yes, but they've only half his intelligence,' Mr Osborne muttered sourly.

'Downstairs!' the sergeant barked at the two prisoners.

'I'll give you a hand with them,' Charlie Dean said, roughly catching hold of the plump man. 'It'll be a pleasure.'

Joel was going to follow when he realized everyone seemed to have forgotten about the little girl. She was pressed against the wall, squatting on her haunches, arms clasped round her knees. Joel saw that she was wearing a skimpy yellow frock, heavily soiled and with one sleeve badly torn. His heart went out to her. Although she had dark brown hair, unbrushed and messy, in every other way she reminded him of their little Sally. They must have been much of an age.

'Hello there, little 'un.' He spoke very gently.

Her eyes widened further and she tried to press herself back harder against the wall.

'I'm going to come over and sit by you.' Joel felt uncomfortably conscious of his enormous size in comparison with her. He seemed like a giant and felt a discomfort that recently, for the first time in his life, his wife had also made him feel: a sense of contamination as a man. What had been forced on this poor waif of a girl? What must he seem like to her? Just another heartless monster come to harm her?

'Don't run away.' He tried to make himself smaller, bending his knees, shrinking down as he walked until he sat himself gingerly on the edge of the grubby mattress. He could see a damp patch on it and there was a pungent smell of urine. The girl flinched, but didn't get up to move away. Close up to her, Joel could see why. Her ankles were tied together with a piece of cord, so tightly that he could see the mauve bite of it where it met her flesh.

'Poor little thing.' He felt close to weeping at the state of her. 'Can you tell me your name?'

'Carol,' she whispered.

'I'm Joel. I won't hurt you, I promise. I've come to help you. Now – let's get these off, shall we?'

Taking his knife from his pocket, he cut the cords away from her ankles and she whimpered at the pain as he did so. She rubbed at the angry welts on her ankles when he'd finished, tears running down her cheeks.

'Now then,' Joel told her gently, 'we're going to get you home safely to your mom and dad, aren't we?'

When Charlie Dean came back up he found Joel sitting on the bed, his arm round the little girl, who was sobbing her heart out beside him.

*

401

When the two policemen ran out in search of Norman Griffin, they got out of the entry only to find that he had already disappeared. For a moment they stood at a loss in the street.

'We're going to get it in the neck for this,' one said gloomily.

'He can't've got far, old geezer like him. You go that way and I'll go this. We'll soon find him.'

They ran off in opposite directions.

Just a few yards away, pressed into the shadows at the back of the house, only feet from the back door, Norman Griffin smiled grimly into the darkness.

Maryann sat at the table in the *Theodore*. In the quiet night she heard the chucking sound of a water bird, which must have strayed out unusually late.

Should be safe on a nest somewhere by now, she thought protectively. *Perhaps it's a young one.* She sipped her tea, feeling very tense, wondering what was going on and where Joel and Charlie had got to. At moments she wished she'd gone with them so she wouldn't have to wait in an agony of wondering. Had they found him? Were the police there? Or had it been the wrong place, wrong person? Had Charlie Dean made a mistake?

She'd put all the girls down to sleep, top to toe, on the main bed. There was no point in her trying to sleep. Filling up her cup from the old brown and white teapot, she sat holding it with both hands, her thoughts spinning round. She thought of Amy Lambert, of what Margaret had said to them, such as it was. Why was Norman Griffin asking about their relatives in Alvechurch? Janet had said that her sister had young daughters. Surely he wasn't planning to track down every member of every family he'd ever been involved with? It was a terrible thought. Her mind moved on to the night the boatmen had found the girl's body in the cellar in Acocks Green and at that she could stand her thoughts no more. She picked up one of Sylvia's old magazines, dog-eared by now, desperate to distract herself. The sight of it brought a faint smile to her lips, remembering Sylvia exclaiming over some of the pictures, but she couldn't concentrate.

Oh, I wish Dot and Sylvia were here still! Maryann thought, giving up and closing the magazine. She missed them more than she could ever have imagined. Thinking back to their arrival on the boats, she remembered how resentful and irritable she'd felt, how all she'd wanted was to have Joel back and for nothing to change. But now he was back and things had changed more than she could ever have imagined. It all felt impossible. She couldn't be close to him or give him what a husband wanted and needed. And it was her that was at fault. There was something deeply, horribly wrong with her to make her like this. Unable to bear the pain of her thoughts, she pushed them away. Tonight, maybe they'd get *him* once and for all. Get him put away, and then maybe her nightmares would come to an end.

Sighing, she picked up the magazine again. Another small sound came from outside and she tensed, listening. But nothing else followed. It must have been one of the other families further along the bank. Maybe she'd even imagined it, the state she was in. Then, a moment later she heard sounds she knew were real: hurrying footsteps and then they were back, knocking on the cabin. At last!

'Coming!' she called.

She undid the bolt and the hatch was abruptly pushed back.

'Did you get him . . .?'

But the questions died in her throat. His form filled the doorway and he was climbing down into the cabin, his ravaged face caught in the lamplight as he leaned in towards her, lips curved into a triumphant smile.

'Hello, Maryann,' he said.

Forty-Four

She could hear his laboured breathing as he slid the hatch closed and shut the door. He'd obviously been hurrying over some distance.

'Sit down,' he ordered.

In that instant it was as if all her will had been stolen from her. Maryann sank onto the side bench as she was bidden, with a wild glance at the back bed. To her relief she saw that the curtains were drawn right across, hiding the girls as they lay sleeping. She prayed that none of them would stir and cry out.

Norman Griffin struggled down the steps. He was a bulky man and unused to moving in this confined space.

'Move up, so I can sit by you, then,' he ordered, and she slid along the bench as if she was programmed to obey him. She couldn't seem to think properly, as if he had scrambled her thoughts. How could she ever get out? She noted that he had not fastened the bolt at the bottom of the door, but even if she managed to get past him, she couldn't leave him with the children. She was trapped in here with him again, and now he was not just her stepfather with his vile, dirty ways. He'd done worse things, terrible things! She despaired, then, paralysed with fear. *Oh, please*, her mind begged, *let some-one, come! Joel, where are you?* She pressed herself as far along the bench as she could, trying to get away from him.

'Don't know how you manage in here.' He lumbered round, stooped to avoid banging his head and squeezed himself, grunting, into the space beside her. 'Like living in a matchbox.'

It was such close quarters that avoiding her cramped proximity to him was impossible, though she tried to shrink away, every cell of her body in revolt.

Norman Griffin laid his hat on the table, and the sight of his face, horribly visible now in the light, the smell of him, of sweat and damp clothing, the press of him against her, turned her into a child again: petrified and at his mercy.

He turned and looked at her, having to swivel his body to fix her with his good eye. Up close she could see with horrible clarity the damaged skin, the way the flames had shrivelled and distorted it. She became aware of her own blood pounding through her veins.

'You always were a nice-looking girl, Maryann. I know the passing of the years takes it out of us. None more so than me—' He made a harsh, self-mocking sound which made her jump and he noticed. 'No need to be nervous ... Yes – you've still got your looks, wench – a freshness about you. Must be living in the open air that does it.'

His voice was soft, wheedling and seductive in the way that she remembered, how he would be before he touched her. The sound filled her with sick dread.

'We go back a long way don't we, you and me?'

You and me. As if there had ever been a 'you and me'!

'What d'you want?' she managed to whisper. She knew she shouldn't show him how frightened she was, but she couldn't control it. She knew her eyes were stretched wide with fear.

'What do I want? Don't be like that!' To her horror he reached for her left hand and pulled it to him, holding it tightly, stroking it. 'You were my daughter once – remember?'

'Stepdaughter,' she corrected, screaming in her head, *You were never my father, never!* All the time he was talking she kept looking round the cabin. How could she get away?

'I used to bath you when you was just a tiny, skinny little thing. And look at you now – a grown-up woman with, how many kiddies is it?'

She didn't answer. *Keep him from thinking about the girls.* She stared back at him as he went on and on stroking her hand.

'I miss having family,' he said plaintively. 'It's a lonely life with no one.'

He paused and she heard his rasping breaths. She felt the dreadful thud of her heart.

'I was sorry to hear about your mother going like that. I went to see her a few times before she died, you know. I've missed her over the years. She were a good woman, Flo was. Good to me. That's why I've come to see you – chew over old times for a bit.'

Maryann almost laughed at the grotesqueness of this. *He's mad.* Her mind was racing. *Stark staring bonkers.* She might have expected all sorts of horrors from him, but not this – not a reminiscence session! Perhaps she should keep him talking, keep his mind off her, off the children, and, pray God, Joel would soon be back . . .

'You used to take us to the pictures.' She managed to make her voice sound almost even and normal. 'Best seats and a nice bag of bulls' eyes. D'you remember? Me and Sal and the boys – all with Mom? Family outing.'

He was listening to her attentively, seemed to be

407

smiling. She watched his face, appalled. Didn't he remember what had happened to Sal? That she'd lain alone with the life blood dripping from her wrist because of all he'd done to her? Didn't he know that? Or was it stored away in some forgotten part of his mind, like a locked trunk?

'We had some nice times, didn't we?' he was saying, suddenly sounding so plaintive that for a second she felt as if there was a child speaking beside her.

'Yes, we did,' she lied.

'We were a family. Amy and Margaret were family too – we used to sit round the table of a night, cosy as anything. I was a dad to you, wasn't I, Maryann?'

This grotesque travesty pierced her so that again she could not speak, but she nodded. What would he do if she told the truth about what he had caused? What if she shattered the shining wall of illusion he was building round them both? She barely managed to hide her shudders at him touching her hand.

'You're trembling,' he said, closing his other hand over hers. 'There's no need to be frightened of your old dad.'

She said nothing.

'I've had a lonely life since ... since Janet and the girls. Walking the streets looking like this. You might as well be a leper. No one'll come near you. I've got my business, of course. I couldn't go on being an undertaker with this face on me – had to move into something else. The business is doing well, thanks to Herr Hitler. And they have to treat me all right. All they want is to feed their families, their kiddies.' There was a savage tone in his voice. 'I'm the boss. I hold the purse strings, see. But other than that, I've taken to going out at night so's I don't get noticed. I'm a wreck of a man, aren't I? I'm loathsome, inside and out.' He looked up at her and all she could do was to stare back, mute. 'Who'd ever look at me now?'

After staring at her for a moment he said, 'I've come to apologize.'

She waited, hardly breathing, deeply suspicious. What was this now? A trick? It would be easier if she knew what he really wanted. But he sounded sincere and abject with self-pity.

'I was never a good enough father to you girls. Never had a father of my own, see. He took off when I was a babe in arms. He was a soldier. And Mother...' he stalled. 'No one ever understood Mother, understood *about* her, should I say. No one knew, you see.'

Maryann thought of the portrait, the sole decoration on the drab walls of his room. Mother's eyes looking out at him from that sternly beautiful face.

Norman was staring down at her hand, stroking it again. Maryann struggled to remember what age he must be. Getting on for seventy by now and sitting here bleating about his mother. It seemed peculiar and deeply pathetic. She was startled by a tiny sound from the back bed, one of the children shifting in their sleep and she held her breath, managing to stop her eyes from moving in the direction of the sound. Norman didn't seem to notice.

'You're a kind mother to your kiddies, aren't you, Maryann? My mother wasn't kind. She was .. unnatural.' He seemed to lose his thread again, then said, 'I've done some terrible things. I tried to tell that young man – that Pastor Owen. Not that other fool, of course – Joyce. Owen's an innocent. He's a real believer. Terrible for someone like me to come face to face with it – with someone who thinks there's goodness. I tried to tell him

409

– never got far. I wouldn't've got him to believe all I've done. D'you know, I abandoned my own son? Never saw him again from when he was seven years old. I don't know where he is to this day.' To her horror she heard his rasping voice begin to crack.

'You're the only one left, Maryann! You know me, don't you?' He was wrestling with his emotions, beginning to sob and she watched, horrified. 'I can talk to you. You know who I am. But even you don't know. You thought your mother was a cruel woman, but Flo was a saint compared with my beloved mother. She was the beloved, you see. My beloved. And I was hers.'

His shoulders heaved and in the second that he loosed her to reach for his handkerchief, Maryann pulled her hand free, nursing it to her as if she'd been stung. The sight of Norman Griffin weeping was horrifying. She shrank back, fascinated yet repelled, her loathing unmixed with any shred of pity. Her body tingled all over with the instinct to run away, but she was trapped.

'She was so beautiful,' he was sobbing. 'The smell of her. She was so soft. Her bed always smelt of her – her soap, her body.'

Maryann sat very still, caught by what he was saying, by the tone of it. His voice had turned into a high, infant whine, and she saw a tear fall from his good eye and drop, glistening, onto the lapel of his coat.

Norman Griffin squeezed his eyes closed and shook his head violently as if to dislodge a picture from his mind. 'Her body – she was always there, with that body.' Looking round at her, he said, 'You're a mother, Maryann: you wouldn't have your own son in your bed, would you? Standing in for your husband?'

Maryann looked back at him, almost unable to believe what she was hearing.

'She was such a cruel woman – so cruel in the daytime when she didn't want me, you know, like that.' He halted again abruptly. 'I've never said this to a living soul before . . .' He tried to swallow, struggling as if there was something stuck in his throat.

'Night-times, most nights – it never ended, the feel of her, making me touch her, and I wanted to in the end, couldn't stop . . . All soft, damp . . .' He closed his eyes, face contorting even further. 'She wanting me to touch her, kiss her. It was all different in the daytime. When she wasn't pleased with me her mouth went straight and hard, eyes drilling into me. She looked as if – as if she couldn't stand the sight of me. And she kept her cat-o'-nine-tails tied to her belt.' There was a silence, then words flooded out.

'She always beat me on my backside. Made me take my trousers down – short trousers when I was younger, of course. Always in the parlour, behind the nets. The things she used to say while she was doing it. She'd reach her arm right up as far as it would go and bring it down, nothing held back in the sting of it. I was red raw when she'd finished. The school chairs were so hard, I could barely sit. She made me bend over the sideboard. There was a china dish on there with a blue glaze on it and I'd always stand by it. I could see my face in it. I'd look at it while she was beating me. If I made a noise she did it even harder, told me I was weak, no good. So I thought, I'll keep my face straight so that boy in the dish will look back at me and he doesn't look bad and he's not having a thrashing off his mom and he can't hear the things she's saying about me being dirty and wicked . . . I'll be like him. It got so's I was always that other boy, hiding with him till she'd finished.' He let out a shuddering sigh.

411

'I never knew what was coming then. Sometimes she'd just go out and leave me with my backside all welts, and she'd close the door very quietly as if there was someone poorly asleep in there and she didn't want to disturb them. As if I was sick. Then sometimes – ' he shuddered – 'she'd pull on my shoulders while I was still bent over and make me stand up. I was half naked and she'd make me put my arms round her and kiss her and she'd press herself against me.

' "It's for your own good, Normie – it'll make you a proper man, like your father was." '

He had his eyes closed, as if trapped in the memories. Maryann eyed the door desperately, sickened by what she was hearing, by him expecting her pity, playing on her sympathy, perhaps even inventing all this for some warped reason of his own. But, worst of all, she knew in her heart by the way he talked that he hadn't invented it.

'Course he was always a proper man, a soldier. She made me feel like . . . nothing. A weak, spineless reed.'

She could hold her silence no longer.

'So why did you do it to us? To my sister – and to Amy and Margaret?' Unbidden, tears came, the surge of grief stronger even than fear in that moment, like a deep crack opening in her onto the pain of it all, the awfulness of being here with this man who had caused it and his monstrous, pathetic story.

When he answered her, his tone had changed as if her speaking had brought him to a different plane in himself. There was a hard coldness which brought her up abruptly and stemmed her tears.

'I have to. It's the only thing that makes me feel better. Feel nothing. For a while. I had to tell someone. It got so's I had to. I tried to tell that Pastor Owen, but he's a man and he's too . . . clean. I had to tell a woman.

Only I couldn't have her spreading it. I started with Amy. She grew up into a right pretty thing. I thought she'd be kind. But she wouldn't listen. I tried to make her hold still, but she kept struggling and she wouldn't let me finish. I had to do it. Couldn't have her telling anyone else.'

Maryann froze again. He'd told all of it to her now, his sad, dirty secrets, the perverted bullying of his mother. She'd been the one to hear it whether she chose to or not, and now ... She had to keep him talking, to keep him calm. She saw him staring at her and his expression was cold and terrible.

'Good at asking questions, aren't you? Wheedling things out of me? You always were a devious little thing – always the one I could never quite get to grips with.' He caught hold of her wrist abruptly, so hard that she gave a yelp of pain.

'Don't,' she panted. 'Don't hurt me. Why hurt someone else? Where does it get you? I've got a family. Just leave us, leave us alone instead of making everything worse. It doesn't make anything better for you – it just goes on and on.'

'But it *does* make me better – for a little while. It makes me happy and light, better than a tumbler of Scotch. As if there's nothing in the world to feel, to worry about.' He was pulling her gradually closer to him and she could smell stale drink on his breath now, see his scarred face looming before her eyes, blocking out everything else. She heard herself whimpering.

'Make me feel better now. You can do it – you know you always could ...' Gripping her hard with one hand, he started to fondle painfully at her breasts.

'Like old times, eh, Maryann?' He breathed into her face. 'You were always the fighter, the little wildcat, weren't you? That's what made you the best one, the exciting one – and you haven't changed, have you? I knew you'd come back to me in the end – that I'd have you in the end.'

'No-o—!' Maryann moaned. He was hurting her, squeezing, pinching, tearing at the front of her blouse.

'Confound it – there's no room to move in this damn place!' He struggled, trying to sit round, but finding his legs caught under the table. He shoved at it. 'Can't you get shot of it? Hold still,' he roared, as she struggled. 'You little bitch, I'm going to have you!'

A sound grated in the air, the broken mewl of a child. Norman Griffin sat up straight.

'What's that? You got one of your kiddies in there?'

No! she wanted to say. No, no! It was one of the twins, she could tell.

'She'll sleep again,' she said hurriedly. 'She's only a babby.'

'Aha – let's have a look then, shall we?'

He flung the table back and lumbered, stooping, to the back bed.

'Well, well. All bagged up together, just like little rabbits. Oh – there's our Sally again. What a lovely child she is!'

As he stood with his back to her, Maryann saw one desperate chance. Eyes fixed on the lamp burning on the little shelf across the cabin, she began to slide herself along the bench. If only she could get there without him noticing! It seemed to take an endless time to inch herself along, holding her breath as she watched Norman Griffin's back. In a moment she launched herself to her feet and swooped towards the lamp. He caught her movement and lurched in front of her, pushing her backwards as he got between her and the lamp. She fell against the

414

stove, banging her head on the wall behind. Ada was still crying.

'Oh no you don't!' He snatched the lamp and held it up. As she stumbled groggily to her feet, Maryann saw his face lit up by the glow of the lamp.

'Thinking of coming that one again, were you? Oh, I don't think that one would work a second time. I saw Margaret the other week, by the way. Fine girl – not that she'll ever breathe the air outside the asylum again. Now – what shall we do with this?' He eyed the lamp, half turned, dangling it over the sleeping children.

'Very fitting, wouldn't you say? Do as you would be done by?'

'No!' She pulled at him with all her strength, trying to get at the lamp. 'For God's sake, have some pity. They're babbies, all of them – my babbies! I never burned you – it was Margaret, not me!'

'But you'd have liked to, wouldn't you? You find me every bit as disgusting as she did.' With his left arm he caught her round the neck and wrenched her in close to him, looking down into her frantic face.

'I could always tell with you. You had too much spirit, too much defiance, my girl. No doubt these little lovelies have your spirit – so let's snuff that out, shall we? Stop it spreading any further. Women with spirit – with their pretty faces and their cruel mouths.'

Maryann threw herself on him, trying to pull his arm back, to get the lamp from him.

'Sally, Rose – wake up!' she screamed. 'Get out – get the twins out of bed!'

Sally and Rose had begun to stir.

'Quickly – *get out*!' She was screaming at them hysterically, but he shoved her off and once more she crashed into the stove. As she fought to get back towards

415

the children she could see what he was about to do, jerking the lamp outwards, swinging it by its handle. She saw it arc to the furthest point, then begin the path back towards the ceiling over the bed.

'Sally!' In that second all she could seize hold of was her daughter's hand to pull on as the lamp hit the ceiling. The glass shattered and burning oil burst from it and scattered flaming over the bedspace where Rose lay with the twins.

Forty-Five

The cabin was full of smoke. No sound but that of screaming. The darkness was broken by the glow of flames licking round the bedding of the terrified children.

Immediately Maryann felt the normal passing of time alter. In those first elongated seconds she was shrieking at Sally, 'Get the doors open – get yourself out! Rose! Get up out of bed! Quick!' Sally tumbled from the bed onto her feet in the small space.

They were hampered by the obstructing bulk of Norman Griffin. Whichever way Maryann tried to move, he was in the way, though she could tell he too was trying to get out, away from the fire. Iron-limbed with fear and determination she turned her body and shoved at him, and in the darkness he seemed to give way, to disappear with a crash towards the door. She heard a yelp of pain, a muffled curse. She didn't care what happened to him as long as he was out of the way. The smoke was thickening, the small space filling with it fast. Coughing, she seized Rose's shoulders and steered her towards the cabin door. Norman Griffin seemed to have gone.

'Get on the bank with Sally – I'm getting the twins . . .'

Her eyes were streaming. The smoke was f the tiny space and she was racked by coughi could hear was the terrified screaming of t' ones in the burning bed. The edge of the

417

caught light, but Maryann shoved them aside and climbed onto the edge of the bed, seeing both of the babies' faces, each end of the bed, mouths open in the murky orange light. Most of the oil had fallen in the middle of the bed and flames were shooting up to the low ceiling. The heat was intense, but she leaned inside, regardless.

'Come here!' she shouted, reaching for Esther, trying to hold her head to one side while the flames leapt hungrily at her. She could feel the bite of them on her cheek and neck. She snatched Esther out, plonked her on the floor and immediately went back for Ada. As she reached for her, she heard her crying, in between choking coughs, with a distressed shrillness that she'd never heard before. She picked her up, and Ada racked up her screaming even higher.

Maryann balanced her on one hip and reached down for Esther, dragging her to the door by one arm. Within a second she was aware of a strange glow accompanying her, then a burning pain in her right ear and realized her hair was on fire. Loosing Esther she swiped at it, panicking, coughing, her hand smarting, until the flames seemed to have died out. All she could do now was get the three of them up the step into the night air. The twins were gagging on the smoke.

She managed to lift the girls off the boat and onto the bank, setting them down to bend over and cough and cough, her lungs straining for air. She gradually became aware of people moving round her, of voices amid the children's crying. The fire had brought others out from their boats who were shouting to each other to fetch buckets and dippers. But as she straightened up she heard Joel's voice, and Charlie's and Sally and Rose shrieking to them, that there was *fire*, fire on the *Theodore*.

418

'Our boat – and our lassies!' Joel was distraught, couldn't seem to see the girls in front of him.

'I'll get them off!' Charlie shouted. He was fully primed to help, to do something. They'd let Norman Griffin slip through their fingers, and now this! 'Where're the lads?'

'On the motor,' Maryann said, and realized with amazement that Joley and Ezra inside the *Esther Jane* must be sleeping through, oblivious to all this. 'The girls are all out – look, here,' Maryann managed to say. Sally and Rose came to her and clung round her, beginning to cry now the immediate danger to them was over and she stood stroking them, beginning to tremble all over herself. Joel had run to the boat, seized the dipper from inside and joined the others who were trying to douse the fire.

'It was *him*! He did it – set the fire – he's gone . . .'

'Griffin?' Charlie Dean demanded. 'What – he came here? Where is he? Where did he go?'

'That way – he ran off along the path,' Sally said, pointing.

Charlie was off. 'I'll get him this time,' floated back as he disappeared. 'I'll get that bugger and I won't let him go.'

Charlie tore along the dark towpath. He was a strong, fit man and fuelled by an almost insane, rage-filled energy, which stemmed from his soft feelings for Maryann and from the memory of that child on the bed in the room above the butcher's shop. He knew they'd been made proper fools of, letting Norman Griffin get away the first time. He ran tirelessly, almost as if he was flying,

419

were it not for his feet crunching on the stones and cinders. There was a half moon tonight, which he could see reflected in the cut, and it seemed to bob about as he ran.

I'll get you this time. He'd given them the slip once, the slimy bastard, and he wasn't getting away again. That lumbering hulk of a bloke couldn't've got far in this time, surely? Charlie stumbled on something in the darkness and only just managed to stay upright. The jerking this gave his body only increased his anger. His lungs were pumping hard.

It can't be far, he thought. *There must be a place where he gets off the path – I've got to get to him before he gets there or he'll be gone and I'll've had it then.*

And a moment later he thought he heard something along the path ahead. Charlie stopped immediately. Now his feet were not pounding the ground, his own breathing sounded terribly loud. Yes, a cough from up ahead, and the sound of hurrying feet. He ran on, trying to be quiet, almost tiptoeing, gaining quickly until he could see a form moving, a deeper smudge of black in the darkness around them.

They hadn't got the fire on the *Theodore* under control yet. Smoke was pouring out of the door. Maryann watched hopelessly as she began to see flames burning their way through the roof, despite the efforts of Joel and the other boatmen. Maryann and the women tried to comfort the children, but while Sally, Rose and Esther were calmer now, Ada continued to give off agonized wails. Maryann was holding her and she'd screamed even more loudly on being picked up.

'What's up, Ada?' she said, despairingly. 'I can't see if she's got burnt or summat. She just won't stop blarting.'

'Bring her into our cabin,' a woman next to her offered. 'And the others. I'll find a drop of milk for them.'

She was a middle-aged woman with the prematurely aged, weather-worn face of so many of the boatwomen and large, kindly blue eyes. She ushered them all into her cabin. Most of her children had grown up and gone, she told Maryann. There was only one son left, working their pair with them. She signalled to Maryann to put Ada down on the table. It was immediately obvious what the problem was.

'Oh, Ada!' Maryann cried.

'Ooh – that's a nasty 'un,' the woman said as they both leaned over the long, angry burn on Ada's leg. 'My word, you're lucky it didn't set her clothes afire!'

'I don't know what to put on it,' Maryann said.

'Here – we'll put a shaking of flour over it,' the woman said. 'That'll help dry it up.' She produced a rusty tin and scooped out a couple of spoonfuls of flour, dusting it over Ada's leg, which made her scream even more. Maryann watched helplessly, though she was glad of the older woman's confidence in what she was doing.

'Let's give them all a nice drop of milk,' the woman said. 'I've just got some in, lucky for you.'

Charlie could hear Norman Griffin's rasping breaths along the path in front of him. *You're struggling, mate,* Charlie thought, triumphantly. *Not so young, are you? Bet you're not used to running.* Charlie felt like a superior, strong animal closing in on its prey. He was gaining on him fast, that inky, lumbering patch of movement. As he drew closer, he could just see Norman Griffin's coat tails flapping behind him like slipped wings.

Charlie felt a further surge of energy as he closed in. He stretched out his arm, straining to reach him, clawing at Norman Griffin's shoulder.

'I'll have you!' he roared and with a final effort threw himself forward onto the man, hurtling into his back and flinging him face down onto the ground. Norman Griffin went down with a loud grunt and Charlie fell sprawling on top of him.

'Got you!' Charlie roared, scrambling up, but remaining bent over the prone figure. 'You needn't think you're going anywhere now, you bastard.'

There was no immediate reaction. He saw Norman Griffin's head lift and jerk from side to side, then there came a long, groaning inhalation as he tried to fill his winded lungs. He pushed desperately to sit up, to be able to breathe after his severe winding.

'Get up,' Charlie said. He watched over him with a feeling of power mingled with revulsion. What a foul wretch he was!

Norman braced himself, panting hard, struggling to stand and slowly lurched to his feet, but remained bent over, crumpled.

'They'll put you away for a long time,' Charlie said contemptuously. 'You're disgusting.' The man was a mess, hanging over like that, limp at the waist as if he couldn't straighten. He'd have to get him back to the wharf. Get the police – see if they could manage to keep their hands on him this time.

The few seconds it took Norman Griffin to rally took Charlie completely by surprise. Righting himself in an instant, he ran at Charlie, who had no time to brace himself. Propelled by a great shove from Norman Griffin, he skittered backwards and over the bank, hitting the black, moonstruck water, which closed over him, cold and filthy, filling his ears, eyes, mouth. For a second all was darkness and confusion in the muffled underwater world, but the cut was shallow. Charlie pushed himself furiously to his feet, above the water, spitting out the oily brew. He coughed, and cursed with rage. Norman Griffin was once again in flight along the path.

'I'll get you – you needn't think you'll get away!'

Clothes streaming, he hauled himself up onto the path, weighed down by his sodden garments. He could hear Norman Griffin's footsteps receding in the distance and, boots squelching, Charlie hurled himself along the path after him.

He soon caught up again, just as Norman Griffin turned off the path and began to scramble up through the nettles on the bank. No wonder they'd never seen him come and go on the wharf: he had this other way down!

'No you don't!' All he could do was throw himself on the man's legs, gripping on to his left ankle with all his strength. Norman Griffin kicked viciously, trying to shake him off, but Charlie gripped on, trying to pull himself up the man's body as if climbing a pole.

'Get off me – don't touch me!' Norman Griffin's shrill words came to Charlie, the voice almost a squeal. He was struggling like a pig at the slaughterhouse, and Charlie was astonished by his strength. As he got a grip further up the man's legs. Norman Griffin began to punch him, blows cracking into his cheek, smashing open his lip. Enraged by the pain, Charlie hauled himself up and lay on top of the older man, pinning him down.

'You fucking bastard!' he screamed into Norman Griffin's face. He could feel blood running down his chin. 'I'm going to make sure they lock you up and throw away the key!'

He barely got the words out as the hands locked around his throat. Charlie didn't even manage to inhale first and within seconds he was in trouble, chest straining, body crying out for air. His throat was held in an agonizing vice and he knew that if he didn't save himself that instant he was going to die.

Drawing on all his strength, he managed to fling his weight forward and clamp his hands on each side of Norman Griffin's head, which he lifted, then smashed down again onto the ground as hard as he could. For a second there was no reaction. He couldn't see the expression on the man's face in the gloom, but the grip on his throat slackened and Norman Griffin's arms, as if controlled by a separate life of their own, flopped to the ground. Charlie sobbed in gulps of air, gagging from the injury to his throat. He staggered to his feet, hands at his neck to try and ease the pain and landed a vicious kick at Norman Griffin's ribs. *'You fucker, you nearly bloody killed me!'* he rasped.

As his first crisis of needing to breathe calmed, he began to sense the silence in the other man. Kneeling down in sudden panic, he peered at him. He found he was starting to get the shakes.

'Here, come on – wake up!' he croaked. He'd only wanted to get him off – had to, didn't he? To save himself. Close up, he could see that Norman Griffin's one good eye was closed. He was out cold.

'Oh Jesus – God Almighty.' It was an agony to speak. He was in a real panic now though. 'Come on.' He slapped at Norman's face. 'Get yourself up, will you!'

Stopping, he listened for the man's breathing, but could make out nothing. His heart? He groped for what he thought was the right spot under the man's heavy coat. Again, he couldn't feel anything. Wasn't there supposed to be a spot where you could feel a pulse? Fumbling around Norman's wrist, he had no more success. He stood up, filled with panic.

'Don't let him be dead!' he breathed. He knew suddenly how cold he was in his soaking clothes. His teeth were chattering.

Backing away from Norman Griffin, he turned, his triumph shrivelled now to fear, and ran stumblingly back towards the wharf.

Ada had drifted into a light, whimpering sleep. The woman settled all the drowsy children on her bed.

'I must go and see what's happening,' Maryann said. 'The boat – my husband.'

The shock seemed to have snipped her mind into tiny fragments so she couldn't hold a thought together. She was beginning to feel smarting pain from the burns on her hand and neck, but she tried to ignore it. In the cabin she could hear the muffled voices of the men along the bank.

When she stepped outside, a terrible sight met her. Though there were no longer flames pouring out of the *Theodore*, the cabin and all their meagre possessions had virtually disappeared; the fire had only been stopped when it had burned some way along the hold. Smoke was still rising into the darkness.

The men were still working hard, filling bucket after bucket of water from the cut. But she saw Joel, no longer even attempting to carry on, a little distance away, bent over with his hands clenched to his knees as if in defeat, overtaken by bouts of coughing, the smoke too much for his already damaged lungs.

Thank heaven above it's not the Esther Jane, Maryann thought, though this was bad enough. The sight of her husband suffering, his defeated stance, filled her with a tenderness she had not been able to feel for a long while. Cautiously, shyly, she walked along to him.

'Joel – love?'

He straightened up and stood looking at her.

For the first time in weeks, she moved towards him and put her arms round him.

Moments later, while they were standing, numbly looking at the smoking wreck of the *Theodore*, they heard running footsteps.

'Maryann!' They heard him before they could see him and Maryann peered into the murk. Was that strained, gravelly voice Charlie's?

'I'm over here!' she called, and a moment later he was in front of her, panting, obviously in a state.

'He's along there – Griffin. On the towpath. I think I've ... I don't know ...' He gulped, struggling for breath. 'There was a fight. I think I might've done him in.'

Forty-Six

Everyone followed: it would have been no good telling them not to. The helpers from the surrounding boats had been drawn into the Bartholomews' drama and could not be expected to miss the next stage of it.

Charlie was already out of sight ahead of them, tearing along. They hurried after him down the narrow path, their only light the half moon. The other boaters followed and she could hear their boots on the path, their voices muffled yet excited. Maryann and Joel were together at first, but Joel was soon overcome by a fit of coughing and had to drop back.

Maryann ran under the bridge, felt for a second its deeper, echoing darkness, and came out the other side, straining to see Charlie ahead of her.

What's happened? What's he done? The questions hammered in her mind. He hadn't stopped long enough to explain. Something terrible had taken place and he thought Norman Griffin was dead. Her mind could not take this in, or the thought of what might happen to Charlie if this were true. Could he be dead? Over and over, tolling like a bell. Could he? Norman Griffin dead, after all this time?

'Charlie!' she shouted, sensing him ahead of her.

'Up here – come on!' she heard and ran on nimbly ahead of everyone else, soon catching Charlie up as he stopped abruptly, looking round.

427

'This was where ... It was, I'm sure!' Charlie ran back and forth, frantic, stamping at the nettles as if they might yield an answer. 'He was lain down there, I'd swear he was! He's moved himself ... that means he can't be dead. I haven't killed him!' Charlie was almost sobbing with relief. 'I thought I was going to prison!' he croaked. 'Thought I'd finished him off!'

'Charlie – ' Maryann gripped his arm, trying to bring him back to his senses – 'if he's not here, we've got to find him.'

'You sure this was it?' Joel and the others came up from behind.

'He was trying to get up there when I pulled him down.' Charlie pointed up the low bank. At the top was the end of a wall enclosing a line of factories and a tree next to it, then a fence. Between the wall and the tree was a gap. Joel and the other four men immediately sprang up the bank and started pushing their way through.

'There's a path here! We can get along,' one of them called. One by one they disappeared. Maryann watched, without hope. It was so dark and Norman Griffin had had so much time to get away. He knew the lie of the land and they'd lost him once again. He was like the strongman they used to see in the Bull Ring, she thought. He'd be tied with chains in a sack, so it looked impossible even to move, but he'd always manage to escape.

Charlie couldn't seem to stop talking, even though he was clearly in pain, his voice rasping. He was explaining what had happened that evening at the house, seeing the young girl and how Norman Griffin had escaped them there and now again here.

'*Twice* we had him, Maryann, and he still got away. I feel such a blithering idiot.'

'It's not your fault,' she said flatly. 'You did your best for us.' In the distance she could hear the others moving away between the factory walls to the road. They'd never find him now, she knew. He'd be long gone, a malignant shadow slipping through the streets to some new hiding place. It seemed he was always destined to be out there somewhere beyond their reach, untouchable. Victorious.

Once Charlie's torrent of speech had rasped to a halt they stood listening. They could not hear Joel and the other men any more and the night was quiet. Something moved on the water close to them, a little flurry and a splash. Maryann became aware of other sounds, a mechanical throbbing from a factory somewhere, a train, its chugging passage building then receding, and, as the quiet descended again, a low, odd noise which didn't fit the usual sounds of night. She listened, alert. Seconds later it came again.

'Charlie – what's that?'

'What? I can't hear anything.'

They strained to hear, but no sound came.

'Come with me.' They began to walk along the path, further away from the wharf. Only a short distance away they found him, his prone figure like a dark stain on the path. Maryann gasped.

'Oh Lor' – ' She felt Charlie put his arm protectively round her shoulders. She was terrified. Unable to see Norman Griffin's face, she felt he was staring up at her through the darkness, waiting to seize hold of her if she leaned over him.

'It's all right.' Charlie released her and very cautiously they bent down. Norman Griffin did not stir. He was lying face down, as if he had crawled here, and as Charlie touched him a groan came from him. Maryann saw

429

Charlie feel round the back of the man's head. He stood up, wiping his hand on his trousers.

'He's bleeding. Banged his head. He won't be going nowhere. I'm going for the coppers.'

'No!' Maryann panicked. 'We can't leave him here! He might still get up and run off. You can't trust him an inch. And I'm not staying here on my own with him. Wait till the others get back, Charlie.'

'All right. Don't s'pose there's any hurry now,' he said, adding tremulously, 'oh, thank Christ for that.'

Hands shaking, Maryann slowly knelt down, her body tensed, heart hammering, ready to jump away at any sign of movement.

'Can you hear me?' Her mouth was so dry, the words would barely come out and she had to try again. 'Mr Griffin. I hope you can hear me. It's Maryann.'

She stopped, unable for a moment to think what to say. But there were things she wanted to say. He had to know she was here, present at the moment when they finally had him, helpless in front of her, wiped out. Defeated. Breathing deeply, she looked up for a moment at the white glow of the moon. What words could ever encompass all the years of fear and shame and pain? But she had to say something. Just something. For herself and Sal, for Janet Lambert and Amy and Margaret.

'It's Maryann,' she said again. 'I hate you for what you did to me and to everyone else. You're an evil, twisted man and you're never going to hurt anyone again. You've destroyed people. You've wrecked and broken them. But you're finished now.' She took a long, shuddering breath and stood up. 'And you haven't got me.'

*

430

Pastor Owen sat on the front pew in the little church, his eyes red from weeping. He was slumped in his large clothes, like a crumpled bird. The pews looked even more outsized in the room than Maryann remembered. The place was empty except for the two of them. Sunlight slanted in through the windows onto the cross and a bird was singing out on the roof. A place of peace, it should have been. But there was no peace. Maryann had been standing, but she sank down beside him on the pew.

'You had no idea, did you?'

Pastor Owen hung his head. He shook it, utterly desolate. Maryann almost put her arm round him, but she held back. She kept her hands in her lap, the right one bandaged and sore.

It was the afternoon after Norman Griffin had been driven away by the police. When Joel and the other men returned to the cut the night before, they had all helped carry Norman Griffin back to Tyseley Wharf, as he gave off faint, semi-conscious groans.

'He's not going to die, is he?' Charlie asked.

'Don't sound like it,' Joel said. 'Take more than a bang on the head to finish that 'un off.'

The police came. This time it was Joel who had his arm round Maryann's shoulders as they carried Norman Griffin into the back of the vehicle.

'That's him gone,' was all Joel said.

Maryann nodded numbly. She could find no words.

More shock was to follow. The police had taken the two men from the house and had them in the cells. One was the butcher, Mr Osborne, something Maryann was still almost unable to take in. The third, round-faced man was Pastor Joyce.

'He's been like a father to me.' Pastor Owen's

shoulders began to shake. 'We've lived in the same house, done the Lord's work together. And all this time – what have I been living with?'

His bony hands clutched to his face, he began to weep. 'They say he took a young girl's life.'

Maryann could think of no words of comfort. She truly felt for him in his shock, for this terrible shame upon his friend, his church. She knew now his genuine goodness. He was an innocent, caught up in a horror he could barely understand. After a moment she laid her bandaged hand gently on his back.

'You couldn't have known,' she tried to reassure him. 'The other one, Mr Osborne, he was always nice as pie to me. Reminded me of my dad. I bought all my meat off him. How could anyone ever guess something like that?'

Pastor Owen lifted his head, cheeks running with tears, face twisting with emotion. He looked so young! So pinched and battered.

'I don't know what to do.' More tears welled in his large eyes. 'I can't stay here. I thought this'd be my life's work, in this place. I'm lost, Mrs Bartholomew. How can I go on?'

Maryann stared back at him. She sighed, a long, deep sigh which seemed to have been waiting there for years to be expelled.

'I don't know. But you will. You'll find the strength, same as we all do.'

Forty-Seven

August 1944

'Mom – Mom!' Joley and Ezra came tearing along the bank where they were tied up near Napton. 'Look – it's Dot and Sylvia, and Bobby's got his arm round Dot!'

Maryann pulled the panful of sausages off the heat and hurried outside, where the faces of her sons, swarthy with a combination of grime and suntan, were lit up with excitement. A pair of boats was chugging steadily towards them and she narrowed her eyes. Sure enough, it was a pair of Grand Union Canal Carrying Company boats heading south towards them, and yes, there was Bobby at the helm, tiller held easily in his left hand, the other apparently draped in a relaxed way round Dot's shoulders. The children were already shrieking and waving and she saw Dot and Bobby recognize them and start waving back. Sylvia was waving from the butty boat as well.

'Sylvia – Auntie Sylvia!' Rose leapt up and down on the path with excitement.

'We're tying up – just up here!' Bobby called. Within a few moments they'd found a place to pull in and all the Bartholomews were hurrying along for a grand reunion on the bank in the late afternoon sun. Rose ran straight to Sylvia, who picked her up, and Maryann smiled at the sight of Rose's dark, curling hair against the paleness of Sylvia's.

'Ooh, you're getting a heavy girl now!' Sylvia said, kissing Rose's pink cheeks.

433

Joel and Bobby greeted one another warmly and stood slightly apart, talking boats and gauges and cargoes, while Maryann and the children all crowded round Sylvia and Dot. At first no one could get a word in edgeways. The children were all asking questions at once. Maryann saw Sylvia making a special effort to draw Sally out. She was still quiet and withdrawn, although she was much better than she had been straight after her terrifying time with Norman Griffin.

'It looks *awful* just seeing you with the *Esther Jane* and no *Theodore*!' Dot's powerful voice rang out above the children's chatter.

'You *poor* things – whatever has been happening to you?' Sylvia planted a kiss on Rose's cheek. 'Let me put you down now, darling – my back won't stand it. Of course we heard through the grapevine that there'd been a fire, a couple of months ago now, wasn't it? And that there was all sorts of to-do at Tyseley, but no one's told us properly. You must have had a terrible time!'

Maryann nodded. A lump came up in her throat at the thought of the last few months, the raw, fearful wretchedness of it all. But she didn't want to let go of her emotion, not now. She swallowed hard.

'We're managing,' she said matter-of-factly. 'Essy Barlow's got us another butty for when we get back this time. Joley and Ezzy are sleeping out in the hold most nights as it's warm. You lot tied up for the night now?'

'Yes,' Dot said. 'Bobby says we'll not get much further than here tonight in any case with them all locking up so early. The water's so low they're rationing who goes through. It's a gamble to try and get over the top at Tring these days – they only let so many through, then close all the locks!'

434

Maryann watched her in wonder as she spoke. She was so suntanned and strong looking and, yes, happy, in a way she'd never been before. Maryann grinned.

'So – I see Bobby's steering with his arm around his first mate these days!'

Dot gave her hooting laugh, and blushed. Sylvia was looking fondly at her.

'Oh, we've got *lots* to tell you. But let's get the tea brewed first, eh? I'm absolutely parched – and famished, as usual!'

'Bobby and me'll be off then,' Joel said. The meal was over, chores finished for the night and the children getting ready for bed.

'All right.' Maryann smiled at him gratefully. Bobby and Joel would enjoy getting a few pints inside them at the inn along the bank, and she knew Joel was giving her the chance to catch up with Dot and Sylvia. It would be a night like old times, even though in a strange cabin, not the *Theodore*, but she was full of a welling sense of pleasure at the thought of female company, a sensation which even now took her by surprise.

On these light, sultry nights it would be hard for the boys to get to sleep outside, so she settled them inside on Joel's and her bed, parting from them all with dire warnings that they must go to sleep and not monkey about. Even now, climbing out of the cabin, she felt a reflex of fear at the thought of leaving the children alone.

Don't start that again, she told herself. *He can't hurt us any more. Never.*

But how long would it be, she thought, weeds brushing her bare ankles as she walked the towpath, before she could say she had recovered from it, from him, and close the door on it all as she longed to do? Would that ever happen?

'Look what I've got!' Sylvia greeted her jubilantly from the back of *Magpie*, their monkey boat, waving a bottle of Johnnie Walker. 'At last I've got someone to share it with! Bobby's an ale man.' Her hair was up in a pale blue scarf and she'd put on her favourite geranium red lipstick.

Maryann grinned. 'Got yourself a sweetheart in a distillery?'

'No – still working on that one!' Sylvia said.

Dot appeared, all in black still, her short shirtsleeves pressing tight into her plump arms. She looked like a nice, wholesome cottage loaf, Maryann thought.

'Let's not sit inside.' Sylvia jumped up onto the cabin roof, using it as a table to pour Scotch into white cups. 'Not until those blasted beasties nibble us too unbearably.'

Dot and Maryann perched comfortably on the gunwales at the back. Another pair of boats was tied up behind, but not too close, a line of washing flapping along the hold and their children out on the bank. The evening was bathed in rich light, and a warm breeze came over the fields. Maryann drank in the moment, this precious evening to enjoy with her friends. A year ago who would have thought it could feel like this?

'Cheers!' Sylvia raised her chipped cup. 'Down the hatch!'

They found they were all laughing just at the sight of one another, out of happiness.

'Too much to catch up on by far,' Sylvia said. 'Where do we begin? Let's take turns. You first, Maryann?'

'Ooh no.' She felt herself tense up immediately. If she

told them what had happened she knew it would lead to questions. How much could she say, even now? She was so used to not telling things that it felt terrifying to be asked. She looked at Dot. 'I want to hear all about what's been going on here. Come on – you can't keep me in suspense any longer.'

Dot looked sideways at her with an irrepressibly jubilant grin.

'Oh!' Sylvia rolled her eyes in mock exasperation. 'I've been living with a proper Romeo and Juliet. Makes me feel quite old and washed up sometimes!'

'There was me thinking you and Bobby didn't exactly hit it off,' Maryann teased. 'I wonder what gave me that idea?'

'Well, we didn't,' Dot said brusquely. 'But we do now. That's all.'

'For "we do now –"' Sylvia leaned confidentially towards Maryann and almost toppled her precious bottle into the cut in the process – 'you have to substitute the words, "We're completely half-soaked and besotted with one another." So that certain people on lock-wheeling duty are standing there in a complete soppy fug and forgetting to close paddles or get back on the boat at the right moment – or getting off it with no windlass and getting a proper mouthful from other boaters.'

Dot was laughing now. 'I only did that once!'

'And in fact, "we do now" actually, I'm almost sure, means the sound of wedding bells will be in the offing soon.'

Maryann was laughing, astonished. 'But how the hell did this all happen, Dot?'

'Bobby's not like I thought at the beginning,' Dot said with dignity. 'I didn't know him, that's all. And now I do, I know him to be kind and he makes me laugh

437

and, well, I just think we'll be able to rub along together, that's all.'

Maryann and Sylvia were both laughing.

'Here speaks one of the great romantics of our time!' Sylvia giggled.

'All hearts and flowers, aren't you, Dot!' Maryann said. 'But are you really getting wed?'

Dot took a sip of tea and her face grew more solemn.

'Next month. Goes without saying we want you all there with your boots blacked. All Bartholomews in a line! Actually – ' she looked shy suddenly – 'I wondered if Joel would agree to give me away. There won't be any of my family there, you see.'

Maryann saw Sylvia looking at Dot with a concerned, sympathetic expression.

'Not your dad?' Maryann asked hesitantly. 'Isn't he going to give you away?'

Dot cradled her cup between her hands and spoke, looking down at the floor.

'Appears not. Course, apart from a couple of stray cousins who I barely know, Daddy's the only real family I've got left now. I took a couple of days' leave and went up there a month ago. Mainly to tell him about Bobby. I mean I thought I should at least *tell* him, although I wasn't too surprised at the upshot.' She drew in a deep breath.

'Odd, being back there. Seeing the house. Garden was a mess. Daddy saying he's doing some sort of war work, hush, hush, but I'm not sure it's true. He's just trying to sound terribly important as usual. I'd gone to stay the night, but I just couldn't. I missed the last train back, so I slept on the platform . . .'

'Oh, Dot!' Maryann was horrified. That great big

438

house, her home, and poor Dot didn't even feel she could take up a little corner of it!

'Daddy and I had a conversation which lasted about a quarter of an hour.' Again she paused. A bee lumbered past. 'He made himself abundantly clear. If I lowered myself by marrying like this, I could forget that I was his daughter – you know, inheritance and so forth. Apart from these inescapable financial factors – ' she looked up now, with her ironic grin – 'forgetting I'm Daddy's daughter won't feel all that new or troublesome.'

'That's terrible.' Maryann watched Dot's face.

'Yes – she's had a rough time,' Sylvia said.

'You must really think a lot of Bobby.'

'Yes.' Dot smiled. 'I suppose that's how it was for you and Joel?'

Again the plunge of misgiving. How much could she say? Yes, she'd loved Joel, but how much more there had been to her running away, her quest for safety. 'Yes,' was all she said.

'Bobby's done wonders for me.'

Maryann could see that he had.

'Of course we'll be at your wedding.' She reached across and squeezed the top of Dot's arm. 'We wouldn't miss it for anything.'

'Thanks.' Dot said briskly. Maryann saw her eyes fill with tears, but she soon had them under control again. 'That means a lot. More than you might imagine.'

'So – you're going to be a boatwoman! Sure you know what you're letting yourself in for?'

'I think I've a fair idea,' Dot said dryly.

'And you still want to do it!'

'Well – would you swap it?'

'No.' Maryann sighed. 'Not most days, anyroad.'

'It's Bobby's life. He doesn't know any other. We just want to carry on working, and Sylvia can crew for us, for as long as they need her – Inland Waterways, I mean. Once the war ends, who knows?'

'Yes,' Sylvia sighed, sliding down from the cabin roof. 'I'm going to have to face up to the mess my life's in. It sounds *awful*, but I almost don't want the war to end. When it does, I'm going to have to decide all sorts of things I'd rather not think about. Come on, girls – let's go in. I'm starting to get nibbled more than I can stand.'

The evening was cooling and they sat in the *Magpie*'s warm cabin, light and a breeze coming in through the door.

'I can't go back to Roy – not after all this,' Sylvia said, pouring more water into the kettle. 'I've thought and thought. I feel I should for the children's sake. After all, what can I offer them on my own? But I just can't. They weren't happy with us at home. That's why I sent them away in the first place. And it'd be like climbing back into a cage!'

'Lion's den, more like,' Dot commented.

Sylvia gave a wan smile, putting the kettle back on the heat. 'You know, I never thought this would happen to me. I used to look down terribly on women who couldn't make their marriages work. As if it was always their fault, for a start! And the truth is – ' she sank down on the side bench next to Maryann – 'mine barely even worked right from the beginning. There's something terribly wrong with Roy, I've known that really. But it's amazing how long you can kid yourself something is working, that it's normal.'

'What will you do?' Maryann asked.

'Don't know. I'll stay here as long as I can. My sister's

been having the children, but she can't manage all the holidays. I'll have to bring them on here for the last two weeks.' She looked solemn, but determined. 'In the long run, I don't know. I'll have to find a job and somewhere to live ... Roy'll carry on paying the school fees. He's dead set on that. But I know now that I can do it. I'd never have been able even to begin thinking that before I came away.' Her face cleared and she chuckled. 'What a year, eh? And goodness me, Maryann, for you more than any of us the last few months, by the sound of things. *Do tell* – what on earth's been happening to you all?'

The question roused the usual mixture of panic and longing in Maryann. The hunger both to tell and to conceal, each equally pressing. It was like a scouring of inner wounds. But they'd shared so much of themselves with her now. She could tell them some of it quite easily of course, about the fire, and Charlie Dean's chase along the towpath. And she did so while they brewed up again and drank tea round the table, Dot and Sylvia listening avidly.

'Charlie was scared stiff he'd finished him off. It was just a bang on the head, though, and he came round all right. Course, there was no doubt about what they'd all done, him and that Pastor Joyce and Mr Osborne.'

'Mr Osborne was always such a sweetie, though,' Sylvia said, bewildered. 'Least, I thought so.'

'So did I.' Maryann knew she sounded abrupt. This was another betrayal which was only now beginning to hit home. 'Anyroad, the girl in the cellar in Acocks Green – turned out Pastor Joyce was the one responsible for her. He was blarting in the witness box, saying it'd all been an accident, that he never meant to.'

Despite the horror of what she was telling them, Sylvia and Dot were taken back by the bitter loathing in Maryann's voice.

'The girl was called Ellen. She was eight years old and she was Janet's sister's grandchild. They live out at Alvechurch and he – Griffin – had gone all the way out there to track her down. God alone knows what they did to her . . .' She couldn't speak for a moment, almost choked by rage and pain. 'It was anyone connected with any of us – my family, Janet's. If we'd've had more relatives . . .' She shuddered. She couldn't look Sylvia and Dot in the eye. The others were silent. Maryann sensed that they just didn't know what to say, were out of their depth.

'But,' Dot stumbled into speech, eventually, '*why*, Maryann?' She spoke very gently. 'He must be completely insane. They all must be!'

'There was a girl that night in the room above the butcher's. She was one of Pastor Joyce's congregation, from the church. They were just the same, the three of them.'

'So – ' Sylvia was struggling to make any sense out of the horror of it all – 'Norman Griffin was the man who killed Jennykins that night and who . . . who took Sally, and all these other terrible things. And you said he was your stepfather? But none of it makes any sense. Why would he do these things to you of all people?'

'Oh – that's his way of being family,' Maryann said with harsh flippancy. She felt as if there were hands around her throat as she looked guardedly up into Sylvia's kind eyes. Her longing was overwhelming, the need to be able to tell someone who had never known Norman Griffin or been touched by him, to lay it all out before them and have them witness and believe her and

442

not condemn. To know that someone understood all the hurt and shame inside her and could accept her. The shame which never seemed to die, and which, roused again by all the events of the last months, still left her sickened and weeping every time her husband tried to touch her, and breaking down at other unpredictable moments. These last two months had been awash with tears. They gave her some release, but still she had not been able to break through Joel's own pain and bewilderment and tell him the truth. She still felt as if she was living behind a mask and no one ever saw the real her underneath, the lonely, trembling her. If she could just lift the mask, even just a corner of it ... But it was so frightening.

Feeling Sylvia looking at her, Dot's eyes on her across the table, she felt herself go weak, her palms sweating. How could she say it? Put the gross truth into words: her childhood, her sister Sal's, Amy's, Margaret's. She clasped her hands in her lap to control her trembling. If she never spoke, didn't he, Norman Griffin, in his cell in Winson Green prison, where he would stay until they hanged him – didn't he still have sway over her? Even when he was dead, how could she ever be free? She remembered her last sight of him in the courtroom before they took him away, hatless for once, sitting hunched forward, trying to hide his face. Even in the packed court she had felt her skin crawl at being so close to him. How could she banish him, and the everlasting sense of dirtiness he had given her, and begin to live properly again?

She knew Sylvia and Dot had sensed her inner struggle. Folding her arms, almost hugging herself, she spoke, staring down at the table top with its rings of stains.

'Yes, he was my stepfather.' She could barely raise her voice above a whisper. It felt impossible, crushing, as if the whole world was listening. 'He came to live with us after our dad died. And ... and ...' She was weeping then, unable to speak.

'Oh, darling.' Sylvia's arm came round her shoulders. Eventually it gave her the courage to go on.

'He wasn't a father to us. He interfered with us. Both of us. But my sister, Sal, most of all.'

The sobbing took over, wrung out of her. Sylvia cradled her in her arms and Maryann was conscious of her head being pressed against Sylvia's shoulder, of motherly, comforting noises, of feeling warm and safe. All she could do was to cry and cry. She couldn't go on speaking, telling it all. Not tonight. But she had lifted the edge of the mask, allowed a chink of light into her darkness. She knew she could go on now. Tell them more, and at last be able to take what seemed the hardest step of all: telling Joel.

She had spoken.

Forty-Eight

'Time to come and get scrubbed up!'

Maryann was ready with the dipper on the table, full of steaming water. They were at Sutton Stop and all six children were out on the bank, among a gaggle of others having conker fights. They were so engrossed in bashing each other's conkers they didn't hear her, and Joel went to hurry them along.

'Boys first!'

Joley and Ezra groaned. 'Do we *have* to?'

Maryann set about washing and dressing them, tutting as the pockets in the boys' trousers and girls' frocks yielded up stashes of the horse chestnuts, polished shiny as leather, and a couple still encased in their prickly shells.

'D'you have to pick up all these? It's not as if they're on the ration.'

'But the others'll get 'em if we don't,' Ezzy yelled urgently. 'And then there won't be none left.'

'Don't *shout* – I'm not deaf.' Maryann scrubbed at Ezra's soot-begrimed cheeks. 'And I don't want any of them conkers in the church, d'you hear?' She attempted to get a comb through his dark curls as he squirmed and moaned. The girls were waiting on the back bed.

'Are we wearing our new frocks now?' Sally asked.

'That you are – and once you've got them on, don't flaming *move* in them until the wedding's over!'

'Oh, Mom!'

'Is Sylvia putting hers on now?' Rose wanted to know.

'Yes – and she's helping Dot. Oh keep still, Ezzy – it's like trying to comb a hedgehog.'

For the past month, every spare moment had been spent sewing. Sylvia, who was very good at it, had taken over the problem of dressing everyone for the wedding. In the last two weeks of the school holidays she had introduced Kay and Dickie to life on the cut, and they had evidently taken to it with enthusiasm. Fetching them had also given her an opportunity to go home and collect some of her belongings. She was a keen seamstress and had found a generous length of pretty blue cotton with trailing daisies on, and devised a simple pattern to make dresses for the Bartholomew girls.

'Oh, I wish I could've brought my sewing machine!' she said. 'It's at home, but it's so heavy. I'll have to get hold of it later. But never mind – we can handsew.' She showed a nervous Maryann how to make the little girls' frocks up, while she concentrated on the other dresses, as well as making outfits for the boys. She had a marvellous collection of material at home, accumulated over years, including a yellow flowery fabric for outfits for herself and Maryann.

'I was going to make this up just before the war,' she mused, lifting the corner of the bright, sunny cloth. 'Somehow I didn't have the heart. I think the colour was too happy for me!'

For Dot's wedding dress she managed to acquire something highly prized from her favourite draper's. Parachute silk!

'This is going to be a fancy wedding,' Maryann laughed, seeing it all. 'We aren't used to all this.'

446

Everyone was gathered at Hawkesbury now: the Bartholomews with the *Esther Jane* and a new Barlow butty boat called *Jonquil*. Sylvia and Dot were tied up behind them and Bobby's family, the Jenkses, were there too. Word had passed also to Joel's brother Darius that there was a celebration in the offing and they were hoping he might arrive in time.

Sylvia appeared in the doorway of the *Esther Jane*, still in her old slacks, hair turbaned up in a scarf. Maryann had managed to finish off the boys and made them sit down with 'Don't move and don't get dirty!' ringing in their ears.

'Aah!' Sylvia exclaimed, seeing Maryann put Sally's dress on over the child's head. Her long blonde hair was newly washed and brushed and she looked very pretty. 'I knew it would match your eyes, Sally. You're a picture! You and Rose will make perfect bridesmaids.' Seated on the coalbox, she reached out and squeezed Sally's hand. 'It fits very nicely, Maryann – you've done so well.'

'It's a blooming miracle.' Maryann laughed. 'I've never been any good at sewing. How's Dot? She dressed yet?'

'No – I'm going to go and help her in a few minutes. Just thought I'd see how you were getting on. Dot's having a wash. Poor darling – you might not think it, but she's really very worked up and nervy this morning. It's good that we got shot of Bobby to the Jenkses' last night – just gives us all a bit of breathing space. And I suspect he'd have been in even more of a flap than her!'

'There.' Maryann finished combing out Sally's hair. She was pleased to see a smile on her daughter's face. The life was gradually coming back to her over these months. 'Rose, you next!' She nodded towards Ada and

447

Esther, on the bed, who were watching with rapt expressions. 'Goodness knows how I'm going to keep those two out of the muck once they've got their finery on!'

The boats set out in convoy along the cut to Longford. Summer was waning, but the leaves were only just beginning to turn, and Maryann caught a whiff of smoke from a garden fire as they chugged along. In the hedgerows were sprays of ripe blackberries and Maryann grimaced, standing at the tiller of the *Jonquil*, imagining all that magenta juice down the front of her offspring's new clothes if they were to catch sight of them later on the bank. She had on her own yellow frock, and, as ever, wore Nancy's gold hoops in her ears. The outfit made her feel very smart and happy, but for the moment she had put her coat over the top to try and keep the coal dust at bay. Dot and the children were all safely inside their respective cabins, keeping well protected.

Maryann glanced at the line of boats behind her and smiled. The sun was coming out and the boats were decked out with as many pots and jars of flowers as they had been able to find on the cabin roofs beside the bright roses and castles on the water cans and dippers. All the boats had been washed and their rope work and Turks' heads were a miracle of whiteness in the sunshine, after a good scrubbing with cut water. At the back of the line they had been joined in the nick of time by Darius's pair, with his crew and the boys, Darrie and Sean.

They tied up at Longford in a colourful, celebratory line. Maryann swiftly went indoors to take off her coat and tidy her hair. Sylvia had given it a trim for her and it felt clean and bouncy, curling at the ends and pinned stylishly back.

'Now you lot—' She managed to drag the comb once more through the children's hair and smiled proudly at them. It was a long time since she'd seen her boys so smart. Joley with his thick blond mop and Ezra very dark.

'You look like princes,' she told them.

'Oh, *Mom*,' Joley groaned, disgusted, 'can us *go* now?'

Rose and Sally, equally contrasting in looks, and being self-consciously careful with their clothes, were next out, tiptoeing along the plank, and then Maryann led the twins out. Ada's leg had healed from her burning, but she would be scarred for life, and the look of the ruckled patch of skin was a bitter one for Maryann every time she saw it.

Joel was waiting on the bank, as proud and upright as his sore back would allow, his beard trimmed and wearing his ancient 'Sunday best', which included an old jacket of his father's. He came to help the twins out and Maryann looked across at him as he took their hands, seeing him afresh for a moment. She knew he was still struggling with the terrible things she had at last told him about her past. Part of his hurt was that she had kept it all from him for so long. But she also knew that he was solid and true, that she knew him so well and trusted him, and that they would endure.

'When's Dot coming out?' Rose demanded.

'In her own time,' Joel told her. 'Come on, little 'un – your dad's tied up back here. Come and see him.'

Rose greeted her father shyly, and when he went to lift her up she said, 'Don't get me dirty!' in a panicky voice. So Darius knelt down and talked to her instead.

449

She was shy with her brothers too, but Joley and Ezra were soon tearing up and down with Darrie and Sean and Maryann knew Rose would come round eventually.

'You all right, Darius?' she asked, tender towards him. She missed Nancy so much – how much worse it must be for him!

He nodded, pushing his hat back from over his eyes. His striking, chiselled face was beginning to look more like old Darius's, with its deep clefts and lines wrought by weather and by the grief of losing Nancy. And he looked dirty and exhausted from a rushed trip, trying to get here on time.

They exchanged bits of news: Joel and Maryann had not long been to Oxford and they told Darius that his father and Aunt Alice were both in good health.

'Better get in and clean myself up,' Darius said, after a time. 'The bride'll've left without us, else.'

Bobby and the rest of the Jenks family went ahead to the church. The others waited on the bank for Dot to make her appearance. Rose kept peering round at the back of the *Magpie*, trying to see what was going on.

'Can I go in?' she asked repeatedly.

'No, you stay out here,' Maryann said, wondering how much longer she could restrain Ada and Esther. She and Joel were each holding one of them to keep them from dabbling in every bit of muck and mess around. As they stood there, the sunshine grew brighter and it became quite warm.

The *Magpie*'s hatch slid back and Sylvia came out first in her sunny yellow dress, lovely as a flower herself. Then everyone 'oohed' as Dot followed her and stood before them, blushing more bashfully than Maryann had ever seen her, sheathed in her silk dress, which emphasized her considerable curves, her nut-brown arms protruding from the short sleeves. Her black hair was pinned in a knot at the back and topped by a little cream skull cap which Sylvia had somehow managed to fashion as well. The children all stood suddenly silent, in awe.

'Oh, Dot!' Maryann exclaimed. 'You look lovely! Sylvia, how did you manage to make all these things, just in there?'

'Well – we managed.' Sylvia laughed. 'By hook or by crook.'

'You all look like three pretty flowers together,' Joel said, and Maryann was touched by this rare romantic outburst from her husband.

'Well,' Dot said, 'this might be the last chance I ever get to dress up properly, so it's jolly nice to be able to do it in style! Now – what about my little bridesmaids? You both coming along with me?'

Sally and Rose came timidly forward.

'Aren't you both beautiful?' Dot said, making them smile, pleased with themselves. 'Now, don't be scared. We've all got to manage this together.' She took their hands, and everyone set off for the church.

Maryann walked with Sylvia, holding Ada's hand.

'Who's that then?' Sylvia nodded towards Darius and his sons.

'Oh – you've not met, have you? That's Darius – Joel's brother.'

They caught up and Maryann introduced them.

'Sylvia's been ever so good to your Rose,' she told him.

Darius shook her hand, shyly touching his cap and clearing his throat. He wasn't used to the volunteers yet, not having worked with any.

'I'm ever so fond of little Rose,' Sylvia told him. 'She's a real poppet. You must miss her terribly.'

Darius nodded. 'We do. It's been a while now and the lads miss her. But our Rose's better off with a woman to see to her.'

They all filed into the cool darkness of the church. Bobby was waiting at the altar, his thick hair slicked as far down as it would stay, looking smart and solemnly nervous. As soon as he caught sight of Dot moving along the aisle towards him on Joel's arm, though, an unstoppable grin spread across his face.

Sally and Rose both looked round at Maryann, needing reassurace as they followed on, and Maryann smiled at them, full of pride. What a picture they made! She filled up with mixed emotions. Most of the time she tried never to think about what might have happened to Sally had they not rescued her when they did, but sometimes she was overwhelmed by still having her with them and safe.

Joel slipped into the pew beside her with Ada and Esther. As Dot and Bobby began to say their vows, she felt him glance at her. She knew they were both remembering their wedding day, which seemed so long ago now. How much had happened! Her heart was scarred by some of the worst times; losing their little Harry, the awful thing she had done to their last child when she just couldn't stand any more, almost losing Sally, and her own pain and confusion. That was not over, even now: it would take time to emerge from, like a dark, confusing forest, because the hurt in her went so deep.

As the vows were pronounced in the shadowy church, Maryann felt Joel gently take her hand and squeeze it. She didn't look round at him, but with her own hand answered his gentle pressure. *We're still here, whatever,* that loving squeeze seemed to say. *Aren't we?*

Forty-Nine

A bird was singing, so that lying in the dark cabin Maryann could tell it was dawn.

She lay wide awake beside Joel's sleeping body, listening to the day coming to life.

Back to work, she thought, with a sense of deflation. These times of rest and celebration were always over so quickly, and then it was back to the grind. Dot wouldn't be wearing a silk dress today or any day from now on. She knew that her yellow frock and the girls' daisy ones would soon be pressed into everyday service and become as worn and grubby as the rest, and it seemed sad how quickly their day of finery had passed.

But she smiled at the thought of Dot and Bobby. At how they used to squabble. But they did go well together, she could see now, like bread and cheese. And the Jenks family, though at first bewildered by their son's choice of wife, had seen Dot's good nature and enormous capacity for hard work, and had taken to her in a shy sort of way.

'Least she's got a proper name now,' Bobby joked, when they came out of the church into hot sunshine and the children showering them with their collection of flower petals. Dorothy Higgs-Deveraux had become plain Dot Jenks and she seemed quite content with the transaction.

Maryann ran over the day in her mind: her children

looking so clean and smart for once, the solemnity of the service, and after – eating and drinking together at the boats, having gathered all the food and drink they could muster, the enjoyment of being able to sit and relax, merry with ale, celebrating outside. She ran her eyes over the faces in her memory. Dot full of happiness and laughter, Bobby grinning as if he still could not believe his luck, Sylvia ... She ground to a halt on Sylvia. Something had caught her attention, but she hadn't identified it at the time. The expression in Sylvia's eyes when she sat out on the grass, talking to Darius. It was something familiar ... With a jolt she matched up what she had seen. Nancy, the first time she had met Darius. That irresistible drawing of the eyes to Darius, in fascination, attraction ... Was that really what she'd seen, or was she mistaken?

And last night, when it was all over and they were dropping with fatigue, she bedded down the older children in the *Jonquil*, as was her habit now, keeping only Ada and Esther with them on the *Esther Jane*, end to end on the side bed.

Joel turned to her in the cosy light of the cabin as they prepared for bed, his eyes solemn, appealing to her. Maryann tensed immediately. *Is this what he expects now?* she thought. *For everything suddenly to be all right again?*

'I don't know.' To her frustration she began to tremble. 'I don't know if I can yet. I'm trying, but ...'

'I know you are.' He stroked her cheek with his thumb. 'Never mind that. Just come here.'

She felt herself enfolded in his arms, held close to that warm, fleshy, comforting body, which she knew like her own, and felt him stroke her back, his lips brushing the top of her head.

'It's all right,' he murmured. 'There's time aplenty.'

They lay down together and once more he drew her into his arms, demanding nothing more than to hold her. She lay with her cheek pressed to his shoulder as he stroked her hair, both of them growing drowsy.

'It's all right, my lovely,' was the last thing she heard him say. 'It'll be all right.'

And sheltering in his warmth she felt herself drift into sleep, safe, comforted. Home.

Glossary

bow-hauling – pulling a boat, usually a butty, into a lock by hand

breast-up – tie boats side by side, at night, or in some cases when going into locks empty

butty, butty boat – a narrowboat which is not powered, but towed as one of a pair

cratch – a small timber and tarpaulin covering at the fore end of the hold

the cut – any canal

dipper – large metal vessel with a handle, used for washing, cooking and laundry

joey – unmotorized narrowboat without living accommodation or covering for cargo. Pulled by horse or tug and usually used for short trips around Birmingham

joshers – slang name for boats belonging to the company of Fellows, Moreton & Clayton, after Mr Joshua Fellows

lengthsman – employee of the Waterways, whose job is to maintain the 'length' of the canals, e.g. keeping clear of trees etc

lock-wheeling – to go ahead on foot or bicycle and prepare the locks for passage by boats

monkey, monkey boat – a power-driven narrowboat which can tow a butty

monkey hole – storage space inside the boat

pinner – apron

to shaft – to manipulate the position of a boat by using the shaft (boathook), a long pole

snubber – towing rope made of coconut fibre and used between the fore end of the butty and the stern of the motor – at full stretch, usually seventy feet long

spare-wheeling – filling in for a crew member when a boat was short-handed

to stove – to fumigate with sulphur to rid the boat of bugs

strap – ropes used for tying up or short-length towing

stroving – working hard

Turk's head – decorative rope fender found in numerous places on all narrowboats

winding hole – wider spot in canal, where boats can turn round

windlass – L-shaped cranking handle used for winding the lock paddles up and down

to work fly – work on one of the fly boats with larger crews, which did the London to Birmingham round trip non-stop in something under sixty hours